A Hunter and His Prey

A Tamalarian Tale

Joshua Calkins-Treworgy

BooksForABuck.com

2008

A Hunter and His Prey:
A Tamalarian Tale

Joshua Calkins-Treworgy

BooksForABuck.com
2008

ISBN: 978-1-60215-084-3

A Hunter and his Prey

Also by Joshua T. Calkins-Treworgy:

From BooksForABuck.com

Damnation of the Realm: Freedom or the Fire Volume One

The Dread Knight's Redemption: Freedom or the Fire Volume Two

From PublishAmerica

The Druid, the Aide, and the Wolf: Book One of Dark Hearts

From Lulu.com

Motor City Shambler

Roads Through Amelia

Continuation and Damnation: Book Two of Dark Hearts

The Last Days of Freedman High

Wraiths of Formuth

Dedication

Firstly, I'd like to dedicate this Tamalarian Tale to my brother Colin, whose physically intimidating presence I thought of when trying to put the main character of this novel together. He had ever been the jester, especially combined with our oldest brother, Newton. I'd also like to thank said oldest brother Newt for first getting me interested in pen-and-paper role-playing games. Without those game sessions, I doubt I would have created Tamalaria.

A Hunter and his Prey

A Word Beforehand

Salutations, reader. I'd like to take a minute before the story begins to tell you how I became inspired to write about this story's primary protagonist, and where I came across my various inspirations.

The main character of this tale, a Simpa (read: werelion) by Race and a Bounty Hunter by trade, came into being from several sources. Firstly, I recall watching an anime (Japanese cartoon) by the name of *Cowboy Bebop*, a sort of science-fiction-Western hybrid set in the vast cosmos. The crew of the titular vessel, the *Bebop*, was an interesting amalgamation. The character who struck me most on that show was Jet Black, the sort of grumpy father-figure of the crew. He was physically husky and old-fashioned in his way. But he, like two of the other crewmembers, was mostly about the money of the profession.

The idea sort of formed itself. I wanted a Bounty Hunter character, but I wasn't quite sure of the Race or the personality. The second source of inspiration for this character came one night while I was channel surfing, and chanced upon *A&E*. This was around one or two in the morning, and though I was groggy, I had the presence of mind to stop flipping the station when I saw what was on. Or rather, who was on.

On my television screen stood Duane "Dog" Chapman, of Dog the *Bounty Hunter* fame. Having never heard about the show, I was ecstatic that blind luck had brought him into my home. His profession fit nicely for the character I was assembling. His lion's mane hair made the second decision in the creation process much easier for me. A Simpa, I decided. Yes, my Bounty Hunter will be a Simpa. There's more of "Dog" Chapman in the character within these pages than that, but I'm sure you'll figure that out.

I took this cobbled together character, and then ran him through a few role-playing sessions with my wife, Audrey. Together, we sort of hammered out his personality and mind-set. I later added in a dash of oddity, and the character himself was born.

There's also a minor character that shows up here largely thanks to my editor/publisher, Mister Robert Preece. This particular character, he said, was 'charming, and shouldn't be left feeling like a plant'. Well, I've addressed that a little by extending his time included in the story, and for those of you familiar with anagrams, you'll find this particular character enjoys ties to another great fictional bird, one who also had little exposure, but great impact.

And so once again I hope to take you into that mythical realm known as Tamalaria, and give you a tale taken from that place. I hope you enjoy your journey into it as much as I enjoy telling you about it.

Joshua Calkins-Treworgy

A Hunter and his Prey

Prologue

It was the year 877 A.F. The land of Tamalaria had barely recovered from the devastating War of Vandross. Now, no warlocks threatened the peace, no monsters ravaged the countryside. The more common, mundane sort of villain and beast roams freely once more, terrorizing their communities and the cities in old-fashioned ways.

But one city could never return to normal after the ravages of the warlock Richard Vandross: the city, of Ja-Wen. Brimming with brigands, thieves, and other merciless ne'er-do-wells, the city relies on a relatively new sort of professional: the Bounty Hunter. Commonly referred to as 'Bloody lawmen', or 'heroes-for-hire,' this group of professionals come predominantly from the fighter Classes, and are typically Human, Elven, or Jaft. But at high noon, where our story begins, one particular Bounty Hunter does not seem to fit this profession. He was a Simpa, or werelion in simple terms. His name was Portenda: Portenda the Quiet.

The noon sun blazed heat on the sprawling city of Ja-Wen, the wind gently churned dust on the town's streets. Only Pocket Town, the district in the northwest, had paved streets, as it was inhabited and independently maintained by the more well off members of the city's society. In the southwestern residential district, the buildings were shabby and worn down, the wood of the homes and apartment complexes stained and rotting from water damage suffered over the years. Down one of the many narrow streets of this hobbled-out area stalked a broad-shouldered Simpa, a man few of the locals recognized, or wanted anything to do with.

The Simpa wore the black leather armor typical to his people: buckles and belts and straps adorned the front of the upper leather shirt-coat. The sleeves had been torn off to the shoulder, exposing the robust musculature beneath his thin layer of golden fur. His pants were off-white, simple and baggy, concealing the chain link greaves that protected his legs. Bare feet curled their toes every few steps as he tested the ground for stability and movement opportunity. His cold, gray eyes swept over the area, scanning for any signs of ambush. He saw none, but noted the escape routes that he or his prey might take in the event of a confrontation.

Slung across his back were three weapons of equal deadliness: a broadsword that held an enchantment of some unidentified sort, a spear for thrusting and piercing attacks, and a chain flail. Though Bounty Hunters were well known for being all show and no skill, most entering the profession thinking it would be quick, easy money, the Simpa looked more than competent. *Then again*, Portenda thought without betraying any sign of emotion, *most died that way.*

At his right hip hung a monstrous crossbow, known to the Dragoon Forts and the Order of Oun militias as an Auto-Crossbow. Composed of wood and steel and springs, as well as a single pair of grind wheels, the bow had a crank on the left side and a circular attachment on the bottom for holding the bolts it fired. If used properly by a highly expert Elf Hunter or Soldier, an Auto-Crossbow could fire fifteen shots in a ten second span.

At his left hip, the silent Simpa kept a strange, ancient weapon, known as a *firearm*. Truth be told, Portenda knew it was once referred to as a pistol of the forty-fifth caliber, whatever that meant. It had taken him nearly four years to learn how to properly wield and maintain the odd weapon, but once he had the hang of it, he kept it as his standard response to ranged threats and targets.

Portenda saw neither his assortment of weapons nor is brute Simpa strength as his greatest assets. True, coming equipped like a one-man army made one appear intimidating, but the weapons and the armor and the fighting skills he had learned over the years did not by themselves make him deadly and effective. His keen sense of observation completed the package. As Portenda stalked down the dusty lane of Ja-Wen, his footsteps carefully counted in his head, he heard the faint rustle of a body standing from being flat against a wooden rooftop. From the faint echo and furtive movements of whoever made the noise, he estimated two hundred yards in distance from his location.

The Simpa stopped his advance, closing his eyes ever so slightly. The familiar clink and snapping noise of a crossbow bolt sliding into the firing position caught his ears.

Not a very well oiled weapon, he thought with a small measure of satisfaction. A quick sniff of the air alerted Portenda that the bolt was purest silver. Someone had done their homework. Few of his targets ever knew he was even coming for them; this one had both been informed and knew to bring silver to bear against the lycanthrope Bounty Hunter.

Using a snake-like slither, Portenda brought his right hand up to the hilt of his broadsword. *Wait for it,* he thought silently, *wait for it.*

His fingers remained open as he brushed the hilt with his palm, counting the seconds. *One, two, three, four,* he counted, waiting for the sound that would send him into motion. Almost a full minute passed before he heard it, the sharp report of the crossbow trigger and the catch of the firing mechanism snapping open.

His fingers closed on the broadsword, and in a single, lightning-quick reflex movement, he brought the weapon down in front of him, cutting the silver bolt in half and deflecting its motion into the ground at his feet. Both metal halves glimmered in the bright sun's rays as he lifted his head to look up at the face of a stunned Jaft Strong-arm Thug. Thug or Pickpocket, Portenda thought as he shook his head, they all think alike.

Whipping the sword back in place with his right arm, Portenda drew the firearm with his left and fired a single bullet back at the target, watching as the stricken Jaft spun around, a bleeding hole opened in his left leg. The force of the impact, combined with the angle, spun him around. From the edge of the inn, he dropped to the ground two stories below.

Landing with a heavy thud and a scream of agony, the blue-skinned humanoid writhed and thrashed about, clutching his wounded leg. "Why won't it heal?" Jafts' regenerative ability was on par with the healing factor of many lycanthropes. This Jaft's wound, however, refused to regenerate.

Well, the Bounty Hunter thought, *here we go again. The same dance of stupidity, foolishness, and cashing in.* He shook his head, trying to ignore the screams rolling from the target over his sensitive ears. *The target,* he thought, his feet starting him in motion towards the downed man. *If I keep working like this, they'll all be targets before too long. No friends, no family, just colleagues and targets.* He would have wondered what kind of life it was, but he already knew. It was a life of profit margins and staying in cold, unfamiliar places full of people he knew damned well didn't like him.

Portenda stopped fifteen yards of the Jaft, pulling a scroll out of his pocket and opening it. He glanced at the target on the ground, and then back to the sketch and the words 'Dead or Alive, five thousand gold pieces' beneath it. The name Roger Barone was in bold, italicized letters above the picture. This man fit the picture and the description. Without a word, Portenda pulled his large, green rucksack off of his back and withdrew several feet of thick, black rope, and slung the bag back over his shoulder.

"I'm not going without a fight." The Jaft sat up and pressed his back against the outside wall of the inn. He drew a wickedly curved and serrated dagger, holding it in front of him as a last line of defense. "You'll have to kill me, Bounty Hunter!"

"That's just fine by me." The Simpa's voice carried through the area though it was barely more than a whisper.

The entire neighborhood stood stock-still and silent, watching this encounter unfold.

Portenda looped the rope around his right hand, and held out the contract scroll for the Jaft to see. The target's face fell, and the dagger wavered.

"D-d-dead or alive?" the Jaft asked in a hushed, humble stammer. With the Jaft's attention on the scroll, Portenda drew his right hand back, and brought it down at an angle into Roger's upper forearm, knocking the weapon out of his hand.

With a howl of surprise, Roger watched his last chance for escape or resistance tumble under the feet of a storeowner.

The Human scooped up the dagger and whisked it away to his shop, where he would sell it for three gold pieces. A reasonable profit for something the man hadn't had to pay for at all.

Wasting no more precious time, Portenda used the rope to hog-tie Roger, slinging him over his burly left shoulder and stalking away from the area, the shadow of Death come alive. He sighed quietly at the drudgery of this routine for he could not recall clearly when last he had taken a break from his career. *Maybe never,* he thought. *Maybe this is all I am. A Simpa who couldn't even cling to the proud old ways of the hill-born lycanthropes.*

Local authorities hadn't been able to catch Barone, so they had issued a general bounty on his head: five thousand gold pieces. In a world where two-thousand gold pieces could buy you a house and a little property, successful Bounty Hunters made a great living.

There weren't very many successful Bounty Hunters in Tamalaria.

A Hunter and his Prey

Chapter One
Standards

In Ja-Wen, nighttime brought out three groups of people: drunks, mostly consisting of the city's blue-collar workers; unemployed 'adventurers'; and thieves. Jonah Staples belonged to none of these sects. He was a young Human male with a dream and a questionable source of information.

He pushed open a set of saloon-style doors, popular in Ja-Wen business buildings, and entered the seedy little tavern. A wooden plank out front named the place the 'Flaming Tongues'.

Jonah stepped into the dim lantern lights of the tavern. He stood at approximately five and a half feet in height, with a skinny, angular frame with an unkempt, shabby appearance. Thick, oily black hair hung in tufts about his head, uncombed and seemingly unwashed for weeks. With a simple woodsman's shirt, cloak and blue wool pants, he looked like an average, everyday citizen. With the thick, black leather-bound book tucked neatly under his left arm, he appeared to be the sort of man who spends his days working, reading, and doing little else.

Unbeknownst to anyone else in the tavern, Jonah carried a logbook. For two years, he had logged both public and private bounty contracts from the cities of Ja-Wen, the Port of Arcade, and Palen in the northeast. Each bounty listing was accompanied by the name of the Bounty Hunter who had collected, information that was free to the public, if the public bothered to inquire.

Jonah Staples was not some drunken wanderer or beggar. He was what is known in Tamalaria as a Scholar Class, a scientist-type. He had dreams of being something more. Jonah Staples wanted to be a Bounty Hunter, and he wanted to learn from the very best. Of all of the names of Bounty Hunters in his logbook, one name appeared time after time, accounting for a little more than half of the bounty head takedowns in the region. Portenda the Quiet.

Aside from being a Scholar, Jonah was well-versed in Alchemy and the principles governing the creation of tonics, tinctures, and potions. He hadn't gotten far into the semi-magical arts of Alchemy, which involved the concept of energy exchange and the reformation of molecules, but that was mostly due to his low income and lack of resources. Manuals on the higher, more complicated concepts of Alchemy cost an arm and a leg, and his job as a farm hand just wasn't paying enough. For a short time he had tried his hand as a potion shop owner, but that business venture had gone south, and he was forced to rely on the menial wages of a farm hand.

Two years previous to entering the Flaming Tongue, Jonah had resolved to become a Bounty Hunter, to train with the very best in the business. This Portenda, whoever he was, certainly qualified.

A month and a half earlier, an odd Gnome gentleman had stopped by the Newman farm, where Jonah worked, a man by the name of Lee Toren. Jonah, having recognized the name from one of his friends in Desanadron, had immediately asked the Gnome Pickpocket where Portenda the Quiet could be found.

11

"Ja-Wen, I fink," the Gnome had replied, weary and travel-worn. "I was just through that way not too long back. Think he's some sort of freelance adventurer or somefing loik that."

Jonah had thanked him for the information, and asked old man Newman to be excused for a while.

The kind old farmer had told him to go ahead, and that he had a job waiting for him when he returned.

The information hadn't been free, of course. Lee Toren had "this damned fuzzy memory," and had remembered the city name after ten gold pieces of reminding.

Now Johan stood looking into the shadowy corners of the tavern, trying to find a Bounty Hunter. Other than a name, Jonah knew nothing of the man. He would have to pester someone for a more precise account of the man. Barkeeps, he had learned in his travels, often had relevant information for travelers and adventurers looking for people or places specific to the region. The Dwarf at the counter looked like a reliable source of info, so Jonah walked awkwardly up to the bar.

"Excuse me, sir?" With a finger pointed upward, Jonah caught the Dwarf's attention.

The barkeep finished cleaning the mug he was rubbing down with a presumably clean cloth, then set the mug down and sauntered over in front of Jonah, placing his knobby hands flat on the counter. His braided beard ran nearly down to his sizable belly, and Jonah had trouble looking away from it for a moment. He had traveled much in his time, but had rarely seen such a gruff looking individual. He tended to take their sort as a sign of danger, and kept his distance. Now, he was surrounded by brutish looking people, and being glared at viciously by a member of one of the proudest warrior Races in the history of Tamalaria.

"Wot you want, stranger? Speak up." The Dwarven barkeep slammed a palm on his counter.

"Oh, yes." Jonah floundered for a moment. "I, ah, I'm looking for someone who might reside here in Ja-Wen. He goes by the name Portenda the Quiet." Jonah gave the Dwarf a winning smile, which apparently only served to aggravate the man, as the Dwarf made a fist and slowly heaved a sigh.

He pointed at the far corner of the tavern from the entrance, where a single Simpa, loaded for bear, sat sipping a drink and reading a town crier of some sort. "Ah, thank you very much sir." Jonah gave the Dwarf a slight bow. As he moved away, someone stuck their leg out at the bar, tripping Jonah up and sending him crashing to the floor.

A burly half-Orc seated nearby pointed at Jonah and giggled.

"Stupid Hu-man," the brute said, pronouncing the word 'human' with an apparent lack of mastery of the common tongue. "You need to watch your step around here. This is not some village in the sticks." The green-fleshed man hopped down off of his stool.

A Hunter and his Prey

Jonah scrambled back on all fours, in time to see several customers leaving through the front door. For a moment, he was nearly paralyzed; he had never seen a Greenskin, and though this man was clearly not a full-bred Orc, his manner and musculature spoke of his ancestry.

Several thugs at the counter spun in their seats to watch this spectacle of bullying first-hand, cheering as the half-Orc lifted Jonah by the collar.

Oh shit, oh shit, Jonah thought, his mind going into overdrive as panic set in. He looked around the room for help, but everyone was either sitting back and enjoying the show, or cowering away in the hopes that this drunken brute would be satisfied by only beating on one person smaller than him.

Wait. A rush of hope ran through him. He looked at the werelion in the corner, who was watching with a detached look on his noble face. *Wasn't he going to do something?* Jonah thought, afraid of what might happen next.

What happened next was painful. The half-Orc reared his head back, and pounded into Jonah's face with a head-butt that felt like a blow from a boulder.

Jonah flew backward, his nose broken and bloodied. Tears blurred his vision, and he tried to scurry beneath a table, but the customers seated there blocked him with their boots.

The half-Orc's crushing grip latched onto Jonah's ankle, and in an instant he was hanging upside down by his foot. The world tilted and wheeled. Luckily, he kept his money tucked in pouches around his waist, but it wouldn't take the brute long to figure that out.

Looking once again to the Simpa, Jonah shouted through bloodied lips. "Fifty gold pieces to anyone who will help me. Fifty!" It might not be enough to sate the Bounty Hunter's tastes, but it should get his attention.

He saw a blur of golden fur as the Simpa darted from his seat to the half-Orc's side, slamming into him with a huge, furious elbow strike to the ribs.

Jonah fell to the floor. As he fell, he saw the half-Orc fly across the tavern, landing on a table and breaking it into a thousand shards.

For a moment, the brute didn't move, and Jonah feared that the Simpa had killed the man. But then his head bobbed up, and he clutched his side.

"Big mistake, buddy," the half-Orc growled at the seven foot werelion. "Big mistake! I'm gonna…" as he tried to regain his feet, he fell back to the floor.

"You aren't going to do anything," the Simpa said in a deep but regal voice. His tone was quiet, barely a whisper, but it carried throughout the tavern effectively. "I struck your quiniod muscle, which as you well know has the tendency to cause muscle failure and spasms in your people. Even half-Orcs have quiniods. You may experience the need to rush to the bathroom, but with your ruptured muscle and broken ribs, you'll have to start crawling that way now."

The lethal Bounty Hunter turned to Jonah.

"Thank you greatly, sir, from the bottom of my heart," Jonah said, reaching for the hand the Simpa offered. But as he tried to grab it, the Simpa moved his hand away, reaching it back down a moment later. "Oh, yes, of course." Jonah untied one his money pouches and sett it in Portenda's hand.

The Simpa felt the bag for a moment, looking at it with those cold, dead gray eyes. He looked back up into Jonah's face as the Scholar got to his feet.

"There is only forty-eight gold in this pouch." There was a slight lilt to Portenda's flat tone, barely enough to keep it from being monotone.

Jonah looked at him as though stricken dumb. He was certain that there were fifty gold in that pouch.

Portenda opened the drawstring and poured the money onto a nearby table, counting it in his head as Jonah counted aloud. Forty-eight on the nose. How had the man known without counting it in the first place? He had merely felt the bag, and declared it two gold pieces shy. This had to be Portenda the Quiet, the Bounty Hunter whose name graced so many pages of his logbook.

"Here's the last two," Jonah said, placing two pieces down from another of his pouches. "You're him, aren't you? You're Portenda the Quiet!"

The Simpa glared at him with a steely gaze.

Jonah contained the urge to jump up and down like a fool. "Can we speak for a few minutes? I have some questions to ask you."

Portenda just shrugged, and returned to his table, leaving the town crier on the table's surface. He took a long pull of his drink, some sort of wine from the smell of it.

The young Scholar sat across from him, thumping the logbook on the table. "Do you know what this is?"

The Simpa didn't speak, didn't move. He made no sign to indicate that he did or didn't know anything, or think anything. *What's going through his head*, Jonah wondered silently? He opened the book to its first set of names, pointing at the pages excitedly. "This is a record log of all of the bounties that have been posted in the last two years for the cities of Ja-Wen, Palen, and the Port of Arcade. Next to each bounty, I've listed the name of the person who brought them in. Of three hundred and sixty-one bounties, you've brought in one hundred and ninety-eight. That's fifty-five percent. You're unarguably one of the best!"

For a long moment, neither man said anything.

When it became apparent that Portenda wasn't going to say anything, Jonah closed his book, somewhat discouraged. Didn't the man say anything? Sure, he spoke to the half-Orc, who was now making a slow trip to the bathroom, and he had even spoken to Jonah about his payment, but aside from that, he hadn't uttered a single word.

Jonah was incensed: how could anyone speak so little about himself? *All right*, he thought. *I'll just come out and ask him.*

"I've kept track of you for two solid years, and I've come to admire and respect your work and achievements. To tell the truth, I've also made a running tally of how much money you've earned off of these bounties." He tapped the book. "The total is nearly one hundred and fifty thousand gold pieces! You've got enough money to buy a city of reasonable size for the gods' sakes. How do you remain so silent, so enigmatic? Why do you still do this?"

"Because it's all I know." Portenda took another sip of his wine.

A Hunter and his Prey

Stunned by the swiftness of the response, and the fact that he got one at all, Jonah tried to assemble his thoughts. How would the man react to his request? *Most likely in a very harsh fashion*, he thought, *but nothing tried is nothing gained.*

"Very well then. Clearly, you're a man of business." Jonah got a genuine flare of interest out of the Bounty Hunter's eyes. The word 'business' apparently was something that got Portenda's attention. "Now, I know you took down a bounty head this morning, and received five thousand gold pieces, I believe it was. Oh, don't worry," he added, closing his eyes and leaning back in a haughty manner. "I have ways of finding these things out." Of course, those ways happened to be pestering the local constables for all bounty information they had until someone gave up resisting. "The point is, you make a handsome living doing what you're doing. I'd like to make that sort of money as well, you see. I'd like you to train me."

The instant the words parted from his lips, the gleam in Portenda's eyes faded into a cloudy gray.

Portenda stood, laid two gold pieces on the table, and stalked away.

Jonah, shocked at the sudden departure, collected his book and his thoughts before running after him. "Wait a minute." He looked at the Simpa's broad back, at his weapons, at his rucksack, noticing the odd weapon on the Simpa's left hip, recognizing it as a rare firearm.

"Why are you walking away? Look, I'm not joking! I want to learn from you! I'm a capable student, more than willing to learn anything! And I can teach you things too!"

Portenda half turned back toward him, the moonlight glinting off of the tip of his spear.

"What can you possibly teach me?"

"I can teach you about that weapon. That's called a pistol."

"I know about firearms," Portenda replied.

Jonah stood stock still once more. *Damnation. There goes that advantage.*

Recovering, Jonah ran up and around Portenda, stopping in front of him.

"Why won't you train me? Is it because I'm not big enough, not fast enough, not smart enough? What is wrong with the idea of training me?"

Portenda didn't move, didn't flinch. His nose rustled slightly as he sniffed the air.

"I know you're not stupid," Portenda said. "Those potions in your shirt and belt are homemade. You're an adept of Alchemy."

Incredible, Jonah thought to himself. *Such powers of observation.*

"Back at the bar," Portenda continued, "you were trying to get to cover so you could pull out one of those chemicals to spray in the half-Orc's face, weren't you?"

"How did you know that?"

"The way you were crawling, with your left hand trying to move you forward and retrieve the vial under your belt at the same time—a blunder, manageable if you had a little more muscle on you." Portenda started to turn away then, but Jonah had misread something in the Simpa's words.

"So you'll train me then?" He pressed his small, Human hands together in front of his chest.

"No," Portenda almost growled. He turned again and walked away, keeping his back to Jonah Staples.

"And why not," Jonah shouted at his broad back, furious and nearly in tears. Two years of work, now walking away from him like he didn't matter a whit. "Are you to full of yourself? Or is it because you can't stand the idea of having someone take an interest in you, other than trying to kill you or take your bounty head?"

At last, Portenda ceased his solemn, silent march. But when he turned around, Jonah began to question the wisdom of having taunted a man like him. Before he could blink, the Simpa loomed over him, the pistol in his hand, the barrel pressed against Jonah's forehead.

"This is the reality of the world around you, little man," Portenda said in that same regal but cold tone.

Formal, Jonah managed to think between bouts of *ohmygod, ohmygod, ohmygod.*

"There are those that can, and those that cannot. You cannot."

Somewhere in the middle of Portenda's short monologue, Jonah's left hand shot out and did something to the weapon in Portenda's hand.

The Simpa raised the weapon into the air, and pulled the trigger.

Nothing happened, no bullet fired, no resounding discharge of powders and metals. Absolutely nothing.

For perhaps the first time in years, Portenda the Quiet looked stunned, an expression that lasted all of a few seconds. But a few seconds was enough for Jonah to notice as he tossed the slide-catch of the weapon up and down in his left hand.

"I told you I knew about this weapon," Jonah bluffed. He had no idea what he had just done, save that it may well have saved him from having a heart attack. The Simpa had clearly never intended to do him harm. If he had, Jonah reasoned, the pistol would have remained aimed directly at him the whole time. A section of weapon still sat in Jonah's hand, but now he offered it up to the proud Simpa, who took it immediately and reassembled the weapon, aiming in Jonah's direction again.

"I thought," Jonah stammered, shocked into disbelief. *Now I've done it,* Jonah cringed with fear. *Now he's going to kill me!*

"Get down." Portenda's facial muscles tensed as he brought the weapon up and pulled the trigger.

The resounding report of the bullet firing from the ancient, mysterious weapon echoed over the nearly twenty-five square miles of residences, businesses, and various stables and taverns of Ja-Wen. Accompanying that sound was the crunch of metal deflecting metal. Only the regal Bounty Hunter heard the 'shink' of a short sword jamming into the ground.

"Be on your way. You've wasted enough of my time, brute."

Jonah turned to see the thug from the tavern, hands still raised over his head to strike the Human dead.

A Hunter and his Prey

With an awkward smile, the half-Orc tucked tail and sped off down the street, leaving a trail of kicked-up dust.

"Well, I suppose I owe you my life, again." Jonah was completely humbled by the Simpa's skill. The bullet had passed within inches of his head, and struck the thug's sword instead of his brains. Portenda's course of action made a strange sort of sense: neither he nor the half-Orc had been contracted targets, so of course they wouldn't be killed unless no other course of action was fitting.

"Come on. We're leaving." Portenda turned and stalking away.

The fact that Portenda had included him froze Jonah for a moment before he sprinted ahead to catch up.

"So what changed your mind? About bringing me along, I mean? Because it would appear to me that I just proved that I'm not up to being like you at all."

"My reasons are my own," the Bounty Hunter said in his emotionless tone. He didn't bother to look at the Human Scholar as he twirled the pistol twice and returned it to its holster. "And from the looks of things, you won't last long without a bodyguard. Don't get me wrong, I'm not going to train you." The Simpa sighed. "I have certain standards, and you're a long way from meeting them."

Jonah Staples was not concerned with meeting the Simpa's standards. While spending time with the Bounty Hunter, Jonah would learn.

Portenda the Quiet thought to himself, *this is going to take a whole lot of work.*

Chapter Two
The First Assignment

Jonah Staples followed the Bounty Hunter's broad back to a run-down, ramshackle apartment building, the inside hallway walls yellowed with age and tobacco smoke from pipes and the recent product of the Gnomes' collective ingenuity, smoke sticks. The floorboards creaked and groaned under his feet, but curiously enough, no sound came from the rotting planks of hardwood when Portenda stepped on them. The faint trickle and splash of water leaking through the building's roof echoed through the halls and stairwell as he and Portenda ascended to the third floor. The smell of ozone filled Jonah's lungs, as nearly a dozen assorted Humans, Jafts and Minotaur residents sat on a long bench on the third floor, smoking their own pipes.

Portenda stopped at a solid, off-white door, pulling a set of keys from one of his various pockets. Without even looking at the smokers, he selected an oblong key with a diamond-shaped head. Inserting into the lock, the Bounty Hunter turned it, turned it back, and turned it again, unlocking, locking, and unlocking the door.

Strange little ritual, Jonah thought.

Opening the door, Portenda leaned in, peered left and right, and then finally entered, waving Jonah along with him.

The apartment was Spartan to say the least: a single huge bed to accommodate the Simpa's thick frame, a fold-down cot for guests, a set of candles on a low topped table, and a single bookshelf stretching from the floor to the ceiling. Otherwise, the apartment was empty.

Jonah looked to the left, finding the door leading to the Gnome engineered bathroom. *Indoor plumbing,* he thought with a sigh of relief. Though many of their inventions and 'inspirations' tended to backfire, indoor plumbing was one Gnome Race project that had never failed for design reasons.

Taking a few steps into the room, and leaning forward, he saw a toilet, a sink, and a shower stall. *Good,* he thought. *All of the basic necessities.*

A cooking pot hung over a set of unburned logs in the fireplace against the far wall from the bed and the cot, which Portenda was now lowering to the floor. The pot looked pristine, and there were no ashes in the fireplace. Of course, there was the Dwarven stove and countertop on the left, probably used just as seldom as the cooking pit. Then again, the whole apartment was very clean. The wood of the floors looked new, freshly cut and laid, and then polished. The tabletop holding the candles almost shone, and the candles were all new, unlit.

Jonah took his rucksack off and tossed it to the floor near the cot.

Portenda picked it up and set it neatly at the end of the cot.

Hum. Opening his rucksack, Jonah spilled the contents across his threadbare cot, making sure to jumble everything together in general disarray.

As Portenda walked out of the bathroom, he entered. Closing the door, he crouched and peered through the keyhole.

A Hunter and his Prey

Through the small hole, he watched Portenda remove his own rucksack, setting it squarely against the wall near the head of his bed. He then took off his weapons and began setting them around the apartment in what appeared to Jonah to be a random fashion. On second observation, there was a weird sort of logic to his placement of the weapons. Portenda placed the ancient firearm under his pillow. On the floor next to the bed, he placed the broadsword. Jonah shifted his position and watched Portenda set his spear upright against the doorway leading into yet another room, presumably empty, Jonah thought.

The Simpa was strategically placing his weapons around the apartment. *How could the Bounty Hunter be so paranoid?* Jonah wondered.

Jonah realized he had spent too much time in the bathroom to feasibly just be using the toilet.

Portenda, he noted when he put his eye back to the keyhole, was nowhere to be seen. An instant later, Jonah nearly died of fright as a huge, gray eyeball filled his field of vision. "Holy shit!" He stumbled backwards, hitting the backs of his knees on the edge of the tub, falling in and hitting his head on the back wall. "Ow," he groaned as the door flew open to reveal Portenda, sans his black leather upper armor.

Jonah looked at the thick, muscular Simpa, his golden fur slightly wavier than most and with a strange set of gray stripes. Scars crisscrossed the entire front of his torso, permanent despite his lycanthrope ability to regenerate wounds. Small patches of fur were gone, somehow unable to grow. And those eyes, Jonah thought. Those eyes held a quiet ferocity at that moment.

Mortal fear slammed into Jonah with the force of a charging bull.

"Very good," Portenda said in his calm, level voice. "You've already taken one lesson in. Observe your target, no matter who or what it is."

Portenda offered his hand, and Jonah reached for it. As the Simpa lifted him up out of the tub, his hand slipped effortlessly out of Jonah's grasp and on to his throat.

Eyes wide, Jonah clutched at Portenda's wrist without result, trying to pry himself free.

"But lesson number two is a harsh one." Portenda narrowed his eyes squeezed the Human's throat. "Never trust your enemy." An instant later, Portenda let go, dropping Jonah in a limp heap of tangled limbs on the bathroom tiles.

"Right," Jonah gasped, rubbing his hurt throat. "Never trust your enemy." Jonah closed the door again, using the toilet and coming out a minute later to find Portenda sitting up in his bed with a book in his hand, and a pair of reading glasses on his face. The werelion looked almost ridiculous with the spectacles, but Jonah suppressed the urge to howl with laughter. He didn't want another 'lesson.'

"So, what do you keep in the other room?" Jonah asked, noting that the door had been shut.

Portenda looked up over the rims of his glasses, then back down at his book. "Go see for yourself."

His attention focused on a book, entitled, Jonah noticed, 'The Dreams of Men', a fiction novel that Jonah had read the previous year. He remembered struggling with the underlying concepts of the novel, looking for the hidden messages and metaphors while he read the book, having to read through it a second time before he had any success. He was pleasantly surprised to see that the Bounty Hunter wasn't all business and gruff, cold demeanor. Perhaps he could even drum up an intellectual conversation on the subject, though conversation was not one of Portenda's strong points.

Curious about the contents of the other room, Jonah walked over to the door and, without thinking, turned the handle and opened it. He heard the click of the door opening, and as he pushed the door open, he heard a second click.

Hmm? A bag of sand swung down, slamming into his face and upper torso and throwing him back onto the hardwood floor of the central room.

As he looked with blurred eyes at the ceiling, a huge, golden face hovered over him, upside down.

"You're fortunate I changed the trap attached to the swing arm. I normally keep a woodcutting axe there. You should have noticed the copper wire bound around the doorknob." Portenda used that cold tone, but actually gracing Jonah with a smile before returning with a heavy thud to his bed, his book in hand and his reading glasses on his face.

"Lesson number three, I'm guessing." Jonah rubbed his jaw and wobbled to his feet. The sandbag still swung in the doorway, and as Jonah pushed it aside, he noticed the woodcutting axe, its edge looking sharp enough to split a hair from his head, leaning against the right hand side of the doorway. Inside the room itself, rows of bookshelves filled the tiny room. Reference guides and textbooks lined bookcases on the left and half the far side of the room, blocking the windows. The other half of the opposing wall and the right hand side of the room was lined with fiction novels. *So many books*, Jonah thought with excitement. *Is that all the man does when he's not on the job? Read and sleep, occasionally eating and laying booby traps around the apartment?*

Perhaps Portenda wasn't such a bad guy after all—little anti-social maybe, and certainly lacking in tact, but not bad overall. Jonah strolled to one of the fiction shelves, watching his step and training his eyes on the ceiling and floor alternately, watching for more traps or pitfalls.

Finding none, he selected a book at random, and pulled it free. Or rather, he tried to, but had trouble doing so. So many books filled that particular shelf that he had to give it several heaves before coming away with a copy of 'Vampire Legends', a novel written several hundred years before.

In the main chamber, he found Portenda asleep with his face buried in his book.

That didn't take long, he thought. Then again, it might have been another ploy to catch him off guard. Leaving nothing to chance, Jonah moved slowly, keeping an eye on Portenda. Kneeling, he set the book slowly, silently, on the floor. Half turning away, he groped for the spear that Portenda had propped against the wall, clutching nothing but air. He turned away from the Simpa for a moment, located the spear a foot away from his grasp, and grabbed it.

As he did, he heard a loud click, and turned back to find the ancient firearm once again leveled at his head.

"Last lesson of the day. The situation is rarely exactly as it appears. But very good of you to try and take advantage of a situation. I heard your heartbeat start to race, counted your breaths." The Simpa stalked over to the bed, putting the pistol back under his pillow.

Jonah stood there, the spear still in his hand, marveling once again at the Simpa's powers of observation.

"From exiting the library to the spear is always two of my steps," the Simpa reported. "I compensated for your stride, knowing it would take four and a half strides for you, but I only counted three when you stopped. The airflow of the room shifted, and I knew you had turned your body sideways to me. That's when I chose to strike. You also failed to notice that my reading glasses weren't on. Someone who wears glasses for reading seldom takes them off if they fall asleep with the book in their hands. But that's all right. You've done surprisingly well for your first day." Portenda actually paid the Human a compliment. "I underestimated your willingness and rate of knowledge acquisition."

"Well, thank you very much." Jonah rubbed the back of his head awkwardly. "I'd like to think that am an apt pupil."

"And this is the first time I've ever taught anyone." Portenda peered over the rims of his glasses before removing them and marking his book, lying back on his bed. "I'll remember not to be so easy on you tomorrow."

Jonah laughed before realizing that there was no joke to be found. The Bounty Hunter intended to take things up a notch in the morning, and Jonah would have a whole day with him, learning in the harsh manner that the Simpa chose to teach.

"Gods in heavens, get me through the day tomorrow and I swear I'll pay each and every one of you tribute," he whispered, making every holy gesture he could think of before laying back on his cot in the dim light of one candle.

* * * *

When Jonah opened his eyes the next morning, he still couldn't see anything but the darkness behind his eyelids.

"What the hell?" He yawned and reached for what felt like a blindfold.

As he grabbed it, a huge, furry hand clamped down on his.

"Leave it on," Portenda said in a hushed whisper. "This is the day's first test. Let us see if you remember how to navigate my den."

The Scholar/Alchemist was at a loss for words; he had at least expected a meal and perhaps some coffee if the Simpa had it lying around, maybe in one of the many cupboards that Jonah had failed to investigate the night before.

"Isn't this a bit much?" Jonah swung his feet off the edge of the cot. He hoped that the Bounty Hunter would reply, giving him an audible clue to his location. He heard only the sound of the toilet running in the bathroom. "I mean, I haven't even eaten anything yet."

Once again, he failed to get a response from the Simpa.

"Hmmm," he grumbled, getting shakily to his feet. He could hardly recall the layout of the main chamber, which was sparse and mostly barren. But the Simpa may very well have laid caltrops or littered the floor with obstacles. Jonah crouched and reached for Portenda's bed, but it wasn't where it should have been. Taking one step forward, he waved his hands, searching for the bed.

While his attention was on the missing bed, his foot landed on something round and slippery. The world spun around him as he launched into the air, a bird falling quickly to the hardwood ground.

As he flopped about the floor, grasping for whatever had tripped him up like a sack of marbles, his hand found a metal pole. He slowly felt up the length of the shaft, not finding the spearhead he expected to be there. It was just a pole, nothing more—but he could use it to his advantage.

From one knee, he probed the area around him with the pole, contacting something wooden, judging by the sound. Portenda had moved his bed a good five feet from its original position.

Getting to his feet, Jonah used the pole as a walking stick, like a blind man navigating his own home. *God,* he thought dismally, *I never realized how much I depend on my eyes to tell me everything.*

Tapping around, he found several more obstacles, making his way slowly and cautiously across the room to the wall. As he pressed one hand against it, the blindfold was removed from his eyes, and the light temporarily blinded him again.

Rubbing his eyes, he looked at the smiling countenance of Portenda the Quiet.

"Very good, Mr. Staples." Portenda held out the man's identification papers.

"Are you all right?" Jonah had expected a much harsher judgment. "I mean, I fell, and had to use a pole to help me get over here. That's all for now?"

"It is." Portenda moved over to the cabinets after Jonah took his papers back. "For now. As for my attitude," Portenda's voice slid toward the same gray, cold tone as his eyes. "Well, I'm a morning person. I get over it fairly quickly. Now come over here and eat." He opened a cabinet door and pulling out a hunk of bread and from a separate drawer, a cold wedge of cheese.

Jonah approached and looked down, seeing that the second drawer was an icebox of some sort. Yet he saw no blocks of ice, just steam from the cooled compartment.

Portenda looked at his puzzled expression, then slid the drawer shut. "Enchanted. A business acquaintance of mine exchanged services for services. An Elven Aquamancer. I found his missing daughter, and he made me an unending icebox. Come on, eat. We've a long day ahead of us."

Portenda didn't any food for himself, Jonah noted. When did the man eat? How early had he wakened? According to Jonah's Gnome timepiece, it was only eight in the morning.

A Hunter and his Prey

"You don't talk about much outside of your trade, do you," Jonah asked between mouthfuls of bread, as Portenda watched him eat with detached interest. The air felt suddenly chilled, and Jonah knew that the Bounty Hunter's attitude was returning to the glib, reserved mode he had been in the evening before. *Quick change over*, Jonah thought bitterly. Maybe that's why he didn't wake me up at the same time as him, aside from setting up the little 'test' as the Simpa had called it.

Portenda simply shook his head, pulling one of the drapes open a bit. The Simpa had already armed himself, leaving his rucksack at the head of his bed.

Jonah moved over to his own rucksack, removing his mortar and pestle, his alembic, his calcinator and his small scales. All of his Alchemy equipment was now arranged neatly at the foot of his bed, and he rifled further into his bag, locating the individually wrapped ingredients but finding that he was out of scuggle root. "Damn it all," he muttered, popping the last of his cheese in his mouth and chewing slowly. He had wanted to make a quick sensory enhancing potion, but without scuggle root, he was out of luck.

"What's wrong?" Portenda loomed over the Human Scholar/Alchemist.

"I don't have any scuggle root." Jonah assumed that Portenda knew what the plant looked like and what it could do. He found that the Bounty Hunter now wore puzzled expression he'd had earlier. "It's a, uh, a sort of plant root. We Alchemists use it in potions of all sorts, and I wanted to prepare one before we went anywhere. It's fairly important to me, and I've got none left." He opened the small satchels and pouches of ingredients and showed them to the Bounty Hunter, who looked with mild interest at the assembled petals, powders and plant parts.

"I have no idea what I'm looking at."

He sounded uninterested to Jonah, who quickly started to pack the ingredients away.

Portenda clasped Jonah's wrist softly. "Leave them out. We'll see if we can find your scuggle root at an apothecary." He stalked to the front door, checking his key ring as he opened the door.

Jonah stood, put his rucksack across his shoulders, checked his belt for the potions he had on hand, and nodded before exiting the apartment.

"So, where are we going so early in the morning? Is anything open around here?"

Portenda looked at him and harrumphed rudely.

"This is Ja-Wen." He performed his locking-unlocking ritual in reverse. "Nothing ever closes. Come." He stalked down the hall nodding to a Jaft neighbor, who sat outside of his apartment, dragging off of a smoke stick and puffing smoke in Jonah's face.

The Human Scholar coughed haggardly, his lungs suddenly on fire. He followed Portenda down the stairwell and out into the morning sunlight, watching as the Simpa stretched and yawned mightily.

The neighborhood was already alive, the streets filled with laughing and playing children of various Races, children whose peoples had warred with each other for generations. A Jaft child, a boy no older than eleven, chased an Elven girl of comparable age. By the calendar, Jonah thought, she was probably around forty years of age, but Elves aged the slowest of all the Races. And they cherished their youth more than most. Traditionally Jafts, the blue skinned, brutal warrior people of the mountainous regions, didn't get along well with the fair skinned, magically inclined Elves of the woodlands.

Jonah enjoyed watching the children play, thinking back on his own youth. He hadn't paid much mind to the Race of his friends, the few that he had. Now, after years of travel, working, and hearing the opinions of his father and mother, he had a slightly different view of the Races of Tamalaria. Back then, leisure time was leisure time, and he was willing to spend it with whoever would give him the time of day. He recalled having a Draconus friend, one of the mighty dragon-men of the southeastern plains and desert region. He hadn't told his parents about the boy for fear that they would forbid him from playing with him. But Talok, the Draconus, had simply stopped showing up in the fields where they played their simple, childish games. Jonah had learned later that Talok's parents found out he was playing games with a Human child, and had forbidden him from ever going out and playing with Jonah again.

"What are you doing?" Portenda waved a huge, golden hand in front of his face.

"Oh," Jonah stammered, coming back to the present day and place. "Sorry, just remembering. Lead the way."

Portenda turned his broad back and stalking away at a brisk pace.

Jonah found the pace that Portenda set reasonable, even heartening, as they took turns here and there, stopping briefly at traveling merchants' wagon stands. Back and forth through the city streets they walked, and Jonah was surprised to find that several Dwarves were already coming out of a tavern, loaded with alcohol and good times shared, stumbling and bumbling down the road. He went out of his way to avoid them, sprinting ahead to walk side-by-side with the Bounty Hunter for a minute. "Those men were already drunk! It's not even," he said, looking at his timepiece. "It's not even ten in the morning yet."

"Overnight miners." Portenda didn't look back at them. "The layer of black and gray soot on their clothes, the drooping of their eyelids, give them away. Imbibing spirits does not make a Dwarf tired. Typically it wakes them up, no matter how drunk they get. Those men are tired from work. Their heart rates are slowed, their muscles tense from cutting rock. Their mattocks were covered in fresh dirt."

Portenda's words sent Jonah into a spiral of confusion as he looked over his shoulder at the fading Dwarves.

"How in the world did you notice all of that? We only walked past them. How do you do that?" He threw his arms around.

"You are drawing unwanted attention to us, Jonah. Please stop waving your hands around or I shall be forced to break your arms."

A Hunter and his Prey

Jonah ceased his ranting and tried to pay attention to his surroundings. *Too easily distracted or put off*, he thought to himself. *Must aspire to be more like this man. I must.* For a while longer, they simply ambled around town, covering about a quarter of the city before returning to the area where the Bounty Hunter resided.

"What was that all about?" Jonah set his rucksack down. Too much walking at too brisk a pace had made his shoulders and calves sore. "I mean, we didn't stop anywhere, talk to anyone, or really do much of anything. What was the point?"

"The sign in front of the apothecary," Portenda said without turning to face Jonah. "What color was it?"

What the hell sort of question is that, Jonah thought vehemently. But he breathed in deeply, calming his frayed nerves, thinking back on the sign. He couldn't remember for the life of him! Most apothecaries and Alchemy shops had the same colored sign though, a dark, verdant green.

"Green," he said, hazarding a guess.

"Good, even though you don't really remember."

"And how would you know I don't?" Jonah asked indignantly, sitting cross-legged on the ground.

"Your heart rate jumped and your jaw bone gnashed your teeth together. You were obviously drawing on other knowledge or memory." Portenda turned to face Jonah once again.

"You're making this too hard. This isn't fair at all." Jonah crossing his arms and threw back his head like an offended noble of the court.

Before he could apologize or explain, Portenda hefted him off of the ground, holding him a good foot over the street by his shirtfront. He was nose to nose with the deadly Bounty Hunter, the hot, reeking breath of Portenda's unclean teeth charging up his nose like a herd of stallions.

"Life, isn't, fair." The Simpa threw Jonah to the ground. "Lesson one for the day."

Clearly Jonah had offended the Simpa, but he was simply stating an opinion.

"That's a worldly truth that you're going to have to suffer with learning," the Simpa said, his eyes opening wide once more as he twitched and helped Jonah up off of the ground. "My apologies," he said flatly. "I lose my temper sometimes."

"Probably from bottling up your emotions all the time," Jonah said smugly. "I read somewhere that that isn't healthy for you." He had in fact read a well-respected Gnome healer's report on the subject of emotional stress and the effects it could have on a person. Without releasing one's emotions, the healer had written, one might very well experience a psychotic episode, as the broad Simpa just had.

"Let's just forget that it happened, okay," he offered.

"No. It was uncalled for. Come. Let's go get that, that, whatever it was you called it."

"Oh, yes," Jonah said, pointing his finger to the sky. He had almost forgotten. "Scuggle root. But let's not go the apothecary, Portenda. I much prefer Alchemy shops."

Portenda shrugged, then indicated that Jonah should lead the way.

Jonah took the lead for the first time, and the pair walked to the business district.

It took Jonah little time to locate the dank little store: they all looked the same from the outside, a single little shit hole building among two or three story ones. A wooden plank sign with a pentacle drawn inside of a square designated the shop, and they walked in.

Rows of candles lit the shop dimly, and scents of assorted spices and herbs filled the air. Portenda's nose shrank back, but he took a deep breath of the air, and appeared to be fine afterwards.

Oh, right, Jonah thought. Lycanthropes have sensitive noses.

"Greetingsssss," the Lizardman proprietor hissed as Jonah gazed around like a child in a candy shop. "What may I interest you in, fair student of Alchemy?"

Jonah had visited this store once or twice before, and each time it had a new owner or shopkeep. *Probably blew themselves up*, he thought with a wry grin.

"I need some scuggle root, sir," he replied, taking a look at a shiny brass calcinator. His steel one was getting old and beaten from heavy use, and he seriously considered getting a new one. He picked it up and tested it with his thumb and forefinger. Good balance, a fairly standard adjustment lever. But the tool didn't have the required range of measurements and adjustments that he needed. It was definitely designed for apprentices of the trade. "And would you happen to have another of these brass calcinators? Maybe one of a Midcuran rank?" Midcuran rank was generally accepted as the fourth of five ranks of Alchemy practitioner, and finding equipment of Midcuran or Uptcuran rank was difficult. Most Alchemy shop owners carried the goods and supplies meant for mid-level understudies, as the owners were more often businessmen first and Alchemists second.

"Asssss a matter of fact, I do," the Lizardman replied, much to Jonah's delight. He looked excitedly at Portenda, who was holding an alembic and eyeballing the tool with a mild sense of curiosity. The proprietor left through a veil curtain, and returned several moments later, a Midcuran rank brass calcinator in hand. "And here is your scuggle root, young man," he hissed, practically slithering over to his adding pad. "Now let'ssss sssee. Carry the two," he muttered under his breath, making Jonah a tad anxious about the overall cost of this endeavor. He might have to ask the man to remove the calcinator from his purchases. "That will be two hundred and seventy-five gold pieces, Human," the Lizardman said with a toothy grin.

Shit, Jonah thought. *I don't have that sort of cash on me.*

Before he could respond, three heavy leather pouches flew through the air and landed squarely on the counter in front of the Lizardman. Portenda looked at Jonah, who stared at him in shock. Portenda nodded slowly at him.

A Hunter and his Prey

"Wait, you're paying for thesssse," the Lizardman asked, his scaly forehead raising what would have been an eyebrow.

"Yes. Now give him his order." The enigmatic Simpa Bounty Hunter exited the shop, letting vibrant sunlight into the store for a moment before he disappeared.

"Your friend is a sssstrange one, Human," the Lizardman said from beneath his purple robe hood.

Jonah tied the pouch of scuggle root to his belt, and grabbed the calcinator, collapsing it to its travel arrangement and using the metal loop to connect it to his belt as well.

"He's not exactly my friend," Jonah said, looking the Lizardman in the eye. "But I agree wholeheartedly," he said with a wry smile. "He is a strange one."

* * * *

It was nearly noon when they arrived back at Portenda's apartment.

While walking back, Jonah tried to think about why a Bounty Hunter like Portenda the Quiet, who easily had vouchers and gold amounting to hundreds of thousands of gold pieces, would live in a place like this. The man could have had a house built to his design for a fraction of his earnings, so why did he live in a dilapidated apartment in a run-down building in the most poverty-stricken part of the city?

Deciding to focus on his work, Jonah sat on the floor of the apartment and set to making himself a pair of sensory-enhancing potions. He needed no guidebook or reference material for this task: he knew how to make dozens of potions and chemical tinctures and compounds by heart. He just needed some water, which Portenda provided, his ingredients, his tools, and some time. An hour, hour and a half, and he would have produced the potions in question and been done. Though he could have been considered an Uptcuran rank Alchemist, he considered himself lacking in that he still knew so little about the semi-magical arts of Alchemy known as Focus.

While Jonah worked, Portenda moved about the apartment, practicing sword techniques, spear attacks and defenses, and his quick draw with his ancient firearm. The man brimmed with energy, a fact that he kept reserved from the general public.

Don't let the target have any idea what you can do, Jonah reasoned. That sounded in his head like something the Simpa would say. He turned his attention back to his labors.

After a while, Portenda set his weapons down and looked at the Human. *Interesting one*, he thought. He removed his lead-lined leather armor, laying it softly across his bed, and walked into the bathroom, closing and locking the door behind him.

Inside, he looked at the patchwork of scars that littered his torso and arms. *So many battles fought*, he mused. *So many targets neutralized and brought into the accepting arms of the justice system.* Not all of his contracts had been confrontation driven. Some of them, like the Aquamancer and his missing daughter, hadn't required a single blow. And certainly this job wasn't like any he'd had.

Once, he had vowed never to reveal his secrets. But that had been almost thirty years before, when he took up Bounty Hunting. He had only been fifteen, barely an adult. But he had learned early on in life how to fight, how to defend himself. People like him often had to.

"Thanks a lot, father," he whispered as he looked balefully at the thin, gray stripes on his forearms. He took a washcloth from the cupboard at his feet, drew hot water over it and washing his forehead and underarms. The thin fur of his face was left clotted to his cheeks and neck, and his underarms no longer stank of sweat. How long had it been, anyway, he wondered. How long since he had actually allowed anyone into his abode? Five, six years? And that had been an unexpected visit from the man he hated most—his father.

Enough of this. He slapped himself hard in the face. *Get dried, get out, and get dressed. Check on Jonah, make sure he hasn't turned himself into a frog.*

Using the single red towel he kept in the apartment, he dried his face and underarms and opened the door that separated him from his Human pupil.

When he came out, he stood frozen where he was. Something revolting filled the air, and he nearly gagged on the stench.

Smoke plumed from one of Jonah's tools, but the Scholar/Alchemist didn't seem concerned. Rather, this appeared to be a part of the whole process.

Jonah turned and smiled brilliantly at Portenda, who quickly donned his leather armor and excused himself for some air.

"I need to get him a breathing mask or something," Jonah said as he watched Portenda slam the door shut on his apartment.

Looking back down at the smoldering liquid in his alembic as he finished the whole process, Jonah glanced at his timepiece. Fifty-seven minutes, he thought excitedly. A personal best. Taking two shatterproof vials from his rucksack, he carefully measured and poured an equal amount of the finished potion into each, corking them when he was done. "Not bad if I do say so myself."

"You can come back in," he yelled to the Simpa, opening a window to vent the room. As it slid open, he heard another of those horrible clicks—but not in time to prevent himself from being doused with tar from a concealed spout in the wall next to the window.

Portenda opened the door and stepped in, stopping in surprise when he saw Jonah. *Hmm. Forgot I put those in.*

Shrugging his shoulders at the seething glare that Jonah gave him, Portenda stalked into the bathroom and drew warm water for the Human to take a shower. "Hope you have a change of clothes in there." He pointed to Jonah's rucksack.

"Yes, as a matter of fact, I do," Jonah replied, wiping tar from his face. But he also knew one of Alchemy's many semi-magical tricks.

He closed his eyes and concentrated, mentally focusing his energy on the arrangement of the fabrics he wore. He made several gestures in the air, and with a whoosh of air and a glow of red light from his fingertips, his clothes were suddenly clean, free of tar.

Of course, now Portenda's floor was covered in it. "Whoops, sorry," he stammered, rushing into the bathroom and locking the door behind him.

Portenda sighed wearily, and got out his mop and bucket.

* * * *

An hour after that incident, Portenda strapped on his weapons and rucksack. "It's time I gave you your first assignment," he told Jonah as the freshly cleaned and shaven young man came out of the bathroom in a clean tunic shirt and forest green pants.

The ruffles on the collar and cuffs of Jonah's shirt gave him the semblance of a poet or an actor, though clearly he was neither of these things. His boyish look did lend him the illusion of perhaps being a young noble, however. Aside from the way he carried himself physically, he could very well have played the part. Had he been a Rogue, Portenda thought, he could use that sort of background as a set up for his lies and cons. Luckily, though, Jonah was no thief. The man had asked for permission to use the Simpa's towel, something a Rogue or any other thief for that matter would take for granted.

"My first assignment?" Jonah's eyes went wide. "But I've hardly learned anything! What sort of assignment could I possibly complete?" The Scholar was certain that the Bounty Hunter was mocking him.

"It's a simple assignment." Portenda opened the door to his apartment and let Jonah step through before doing the lock-unlock-lock routine. "Being a Bounty Hunter isn't all about combat and confrontation. Some contracts are simply requests for information, or the collection of an item or retrieval of a person. You're a talkative person, and believe it or not, that's to your advantage," Portenda said in that cold monotone of his. "People are more willing to part with information if the person asking is, amiable. Are you ready?"

Puffing out his chest, Jonah's eyes sparkled. Maybe this wouldn't be so rough after all. "Yes, I'm ready. What's my objective?" He tried too hard to sound professional and instead sounded hokey.

"Your task is to find me before sundown." Portenda put a blindfold over Jonah's eyes once again. "Keep it there, and count to two hundred. I will be hiding someplace in the city. If you run into trouble, don't worry." He retrieved a whistle from his pocket, the one his mother had used to call him in for dinner. It was all he had left to remember her by. "Now, bear this in mind. This item is very important to me. Lose it, and I will kill you."

Jonas laughed half-heartedly, hoping it was a jest.

"That is not a joke. I will kill you if you lose that. And remember, I'm very good at finding people."

The thinly veiled threat struck a chord in Jonah, sending a wave of darkness through his mind and soul that the sun's bright rays could never pierce.

"I completely understand your position," Jonah stammered. "But, what if it's stolen?"

"I will find the one responsible, and kill them," Portenda replied without pause. The quality of ferocious, territorial instinct in his voice did not escape

Jonah's notice. He nodded, and accepted the blindfold without complaint, counting aloud. As he counted, he tucked the whistle into a small pouch he kept around his neck, which held a single ring, an emerald set in the middle of it. His only sister had given it to him as a parting present when he had left home three years before she too had briefly gone out into the world. He wondered for a moment how she was doing, and resolved to write her a letter when he had the chance.

When he finished counting to two hundred, Jonah removed the blindfold and tucked it into one of his pants pockets. *All right*, he thought. *I have an entire city to search.* He checked his timepiece once again. *Six hours, roughly, before sunset.*

He darted down the hall, to the stairwell, and out past the many residents of the building. Outside, he looked left and right down the main street, trying to think of where the Simpa might take shelter in this little exercise. He tried to clear his head and think like Portenda the Quiet, but found it too difficult. He hadn't yet formed a full impression of the man's mannerisms and style, so he decided to head where he himself would most likely never go: the labor district.

The labor district of Ja-Wen lay on the opposite side of the city, but it took him only a little more than half an hour to negotiate the crowds of people and traveling merchants and find himself at the outskirts of the labor district, where most of the city's blue-collar residents worked.

There was a printing building for the town crier, filled with Gnome and Dwarven mecha from the Age of Mecha, when technology and science were at their height. That was eight hundred and some-odd years previous, though. Hence the A.F. on everyone's calendar, standing for After the Fall of Mecha.

A foundry, where the city's crops were compressed into canned foods, stood in the center of the district.

A mecha junk shop stood adjacent to the looming foundry, a Gnome shopkeep standing out front, trying to attract customers. And off in the distance, almost outside of the city, was the entrance to the iron ore mine where most of the Dwarves of Ja-Wen worked.

In addition to these places was the city's prison, a mammoth of a building, standing easily ten stories high. Ja-Wen seemed to attract some of the land's most dangerous and foolish criminals, and Jonah decided to keep as far away from that building as possible.

Several city constables, a Human, an Elf, and a tan furred Werewolf, stood near the junk shop, chatting amiably with the Gnome out front.

Werewolves, Jonah thought, *have the keenest noses of the lycanthrope Races*. He resolved to question the officer about a Simpa scent.

He approached with loud, clear footsteps and the trio of officers turned to face him.

"Good afternoon, citizen." The Human constable's chain mail caught the sunlight and reflected it into Jonah's eyes.

All three stood straight, their duties to the general public brought back to mind as they adjusted their uniforms. Each wore a wool overpiece, open on the sides and without sleeves, over their armor. The cloth had an emblem of a wolf's head on it, the red background edged with a yellow trim around the wolf's head insignia, indicating that they were indeed Ja-Wen constables.

"Good afternoon, sirs," Jonah said, hands clasped behind his back. "I was wondering if I could ask you a question."

"Certainly, citizen." The Elf's three bars indicated he was a Sergeant, while the two men with him had no such stripes on their persons. The Ja-Wen constables, preferring not to wear sleeves, wore badges on their collars instead, like regular army officer ranks. "How may we assist you?"

"Well, I'm looking for somebody, as a part of a sort of test, you see. I was wondering if any of you have seen or smelled a Simpa in the area recently." He tried not to be too specific. The constables might not be so willing to help if they knew Jonah was associated with a Bounty Hunter.

"No, can't say as we have." The Elf looked to his companions for confirmation, but both agreed that they hadn't seen or smelled anything.

"You said this is for some sort of test? Perhaps we shouldn't give you too much help. Proving your own capabilities is important in any society or Class. You should try talking with the common people," the Elven man suggested politely. "They tend to notice non-criminal activity much better than we can."

Jonah nodded in agreement, thanked them for their time.

Damnation, he grumbled inwardly. Five and a half hours left, and he had the whole of the rest of the city to search.

Jonah held tight to the straps of his rucksack, and jogged back toward the business district of the city. Perhaps speaking with bartenders would work, as it had the evening before. He wouldn't be going back to the Flaming Tongue, however. He didn't want to risk yet another encounter with the half-Orc brute. Portenda wasn't there to help him out, and he sincerely doubted that the thug would give him the time to use the whistle and call for help.

Keeping his head up, Jonah stopped in a circle surrounded by eateries and grocery stores.

Speak with the common people, the constable had said. Everyone needed food, even the most humble of folk.

His stomach growled at him as he approached a dining hall labeled 'The Meeting Place'. Perhaps he could stop for a quick bite to eat while he was at it.

Jonah pushed open the solid oak door, and found himself standing in front of a register.

The place was set up like a buffet restaurant, plates and containers of steaming food set on long benches and tables. A perky young Human girl at the front counter bobbed her head as she came up to him.

"Just one?" she asked in a high, bubbly voice.

Gods, he thought, unable to stop the perverse images from flooding through his mind's eye. *How long has it been, Jonah?* Three long years, he thought in glib response.

"Yes, just one please. Oh, and have you had any Simpa stop by, or seen one coming through the area?" He was going out on a limb here, but was more concerned with filling his stomach at the moment than finding Portenda the Quiet.

The girl cocked her head to one side.

"We have one sitting in the dining room. Is he friend of yours?"

"I don't know," he replied. "Is the man in there armed to the teeth?"

"Oh, no," the girl replied with a bounce and a giggle. "He's just a local we get in every now and then." She used the Dwarven adding machine to calculate his cost of a meal. "That'll be two gold and five silver." She held her hand out.

Jonah hurriedly paid her, and grabbed a plate, loading it with whatever caught his fancy.

Seating himself at the far end of a long table from the solitary Simpa customer, he began eating like a starved man.

"Easy there, sport," a familiar and unwelcome voice said from his left. "Too fast and you'll choke."

Jonah found himself looking at a tall, elegant Elven female of young adult age. Her skin was pale, like that of the Illeck, or dark Elf as they were commonly called. Raven black hair hung loosely about her shoulders. She was short for a woman of her Race, with sultry, dark blue eyes peering out from beneath a high forehead. Her slim, angular nose jutted in his face. Her trim, slender arms propped her head up on her palms, the sleeves of her navy blue dress practically hanging off of her gaunt frame.

Nareena Finch, an old friend of Jonah's until the two of them began to compete for dominance as the area's greatest Alchemist. In the short time he had lived down the road from her in Palen, they had become good friends, until each found out the other, too, was an Alchemist of some considerable skill. Since then, they had shared a bittersweet rivalry.

"Of all the places to run into you, Nareena." He had never been comfortable being close to her after finding out that the Elven girl created poisons of all sorts, as well as narcotics for commercial sale. The high demand for her products had made her a financial success, while Jonah had failed at even being a part-time vendor of healing potions. "What in blazes are you doing in Ja-Wen? What do you want with me?"

"Oh, nothing," the Elven woman cooed mockingly, letting her breath flow against the side of his neck and ear.

Gods, he thought, trying to control the urge to spin on her and take her then and there for everything she'd give.

"I just couldn't believe it was you, after so long. Tell me, Jonah," she said, inching a tad closer to him, and rubbing his back with her right hand. From years of hearing tales about her particular methods, Jonah put down his fork, reached back suddenly, and grabbed her wrist with his own scrawny left hand, pulling her hand up on the table.

"What the Hells are you doing?" she stammered. Jonah used the spoon in his right hand, and tapped Nareena's now clenched fist.

It sprang open, revealing small, thin sticking implement, like a thumbtack or pushpin. But this object had the slightest trace scent of vinegar and wildflowers —a truth serum.

"How very droll, Nareena." Jonah stripped the sticker from her palm, placing it in a separate, empty vial from his belt. "Thinking to slip it up under my shirt, or say the Hells with it and go through it. This wasn't some chance encounter, was it? You've been looking for me."

"Yes, actually, I have been." Nareena reached into a satchel on the floor at her feet, beneath the dining hall table and took out a modest sized book, bound in a yellow cover of some sort of animal skin. She set it down on the table, and pointed to it. "Jonah, I found this a couple of months ago in a set of ruins in the northwest, just north of Desanadron. Now, try as I might, I've never been much good with languages, and nobody else would help me." She ground her teeth for a moment, "I need your help."

"Piss off," he replied through a mouthful of food.

He stopped then, shocked at his own rude behavior. *What has come over me,* he thought. *I used to practically be in love with this woman. Why am I treating her so unkindly?*

Easy, a little voice in the back of his mind told him. *Because she tried to use truth serum on you!*

Oh, right, he thought in response. "What makes you so sure I'll be able to make heads or tails of the thing?"

"You've always been good with languages, and things that don't make much sense." Nareena picked at her own food with mild disinterest.

For nearly five long minutes, the two Alchemists sat in silence, the only sound the digging and scraping of Jonah's utensils as he ate his meal.

After he finished, Jonah pushed the tray and plates away from him, and got to his feet.

"Tell me Nareena, do you still have that carrier bird, the one that can deliver letters?" he asked as he picked up the yellow bound tome.

Hope flickered in the Elven woman's eyes.

"Of course. Writing to your sister again? What was her name?"

"Eileen." Jonah perused the book. He had the advantage of a more thorough personal education outside of Alchemy and Nareena often came running to him for help on matters outside of their chosen art. Letters by postman took too long to get where they were going. Even if the rider didn't get mugged on the way, a few letters always went missing by the end of his or her route. Nareena's trained crow, in contrast, never failed to deliver quickly.

"I'll tell you what," Jonah said, mentally translating the ancient Cuyotai script as he flipped through the pages. An arcane and unused form of the werecoyotes' tongue, the text came easily enough to him, though a few characters remained beyond his ken. "I'll translate the text for you, in return for the use of your bird. Fair enough?"

"Fair enough," Nareena replied with a genuinely warm smile.

Jonah put the tome in his rucksack, along with his other belongings.

His whole world was in that bag, he thought dismally. But he found himself smiling back at Nareena for a moment, their past troubles and rivalry set aside for this one, perfect moment.

Then Nareena stood and got too close for comfort again, and Jonah found himself reflexively stepping back, his left hand easing toward the only weapon he kept on him, a steel long knife.

Sensing his mistrust, the Elven woman gave him an awkward smile.

"So, how long should it take?" She scanned the room briefly. People had been watching them since Jonah had grabbed her hand and fairly slammed it down on the table. His reaction had been more violent than anything she would have expected from this calm, polite and quiet little man. He had changed—and recently from the feel of the air around him.

"Three days, tops." He took in a deep breath. *Gods, that same perfume as before, with the trace hints of jasmine and sage.* It radiated off of her, and combined with her pale complexion, vibrant eyes and graceful, bountiful curves, Jonah found himself once again attracted to her in a way that made him almost blush. "Meet me here in two days, around this time. If I'm not finished, I won't show up. Just come the next day, and I'll have everything ready for you."

"Jonah." She put a gentle hand on his shoulder to stay him for just another moment.

He half turned to face her, determined to deal with whatever she said or asked in a fashion akin to the Bounty Hunter. After all, he was trying to be more like Portenda the Quiet.

"Do you ever wonder," she asked, "what might have been? If we could have, you know, gotten past our differences?"

He saw the genuine, heart-felt interest in her eyes, heard it in her voice. Her touch was almost a plea for a positive answer, but unfortunately, he had no positive answer for her.

"Yes, I've wondered. But then I remember that you make your living by helping others take people's lives." *Gods,* he thought. *How can a man live like this? Always putting people off, not keeping any friends to speak of.* Did the Simpa have any friends? He resolved to ask him when he found him.

Checking his timepiece, he saw that he only had about four and a half hours left to do so. He refused to fail this first assignment.

* * * *

Jonah's scent wafted through the air, mingling with many hundreds of others, but Portenda had no trouble catching it.

From the building he stood atop, he looked down over the sprawling masses of the people going on about their business and their personal affairs with the ease that comes from being common civilians. He wondered what drove them, what kept people going from day to day. Most people led common, uneventful lives, filled with the tedium of routine and familiarity.

Then again, so did he, jumping from contract to contract, bounty to bounty, without much of a break in the pattern. Only once before had he taken time out from his business, and that had been when his father had stopped by to visit.

"The bastard," Portenda growled, leaning against the edge of the roof and clutching the cement barrier that kept people from just falling off of the building.

Portenda had been in his apartment, minding his own business, reading through his first copy of *A Tall Tale* by Whitney Rogers, an autobiography about a Giant's life among the short Minotaur tribes of the north central mountain ranges. His father had kicked down the door, and stood there smiling like a drunken idiot, which nine times out of ten, he was.

His father, a slightly more beige hued Simpa, had fallen flat on his face, affected by something that the Humans referred to as 'alcohol poisoning'.

Portenda had been forced to go and buy a cot and treat his father's sickness for three days, listening to the offensive banter he spewed about Portenda's mother and how much Portenda disappointed him.

"I, am ashamed, to be your father," the old coot had growled at him on the second day, spitting a huge wad of phlegm right in Portenda's eye.

The icy Bounty Hunter had wiped his face with a rag, and for the second time in his life, lashed out at his father, screaming and raging like he never had before. So enraged was he, so livid at his father's insults, that he had hurled a novel at the older Simpa's head, striking him in the forehead with the spine of the book.

The old man had fallen silent then, and the two didn't speak again, even when Portenda showed him out of the building on the evening of the third day of his unwelcome and unexpected visit.

For a solid week after his father's departure, Portenda had scrubbed the floors of his apartment to get rid of the stench of his vomiting. In the end, he had given up and torn the floorboards up, replacing them with better cuts of hard oak.

That had been his last visitor until Jonah Staples showed up at the Flaming Tongue.

Few members of the smaller Races intrigued Portenda quite as much as the diminutive Scholar/Alchemist. The man had intelligence, that much had been obvious from the start. And he possessed a sort of sophistication better suited to the upper classes, though he appeared more like a blue-collar laborer than nobleman. Portenda had never before met a man who could easily browse through his personal library and tell the Bounty Hunter, 'well, I've read most of these.' Yet Jonah had. An interesting man, indeed.

But the Human only had about four hours left to find him, and Portenda felt genuinely worried for him. If he had time to use his chemicals, the Human posed a threat, but his reflexes were simply too slow. How Jonah had dismantled the ancient firearm in the blink of an eye still puzzled him, but Portenda was starting to think he knew how it had been pulled off. Firearms were the result of science, mecha on the forefront of history's progress. And Jonah had told him that he was a Scholar and Alchemist from the start, both

Classes of scientist type. Perhaps there was a natural connection between the nerdy Human and mecha. Many mages believed science to be a part of nature, defined by logic and reason. Natural connections, in that case, weren't impossible.

Portenda stalked across the rooftop to the access door that would lead people up to and down from the roof, leaning against the stone structure. He felt suddenly fatigued. His body slumped, and he slouched against the side of the stairwell access, his muscles burning as though he had just run for a week straight without stopping. He had almost done such a thing when he was nearing the completion of his self-training, before his career as a Bounty Hunter. He had run six days flat-out, making the trek from Palen to Ja-Wen in a record time for foot travel. Of course, no one documented his achievement. Like most of his accomplishments in life, it had gone completely unnoticed and unrecorded. Yet, Jonah had kept a record on him. A record of two years out of the thirty he had been in this line of work.

With no preamble, and no real reason to stay awake, Portenda let slumber carry him off.

* * * *

"Screw it." Jonah drew out one of his sensory enhancing potions.

Pulling the cork with a loud pop, he drank. The taste of week-expired custard and thyme washed over his palette, nearly causing him to gag. Swallowing hard, his eyes squeezed shut with disgust, Jonah mentally adjusted himself as the liquid took immediate effect.

A loud clack-clack-clack resounded in his eardrum, and he opened his eyes to look at the building wall to his left. A large wolf spider, its web not yet constructed, shuffled along the brick outer wall of an eatery. He focused his attention on his vision, and could immediately see the swollen membrane along the spider's underbelly. It was about to be a mother.

He scoured the area with his eyes.

Prismatic rays of light filled the central area of the dining sector, the slowly waning sunlight trickling gracefully through the sky. He could detect the faint scent of perfume, and turned to see Nareena walking out of the diner area.

Wait a minute, he thought. *I don't even know what a Simpa smells like.* Jonah raced back past the hostess and stopped behind the Simpa customer. Taking a mental note of the particular scent, he dashed back outside.

Ah, he thought excitedly. *A trace of it, due south from here.*

Sniffling at the air every few yards, he walked down the street, calm and collected.

When he reached the midpoint between his start and his final destination, something that reeked of stale food and booze blocked his path.

Following his nose, he had ceased to pay attention to where his feet were taking him.

He was in a long, narrow alley. At the far end stood the half-Orc brute from the Flaming Tongue. This was exactly what he had been trying to avoid, a confrontation that he might not be able to get out of easily.

A Hunter and his Prey

Jonah spun around, but found a menacing Human patting a club on his left palm in a threatening fashion.

Go ahead, the man's rough, oft broken countenance said, *try something funny*.

"Hey there, bub," the gruff half-Orc intoned to his back. "Remember me? We have business we didn't have a chance to take care of at the tavern," The stepped forward and drew a long knife from his hip.

It cleared its metal sheath with a deafening shriek of metal scraping metal, but Jonah knew that this was only his perception of the sound. With his senses finely tuned, he could hear the two thugs' labored breathing as they approached.

Think, Jonah, think. You can take care of this on your own.

"No more hesitation," he whispered. The Alchemist drew out and threw a vial of blood-red fluid.

The fragile glass vial broke open against the half-Orc's chest and the tincture engulfed him in roaring flames.

Shrieking like a banshee, the green-hued humanoid flailed about, thick black smoke pluming from his clothes.

Whipping around and facing the Human thug, Jonah hauled back his left arm, a green powder from one of his many pouches in his hand. "Just try it, villainous cur,"

The bruise-laden man stopped in his tracks, his club poised to strike.

"Go ahead! Your organs will be turned into a collection of flayed meat and pools of blood when I blow this stuff in your face." Jonah felt rather proud of his bluff. The powder was Cutsen Powder, made by grinding the bones of a dead Aeromancer. It would turn into a set of Aeromancy cutting blades. The damage they inflicted would be minimal, but this brute didn't know that, just like he didn't know that the half-Orc wasn't really on fire. The chemical compound in the vial that Jonah had hurled against the green man created flames that only consumed cloth and metal. Lethal against a Dwarf, due to the nature of their skeletal structure, with the traces of iron ore in their bones, it was harmless to other Races or animals.

The Human turned around and ran, his heart hammering in his chest like a horse running at full tilt.

Jonah chuckled softly, put the powder back in its pouch, and turned to face the half-Orc, whose flames were petering out.

Jonah drew the long knife from his belt with casual ease and leaned against one of the alley walls. As the last traces of the flames snuffed out, the half-Orc glared at Jonah with murder in his eyes. "Is that all? A cheap trick?"

"Not exactly cheap," Jonah said, smiling to himself and peering at the man from the corner of his eye. "It cost you plenty. Notice a draft?"

The half-Orc looked down, saw that he was standing there in the nude, and immediately broke out in a cold sweat. He grabbed a trash can lid and covered his shame, keeping his rear end covered with one hand.

"You'll notice your weapon is gone, too, as well as all of your money. That stuff just eats right through everything but flesh, bone and soil. You may want to consider leaving." Jonah pushed off of the wall, twirling the knife in his hand inexpertly. Still, the overall look of the action made him seem rather nonchalant and quite deadly, or so he hoped. "Or perhaps you'd enjoy having a few body parts go missing. Or rather, one, body part go missing." He smiled like a demon as he pointed the tip of his long knife at the trash lid the half-Orc held.

Looking to where the weapon pointed, the half-Orc stumbled backwards, shouting in panic as he turned and fled through the city streets of Ja-Wen.

"Idiot," Jonah muttered as he put the weapon away and reviewed his stock of Alchemical compounds and mixtures.

The whole incident had taken little more than four minutes, but Jonah was overwhelmed by the adrenaline flowing through his system. He had to sit down, take a moment, and breathe deeply.

His thoughts came into line, and his sense of logic honed itself down to a fine tip; everything seemed clear, and he found himself trying to think of the simplest, quickest way to find the Bounty Hunter.

Wait a minute, he thought excitedly.

He drew the whistle from his pouch at his neck. He had the means to get the Simpa from the very get-go, but he had never thought to use it that way.

Neither had Portenda the Quiet.

* * * *

Somewhere between sleep and consciousness, Portenda heard the high-pitched tone of his mother's whistle. Jonah was in trouble.

He shrugged off the shackles of sleep, checked his equipment hastily, and darted toward the edge of the rooftop, leaping over the shin-high stone barrier and flying through the air like a huge, graceful bird. Or rather, he could have been said to fly like a bird bearing down on a small army. By itself.

Landing in a skidding crouch, sliding along the next rooftop without making a single noise, the Simpa wondered what situation Jonah had gotten himself into. The Alchemist's pride scurried along behind his eyes, trying to remain hidden and unnoticed, Portenda thought.

He hurried along to the iron fire escape steps, jumping off of the side of the building he'd landed on and latching onto the lowest railing as he fell like a rock.

The Bounty Hunter had miscalculated the height from which he dropped. As he latched onto the railing of the fire escape, he heard a loud pop.

His body dangled from his failing right handed grip, his shoulder out of joint.

Terrific, he thought, disgusted with himself. He looked down to the dirt alley below him, dropped in a three-point stance, and rose to his full height.

Holding his right arm across his torso at an angle, he slammed his shoulder into the nearby wall. Another pop, and his shoulder was reset.

Portenda paid little or no heed to the shocked and frightened faces of the people he raced past. Men, women and children leapt to get clear of his path. A heavily armed Simpa with a face full of worry and rage was flying down the street at them. Of course they cleared the way.

Once more the whistle sang out, sending mental images of the Human's impending beat-down through his head.

A Hunter and his Prey

Portenda the Quiet ducked down an alleyway, and stopped abruptly, sweeping the area with his eyes, nose, and ears. He heard a human's racing heartbeat and could smell Jonah. He was close.

Portenda closed his eyes, and felt the flow of the air around him. He reached out, grabbing something solid.

When he opened his eyes, he had Jonah in his hand, the Alchemical effect of his temporary invisibility potion having run out.

Jonah smiled at Portenda, and tapped him on the shoulder.

"Found you." The Human grinned.

"What? I," Portenda started, at a sudden loss of words. Something had happened here that he hadn't thought to factor in. He had allowed it to happen, because he hadn't made very basic ground rules.

"You gave me a very useful tool." Jonah held up the whistle, which Portenda snatched out of his hand. "You let me have something that would give me almost instant access to you at any time I chose, and you never thought to restrict me from using it in such a fashion. One of the quotes in the unwritten rules of the Bounty Hunter is, 'Use everything at your disposal,' isn't it?"

Portenda looked at the whistle before he tucked it away, and he let out a sound that nobody had heard from him for nearly ten or eleven years: he chuckled, a low, growling laughter deep in his stomach, rising up and stopping at his clamped mouth. He turned, put a huge, hairy arm around Jonah's shoulder, and began to walk with him that way.

"Very good. You've passed your first assignment with flying colors, Mr. Staples." Portenda let Jonah go before they exited the alley.

Chapter Three
Trouble at Home

The next morning, Jonah wrote a lengthy letter to his sister, telling her about the last forty-eight hours' events, and asking about her own daily goings-on. Eileen led a fairly simple life with their mother and father in Desanadron, where their father had a job as a night watchman.

Jacob Staples, their father, had never understood his son's interests in the sciences, or his daughter's fascination with animals. A man in his mid-fifties, he had always been Soldier Class, learning early the arts of warfare and combat. During the War of Vandross, he had served as a foot soldier in the army of the rebuilding city of Desanadron. Now, retired from the regular army with a nice pension, he needed something to do to kill the time at night.

The Staples children's mother, Anna Staples, had never worked out of the home since marrying Jacob shortly after the war. Jonah, their first child, had been born several years into their marriage, when Jacob was out on assignment as a border patrolman. He had not seen his son until the boy was four months old, and hadn't known that his brother, Allen, had spent most of that time helping Anna with the newfound venture of motherhood. Allen had four children of his own already. When the soldier had returned home from assignment he had been immediately assaulted with a barrage of hints, tips and examples from his older brother.

Uncle Allen had been an Alchemist and Engineer, both Scientist Classes. Growing up, Jonah had seen his uncle more often than his father, but he'd sympathized with the soldier. "He needs to earn money," he had told his mother once when she tried to apologize for daddy not being around to help with his little sister. "Or we wouldn't have a home."

Five years separated the two siblings, making Eileen sometimes seem a tad naive to Jonah. Yet, the two had kept contact through written letters every few months.

As he finished his good-byes, Jonah looked at his timepiece. It was fast approaching midnight, and he needed some sleep. He was certain the Simpa would have another rigorous day planned for him.

Rolling the scroll up as small as he could, Jonah placed it inside of a carrier bird tube, which Nareena could attach to her bird's leg. He resolved to start translating the ancient Cuyotai text the next day. If he had a chance, he amended mentally. Gods only knew what Portenda the Quiet would have in store for him.

Since returning to the apartment, the Simpa hadn't said a word, and presently slept as soundly as a newborn babe. *Sleep*, Jonah thought wearily. *Sounds good.*

Jonah's dreams were filled with memories of how life had been in the last year or so he had lived with his mother, father, and Eileen. He spent many hours slaving away in the laboratory that his parents let him keep in the basement, often receiving instruction from his uncle and the various textbooks that the man kept with him. Allen Staples, while intelligent and well read, didn't have a capacity for memory. The man kept reference manuals and handwritten books of notes and diagrams on hand as a result, and Jonah had learned a great deal from them. The diagrams, for some reason, stood out boldly in his mind while he dreamed. He seldom saw them anymore, knowing that the knowledge of them was somehow secretive, sacred in some way. Why, he could not clearly recall.

Then, someone was shaking him. "Get up," Portenda whispered, his face inches away from Jonah's.

The Scholar/Alchemist had fallen asleep on the floor where he had written his letter to Eileen.

The look in Portenda's normally emotionless gray eyes told him that something was terribly wrong. Jonah sat up like a bolt of lightning, getting to his feet and putting his hand on his long knife's handle.

"What's going on?" He checked his timepiece. He had only been asleep a couple of hours.

"Someone just knocked on my door. I don't get visitors." Portenda checked his broadsword. "Elven, female from the smell of her," Portenda said, his tone flat once more. "Wearing some sort of expensive perfume. She's slender, her heart beats almost right against her flesh. The knock had little strength behind it."

Jonah tried to prepare for whatever might be on the other side of that door. He hoped they simply had a wrong address.

"Open the door." Portenda took a position against the wall, weapon at the ready.

Jonah walked up to the door, and tried to look out of the peephole, but found that it was blotted over. This person wanted their identity to be a surprise. Jonah was almost certain that it was some drunken woman who had gotten her boyfriend's address wrong.

He turned the knob and opened the door, and found Nareena standing there in all her glory.

Half-asleep and lacking in the proper judgment, Jonah found himself almost uncontrollably attracted to her as she smiled that coy smile at him, her rose-hued lips looking so inviting.

"Oh, Nareena." He glanced at Portenda, who sheathed his weapon when the woman was identified.

A low growl escaped the Simpa Bounty Hunter's throat, and Jonah woke up rather quickly. "Um, how did you find me?"

"I didn't," the Elven woman said, extending her arm, where her crow was perched. "He did. I needed to see you again, about that text."

Her lie was rather transparent. Jonah could smell liquor and smoke on her breath and on her clothes. Gods, he had never actually seen her drunk, though he had heard stories from his peers in Ja-Wen and Palen. She became rather 'friendly', as they had subtly put it.

"Can I come in," she asked, lowering her chin to her chest seductively.

Oh, how he wanted to forget their long-standing rivalry, grab her, and take her to his cot. But this wasn't his home. For all he knew, the Simpa would be incensed and throw him out on his ear. He looked over to Portenda, who just stood with his arms crossed over his chest in a very paternal fashion.

"Um, look, Nareena, this isn't even my place," Jonah stammered.

The Elven woman poked her head in, leaning forward while holding the doorframe, exposing her ample cleavage to the Scholar/Alchemist.

He tried not to stare, but found his eyes locked on her bosom. She looked directly at Portenda, and smiled sloppily.

"Oh, hey mister," she slurred, almost falling forward onto Jonah. The crow fluttered up onto her shoulder, twitching its head this way and that, its eyes finally settling on the Bounty Hunter.

"Hello," Portenda said in his slow, cold fashion. He moved away, toward the Gnome coffee maker, and then sauntered into his bathroom and started a shower running before coming out and clamping a hand on Jonah's shoulder. "Get her inside. Get her into the shower, try to sober her up. There's a spare towel tucked under the tub." He started the coffee brewing as he kept his back to the Human and Elf.

Jonah stared at him with surprise: he wasn't pissed off at this intrusion of his privacy? He didn't mind that someone had followed him, and inadvertently found the Bounty Hunter? Jonah grasped Nareena softly by the hand, leading her inside and closing the door behind them. Her crow took wing out into the kitchen area with Portenda, perching on the counter just out of hand's reach from the looming Simpa. As Jonah turned to lead her to the shower, she threw him back against the door and pressed her mouth to his, kissing him roughly.

For a moment, he let it happen, but then he felt Portenda slip his huge, powerful hand between the two of them, pulling Nareena easily away from him. He gripped the Elven woman by the shoulders gently, giving her an easy smile. "Miss Nareena, you are heavily inebriated. Let Jonah help you into the shower."

Jonah once again felt shocked to the core; the man was showing an impressive range of emotion and compassion for one so generally cold and unmovable.

"Sure, whatever." Nareena brushed the huge, furry hands away and grabbing Jonah by the hand. "Lead the way, stud." She gave Jonah a look that cried out to him in a primal, feral way.

He led her into the bathroom, where steam sprang up like mist from the warm, running shower.

"Get undressed and get in." He tried to sound like the authority figure in the apartment.

She grabbed him by the crotch, and he went icy cold and still to the bone, paralyzed by the venom of sexual desires.

"You wanna help me with that." She licked his cheek.

Gods that's unattractive, he thought, genuinely disgusted at the damp tongue against his face.

A Hunter and his Prey

"And I've got this spot on my back I can never reach." She laughed drunkenly.

Jonah almost lost control, but cleared his throat, and resolved to do the gentlemanly thing.

"I'll help you undress, but that's it." He reached under the tub and found a yellow terrycloth towel, much softer than the one that Portenda used. Jonah aided Nareena as best he could, trying not to touch any one part of her body more than the others, and helped her step into the tub. Once she was in, he closed the shower curtain, and moved out into the main den, closing the door behind him.

"Leave it open," Portenda said to him from his seat on his bed. He kept his eyes locked on the crow, which appeared to be smiling at him, as if it held some secret from him. "You'll have to check on her now and again, make sure she hasn't drowned."

"How are you all right with this," Jonah blurted. "I mean, I apologize for letting her follow me, but I must say, you're handling this much better than I am." He flopped down on the edge of the bed next to the Simpa.

"Yes, well, I'm not attracted to her nearly as much as you are," Portenda replied.

Jonah sat straight like a bolt. His heart hammered like one of those ancient Dwarven mecha tools. What did they call them, he thought. Oh, yes, jackhammers.

"Carnal desires are a natural part of the living experience, Jonah," Portenda said. "So, for most mortals, are drunken stupors."

Jonah heard, on the outside of his audible range, sobbing in the bathroom.

"You might want to go to her now. I think she's coming around."

Jonah cautiously crept into the bathroom, hearing Nareena's moaning sobs over the running water.

"Nareena?"

She gasped, and swallowed hard. "I'm, I'm confused Jonah." She turned the water off and threw the curtain open.

Jonah averted his eyes from her slick, slender frame. *Like the road between Arcade and Palen*, he thought, offering her the towel. *Curves in all the right places.*

She took the towel and wrapped it around herself.

"I'm covered," she said.

Jonah looked to find that she was rubbing her blood-shot eyes.

"I'm so sorry about this," she said, sobbing and laughing at the same time. "I, I don't know what came over me." "I just asked Talonz to find you, that was all," she said, referring to her crow.

"I'll let you get dried and dressed." He closed the door behind him. He had been handed the opportunity of a lifetime, and he'd blown it by being, well, Jonah. *What the Hells is wrong with you,* his sex drive shouted at him from the dark recesses of his mind. *She was primed and willing!*

I know, he answered himself. *But it wouldn't be right.* "It wouldn't be right," he muttered, moving toward the cupboards and getting himself a drink from the icebox drawer.

"Jonah, what are you thinking." Portenda barely fit on the small cot but Jonah saw that his eyes were already closed.

Did the Simpa plan on sleeping in the cot, letting Jonah have the bigger bed for the rest of the night? He could easily fit on that thing twice over, he thought. "I'm thinking," Jonah said as he sat at the edge of Portenda's bed, "that an opportunity was there, but it would have been taking advantage. And besides, I'm still not entirely sure how I feel about her."

"You're a good fellow," Portenda said levelly. "Not the sort to do that kind of thing to a woman. She might have woken up to regret it. But you've spared her that." He opened his eyes briefly to look at Jonah. "Had you chosen to, I would have told you to do what you would with her and get her out of here. For tonight, though, you can take my bed. The two of you."

Jonah was touched by the Simpa's empathy. A moment later, when Jonah tried to say something to Portenda, he heard the big werelion's soft snore.

"Thanks," he whispered to the Simpa's back. He turned at the sound of the bathroom door opening, and saw Nareena walking toward the coffee's aroma. She moved in a daze, opening several cupboards in search of a mug.

Jonah got up and crossed the room to her, locating one for her (searching all the while for booby traps). Finding no traps, he handed her the mug, and she smiled appreciatively at him. As he turned away, she set the mug down, spun him around, and locked onto him in a hug that nearly shattered his ribs. She said not a word, squeezing tighter until he returned her embrace, and then she let out a heavy sigh.

He patted her on the back, and pulled away, smiling at her in return.

"I've, uh, got to get some sleep," he said. Forgetting the coffee on the counter, she followed him. Nareena looked over at the massive Bounty Hunter, and wondered what he made of her pet perching on the head of the bed she would be sharing with Jonah.

Cradled together like a pair of spoons, they fell quickly asleep on Portenda the Quiet's bed.

You're very welcome, Portenda thought.

* * * *

Morning rarely takes so long in coming, Jonah thought as he was gently prodded awake. The aroma of cooking food, eggs, bacon and toast, filled his nostrils like a long awaited guest.

He rose slowly, and when he looked over for Nareena, found she stood at the Bounty Hunter's stove. Talonz pecked at breadcrumbs she sprinkled on the counter next to the appliance, giving Jonah a dark stare every few pecks. Portenda was nowhere to be seen, but the door to his library was slightly ajar.

Nareena looked over at him, freshly washed and looking pristine and lovely.

A Hunter and his Prey

Wonder if she's planning to poison my food, he mused. Sober and aware of the events of the previous night, the Elven Alchemist might have turned back to her old ways. Jonah didn't want to be skeptical, but didn't think he had a choice.

"So, who is he, really?" Nareena placed portions of food on two plates and brought one over to Jonah, sitting next to him on the edge of the bed with her own meal. "He wouldn't say a word to me this morning. When I woke up, he was swinging that huge sword of his around. Nearly took my head off, but he stopped it an inch from my neck. How does he do that?

"He's a Bounty Hunter." He sampled his breakfast. Not bad, he thought, chewing thoroughly. And not a trace of poison. "His name is Portenda the Quiet."

"Fitting. Well, after he stopped his sword, he set it next to our bed."

"His bed, actually. He let us use it so we'd both fit."

"Oh. Nice of him." She finished her meal without speaking again. She got up, smoothed her dress, and set her dish on the counter by the sink. "Well, I'm off. Thanks for not, you know," she stammered, but Jonah put up a hand to stop her short.

"Think nothing of it, Nareena," he replied gently. He set the plate on the bed, and stood, walking over to the door out into the hallway. "I assume you'll be on your way?"

"Yes, actually," Nareena said, collecting her thoughts and her bird from his perch on the bedpost.

Jonah opened the door for her, and before she left, she turned and put her arms around his neck, pulling him close and giving him a soft, warm kiss. As she pulled away, she said, "You know, we could've been great together."

"We might yet," he commented with a wry grin. "I'll see you about the book," he said, nodding toward the Cuyotai text.

"Okay. See you then, Jonah. Oh, do you have that letter for your sister," she asked, turning toward him fully and holding out the crow.

"Ah, yes," Jonah spurted suddenly, tying the letter tube to the bird's leg. "There we are. Well, tomorrow then," he said, starting to close the door slowly.

"Tomorrow," she replied, giving him another peck.

The crow cawed rather more loudly than need be, and Jonah got the sense that it didn't approve of the intimate contact. Probably why the damned thing hovered over us on the bedpost.

She walked down the hallway, and Jonah shut the door. Knowing that Portenda was right behind him, feeling his presence more than actually sensing him by other means, Jonah spun and ducked down, keeping his hands up.

"Good." Portenda said, his tone cold and hard. "I have an assignment today," he said, hefting up his rucksack. "Keep an eye on things here. I'll be back by nightfall."

When Jonah had heard the word *assignment*, he had felt a tiny rush of adrenaline. But seeing as it was a contract taken by the Bounty Hunter, he felt disappointed.

"Oh, all right. So, you want me to stay here?"

Portenda opened the door, rummaging through one of his many pockets and producing a key.

"I had this copy made this morning. If you decide to go out, lock up. Remember, lock, unlock, lock. It sets the security traps." Portenda left without another word.

Jonah suddenly felt very alone, but he found a little satisfaction at being left to his own devices. He could work on the text translation, which in truth would only take a few hours. Then he could make some more potions and powders, maybe peruse Portenda's library once more.

Sitting cross-legged on the floor, Jonah took out an empty notebook, purchased several weeks ago for this sort of thing, and the Cuyotai textbook. Pouring over the text, he translated as best he could into the blank notebook. Often, when he translated languages, he wrote down the meanings of the foreign words without thinking about their meaning. After a half an hour, and an entire chapter of translation, he read over the notes he took. The first chapter of the Cuyotai text read like a long, exhaustive list of Alchemical ingredients and natural plant life. No wonder Nareena took an interest in it. Those ruins must have belonged to pre-Fall history, back before mecha even rose to the forefront of society. Back in those days, centuries before the Age of Mecha, only a few Races were bold enough, or foolish enough, to experiment with Alchemy. The Cuyotai had been one such Race, willing to try anything, provided there was some merit or fun to be had in it.

For three more hours he slaved, translating every last word, until his stomach grumbled and he knew he needed to eat again.

His feeding habits hadn't been all that great, and having a large meal at the diner the day before, along with a decent breakfast, complements of Nareena, combined to give him an appetite again. He got up and rummaged through the icebox, finding some fresh fruit, some cheese, and in another drawer, not chilled, were three untouched loaves of bread. He used his long knife to cut out a nice hunk of bread, closed the drawers and sat back on his cot.

As he ate, he read over the notes. Even translated, the words were jumbled. Water, iron, zinc, sodium, urea, proteins, carbohydrates, and a host of other ingredients were listed in the second chapter. The last chapter he hadn't translated so much as copied, as it was a collection of diagrams and symbols, all drawn roughly with side notes. He had translated the side notes as best he could, but they too were jumbled.

On the final page on which there was anything written or drawn, Jonah found splotches of rusty stains. Blood, he knew from the look of it. The notes were scrawled, and the diagrams were unfinished. Whoever had written this tome had either been murdered, or blown himself up halfway through his final report. The symbols all seemed so familiar, however.

A revelation struck Jonah like a bolt of lightning. Those symbols were used in the rearrangement of molecules and energy. They were the basis of the quasi-magical powers of Alchemy. Jonah shoved a piece of cheese in his mouth, took out a piece of chalk from his rucksack, and drew the simplest of the symbols on the floor— a simple box with a slash mark in each corner of the box, diagonally through the corners.

He pressed his palms against the symbol and a flash of brilliant white light filled the room. Thrown back by the sudden force, he fell on his rear end, and found himself shortly looking at a short sword made of steel.

While he considered the sword, he heard a loud crash as the mattress of his cot crashed to the floor, the frame half-gone. He had succeeded in art of molecular and energy rearrangement. He had finally accomplished what he previously could not for years.

But Portenda was going to be furious about the destroyed cot. The smell of rotted meat filled the air as smoke curled up from the symbol on the floor.

That's it, he thought. *I'll make another sword, and let the mattress lie on the floor.* Pressing his palms to the symbol once again, he closed his eyes and felt and heard the whoosh of air and energy. When he opened his eyes, he saw another short sword, though this one had some serious flaws. He darted to his notebook as the bed mattress flopped onto the floor behind him. One of the side notes he had translated stated, quite clearly, 'A symbol should not be used more than once, as the second result will be flawed in some essential way. Weapons symbols especially suffer this side effect.'

Damn, Jonah thought. *Should have read everything over again before I tried anything.*

Pleased in any event at his achievement, Jonah reached once more into the icebox, and took out a single bottle of amber-colored ale. Portenda didn't keep a lot of the stuff around, probably wanting to keep his senses as sharp as possible.

Jonah now had an edge over Nareena, though he tried to dismiss the thought as unwarranted. He had shared something with the Elven Alchemist the night before, and that very morning. It was as though all of their time as rivals had melted away, leaving them in the almost romantic relationship they had been in before discovering their competitive natures.

When he heard something slide beneath the door, Jonah spun and looked. A manila envelope, sealed shut but weighted with something metallic, lay on the floor.

Jonah took a swig of ale and opened the envelope. The front just said 'Roger' in bold, crudely written letters. Inside was a single gold piece.

He set the envelope, the coin still inside, on the counter of the den/kitchen, not giving it a second thought.

* * * *

Portenda sat patiently in the corner of the Flaming Tongue, awaiting his contact. The letter had said that the man would arrive at about four hours past noon. Not wanting Jonah to get curious, and thus have to explain himself or his lie, he had set out early, wandering somewhat aimlessly about the city until about three.

At a little past four, the contact sauntered into the tavern, already smelling like booze.

The man was a barrel-chested Simpa, his dark, golden fur matted in unclean patches. Staggering slightly to the counter, the Simpa ordered a pitcher and a pair of glasses, took them without paying, and set them down on the table between himself and Portenda.

"Why have you come again, father," Portenda growled, unable to contain his quietly building fury. His father had come to visit once again—unwanted and unbidden. He had, at least, written his son this time, but that didn't change the fact that Portenda the Quiet hated the man with a passion unmatched by the brilliance of the sun on a clear day. *In the desert*, he amended. The scent of cheap liquor stained his father's labored breathing, and the man's shabby, tattered pants indicated that his father didn't care a wit of other people's opinions.

"Is that any way to greet your old man?" The habitual drunk poured himself and his son each a glass from the pitcher. "Come on, have a drink with me. S'the least I can do for taking care of me last time I stopped in." He pushed the second glass toward the tense Bounty Hunter, who knocked it to the floor with a loud clinking, shattering tinkle.

"Oi, you gonna pay fer that glass," the Dwarf shouted. He came up short when he saw which customer had dropped the glass. He had first-hand knowledge of what the Bounty Hunter was capable of, and had even hired him on a few occasions. He knew that Portenda the Quiet was good for it, and knew further that aggravating the man could mean certain agony and probably at least a hospital stay.

"I don't want a drink with you, you bastard," Portenda growled at his genetic forbearer. "Just tell me what you want. Is it money? Did you already spend what I sent you last year?" He slammed his heavy fist on the table.

The older Simpa sat there, grinning like an idiot.

"No, it's not money," his father said.

Why couldn't he keep his emotions under control when he was around this infuriating man, Portenda wondered? His father had an eerie ability to break down people's willpower, their mental and emotional barriers.

The old drunkard never revealed the secret of his ability to anyone, least of all his own flesh and blood because he knew the boy would then find a way to negate the effects. And he enjoyed watching the little freak squirm. Neither man had much of anything good to say about the other, but whereas Portenda openly hated the old man, the father himself loathed his son more quietly, more discretely.

"It's about the clan," the father said. "They've decided to let you back, if you ever want to come back to their village in the Allenians."

The Allenian Hills, Portenda thought with mild disgust. Home. The place of his birth and banishment. He hadn't been there for years, when he had taken a contract that led him right in. He had been harassed by clans of Khan and Simpa both, the dominant Races who warred over ownership of the region. But none had tried to stop him, knowing what the now grown man was, and what he was capable of.

A Hunter and his Prey

"Tell them I don't care about their welcomes and traditions, father," he replied, mouthing the word 'father' like it was the foulest of curses. "Tell them they can blow me. Tell them the son of Makira does not want anything to do with them."

"Why not the son of Telroke," his father said, speaking his own name.

"Because you're not my father," Portenda said, getting to his feet. "You're just some drunken idiot who had his way with a naive young woman when she was vulnerable! Now stay out of my way, and get out of my life." He grabbed the pitcher and tossing the ale on his father's face.

Telroke closed his eyes and giggled.

"And what will you do now, you stupid little freak," his father growled low in his throat. He too rose to his feet, standing nose to nose with his son. "What do you intend to do, hmm? Spend the rest of your life in this city leaving whenever there's a contract out on someone's head? Will you remain a drifter, a stranger to everyone you meet? When will you come to your senses and take up the responsibility of every Simpa of the Allenians? When will you acknowledge your heritage?" Telroke shoved Portenda as hard as he could. He barely managed to move the boy, though. A moment of clarity advised him against taking any further sort of aggressive action against Portenda. *He isn't a boy any more*, the little voice of reason warned him. *He's a fully-grown man, and he's more dangerous than anyone you've ever met*. But the voice of alcohol and old regrets surfaced once again, drowning out that tiny voice of reason as it usually did. *Don't just stand there, it called out to him. Slap the boy a good one, he deserves it*. Telroke took a step forward and swung.

His arm was almost immediately clamped in an iron grip, twisted to an uncomfortable angle that forced him to his knees rather more quickly than he thought possible. Portenda stood silently, holding his father's palm and wrist turned upward. His sterile, steely gaze fixed on father's eyes, and Telroke Manewa, of the Allenian Hills, heard the Sacred Visitor, as his Race referred to Death, in Portenda's voice.

"You will leave when I let you go. Or I will kill you where you kneel. Your choice doesn't matter to me. I will not join you or the others. I will not wage war against the Khan. Mother wouldn't have approved." He let go of his father, who tucked and rolled away with surprising agility, considering his blood alcohol level.

"So what, you're going to fight for them?"

"I fight for no one, except my current employer at any given time. And don't think I'll accept any contract from the Allenians. I'm not that much of an idiot." Portenda took two steps toward his father, drawing his pistol and aiming it at his father's forehead. He cocked the hammer back, his trigger finger on the circular guard.

"All because of your bitch of a mother and your love for her. Whatever," Telroke said to his only son. "Do what you like, traitor!"

When his father stormed out of the tavern, Portenda put the pistol away and approached the bar, placing several gold pieces in front of the Dwarven barkeep to pay for the drinks and the broken glass.

The Dwarf gave him a curious look. "What did he mean by traitor? And how could 'e say such things about your mum."

"He calls me a traitor and calls my mother names for the same reason," Portenda said, pulling up one of his leather sleeves, revealing faint, gray stripes. "Because she was a Khan." He rolled his sleeve back down and left the establishment and the bewildered Dwarf, behind him.

* * * *

It was nearly eight in the evening when Jonah heard the door open and looked up from his book. He had set the swords he had made on the floor between their two beds.

Portenda raised an eyebrow as he walked in, closing the door and locking it behind him. He then stopped as he saw the symbol drawn on the floor. He would have commented on it, but didn't yet trust himself to remain detached. Instead, he simply pointed to the symbol, the swords, and then looked hard at Jonah, who peered timidly over the cover of a book. Not one of Portenda's, the Bounty Hunter noted, but a notebook of some sort.

"I used that," Jonah said, indicating the symbol on the floor with a tilt of his head. "To make these," he said, touching the short swords.

One of them was quite ragged, Portenda noted, while the other was expertly shaped and weighted. Resisting the urge to slam it into a wall, he looked down at Jonah and noticed that the frame of the cot was missing. He raised an eyebrow again.

"Oh, it's an Alchemy thing. When rearranging molecules and energy through the art of Alchemy, the saying nothing lost, nothing gained really comes into play."

"And that would explain the cot frame's absence." Portenda pulled his weapons off and arranged them around the room in the usual places. The only weapon he didn't put back where he'd gotten it from, was the spear. Each night he changed its position, so that when he awoke the next morning, he would know a brand new day was starting outside. He had covered almost every inch of the main room, upside down and right side up with that spear. He had laid it every which way he could think of in his waking field of vision. Pretty soon, he would be out of options, have to set a spot aside for the spear and move on to the auto crossbow.

"This is an Alchemical symbol," Jonah rattled, "known as a Focus Site. These symbols come in thousands of types—I believe."

"You believe? I thought you knew what you were doing with all of this Alchemy business."

"Chemical compositions and the making of potions, I'm very, very good at it. But the art of Focus Siting is something that is reserved for only the best and brightest, very secretive and well-guarded information. Most Alchemists give up after a few years, and settle into the routine of making potions, tinctures and powders. A select few, however," he whispered, clearly admiring the power of the Focus Site as he stared at it. "A select few master the Focus Sites. And they go into the annals of scientific history. The first firearms were invented and produced by Alchemists. They had no idea how they would work, but their imaginations, and the power of the Sites created the first of the mecha weapons." He wiped the symbol away with his sock. "Anyway, how was your job today?" He flopped onto his mattress with a heaving sigh.

"It wasn't a job." Portenda removed his leather armor and leaned against the wall next to one of the windows, looking out into the torch-lit streets of the city. "It was a meeting with a very trying man. A man I never want to speak to again." He turned to ask Jonah if he wanted a new bed-frame the next day, but the Human was already fast asleep.

I'll get one anyway, he thought.

Leaving Jonah, Portenda found the envelope from Roger resting on the right hand counter next to the sink, with the old, deaf Jaft's one gold rent payment inside. He took the coin, and walked silently out into the hallway.

Moving on cat's feet, he climbed to the roof of the apartment building, moving in a crouch to the edge of the roof. Taking the length of rope he kept tucked in a hidden compartment in the roof's edging out, he tied it securely to an eyehook, one of many he'd had installed, and slowly descended down the side of the building. When he came level to Roger's window, he looked at his pocket watch, pulling it out of his pants with one fluid motion. Nine thirty—Roger would be in bed. Portenda cranked the window open, peeked in and found Roger fast asleep on the other side of the room, opposite the window.

The Bounty Hunter eased himself inside the room, moving in a Ninja-like crouch. He had learned many of the techniques of the mysterious Ninja Class warrior-thieves, and found that they were best used in non-combat situations. Portenda preferred other martial arts systems, most belonging to the Monk Class, for confrontation. Ninjitsu just wasn't suited for a man of his size and power and speed.

Stalking through the room, he knelt down next to old Roger's dresser, and slipped the gold piece under it. Roger would wait patiently for three days, and then check under the dresser for his rent money. A few years ago, when the deaf Jaft elder had moved in, his grandson had helped him, and told Portenda that he wasn't sure if his grandpa could continue to pay the rent for long. Portenda had said that he understood; the elderly Jaft had ten or eleven years left before age claimed him, and was too frail to work. He had told the young Jaft warrior that he could make arrangements.

For three years, Portenda had taken the same gold piece, and had secreted it back into Roger's apartment each month. Often he left it under his dresser, but when Roger wasn't home, he would slip it between the old man's mattresses. Roger was a scavenger, and constantly checking his apartment from top to bottom for signs of intrusion. He always managed to find the extra gold piece and, his memory shot to Hells, he would wonder if his grandson had sent him money that he had simply forgotten.

The money planted, Portenda took a good look around the rooms, the bedroom, the kitchen, the den, and the empty spare bedroom. Portenda took a mental note to do some repairs on the apartment, seeing a good number of improvements that could be made. He had learned sign language from the old man over the course of a few months, and would come knocking and explain that it was about time to do inspections the next day. For now, though, he left the apartment silently, ascended the outer wall, and put the rope away. That accomplished, he sauntered to his apartment, and slipped into bed.

* * * *

Jonah awoke from his deep slumber, and found that he was looking up into darkness again. "Oh, Hells," he muttered. "This again."

He got no response.

Oh shit, he thought. *He isn't even going to give me a clue.* Jonah stood perfectly still, trying to hone in on his sense of hearing. Without a sensory enhancement potion, he had difficulty.

He reached down for where he'd left his chemical belt lay at the foot of the mattress, and discovered that it, along with his rucksack, were gone. Or at least moved from where he'd left them.

One thing, however, remained to him.

He reached for the chalk in his pants pocket, grabbing it like an ice pick, and kneeling next to the mattress.

He tried to recall one particular symbol in the translations, hoping that he could draw it properly without his eyes to guide him. He tried to concentrate, thinking back on the translations. The symbol he considered had been mentioned as an 'extension creation', though no explanation had been given except that the Alchemist should stand directly in the center of the Focus Site while activating it.

He used the chalk and, with great care, drew the Focus Site from memory.

He knew that Portenda had to be watching, but he didn't care—this wasn't just an exercise for his perception skills. It was testing of his capabilities and his ability to adapt to the situation.

Finishing his drawing, Jonah stepped into the center of the Site. He clapped his hands together, and pressed his palms to the Site, kneeling atop the symbol.

A harsh wind of force blew over him, feeling like a thousand dragons had just got together and decided to blow him over a cliff. His hair flew up over his head, and he had to hold the blindfold over his eyes to keep it from flying off as well.

Whispers echoed in his ears, voices that sounded thousands of years old, ancient and secret. The scent of burning plants swirled through his nostrils, flooding him with a sudden sense of dread. What had he done?

Pain ravaged his body, and Jonah dropped to the floor in a twitching writhing heap, his body convulsing back and forth. Drool slopped over the sides of his mouth, and from some faraway place he heard Portenda shouting his name.

A Hunter and his Prey

Something coiled and grew in his arms, and he flopped onto his back, still shivering and shaking like a dying chicken. Something sprang forth from his flesh, spouting gouts of blood all over the apartment, the agony of the transformation nearly knocking him out.

After a long moment, he felt better, more capable. Jonah got to his feet, feeling the extensions in his arms as they slithered about.

Portenda, meanwhile, had pressed himself into the corner of the main chamber. He'd watched as Jonah had dropped to the ground. He had, an hour earlier, woken up and moved Jonah's belongings to the library. He had known that something was in Jonah's pocket, noting the lump when he removed the Human's long knife. He had carefully removed it without waking Jonah, and decided to let the man keep it. After all, he had taken every other tool available to the young man, and Jonah had seemed so eager to try out these, what did he call them? Ah, yes, Focus Sites. Now the half Simpa watched in fascination and concern as verdant, spiked vines grew from Jonah's body. When Jonah's face contorted with pain, he called to the alchemist.

"Jonah," he had screamed, trying to make himself louder than the rushing force that howled through the room. He failed, miserably, and watched as Jonah got to his feet.

Jonah, meanwhile, was amazed. His vine extensions received new sensations of touch, taste and smell.

He forced the vine from his left arm to extend further, and felt along the floor and eventually the far wall. *Good, the wall near the counters and sink*, he thought. He concentrated his will, focusing on that vine, and making it snake its way along the wall, touching the sink faucet and moving on. Metal had a strangely eerie, hostile feel when experienced through the senses of a plant.

"I never could have imagined," he whispered, awed by alien sensations.

Portenda stood there, stunned into paralysis.

A minute later, the vine that Jonah had forced out made contact with Portenda's right arm. Out of instinct, he spun away and brought his broadsword down through the vine.

"Haaaauuuuugh!" Jonah screamed. He dropped to his knees as green fluid and red blood flowed from the severed vine.

Portenda's mind raced, and he realized that the vine was now essentially a part of Jonah.

Enough of this, the Simpa Bounty Hunter thought. He rushed to Jonah's side, removing the blindfold and holding the frail Human on his feet.

"Jonah, come back to me," Portenda said, his emotional control once more shattered. "Come on Jonah, snap out of it." He slapped the alchemist lightly.

There was another whoosh, and the thorny right-hand vine lashed out, slashing Portenda's leather armor open, tearing through even the lead plating that lined the interior of the armor.

Blood spilled over his front, but Portenda ignored it; it would heal over in a few minutes, though not as quickly as would a purebred Simpa.

The vines then retracted back into Jonah's body in a flash of green and white light. Jonah opened his eyes and stood wobbling to his feet, clutching his forehead. "Incredible," he whispered. "That was, incredible!" Then he noticed the Simpa had turned away from him. "What's the matter? Portenda?"

"I should not have let you keep the chalk," the Bounty Hunter said flatly.

Jonah was out of harm's way, now, and he could think clearly. "Or at the very least, I should have left the blindfold off. I meant for you to find your belongings while avoiding the traps." He went to the front door deadbolt and deactivating the traps in the apartment. "I don't think I can train you any further."

"Nonsense." Jonah waved his arm in a dismissal. "You and I simply have different ways of doing things. Portenda, I'm an Alchemist. I always have been, and always will be. You're, uh, I'm not clear as to what your Class is, but you're obviously a warrior." He took a seat on the edge of Portenda's bed. "We cannot change what we essentially are. For example," he said, grabbing one of his short sword creations. "I know how to use one of these, but not very well. I could be instructed further, certainly, but the point is, I'll never be as good at this sort of thing as you." He tossed it lightly to Portenda, who caught it deftly by the hilt. "Being a Bounty Hunter, I think, is not so much about Class and skills and training! It's about the techniques of information collection, tracking, and tracing. Negotiation, deliberation and stalking. Those are the things I want you to show me, to teach me."

There was a long silence, which Portenda finally broke after he retrieved a hunk of bread from his drawer.

"You know, most in the business would say that's a load of shit," he said coldly.

His eyes were unreadable to Jonah, whose senses were still taking a rocky trip back to normality.

"But you have a point. Some of my more capable colleagues are mages and clerics, or even thieves. But tradition, though traditions for Bounty Hunters mean little and have only been around thirty or so years, states that you need fighting skills." He ate his bread silently, and slid the short sword back across the floor to Jonah.

"So where do we go from here?" Jonah asked.

"We go to the bookstore." Portenda went into his library.

Jonah sat confused, and waited patiently for the Simpa to return.

Five minutes later, the bounty hunter came out with Jonah's things and several dozen pouches of money tied to his waist. Jonah found himself staring at the regenerating wound, horrified that he had actually harmed the Bounty Hunter.

"I didn't hurt you, did I," the Human Alchemist asked sheepishly.

Portenda looked down as the wound finally closed shut, leaving a permanent scar behind.

A Hunter and his Prey

"Just wounded my pride a little," the Simpa replied with a wry grin. His eyes danced for a moment with life, and then returned to that ashen frost that Jonah had become accustomed to.

He caught his rucksack and belt as Portenda tossed them at him, strapping both on. "Come on. We're going to go get you some books of your own." Portenda opened the apartment door and waiting for Jonah to follow.

As Jonah exited, he cringed at the long holes that his vine extensions had torn in the walls.

"I hope your landlord isn't too angry about the noise or the damage to the apartment," Jonah said as Portenda locked, unlocked and locked the door again.

"I am the landlord," Portenda replied simply.

Jonah spun on him, arms at his sides and his face wide with surprise.

"You own this building," he nearly screamed. "Why didn't you tell me?"

"Didn't think it was worth mentioning. Besides," Portenda said quietly. "It never came up." The two stalked down the hallway, down the stairs, and out into the waking city of Ja-Wen. Jonah never noticed the eyes that watched them like a hawk.

* * * *

"Ah, good day again Mr. Portenda." A creepy, raspy voice echoed through the dimly lit store as the Simpa and Jonah entered.

Jonah searched for the source of the voice, and a moment later, a little Goblin poked his head over the counter.

The Greenskin wore a fabulous tunic and robe, each decorated with yellow stars overlapping purple fabric. On his head, sat a strange, square cap, with a red, frayed tassel. Thick lenses made the little man's eyes as large as an insect's, and Jonah felt ill at ease under that stare.

"What can I do for you and your little friend?" the Goblin asked.

"Tell him." Portenda pushed Jonah forward then stalked off to peruse the fiction section.

Jonah rubbed the back of his head awkwardly. Was Portenda going to pay for the books he wanted? He certainly hoped so, because Alchemy books dealing with Focus Sites were expensive.

"I need some textbooks on Alchemy," Jonah said. "Focus Sites, mostly. Actually, that's all I need—books on the art of Focus Sites." He rushed his words in the hope that rushing would make the books appear faster.

The Goblin smiled and shook his head. "Those books are very, very expensive sir. Frankly, you don't look like you can pay."

"I'm paying." Portenda slammed a stack of books on the counter. "Put his with these, Marvin."

The Goblin grinned from ear to ear.

"Of course, Mr. Portenda." He darted into a back room. A minute later, he returned, half a dozen tomes thicker than Portenda's entire stack floating directly ahead of him.

A Goblin mage, Jonah thought with wonder. Now I've seen everything. The tomes floated down onto the counter and came to rest a full foot above the top of Portenda's pile.

The two men looked at the stacks side by side, then to each other.

"I think we're going to be busy for a couple of days," Jonah said.

"Perhaps," Portenda replied as the Goblin took out a sheet of paper and started calculating the total cost.

Portenda leaned in close to Jonah. "We were followed."

"Three hundred and twenty-five gold pieces, Mr. Portenda," Marvin said.

Portenda took six pouches off of his waist, and emptied another half pouch onto the counter.

"No need to count it," the Goblin said, as Portenda prepared to open the first pouch and count it aloud. "I know you're good for it."

Portenda opened his rucksack, which he had emptied prior to coming, and shoved his fiction novels inside. Jonah opened his own rucksack, and found that he only had room for three of the alchemy books. By the time he'd figured that out, Portenda had already put four of the Focus Site tomes in his own rucksack, slinging it over his shoulders. Jonah took the remaining two and packed them away, also slinging his rucksack.

"So who's following us?" Jonah asked.

"I'm not certain. But he's tense. The smell of sweat is all over him. And his leather boots creak with every step he makes. His heart rate is threateningly fast right now." Portenda headed slowly back toward the apartment building.

Jonah's eyes were glued, at the moment, to a flower shop and its lamenting owner, an Elven man whose entire stock of plants were mysteriously missing. My god, Jonah thought, looking at his hands and then back at the flower shop. Is that where the vines came from? Transference, he thought. Nothing lost, nothing gained.

Portenda listened carefully, hearing the distant and slow sound of a mace clearing its holding loop. "Jonah, get ready. He's making his move."

Portenda walked toward an apple cart. The Gnome proprietor smiled at him brightly, revealing the few teeth in his black-gummed mouth.

"One silver piece, sir," the Gnome said, then quickly tried to apologize. "Oh dear, sorry sir. I forgot your people don't touch silver."

Portenda gave the man a gold piece.

"Keep the change," he said.

Jonah ducked as Portenda spun in toward him, hurtling the apple at full speed into the face of a charging Human.

The fruit exploded against his forehead, and he spiraled through the air feet first in a full circle, landing heavily on his face and chest.

Sprawled out on the dirt ground, Jonah recognized the man as the Human strong-arm thug that had accosted him with the half-Orc from the Flaming Tongue. These people just didn't learn.

Portenda kicked the mace away from the man, who got to his hands and knees and touched his nose. His hand came away slick with blood.

A Hunter and his Prey

Portenda hauled the man up into the air by his suspenders, holding him like an animal by the scruff. The strong-arm thug thrashed around, kicking and spitting, but Portenda grabbed one of his flailing feet and spun him around by it like a child's toy.

When Portenda grabbed the same leg again, the man came to a stop and vomited.

"What are you doing," Portenda asked.

Jonah looked around and saw that they had an audience.

"Um, Portenda, perhaps we should leave." A few toughs in plaid work clothes came to the front of the audience, one of them a Sidalis, judging by the single horn protruding from his otherwise Human face. The other was a Minotaur with a woodcutting axe in his left hand. *Lumberjacks*, Jonah thought. *Strong men, and I don't want any part of them.*

"Not yet," Portenda said, a trace of menace in his voice. "Why were you attacking us?"

The man stammered as he tried to speak.

"I, uh, I just wanted the little guy," the man said. "He, uh, he, uh, he threatened me the other day, yeah, that's it. He's a freak." The man pointed an accusing finger at Jonah.

Portenda tapped a spot on the back of the man's neck with a single finger.

"Hey, what the heck was that?"

"I've struck your min-nori key point. Pressure is going to start building in your spinal cord."

The man felt a sudden inflammation at the point where Portenda had struck him.

"The fluids have been cut off from your brain. If I do not release the pressure in a few minutes, you will have an uncomfortable experience. It is a rather painful way to die. I have done this because you are lying. Your nervousness, the stammer of your speech, and the sudden intake of air before you spoke gave you away. I don't like being lied to."

The Human shook as the min-nori key point swelled further with blocked fluids.

"All right. Me and my buddy, Tugot tried to jump the little nerd the other night. He set my buddy on fire and he was gonna kill me!"

"Fitting. You'd have done the same to him, had you been given the chance." Portenda struck the min-nori key point again and let the man drop to the ground, alive.

The Human rubbed his neck and stared at the Simpa in awe.

Portenda brought one heavy foot up, and sent it crashing down in a violent thrust kick, breaking the man's kneecap.

The Human screamed, and the spectators all stepped back from the Simpa and the Alchemist.

Rolling over and trying to hug his leg, the broken Human just moaned and congealed on the ground.

Constables came running toward them, and Jonah feared that these people, more afraid of him and Portenda than anything else, would accuse them of starting the fight.

One of the constables, a stalwart looking Dwarf, stopped only two feet shy of Portenda.

"Oi, wot's all this den," he asked the crowd as a whole, hefting a battle-axe toward the Bounty Hunter.

Jonah stepped forward to explain, but the Sidalis with the horn in his forehead spoke first.

"That man," he pointed at the broken Strong Arm Thug, "attacked these two with that mace." He pointed now to the weapon that Portenda had kicked away. "But the big fella here pegged him with an apple before he could swing, took him down pretty easy."

The crowd, on the whole, muttered their agreement. The Dwarf looked up at Portenda and gave him a scowling grunt.

"Roit, then. Boys, haul this one to jail," he said, indicating the man on the ground with a bob of his head. He took a step closer to Portenda, standing only up to the Simpa's waistline. "And as fer you, Bounty Hunter." He spit the words as though they left a foul taste in his mouth. "I've always got an eye on you."

"Must make it difficult to do your job then," Jonah said before he could stop himself.

The Dwarf whirled on him, and Jonah stumbled backward, tripping on his own feet. As he got to one knee, the Dwarven constable gave him that same withering glare as he'd given Portenda.

"Don't go gettin' woise wif me, boyoh." The Dwarf patted his axe handle in his free palm. "You wouldn't loik spendin' a week in lockup fer bein' a woise arse, would ye?"

Jonah shook his head fervently.

"I'll be watching out fer you too, boy." He walked away with his two men in tow, the unconscious Human between them.

As soon as the constables disappeared from view, Jonah heard hands clapping, slowly at first, and then gaining momentum as the crowd joined in. He was confused, but Portenda just stood there, raising an eyebrow of inquiry.

"I don't get it," he whispered to Portenda.

"Nor do I," Portenda whispered back.

The Sidalis extended a hand that each took and shook in turn. "Geez, it's great to finally have someone who's willing to stand up for people around here." The mutant flickered in and out of view for an instant.

"What do you mean?" Jonah asked.

The Sidalis looked around at the crowd, most of whom were going back to their business.

"This is Ja-Wen, man. Nobody stands up for the common people. The police are a joke, and half of them are in the pockets of the brigands and gangs that actually control this city. And you guys just took that guy down like it was nothing. Well, you did," the mutant amended, looking up at Portenda the Quiet's ashen eyes. "Is it true? Are you a Bounty Hunter?"

"I am the Bounty Hunter, Portenda the Quiet," the Simpa whispered.

He turned to Jonah. "Let's head back. We have studying to catch up on."

The pair walked away, and Jonah turned back to wave good-bye to the Sidalis, finding that the man had disappeared again. Sidalis and their mutant powers fascinated Jonah, but for now, he had other things to be curious about.

When they got back to the apartment, Portenda emptied his rucksack on his bed, handing Jonah his tomes one by one, so he could stack them against the peeling paint of the wall next to his mattress. "You really ought to think about redecorating," Jonah said. "This place is so barren."

"I'm a minimalist. Besides, I need the room to practice."

"I understand, but some more decoration would add some flavor to the place. I mean, this is your home." He spread his arms wide to indicate the apartment as a whole. "You own the building, so why not fix the place up? Maybe get yourself some creature comforts. A couple of chairs would be nice, for instance, instead of always sitting on the bed or the floor."

"They would just take up space," Portenda retorted. "I'm not going to waste money on things I do not require."

He sat on his bed, put on his reading glasses, selected a book at random, and started reading. "Now leave me be for a while. I'll get another cot frame from the basement this evening."

"Oh, all right." Jonah selected the first tome in the series, and opened it.

Each page in the first book he had opened had a large drawing of a Focus Site up top, with an explanation below, written in fine cursive handwriting.

For most of the rest of the day the two sat like that, occasionally getting up to grab food or use the bathroom. Near evening, Portenda set his book aside and put his glasses down, rubbing his eyes as he left without a word.

Jonah, ever the speed-reader and having a keen knack for retaining information, had finished the first tome after eight consecutive hours of reading. He too rubbed his eyes, and resolved to go with his translations of the Cuyotai text, to the diner where he had agreed to meet Nareena.

He glanced at his timepiece; he had a half an hour to get there, and would have to leave right now. He scribbled a quick note for the Bounty Hunter, and left it on his bed.

Curiously, he didn't see Portenda on his way out of the building, but remembered that he had gone down to grab a new cot frame.

He probably had to assemble it yet, Jonah thought, whistling to himself as he made his way through the dusty, mostly uninhabited streets of the city.

Odd, he thought, that so few people were out this evening.

Shrugging it off as just an early night for most people, he walked all the way to the diner, and entered the building without halting.

The torches were unlit as he stepped into the reception area. He looked over to the left, expecting the bubbly girl to be waiting for the next customer, but nobody was there. None of the serving trays at the buffet had any food in them, either; it was as though the whole place had just been very quietly abandoned.

Jonah crept through to the main dining hall, where a single figure, dressed in a shimmering purple dress, sat waiting for him. At least Nareena had shown up.

But the look on her face told him right away that she was troubled by dark thoughts.

He sat across from her and inhaled. The scent of her jasmine perfume warmed him in a way he hadn't felt since they had parted the day before. "I have your translations for you." He pulled out his notebook and the yellow Cuyotai text.

She gnawed at her lip nervously, casting a suspicious glance around the room.

"What's with you," he asked in a whisper. "What's going on in this town?" Talonz let out a series of short, sharp caws like mocking laughter, shaking his head knowingly.

"It's collections night," she rasped at him. "You haven't been here long, and neither have I, but I have friends here. They told me this would happen." She held out a small tube that had been attached to her crow's foot. "Oh, and this is yours. I think it's from your sister."

Jonah simply pocketed the tube, and looked around the dining hall.

"What the devil's collections night?"

"It's the night when the gangs all come out of hiding and collect money from anyone they see, and any business they can get into." She pulled a vial out of her sash, filled with a bubbling yellow liquid. "Jonah, I wish there was enough of this stuff for the both of us. But I have to look out for myself. You understand, don't you?" Tears ran down her cheeks.

"I'll just head back to the apartment," he said, just before he heard a woman shriek outside in terror.

"You don't understand, Jonah. Even the guards stay inside on collections night." She uncorked the bottle and drank its contents. A moment later, she vanished. Her crow cawed again in mock laughter, and took wing out of the building.

Invisibility potion, good one, he thought.

"Jonah, if they find you, they're going to kill you."

His heart sank. These brigands would just kill a man for a few gold coins? He had to think of a plan, and think of one quickly, because a moment later, he heard Nareena push open the diner doors, and leave.

Oh gods, he thought. What am I going to do?

* * * *

Portenda re-entered the apartment, adjusted the cot frame and set the mattress.

He scanned the main room—no sign of Jonah. He walked over to the doorway into the library—still no Jonah. And the bathroom door was wide open.

He decided that the Human had simply nicked off for a quick walk. Until he looked outside of the window, and saw that the streets were empty. *Ah, that's right*, he thought. "Collections night."

Portenda the Quiet didn't even bother to close the door behind him as he burst out of his apartment.

* * * *

A window somewhere nearby shattered, and Jonah cowered behind the diner's check-in desk.

How could he get himself out of this mess? He had left his vials and chemicals back at the apartment! All he had was his long knife, his wits, and a piece of chalk. If he attempted a Focus now, however, he would be under attack before he could take a second step toward getting home.

His real home, he thought, was a little house in Desanadron, where his mother, father and sister would be more than willing to take him back. Ja-Wen and this whole Bounty Hunting business was starting to look terminal.

Then he heard something else, a sound he hadn't expected to hear from the gruff, uncaring voices of the brutes in the streets. "Holy shit! Andre, Andre! Get some backup over here, this guy just tore Vinny in half!"

There was a loud crunching noise, followed by the vague tremor in the air that Jonah had started noticing whenever there was violence in his vicinity.

He slunk out from behind the check-in booth and crawled to the door of the building. Opening it ever so slightly, he peered out into the dark streets to find Portenda standing there, his broadsword soaked in blood.

A pair of bodies, one bent in ways Orcs weren't meant to be bent and one cleaved cleanly in half on the diagonal, lay at the Bounty Hunter's feet.

Jonah watched as the vicious, efficient Bounty Hunter sniffed at the air. His eyes caught Jonah's for an instant before another thug, a Jaft in chain mail armor, flew at the Simpa out of the shadows. The two went down in a frenzying heap, rolling back and forth, struggling for possession of the sword.

Jonah's heart skipped a beat; he had distracted Portenda by catching his eyes. He had to help.

No sooner had Jonah stepped outside than a thick, splintered baseball bat slammed him in the chest, sending him coughing and sprawling back inside and to the floor of the diner.

A smush-faced Illeck entered after him, bat in hand. The dark Elf brought the wood up over his head, ready to strike.

Before Portenda had arrived, Jonah had prepared a number of Focus Sites on the diner floor, for defensive purposes.

Rolling to his right, avoiding what could have been a skull-splitting strike, Jonah hefted himself up to one knee and clapped his hands together. He then slammed the palms down hard on a Focus Site that was little more than a triangle with a circle inside, and another triangle inside of that circle.

The basic effect, he had read in the tome earlier, was to create a barrier capable of being used as a weapon.

Jonah had used the chemical symbol for iron, writing it in small letters at the north-facing point of the outer triangle. The now familiar rush of force and energy filled the room, and Jonah suddenly stood behind a large, rolling iron cage wall covered with spikes.

The Illeck slowly backed away.

No use, Jonah thought with a grim satisfaction. A second set of spikes was moving toward the dark Elf man from behind. He was going to be crushed.

But Jonah wasn't certain how long that would take, and he now couldn't see Portenda, thanks to his own clever trap.

"To Hells with it," he muttered. He sprinted to the wall to his right, where he had already drawn another Focus Site, this one generally referred to as the 'Blasting Focus'. Jonah pressed his left palm to it, and as the force blew his hair back over his head, the concrete wall exploded open in a shower of meteor-fast debris.

Several goons were struck and knocked to the ground by bits of flying wall. Without waiting to see whether the blows killed them, Jonah raced around to the front of the diner, and found that Portenda now stood over the Jaft who had tackled him.

The man had been clawed and torn apart, so severely that even his Racial regeneration wouldn't keep him alive. A set of wicked tooth marks pocked his throat where Portenda had bitten him, tearing his throat open and killing him. Thick, foul-smelling Jaft blood ran down Portenda's leather armor and his arms and face. He had the appearance of a maddened killer on the outside, but the sparks in his eyes told a different story: he was disappointed. Then he looked over and spotted Jonah, just as an earth-shattering shriek of agony exploded from the diner, accompanied by the sound of metal scraping on metal. Ah, Jonah thought, the spike walls.

"Jonah, are you all right?" Portenda asked as the frail, skinny Human approached.

Jonah rubbed his sore ribs. "Nothing a little rest and a potion can't cure. Can we go home now?"

When they got back into the apartment, Jonah asked why the door hadn't been shut.

"No time," Portenda said flatly, removing his armor and walking into the bathroom for a quick shower. Jonah was fast asleep by the time he got out, clutching his pillow like a child would a stuffed animal. It must have been quite an ordeal for him, Portenda thought, rubbing his face with his rough towel. The Simpa read a little bit, then hit the rack himself.

* * * *

Jonah sat up on the cot, rubbing his temple. A nagging feeling that not all was right with the world hit him like a ton of bricks.

The letter, he thought, half-asleep still. He reached into his pocket for the tube, and popped it open as he watched Portenda go through some sort of unarmed movement exercises. Jonah opened the letter, which appeared to be very short, and written in his mother's handwriting, not his sister's. The contents of the letter woke Jonah up faster than any coffee or exercise ever could.

Jonah's family had always been caring people, open and inviting. His father, though a Soldier for most of his natural life, was a fair man, and often allowed drifters and adventurers passing through Desanadron into his home for the evening. His mother had never questioned the intentions of young people who wished to stay with them, only keeping a closer eye on Eileen, who was young, naive, and given to ideas of romance.

Several days before Jonah's letter reached them, the letter said, a man dressed in sky blue robes and smelling of sea salt had asked to stay with them. He was familiar, Jonah's mother had written hastily, though they didn't know why. The man had taken the bedroom that had been Jonah's. The extra room in the attic had been made into a storage room for his father's things collected from the battlefields over the years. In a frantic scrawl, the letter said that when Jonah's parents woke the next morning, the stranger and Eileen had both vanished. Eileen's room had been in tatters, and there was blood on the bed and the floor leading to the window.

His sister had been abducted.

Jonah sat in stunned silence, his hands shaking so bad that they made the parchment sound like a maraca.

"Jonah," Portenda looked up from cleaning his armor in the sink. "What's the matter?"

Jonah just sat there, tears rushing down his cheeks unbidden.

"Jonah?"

The dam burst, and Jonah wailed like an injured child, covering his face with the letter as he crumbled forward, folding himself in half. His body was entirely wracked with remorse and fear.

Portenda gently negotiated the letter from his grip and pored over it before folding it neatly and setting it on Jonah's pillow. Then the Bounty Hunter disappeared into the library for a few minutes, and Jonah started to pack his things. He had to go home, now. Forget about training, forget about Alchemy, just get home and start looking for his sister.

A minute later, Portenda returned into the main room with an odd, yellow rucksack. He tossed it at Jonah, who caught it more out of reflex than anything.

"What's this," he asked, drying one eye with the back of his hand.

"Enchanted bag. Holds anything. Pack your things." Portenda strapped the last of his weapons, the ancient mecha pistol, into its holster. "We've got a job to do." His gray, ashen eyes shimmered with anticipation.

"What the devil do you mean?" Jonah grabbed the letter and waving it in Portenda's face. "I have other things to do right now! I have to leave, I have to go—"

"Home. Desanadron. I know." Portenda opened the door to his apartment. "We have to get your sister back."

Jonah couldn't stop himself from throwing his arms as far around the Simpa as he could in appreciation.

Portenda just stood there, cool and calm as an iceberg, holding the apartment door open.

After a moment, Jonah, more than a little embarrassed about his response to Portenda's offer of aid, took a few steps back and rubbed the back of his head awkwardly.

"Um, look, about that," he stammered, but Portenda put his hand against Jonah's face, covering it entirely with his huge paw.

"Forget it. Let's go." He gently shoved Jonah out into the hallway, then stepped out himself and locked up. Finally, Portenda pulled a piece of parchment out of one of his many pockets, and jammed a throwing knife through it, pinning it to the door.

The parchment had a skull and crossbones drawn on it, with the words 'Back Whenever' underneath.

Together, the Human and the Simpa darted out of the building, and into the streets of Ja-Wen. Portenda led the way, and Jonah followed, unsure where they were headed, and not really caring, as long as they got to Desanadron as quickly as possible.

Chapter Four
Nemesis

"It'll take too long to get to Desanadron on foot, or on horse," Jonah wheezed as he jogging behind the stampeding Simpa. "It's clear on the other side of the continent. It would take a month on foot, and two weeks on horse. Where are we going?"

"I have a business associate who owes me a favor. We can get a scroll of Teleportation from him. He does a lot of traveling, so he's bound to have one that will take us to Desanadron in the blink of an eye." Portenda took another turn down an unclean, bum-littered alleyway. Grubby, dirt covered hands reached out for purchase of his money pouches, and he delivered a few slaps and one harsh kick to a Human vagrant's groin to keep them at bay.

"And you know where to find him at this hour?"

"Whenever he comes to Ja-Wen, he goes to the same place at night."

Jonah noticed that they were headed for the manor district, where the heads of the city resided in upscale houses and manors. The streets were suddenly very solid under his feet, and Jonah spared a quick glance down at the cobblestone, looking up just in time to collide with a torch post.

He fell back in a heap, groaning and rubbing his quickly swelling forehead where he had slammed into the metal pole. The speed he was running at had been considerable, and he was certain that he had given himself a concussion. Portenda hauled him to his feet, and walked ahead at a pace that was brisk but nothing that Jonah couldn't handle.

The Bounty Hunter stalked through the streets for a while, and then suddenly darted into a set of bushes on the edge of a High Council member's property.

Jonah looked around. The next instant, he was being hauled through the air into a thicket of bushes.

Portenda set him down, and put a finger to his lips.

Jonah nodded, understanding the need for stealth. Trespassing on a High Councilman's property was punishable by a maximum of twelve to fourteen months in the Ja-Wen prison.

Portenda checked his timepiece a couple of times over the half hour that they sat and waited, covered and surrounded by greenery.

Jonah looked at the bush, and clipped off a few leaves as well as a twig. He opened the yellow rucksack, and found nothing inside. What the devil? He caught Portenda's attention and pointed into the bag.

The big Simpa leaned in close and whispered to him, "Think about what you want to take out, and tap the clip before opening it."

Jonah thought of his sample collection vials, tapped the clip, and opened the bag. And there they were, just as Portenda had said they would be.

A useful item, he thought. Hope he lets me keep it. He placed the leaves in one vial, the twig in another. After all, this sort of bush didn't grow naturally anywhere near Ja-Wen, and he wanted to analyze the plant at the next opportunity.

After another ten minutes, someone jumped into the bushes with them.

Jonah nearly screamed as a white bearded Gnome, wearing dark tan leathers, a white tunic shirt, a brace of lock picks and other thief's tools, landed between him and the Simpa.

The Gnome's eyes went wide for a moment, then Portenda clamped a huge, hairy hand over the Gnome's mouth, and dragged him flailing and kicking out onto the street.

Jonah following closely behind, praying that nobody was watching them.

Portenda put the Gnome down.

As the Gnome spun to face him, he whipped a throwing knife so fast at the Simpa that Jonah almost saw a vapor trail behind it. What speed, he marveled. But Portenda had whirled in a circle, and when he came to a stop, he had the weapon not in his arm or chest, but between his fingers on his left hand. He twirled it around a couple of times, and lofted it back to the Gnome, who smiled and clapped his hands, the sound of it echoing through the barren streets of the manor district.

"Well met, Portenda the Quiet," the Gnome thief said.

Jonah recognized him now—it was none other than Lee Toren, the self-professed master pickpocket and gentleman.

"Who's the lad?" The gnome pointed at Jonah unceremoniously.

"His name is Jonah Staples." Portenda cracked his knuckles. "How have you been, Lee Toren?"

Lee Toren shrugged his shoulders and smiled. "I suppose I've been all roit." Lee stepped towards a bench backed by a small flower garden that was cared for by High Councilman Pfnog and his wife. Being the only Werewolf Councilman in Ja-Wen, Pfnog tried to be as friendly as possible, and had placed a bench near the garden, and ordered the guards in the area to protect the people by watching for miscreants.

"And my uncle," Portenda asked, to which Jonah raised an eyebrow.

"His mum's brover, lad," Lee said, catching Jonah's attention. "Amon is doing well, too. 'is arm acts up now an' agin, but it ain't noffin he worries 'imself about."

Lee started to his feet but Portenda hefted a huge, heavy foot against the Gnome's chest, gently pushing him back onto the bench.

"Ah, come off it then. Wha' you want wif me?" Lee Toren might have been a coward, yes. A liar, certainly. But he most assuredly was not an idiot. He didn't move a muscle as Portenda applied pressure with his bare foot.

"You know you still owe me/" Ice hung like shards of glass to Portenda's words. The smell of cold sweat filled the area, and Jonah saw that both the Gnome and the guards in the distance, who now stood directly under a torch lamp, were sweating bullets. The guards apparently knew who they were looking at across the flower garden. The two men had beads of nervous sweat across their fine Elven features, and the faint sound of muttering fluttered into Jonah's ear. He couldn't make out what they were saying, but the tone was one of nervousness, the sound conveyed with an edge of real, mortal fear. The two armed Elves beat a slow, cautious retreat.

"Yes, yes I do at that," Lee said.

Portenda took his foot off of the gnome. "Guards gone, lad?" he asked Jonah.

"Oh, you thought 'e was serious wif me just now," Lee asked, giving Portenda a broad grin.

Portenda gave him a quiver of a grin back, but his face fell immediately back into his usual unreadable countenance.

"It's a rule of moin ta never discuss business near lawmen," Lee explained. "S'the only reason I can think of fer the Quiet 'ere to plant his big stinkin' foot on me. So," Lee said, putting down his rucksack. "What ye' need?"

"Teleportation scrolls," Portenda replied in his whispery voice. "To Desanadron."

Jonah removed his boots for a minute, testing the feel of the cobblestone beneath his feet. They were chilly and gritty, loose dirt and cement from between and beneath the cobbles scraping roughly against the soles of his feet. How did he do it all the time, he thought, referring to Portenda running around without footwear.

"I fink I've got some around." Lee Toren could be heard muttering, but Jonah was busy removing masonry from the bottom of his feet. With the offending stone out of his skin, Jonah readjusted his boots, and walked over to the Simpa and Gnome.

"You know," Lee said, "I remember once having a similar meeting to this one a long toim ago. Big fellah, friend of moin, met me in a tavern wif a relatively scrawny Cuyotai. Not as small as you, mind you," Lee amended, waggling a finger at Jonah. "And the boy turned out ta be tough as nails. I'm not sure why, but I just seem to 'ave a knack fer meetin' people loik you, Portenda. And eventually, ye bring around somebody loik this."

He opened several concealed pockets in his rucksack, cleverly sewn into the inner lining of the sack, in case of search and seizure. "Ah, here they are," he exclaimed, standing and holding out two scrolls. "Two tickets to Desanadron, gents. And, uh, I believe this makes us square, does it?"

He smiled sheepishly at the Bounty Hunter, who merely nodded and snatched one of the scrolls from Lee's left hand. He rolled it open, and looked it over. He then handed it to Jonah. "Make sure it's authentic."

Lee's face scrunched up and turned beet red. "Hey now! I wouldn't fleece you loik that! They're the real deal, honest. I stole 'em from a bona fide Enchanter I did."

Jonah rolled the scroll open, and attempted a quick translation of the old Elvish script. The writing itself was fairly recent, but the most potent scrolls were best written in the old tongues, and someone had clearly been going for effectiveness rather than appearances with this scroll. Loosely translated, it read, 'Swiftest travel, fast as light, let the reader of this scroll take flight. Off to go, from parts beyond, take them now, to Desanadron.' Satisfied with the authenticity of the scroll, Jonah rolled it up.

"It's all right, Portenda. They're the real deal. And very well made," he added, feeling the scroll with his thumb and forefinger. Written on dried out sheep's skin. Very good work, made by someone who knew exactly what they were doing.

"That is excellent," Portenda replied, his voice slightly lilting with satisfaction. "Lee, I think you're right. We're even, now. But don't think I won't be calling on you again some day in the future." He took the other scroll from Lee's right hand, and opening it as well. "Hm. Good. They're exactly the same."

"You do know how to use one of them, yes?" Lee looked around the area for guards again.

"I've used them before, Lee. I don't mean to be curt with you, but we must be going. Now." He rolled the scroll open and held it out with both hands.

He gripped the ends hard, and shook the scroll; an instant later, there was nothing left, save a wisp of smoke where he had stood.

Jonah fumbled with his own scroll, and repeated the process. He had never used Teleportation spells or scrolls before. As reality melted around him, he found himself being hurtled through a tunnel of some sort, screaming all the while.

* * * *

To the best of her knowledge, Eileen Staples had never done anything to offend anyone, except, perhaps, for Natasha Mikal, an Illeck girl who fancied herself the most beautiful young woman in the world. Eileen had gone on a rather long rant at Natasha about how only Illeck men and Humans with extremely low standards would ever be attracted to her, and the two had gone down in a heap of flailing slaps and tugging of hair. It had been declared the most spectacular catfight the neighborhood had seen in a long time.

But she and Natasha had long-since made up and even if they hadn't, that hardly warranted the assault the drifter who had come to stay with her family made on her. Wearing an ivory mask, the man's hot breath had wakened her in the middle of the night.

She had put up a hell of a fight until the man had slashed her chest with a dagger that carried a hint of blue liquid on the tip. Then she'd gone drowsy, and stumbled around the room, knocking over this thing and that as she tried to find her balance. Her field of vision had blurred and an overpowering sense of disorientation swept over her body and mind as she tried to find a grip on something.

The ivory masked stranger had waited as she flailed around and fell over, toppled like a rag doll.

She had awakened, sore and stiff in her joints in a chamber only slightly larger than her bedroom at home, however far away home was. Eileen couldn't be certain how far she'd gone, but she had felt like she had slept for days.

There were no windows in her personal prison cell, just a floor and ceiling made of steel slabs, bolted together to prevent potential escape, and four walls of similar material. Aside from the cot and a table made entirely of metal, and a single steel folding chair that lay on its side from one of her fits, the room was barren.

A slot in the bottom of the door opened, and a tray of food and a water skin were passed inside before the slot shut again.

Eileen shuffled toward the tray like a trapped mouse, unsure if touching the food would give her a jolt of lightning, or the sustenance she required. With no windows, and no timepiece, she had been trying to measure her time by meals. This had been the tenth meal given since she had awoken. If the man, or creature, whatever the masked menace was, operated on the same sort of schedule as her parents, then there would be four hours between each meal, fourteen between every third and fourth meal. Trying to think within reason, that would mean she had been in this dreadful place for three days, and part of a morning.

Her father, she knew, would be busying himself with hating himself for allowing his darling daughter to be abducted, and petitioning his former colleagues for their aid in apprehending the villain.

Eileen focused on the food a few feet in front of her, the aroma of well-prepared sweet meats and freshly baked bread filling the room. As it had been every time, it was homemade food, not just some slop that had been thrown together. This raised questions in her mind. She would have imagined that she would be bound and gagged when she awoke, kept in some dank cellar, filled with snakes or scorpions like she had read in her books. Then again, they were works of fiction, she thought to herself.

This treatment almost made the kidnapping seem personal in a way. Not one of her meals contained a dish or food that she didn't care for. And the cot had been well made and covered with a thick, pink, down-feather filled comforter. It was as though the mysterious abductor knew her and had gone to great lengths to make her comfortable.

She picked up the tray and took it gently over to the table, picking up the chair and sitting down, then picking slowly at the food.

As she finished her humble meal, using the bread in slices to put the meat on for little sandwiches, the door slid open.

The masked man, wearing the same black leather cloak and formal lord's clothes as when he had showed up at her parents' doorstep, stood in the doorway.

"I trust you are doing well," the man rasped from behind his ivory mask. "I have tried my best to make you comfortable."

He knocked aside the food tray aside as Eileen hurled it at him.

"That's no way to treat your host," he rasped again, the sound like a man trying to speak through water in his throat.

"Why am I here," Eileen asked, her voice trembling as she stood and backed away. "What are you? What is this place, and why have you brought me here?"

A wave of nausea washed over her as the masked stranger took two long, powerful strides closer, the ivory mask catching the faint candlelight from the burning wax on the circular table. He looked more phantasm than humanoid, but fear, Eileen knew, had a way of warping one's perceptions.

"My dear," rasped the masked man, picking up her fallen chair as she sat on the edge of the bed. His eyes, visible for the first time to Eileen through the slits in his mask, were vibrant blue and clear, and held a sad, wounded quality.

Her abductor, as she had referred to him in her better moods, might not be a completely horrible person after all. "Years ago, six to be exact, I had a family. A wife, whose beauty could hardly be rivaled. Except by one as lovely as yourself," he amended, giving Eileen a once-over. "I had four bright, energetic children, the oldest about to go off to join a Monk monastery and complete her training in the martial arts. We didn't have much, but we were content with what we had, so long as we were together." The masked man choked back tears and sobs.

"My goodness," Eileen whispered. "What happened to you and your family? Are they not here as well?"

Ocean blue eyes peered out from behind the ivory mask at her, more tears welling up.

"Our home was a two story house, seven miles west of the Allenian Hills. We had a small plot of farmland, which I tended with my wife in order to make a living at market in Manewa, the only free city in the Allenians. The Khan and Simpa clans allow other Races free passage to the city of Manewa, and we made a trip once a week to sell our produce there. In addition, as an Alchemist, I sold potions and powders at market, making the majority of our money with sales of my poisons.

"But the road to Manewa, one week, had been clogged with other merchant traffic, and so I led my wife and children off the free road, so that we might get around and into the city without delay. The children loved to play in Manewa, because every Race is represented there, and they enjoyed learning the unique games children of other Races play. My children were like that, Miss. They were always curious, and very open-minded. But as open-minded as they were, and as kind and gentle as my lovely wife and I were, their curiosity quickly became our collective terror.

"We had strayed farther from the free road than we had wanted to, and when we came over the crest of a hill, we found ourselves staring at a roving pack of Khan Hunters." The masked man straightened, standing to his feet and walking toward the door. His gaunt frame was outlined a moment later by torchlight coming from the outside hallway. "The tiger-men are a cruel and vicious Race, incapable of mercy or understanding. Brutes and savages, all of them!" The masked Alchemist slammed a gloved fist into the wall beside the doorway, and a strange symbol flared to life next to the door, a rush of force blowing through the room and illuminating the steel walls and floor for a brief moment. When the light faded, Eileen found that a rose bush had sprouted from the wall.

"What, happened then," she ventured in a mousy whisper.

The masked Alchemist turned and looked at her, his eyes distant, lost in the memories of years gone by.

"Years have passed, miss, but I remember it as if it happened yesterday. The Khan pack assaulted us, tearing the throats of my wife and oldest daughter, and breaking my other children's spines over their knees. I managed to escape thanks to the Focus Sites of Alchemy, making myself disappear. I remained invisible, bodiless, scentless, soundless all to them. When a few minutes passed and they could not find me, they left, not bothering to dispose of my family's bodies.

When they left, I buried my family, opening the ground with my Focus Sites and closing it over their torn bodies." Suddenly, his head snapped up, and his eyes gleamed with madness. "But I have spent years studying, trying to find a way to bring them back. And I found one, miss, oh yes, I found one! You will help me in this. I have discovered a way to make a person's body into the body of another, perfectly matched to be whomever I want them to be. I shall return my wife from the grave."

Eileen's heart sank, and she realized with horror what the masked madman intended.

"Your flesh shall become my beloved's, and your soul shall be removed, to make certain that I can recreate her in every way. Her personality, her likes, dislikes, and her whole being shall replace your own. I shall have my wife back, and then, my children!" He grabbed the door and pulling it tightly shut behind him.

The slot in the door opened once more, and Eileen could just barely hear his parting words over her own pounding heart. "Nothing can stop this transformation. I shall have my family back."

* * * *

When the rushing sensation finally passed, there was a flash of light, and Jonah found himself standing in the familiar streets of Desanadron.

Portenda knelt in a predatory crouch next to him, panting heavily.

Jonah put one hand on the proud Bounty Hunter's shoulder, but Portenda shrugged him off. "I'm fine," he said evenly, standing erect once again. "I've never gotten used to it is all."

Jonah nodded. "Can't disagree with you there. That was terrible." Though he still felt queasy, he also felt relieved and grateful—he was standing on home turf, a city so familiar to him that he recognized the area they had arrived in as Craftsman's Square. It was a section of the enormous city devoted entirely to craftsmen, from smiths to Alchemists like himself. Craftsman's Square was also home to the city's only Beastmasters, a pair of Lizardman brothers who owned a stable on Silver Street. They trained and sold beasts of all sorts, and were the kind of folks who didn't mind if someone just came in to browse and chat with them. They weren't purely businessmen, and often offered to train the common pets of the citizens in the city for a fee of one gold piece. Good men, all in all, Jonah thought.

"My eyes do surely deceive me, for I know that can nay be Jonah Staples," called a gruff but familiar voice.

Portenda and Jonah spun around to find a smiling Dwarf, all rough edges and muscles, holding his smithy hammer head-down on the ground. The Dwarven man had a short, well-kept beard—a sign of Dwarven youth—that was as red as blood from a fresh wound. His eyes were purest brown, a raw, earthen quality in his countenance that reflected well his profession and personality.

"Boris Rockmight, son of Morek, it is truly a pleasure to see you again." Jonah stepped forward and leaning down to embrace the Dwarven blacksmith. From heavy clap on the back, Jonah coughed roughly, and stood away from the powerful Dwarf. "I wish I had time to talk, but we're in a bit of a hurry, my friend and I," he said in a rush.

"Not many good reasons to use a Teleportation scroll otherwise, I'd imagine." Boris Rockmight had inherited his gruff father's distrust of all things magical. Where his father had been a noble Boxer and leader of Traithrock, the capital of the Dwarven territories, Boris had followed the path of a Soldier for many years until he discovered a talent for making weapons and armors. Leaving the Classes of Tamalaria behind, he had moved to Desanadron, where he was respected as one of the finest smiths in the western regions.

Part of his reasoning for changing careers was that he could never equal his father's accomplishments on the field of battle. Morek Rockmight had been one of the heroes of the War of Vandross, fighting alongside the Dread Knight, Byron of Sidius.

"Jonah, let's head to your parents house first." Portenda sniffed the air. "You lead the way," he mumbled after a moment, and Jonah gave him a sidelong look.

"I have only been to this city a few times before, Jonah. I don't know my way around," he offered coldly.

Jonah shrugged his shoulders, bade Boris farewell, and led Portenda through the streets of his hometown, Desanadron. He smiled and waved to dozens of familiar faces he passed by—in the dining patios, in the merchant shops, and outside of the towering apartment buildings and private homes. He took cutbacks and shortcuts through alleys that were cleaner than the public streets of Ja-Wen.

This city seems very secure, Portenda thought to himself. *Wonder why?*

He had his answer not long after that thought. As Jonah led him along, he took in all of the scents and sights, the sounds of the bustling city foot traffic, he noticed that members of Desanadron's regular army were posted at every turn. They stood in even numbers of two or four men and women, heavily armed, but smiling and conversing with the common citizens.

A city-state with a strong belief in showing the force of its army, it was apparently a clean and orderly city-state. Portenda found this use of the military both effective, and a little offensive. History had shown no great love for military states, and he tended to agree with history.

A Hunter and his Prey

Jonah finally came to a halt on the outskirts of the residential district. He stared gloomily at a two-story home, a humble, wooden affair, the outside paint starting to peel and chip away. A plaque above the front door said simply, 'The Staples' in bold lettering, and Jonah heaved a deep breath before approaching the door, the Bounty Hunter staying a respectful distance behind him.

Jonah took the three front steps in stride, and knocked heavily on the front door. He looked back at Portenda, who maintained his distance.

The front door opened, and Portenda saw a tall, regal woman standing there, her eyes swollen with tears, her commoner's clothes ragged and unwashed. Her face and her aura radiated strength and pride, despite the fact that she appeared to have been crying ever since she had discovered that her daughter was missing.

For a long moment, she just stood there, but then she clutched her tall, gangly son, balling like a woman grieving for the death of a family member.

From around the side of the house came an older man, his hair streaked with shocks of gray the same shade as Portenda's eyes. His frame was squat and powerful, his eyes reflecting the long years of conflict he had seen and lived through.

Jonah's father, Portenda thought. He watched as the man carried a basket of some sort until he looked up at the sound of his wife's crying, and dropped the basket to the ground to join the other two members of his family in a tight embrace.

After a few minutes, held together by the bonds of arms, hearts, and blood, the Staples stood apart.

The senior of the family, standing beside his wife, looked past Jonah at Portenda the Quiet. "Sorry, sir, I'm not interested in joining the army again."

"No, dad," Jonah said. "This is my friend, Portenda. He's going to help me look for Eileen."

Jacob Staples graced the Bounty Hunter with a smile, stepping down off of the porch and extending a rough, work-worn hand. "A pleasure, sir. Any friend of our boy is a friend of the family, especially if you can help us with our problem."

Jacob Staples was a dangerous man, once, Portenda mused. Even in his elder years, and being a Human, he had almost caused the Simpa a bit of discomfort with his grip.

"Do you know the situation, Mr. Portenda?"

"Just Portenda shall do." The Simpa tried to sound friendly, but he came off sounding gruff and uncaring, as usual. "And yes, I have been appraised of the situation. Your daughter, Eileen, has been abducted. I shall assist Jonah in any way I can."

He followed Jacob, Jonah and Anna Staples into their family home. The front door opened into their kitchen, which was kept pristine when Anna wasn't making a meal. Pots and pans and utensils of all sorts hung from a series of ceiling hooks that Jacob had installed with deft skill. A long, oak table sat in the center of the room, just to the left of the Gnome-engineered cooking stove and the hanging utensils, with five hand-crafted chairs, each made from a single piece of wood. Portenda admired the quality of the craftsmanship, noticing the slight imperfections here and there. There were little pots on the counters and hanging in the window, with flowers of various sorts growing in them. All in all, the room had a feeling to it that Portenda knew the word for, but had never before actually experienced: the room was cozy. It had a sense of family and home that made the Simpa ill at ease. He rubbed the back of his furry head awkwardly, hoping that they would move on to the den or some other room shortly.

But as he followed the family into the living den, he found that same sensation, in a more overpowering quantity. The den was slightly disheveled, but otherwise neat and well kept. There was spongy green carpeting the hue of forest floor grass. Several comfortable looking chairs, and a couch for the family to sit on, faced the center of the room where a long coffee table rested. A wood burning fireplace was set in the far left corner of the room from where Portenda stood, clearly designed to spread heat and comfort to the entire den. He felt out of place and out of touch with reality; was this how a real family lived? His own family had been, well, slightly broken.

"Portenda, are you all right?"

He snapped his attention to the recliner where she had taken a seat.

Mr. Staples stood in front of a display set of weapons on the right-hand wall, looking over the various instruments of death he had employed in his younger years.

Here at last, Portenda thought with a relaxing sigh, was something he could identify with. A moment later, he noticed that all of the weapons had been purposely dulled and blunted. His heart sank into his stomach; he didn't belong in a place such as this, surrounded by creature comforts and the homey, friendly atmosphere.

"I'll be fine," he said.

Jacob took his left arm and guided him to a thick, velvety chair. He eased Portenda down in the seat, giving him a concerned look.

"Do you need something to eat, something to drink, maybe," the older Human asked with genuine concern. His bushy gray beard hung about his face like a halo, Portenda thought. "Are you ill?"

"I'm, not certain," Portenda lied, knowing what the problem was. "I could use a glass of water, if it's not a problem."

Jacob Staples smiled and returned a minute later with a pitcher of water and a glass for the Simpa.

Portenda took a long pull, drinking an entire glass as he collected himself.

Jonah was giving him a look that was simultaneously worried and puzzled.

Portenda took a deep breath, centering himself. When he opened his eyes again, he found he was feeling much better. "I'd like to see her room, if I may."

"Of course." Anna got to her feet slowly.

Portenda rose and raised a hand to stay her.

"No, you rest. Your heart rate is still fast, and your muscles are worn."

A Hunter and his Prey

Both Anna and Jacob's eyes went wide. "There was water dripping on the floor from the pots and pans in the kitchen. The pilot of the Gnome stove was clicking on and off," he said, taking in all of the sights, sounds and smells of the entire downstairs. "Your meal isn't yet bubbling, which means you've only just finished preparing it before we arrived. You put it in the stove just before you opened to door to find your son and I standing outside. And you, sir, should take better care of yourself, for her sake." He moved his eyes, but not his head, toward Jacob.

The elder Staples man's eyes reflected his shock and wonder at Portenda's observations. Beneath that surface surprise, the Bounty Hunter saw something else brewing: a wariness born out of years of experience and conflict. Anyone who can know so much from so little time and observation, must be watched and considered carefully.

"Jonah can show me up," Portenda offered, watching as the Human Alchemist stood up and whispered something in his father's ear.

"Always," his father asked, bewildered. He looked at Portenda and smiled knowingly. "You're a Bounty Hunter, aren't you? You people are good, I'll give you that. Astute powers of observation. I've never met one, but I've heard stories about some of your people. You must be one of the best."

Jacob relaxed, much to Portenda's silent relief.

"Well, Jonah," Jacob said, "show the man up. I'm going to go down to the corner and get one of those new Gnome ice boxes the Deltoroes are always telling me about." He smiled at his son and gave him a quick, bone-crunching hug. "It's good to have you home again, even for a little while," he whispered in his son's ear, though the Bounty Hunter heard him clearly.

Jonah led Portenda up an aging set of steps to the second floor, to the closed door of his sister's room.

Before he entered, he turned and gave Portenda a hard look. "You really scared them back there, you know. My mother's never met a man of your size or skill, and my father trembled when he hugged me. I can tell he's really been on edge since Eileen went missing."

"I'm sorry Jonah," Portenda said, a hint of sadness in his voice as he hung his head.

Is he ashamed? Jonah wondered. *Why?*

"It's just," Portenda continued, "I've never experienced a feeling like I did down there. Your father was obviously a great warrior in his time, and I suspect that he doesn't understand the path you've chosen."

"That's right," Jonah said, in a 'so what' tone.

"But he loves you anyway, doesn't he?"

Jonah nodded, and thought for a moment he saw where this was going. He wasn't sure he wanted to hear any more from the Bounty Hunter, because he was certain it was going to be a depressing speech.

"I'm not sure I've ever known that feeling. I've never really known what it means."

"What what means," Jonah asked.

Portenda turned his attention on the door to Eileen's room, sniffing the air closely. "Family," he said, opening the door and stepping through.

Jonah, befuddled more than he had thought possible, followed him in.

The room was in shambles, his mother and father unable to bring themselves to enter the room.

"Your father stood here for a long time, several hours at least," Portenda reported. "He feels personally responsible for this."

Jonah stutter-stepped to his sister's dresser, where her diary lay, opened and facing down. He turned it up, and decided to take the opportunity to read the latest entries for any trace of a hint as to what exactly had happened.

In her letters to Jonah, Eileen had confessed that she had, unbeknownst to their parents, begun studying Q magic—the art of status-effecting spells and minor destructive and defensive magic. She had been studying ever since Jonah's last year living with them, which would make this her fourth year of study. She had told him that she had been finding it difficult to cast the few spells she had memorized on or through steel or iron, and had resolved to inquire about the properties of steel with Jonah himself or one of the other Alchemists in town. Perhaps, she had written, the old half-Orc Q Mage down the street, Balbous Barabus could help her.

But her diary made no mention of her study of sorcery. *Mother most likely read her diary regularly,* Jonah thought, *so of course she would leave that sort of thing out.* It read more like a bad romance novel, a running record of her failed romances and few boyfriends, all of whom she had tried to keep secret from their folks. But the very last two entries, he saw, described a stranger who had blown into town, a man wearing a black, leather cloak, and a strange ivory mask. After that, there were no entries. "Portenda, I think I've found a clue." He handed the diary to the Bounty Hunter, who had been standing there in the center of the room like a statue.

Portenda took the diary gently, respectful of the fact that it was someone else's property. He browsed the final pages of the diary, raising his eyebrows a couple of times and then giving Jonah a flat stare. "You only had to read the last entry, Jonah. Why did you read the rest?"

Jonah blushed and turned aside, crossing his arms and harrumphing. "I'm her older brother. I think I have a right to know what's been going on in my sister's life."

Portenda shook his head and returned to his observations. The scent of blood still clung to the air, old and dried. But there was only one source, female, similar to the smell of Jonah's blood, a scent he now knew quite well. But there was also the trace scent of a chemical of some sort. It was familiar, a sedative he had sometimes used to get himself to sleep.

* * * *

Jonah stared from his sister's open window down onto the streets of Desanadron. Impossible, he thought, that someone could have taken his sister out this window without raising suspicion. Someone out there knew what had happened and hadn't done a thing to stop it. Perhaps, he thought, they even helped the villain escape.

"I smell something here," Portenda said. "A chemical of some sort."

"Can you describe the smell?"

"I know it was a sedative." Portenda closed his eyes and tried to concentrate. Something else in the room, something he felt more than smelled or saw, made him uneasy and uncomfortable, slightly skewing his senses.

Jonah thought through his mental catalogue of every sedative that could be delivered in a drink or on the end of a weapon.

"It smells slightly like pine needles," Portenda said, and Jonah's eyes snapped open.

"Renval Ink," he said. "It's used as a sleep aid for lycanthropes! My gods, if the bastard used that on her, she could easily have been knocked out for days."

The Bounty Hunter wobbled and broke out in a cold sweat.

Oh shit, Jonah thought. Eileen's jewelry box is full of silver trinkets.

Jonah moved over to her vanity desk, grabbed the bronze jewelry box, and carried it over to her closet. He knew she kept a copper safe box in there, on the floor at the back, where she stashed away her most prized possessions. Copper, Jonah had discovered in his studies of metals and their properties, could act as a buffer for the effects of silver on a lycanthrope.

"What did you do," Portenda asked, more interested than Jonah would have liked. He felt as though the Simpa was boring through his soul with those great, gray eyes.

"Eileen wears a lot of silver jewelry when she goes out on dates and the like. I just put her jewelry box in her copper safe. Silver's effects on a lycanthrope are negated when it is placed in a copper container. It's like a natural buffer."

Portenda nodded, and his face went back to its normal look of detached curiosity. "A lesson I shall not soon forget." He stalked over to the window, and found the intruder had left not even a trace scent of himself. "Jonah, come here," he said.

The Alchemist took one final look around the room before he approached. "What is that?"

"It's a piece of his cloak," Portenda said.

Jonah finally felt a sliver of hope pierce the darkness of his heart.

* * * *

"You're certain you can't stay the night," Anna Staples asked once more as Portenda the Quiet and Jonah Staples stood on her front porch.

"We shall return, but not until the morning, Mrs. Staples," Portenda said. "This cloak was very special, unique even. I have a very reliable source of information in the forest just north of this city. We shall require food and drink when we return, and plenty of it. It shall be a very taxing evening."

As midnight approached, Jacob walked out onto the porch, and handed Jonah a gleaming, finely edged short sword. "I know you're not much good at fighting, son, but take it anyway. You may need it out in that forest."

Jonah noted the strange, glowing runes carved into the blade.

"It's enchanted, son—Paladin magic. High Commander Hayes of the Order of Oun gave it to me after the war. That, and a healthy amount of gold," he amended with a smile.

Jonah took the weapon and sheath, securing the sword to his hip.

"Oh, and I packed you a meal, just in case." Anna handed Jonah a small bag of wrapped foodstuffs.

"Mother, please," Jonah protested as his mother shoved the bag into his hands. "I'm not twelve anymore, okay?"

Portenda gave Jonah a light slap to the back of the head, surprising both Jonah and his parents.

With a grumble and a smile, Jonah put the sack lunch in his rucksack, keeping it separate from his chemicals. "Thank you mom," he muttered

Anna gave him a brief embrace and a kiss on the cheek.

"You'll keep him safe, right?" she asked Portenda, a look of fear and concern for her son's welfare impressed in her eyes and voice. She wanted her boy to stay home, he mused. Jacob, on the other hand, appeared to want the boy to go out into the world and gain valuable experience. A Soldier through and through, he thought with an inward smile.

"Of course I will, ma'am."

"Good." Jacob Staples put his arm around his wife's waning waistline. "Because if you don't, you and I shall have to tangle."

Portenda realized that the elder Soldier meant every word of his bold statement. Jacob would try in earnest to kill him if Jonah came to harm. *This family has already been through enough,* he thought vehemently. *I shall not fail this mission.*

"Jonah, come." He led the Human north through the city streets. At night, the city of Desanadron was much like Ja-Wen, lights still glowing in various pubs and stores.

Jonah rubbed the sore spot on the back of his head until they were out of earshot of his parents' house, and then addressed the Bounty Hunter. "Why did you slap me back there? That really smarted."

Portenda wheeled so fast that Jonah saw nothing but a blur of golden fur until he was pressed nose-to-snout with the big man. There was no trace of malice in his eyes, only a sort of sadness, its source unknown to the Alchemist.

"You were being insolent to your mother. She brought you into this world, Jonah. The least you can do for her is suffer her affections, however embarrassing they may be. Now, let's continue."

Jonah followed in silence for a while, nodding to one of the northern gate guards, a man he had grown up with.

The Minotaur smiled and nodded amiably back at Jonah. "Jonah Staples, it is good to see you in prosperous health." The Minotaur Sergeant's steel armor caught the light of the torch in his left hand.

Jonah looked at the stripes on his tunic sleeve and whistled. "Ah, a Sergeant now, Manny. You've done well for yourself. Tell me, how's the baby?"

A Hunter and his Prey

Portenda shuffled aside, observing this interaction.

"Well, he's walking around, destroying everything he touches," Manny replied, and the Private next to him chuckled softly. Manny introduced the Elven man. "This is Private Seth Estoc. Private, this is an old friend of mine, Jonah Staples. I told you I wasn't a racist," Manny said to the nervous Elven man.

"A pleasure to meet you, citizen." The Elf extended an armored hand.

Jonah shook it, and the Private immediately snapped back to an attentive posture.

"Breaking him in, eh?" Jonah gave the lumbering Minotaur a wry smile.

"Just busting his balls. It's his first night on duty." Manny smiled broadly at the Human. "Where are you and your quiet friend heading?"

"The Taiwok Forest," Portenda replied.

Both the Minotaur and the Elf gasped in fright. Jonah had never heard anything about the Taiwok, except that he should stay away from it.

"You're joking, right?" The muscular Minotaur looked at Portenda with his face but at Jonah with his eyes.

Jonah shook his head and shrugged his shoulders.

"Jonah, I can't allow you to go there. Your mother and father are already worried sick about Eileen." He put a big hand on Jonah's shoulder.

The Alchemist gripped his wrist hard, pressing himself forward. "What do you know about Eileen?"

The Minotaur rubbed the back of his head as he pulled his hand away. "Just what your dad told us. Some drifter came through, stayed with them, and then took off with Eileen. We don't have much to go on, but we are investigating."

Jonah nodded. He wasn't entirely satisfied with the Minotaur's response, but for now, it would have to do.

"Look, Manny, thanks for the information. But now we do have to go, both of us, to the Taiwok," he said, moving away.

"Hey, if you're going, Jonah," the Minotaur said, a concerned expression plastered to his face. "Just, just be careful, huh?"

Jonah nodded. He followed behind Portenda, who had already moved away, out of the gates of Desanadron, and into the plains beyond.

* * * *

"*Mak Don*," Eileen shouted, casting another Raybolt spell at the steel floor. All of her energy only managed to scorch the surface a little.

She slumped to the floor, exasperated and drained from the spells. Two meals had passed since the masked freak had visited. At the last meal, the man had slipped a note through the door with the food, with a single name on it—Genma.

So that's his name, she had thought, using it as a focal thought for her spells. But the more she tried, the more she simply wore herself out. Now she desperately needed food and rest.

Another meal slid through the slot as she thought about her needs, and another note accompanied it. As she wolfed hungrily at the food, leaving the

79

tray on the floor and eating like an animal, she checked the note. It read as follows:

'Dear child, you know that all that spell casting will drain you. I have thus far tolerated it simply because I know that you can have no success. I shall allow you to work yourself into a tizzy tonight, but when the sun rises, your foolishness had better stop. I have tried to be reasonable and patient with your ignorant attempts to free yourself, but tomorrow, you shall stop. I shall be visiting you again tomorrow around lunchtime, and expect you to be cooperative. I have some important information that I must gather from you, and you will comply. If you do not, I shall be forced to make things very uncomfortable for you.' —Genma.

Great, she thought, frustrated beyond belief. *I'm locked in some room, held captive by a total nutjob who wants to remove my soul and turn my body into a copy of his dead wife. Lords only know what kind of stuff that creep wants to do with me tomorrow.* But being angry wasn't getting her free. To stand a chance, she would have to take the opportunity he would be presenting her at lunch the next day.

Using her limited knowledge of locking spells, an art that was tricky and very tiring, she locked a number of minor offensive spells on her body and clothes. She also locked a strength-draining spell on the door itself, setting the trigger condition to be when Genma opened it. After her preparations, she felt like slipping into a coma, but settled instead for lying under the comforter on her cot, and falling fast asleep. *I'm not going to let him touch me without leaving a few bruises*, she thought as she slipped into slumber.

* * * *

Midnight. The moon hung high overhead, the perfect mirror of its sister the sun at noon.

Jonah followed Portenda the Quiet through the Taiwok Forest, avoiding branches and piles of leaves when he could. Portenda stepped easily over and around these little problems, making no sound as he passed through the thick maple and pine trees of the forest.

Jonah hurried to keep up, now and again tripping and falling into foliage and underbrush with a "Hoomph!" After a while, he wondered where they were headed. He glanced at his timepiece: half past midnight.

Portenda stopped just outside of a small clearing in which stood an odd little cottage erected entirely of blackened wood.

Jonah had never seen wood of that hue before—it wasn't painted black, the wood was simply dark as night. He stood just behind and to the left of Portenda, who squinted his eyes and sniffed the air.

"One of them is nearby," the Bounty Hunter said. "I can feel the wind breaking over his body." He forced Jonah to duck as he launched a roundhouse kick to the face of a pale, humanoid creature that had charged at them through the air.

The man landed in a heap of purple, velvet evening attire, the sort that diplomats wear to charity balls.

A Hunter and his Prey

Jonah stared in fear and shock as the man stood, brushed off his clothes, and smiled at them, revealing four fangs even longer than Portenda's.

A Vampire, Jonah thought, horror seizing his entire body. *Oh gods, we're screwed.* He scrambled to his feet, drawing the short sword his father had given him.

The Vampire threw his head back and laughed at him and Portenda put his hand back toward Jonah, signaling him to put the weapon away.

"My goodness, Portenda," the Vampire said. "He's a feisty one, isn't he?"

Jonah stared in disbelief at the Vampire and the Simpa. "You, you know this thing?"

Portenda gently took the short sword from Jonah and planted it, tip first, in the soil.

"Oh, listen to him," the Vampire said in a thick, northwestern region accent. "He ist precious, istn't he? Vell, if my friend here von't introduce me, I shall introduce myself, no?" The Vampire rolled his hand forward and bowed, a graceful motion in the moonlight. "My name ist Richard Tiverski. I am the eldest of the Tiverski brothers. Please, follow me," the Vampire said, walking past Portenda and Jonah.

The Alchemist gripped Portenda by the leather armor, pulling himself up his front.

"What the devil is going on here, Portenda? How do you know this, this," he stammered, trying to think of an appropriate term.

"Man, Jonah. He and his brothers are men, even though they are Vampires. Trust me on this one." Portenda grabbed Johan by the back of the shirt and set him on the forest floor. "These are not bad men."

"Not bad men?" Jonah now realized why Manny had warned him against coming here. "They're Vampires for the gods' sakes! You know, black magic, sucking people's blood, turning them into slaves, that sort of thing? You do know that, don't you?"

Portenda simply followed Richard Tiverski.

"This is a bad idea," Jonah muttered to himself as he sprinted to catch up to the long, loping strides of the Bounty Hunter.

The three men entered the cottage, and stood in a den not unlike the one at Jonah's parents' house. Here, though, the wood burned without smoke, and let only a moderate amount of heat into the room.

On the couch, facing the fire, sat two more Vampires. One was clad all in black from head to foot, his waist-long hair draped over the back of the couch. He was large and muscular like Portenda, and broad in the shoulders as far as Jonah could see from his angle. His ears were slightly pointed, a sign that he had once been an Elf. As Jonah angled around the couch for a better view, he saw that the Vampire had a huge scimitar resting against the couch next to him. His arms were crossed as he glared at the fire, his upper fangs jutting just slightly over his lower lip, and his eyes suddenly snapped over to Jonah, who let out a girlish shriek as he stumbled backward, tripping over a footstool and crashing to the floor.

"Please, do not vorry yourself," Richard Tiverski said as he flopped into a chair opposite Jonah. "Trent has that effect on people. These are my brothers, Trent Tiverski, the brawn of our trio." Richard waved his hand at the morbid looking warrior. "And Simon Tiverski, the most talented magic vielder among us." He indicated the third Vampire, a short, gaunt figure who wore a forest green robe with blue runes stitched into the fabric. Simon's head was completely bald, and his eyes were set deep in his face, the red irises barely visible amid the darkness of his face. All were pale, tallow-skinned creatures, but none of them, now that Jonah looked at the three of them, seemed inherently vicious. Trent had an aura of violent potential about him, sure, but Jonah expected that from any Vampire. This was, after all, his first and only actual encounter with the species.

Portenda stood behind the couch, rummaged through his rucksack, and producing the piece of leather cloak.

Aside from the color, it looked exactly like the purple cloak that hung on the wall behind Richard, who had gotten up and returned now to his seat, a glass with suspicious red liquid in it. "Oh, don't vorry about dis," Richard said with a sheepish grin at Jonah.

"Pig's blood," Portenda uttered to Jonah, who looked on with shock as Richard Tiverski tipped the wineglass back, draining every last drop of its contents.

"I don't understand," he said, moving in front of the fire. "You were clearly born a Vampire," he said to Richard. "But he was once an Elf," he said, pointing to Trent, who made a face at him. "And he doesn't look related to you at all." He pointed in turn at Simon, who gave him a slight smile before returning to his thoughts.

Richard laughed heartily as Portenda handed him the piece of leather cloak.

"Ve are brothers, little Human, make no mistake about that. Ve are not related by blood, that much is true, but ve haf taken an oath, the three of us. Ve have vowed never to drink from the throats of mortal men and vomen. Ve flatly refuse to be the monsters that go bump in the night, young man." He got up and rinsing his glass out by a water pump in what appeared to be the kitchen, attached to the living den. "May I offer you a drink off something? Ve keep ales and tonics in the icebox, in case ve get company, vich, by the vay, doesn't happen often."

"Any idea who made that cloak," Portenda asked suddenly, interrupting Jonah and Richard's conversation.

Richard did the talking for the group, Jonah surmised. And why not? The man seemed to have a natural charm. And he was, aside from the accent, very well spoken. A fitting representative for the trio.

"I'm not entirely certain just yet, but you vere right to bring it to me. It definitely hast the same qvalities of our kind's cloaks." Richard returned with a fizzing, bubbling beverage, which he handed to Jonah.

"What is it?" Jonah took a whiff of the drink. *No traces of poison*, he mused, unable to stop himself from checking anyway.

A Hunter and his Prey

"The Dvarves make this stuff. They claim it's like drinkink cold, sugary coffee. They call it, soda, I think the vord is." Richard raised an eyebrow at Jonah. "Vat is that horrible smell coming from your bag?"

Oh, Hells, Jonah thought, thinking about his lunch and tapping the snap on his rucksack. "Ah, it's gone now," Richard said, moving away in any event.

"Sorry, but I'm an Alchemist," Jonah explained. "I keep shaved garlic and garlic powder for combining potions and the like."

Richard, Trent and Simon all cringed simultaneously.

Portenda looked at Richard and cleared his throat gruffly.

"Ah, yes, of course. It is as you suspect, my fine, furry friend. But this cloak ist not like mine, or those off other, more traditional Vampires." He took down his purple cloak and put it on, clipping the neck clasps together. "Observe, if you will," he said more to Jonah than to the Simpa.

Richard Tiverski furled the cloak in front of him, and before Jonah's eyes, the purple, velvety material hardened into a sizable shield.

Portenda hefted the auto crossbow from his hip and turned the crank, firing round after round of bolts into the fabric.

They all stopped, repelled by the cloak as Richard giggled behind his shield.

Portenda, having helped demonstrate the cloak's powers to Jonah, put his weapon away and retrieved the fallen bolts. "Now, Jonah, vatch closely." With another furl of the material, he lashed out at Portenda with a sharpened edge of the cloak, a blow that Portenda easily knocked aside with his extracted claws.

Richard then spun around in a circle, and completely disappeared, the cloak turning to liquid and seeping through the cracks in the floor.

He reappeared a moment later, his cloak appearing to be part of the dark shadows thrown behind the couch by the fire's light. He spun back into being, and flourished his arms and fangs as he bowed deeply once again. "You see, Jonah, the cloak ist an ancient, sacred item to our kind. I vas vonce a monster, just like the majority off our kind." He took off the cloak and hung it on the wall with a heavy sigh. "I vas foolish, and craved the power that my father vonce had. I vas born a Vampire, I knew no other vay. But many years passed." He looked back at the cloak. "And as I surpassed my father, I began to think about the thousands off mortals I had drunk from, taking their lives or turning them into more of us. I svore then, that I vould no longer drink from the throats of mortals. I vould take only vat they villing give me, in a separate container. Some of mortal kind find our existence fascinating, and seek us out. They ask to join our ranks, the fools that they are. I simply ask them to make a cut on their arm or leg, pour in a bowl, and then take their leave from me." Richard Tiverski turned again to Portenda. "This cloak, by the vay, vas not made in the vays of old. Some magic or science produced this." He tossed the leather piece back to Portenda with mild disgust.

"Thank you, Richard," Portenda said.

Trent got up and excused himself quietly from the room.

"Some magic, or science you say?" The Bounty Hunter asked. "What makes you so sure?"

"Vell." Richard put his chin in his palm, thinking carefully. "First of all, the old cloaks are made from the flesh of Doppelgangers, to allow for the morphing capabilities. They're alvays easy to find for a Vampire," he explained to Jonah. "They seem to flock to our kind. Ve have the ability to control them, so I suspect it's a natural instinct. Secondly, there is no trace off verevolf blood on it. They are our kind's most hated enemies, Jonah," he said, again addressing the Alchemist instead of the Bounty Hunter.

Why the fascination with me? Jonah wondered. *Portenda's the one who asked.*

"Ve have no problems vith them, but they know us, and vat ve are about." He lowered his chin to his chest. "Lastly, I can sense that the art used to make this cloak hast been around for thousands of years, long before the Age of Mecha. The cloak itself isn't that old, of course, but the art used to make it is. It seems to have the same abilities as my cloak, but it is of a vastly different nature."

Portenda nodded, and walked into the kitchen, opening a large cupboard and pulling down an empty jar.

What happened next made Jonah so ill that he had to rush to the Tiverski's front door and throw it open to vomit outside. Portenda extracted the claws of his left paw, and carefully, deliberately carved his right forearm open, pouring his own blood into the jar.

The thick, musty odor of Jonah's stomach contents wafted into his nostrils as they splashed to the mossy forest floor outside, and he collapsed to his knees, mere inches away from his own waste. He could hear the trickle of Portenda's blood in the background, filling the jar as he bled himself into it.

"Ah, very much obliged," he heard Richard saying behind him. "Jonah, are you all right?"

When Jonah returned to the den, he saw that Portenda had crashed, bleeding and unconscious, to the floor. Simon was casting a spell on the wound, and it closed an instant later, glimmering with soft emerald light.

The smell of blood filled Jonah's lungs, and he felt like he was breathing in tar.

"My sincerest apologies," Richard said, patting Jonah on the shoulder. "This is how he repays us for our assistance. He's a very generous man."

Jonah hauled back his fist and punched the Vampire squarely in the face, sending him sprawling against the door to Trent's room. Simon yelped in surprise and shock, leaping back over the couch as the huge, warrior Vampire thrust his door open and looked down at the eldest Tiverski brother.

Murder filled his eyes as he glared menacingly at Jonah, whose hand felt like it was on fire after punching Richard. The warrior Vampire cracked his knuckles and stepped forward, his midnight black cloak fluttering in preparation for slaughter.

Richard reached up and grabbed Trent by the wrist, shaking his head.

The Vampire brute looked up at Jonah again, and down at Portenda.

"Count your blessings." Trent's deep, booming voice caused the air to quiver around Jonah, shaking him to his bones.

A Hunter and his Prey

Richard had regained his feet at this point, and smiled crookedly at the Alchemist.

"I, I don't know what to say," Jonah stammered, still concerned for the Bounty Hunter's health. "I just, I lost my temper, Mr. Tiverski. Maybe I should leave."

"I don't think so. You may have been fine coming in to our forest, but finding your vay out vithout Portenda, vell, zat might be impossible." Richard folded his arms in a haughty manner.

"What do you mean?"

"Vell," Richard began as a groan issued from Portenda's mouth.

The Simpa was regaining consciousness thanks to Simon's magic.

"Mostly, it's the wraiths that I vould be concerned vith. They leave our mutual furry friend here alone, because on previous visits to us, he hast slain several of them." Richard's tone hinted at the great respect he held for such an accomplishment. Wraiths stood among the most dangerous abominations in all of Tamalaria. Undead creatures, wraiths took a semi-solid state when they chose in order to rend their victims to shreds with their spectral claws and fangs, but they relied on fear and black magic to break their victims' defenses down. But a wraith, Jonah also knew, could not harm a mortal if he or she showed no fear of them. Portenda, it often seemed, wasn't afraid of anything.

A moment later the Bounty Hunter was on his knees, his palms pressed flat to his thighs as he shook his head.

Gods, Portenda thought, *that was draining. Need to cut back on how much I give them.* He kept his chin tucked against his chest, his eyes closed as he tried to meditate. He focused on the drone of voices a few feet in front of him, not so much the words, but to take a rhythm from them.

A small mental trigger went click, and his mind snapped into place. He would be fine, now, so long as food waited for him when he returned to the Staples residence. Like a possum getting up from the spot in the merchant road where it had laid all day, playing dead, Portenda got to his feet, making certain as he slowly rose that he wouldn't be brought back down.

He wobbled for a moment, and then found that he had solid ground under his feet, instead of under his face.

"Good, you're awake." Jonah smiled. "Can we get out of here and head back to my parents' house?"

Portenda nodded and grumbled something unintelligible under his breath, walking unsteadily over to the Alchemist. Jonah let Portenda lean a little on him, though he didn't quite feel fully capable of supporting his weight.

Ah, he thought, *I can fix that.* "Richard, I'd like to use a Focus Site. May I?"

The Vampire leader gave him a queer look, and Jonah realized that he would have to explain.

"In Alchemy, the semi-magical art known as Focus is the pinnacle of study. Only the most devoted Alchemists master it. I'm no master," he said, putting his hand out to stop Richard from asking any questions about his knowledge of

Alchemy. "But I know many of the Sites by heart, and I have reference texts. I just need to draw a Site with chalk on your floor."

"By all means, go ahead." Richard bowed deeply and slipped back. "I am most interested in this, *Focus.*" He rolled the word out with a hint of mystery.

Jonah pulled out his stick of chalk, which was getting shorter every time he turned around, and drew a simple Focus Site diagram on the floor. The Alchemist knelt on the Site, thrusting his palms into the floor.

The now familiar rush of force, accompanied by the scent of wet wool, blew over his body and through the chamber. Jonah felt fire race through his muscles, an inferno of power raging in his blood as his heart hammered faster in his chest.

The pain was much less than when he had used the extension Site to grow vines from his wrists. Pure, physical strength powered him, and he mentally sighed, relieved that his use of the Strength Site had gone off without a hitch.

Jonah lifted Portenda, who looked at him with an eyebrow raised.

Jonah grinned impishly, and helped him to the door. "Thank you for your help, Richard," the Bounty Hunter said as the senior Tiverski brother handed him back the piece of leather cloak.

"Any time, my friend. Ve are alvays here for you," Richard opened the door for the two men, who eased out into the night.

After about ten minutes of slow marching, Portenda spoke quietly to Jonah.

"Our enemy is very resourceful, it would seem," he said.

"Maybe so, but I think we can get the job done," Jonah said. "So what do we do when we get back?"

"Simple," Portenda said. "We assemble a list of suspects and get any information that the guards have. Information is the best weapon, Jonah, when tracking a true nemesis."

A Hunter and his Prey

Chapter Five
Collection of Information

Jonah Staples and Portenda the Quiet were halfway out of the forest when strange noises first echoed through the trees. At first, to Jonah they sounded like something far away moaning or congealing, like a dog caught in a bear trap. As the sounds increased in volume, and multiplied, coming from all directions, he knew that it was what he had feared: wraiths were coming. "Portenda," Jonah whispered, coming to a full stop.

"I know," the Bounty Hunter whispered. He lowered himself off of Jonah's shoulder, standing tall and drawing his broadsword.

Jonah's mind reeled, and he searched the forest floor for a hard surface to draw a Focus Site on. His potions and powders would have no effect on spectral creatures like wraiths, ghosts, or wights.

The slurping, moaning noises continued, and the ghastly, otherworldly lime green lights of the wraiths appear around them, initially several dozen yards away. They approached slowly, but purposefully.

Jonah noticed that the faster his heart raced, the brighter the wraiths glowed. Still, from the accounts he had read of survivors' encounters with these spectral undead creatures, he expected them to be even brighter, their grotesque features visible from a good fifty yards off. *Portenda*, he thought. *He doesn't fear them.*

Then he recalled, from the first reference tome, that a Focus Site doesn't need to be drawn with or on anything specific. "I've got it," he whispered to himself.

Jonah lifted his right foot, and planted his heel in the soil of the forest and dragged his foot in a full circle. He then knelt to draw the detailed symbols with his finger.

Once he had it completed, he looked and saw that the wraiths had made no further progress in their approach. Portenda stalked about in a wide circle, glaring at them all and baring his teeth, growling like an animal.

Jonah drew the enchanted short sword his father had given him, holding it in his right hand, as he pressed his left palm to the Site. For a moment, nothing happened, and his heart skipped a beat.

"Jonah, stay centered," Portenda shouted.

During that moment of panic, the wraiths had floated a good ten feet closer. Then he felt the rush of force from the Focus Site. Instead of white light, a bronze mist issued forth from the Site. The scent of burning flesh exploded into the air around him, and he took several steps back as a dome of translucent crimson force sprang forth from the Site and closed over the small area that Jonah and Portenda inhabited. The Simpa looked around him, and then over to Jonah with a grin.

"It's called a Rolling Barrier," Jonah explained, sauntering over to Portenda, his short sword still in hand. "It'll only last about fifteen minutes, but where we move, it moves."

"And anything that it rolls into?" Portenda looked at a wraith that was trying to break through the barrier.

"Well, if it isn't a threat to us, nothing. If it's hostile to the creator of the barrier, it bursts into flames." Jonah straightened his back. A second later, he almost collapsed as the effects of the Strength Site drained away. He felt suddenly sluggish and incapable of moving, though the need to was great.

Portenda supported him for three minutes as Jonah regained his bearings.

"Damn, we've lost time. Let's get moving." Jonah followed Portenda, who jogged ahead at a mild pace, as best he could.

Several wraiths erupted in gouts of spectral and Alchemical flames as the barrier rolled into them, their moans transformed into shrieks and howls of agony and unnatural pain. Fragments of their skeletal, semi-solid bodies littered the ground as Jonah and Portenda passed through the forest, and finally, into the open plains north of Desanadron.

The wraiths stopped the pursuit at the forest's edge, but the two still jogged on. Just before they reached the gates of Desanadron, the barrier fell apart, evaporating into the air in a cloud of red smoke.

When they finally got back to the Staples' residence, they both took a momentary breather on the porch, and watched as the sun came up.

* * * *

Lunchtime came much sooner than Eileen would have cared for, but only because she slept so late. Her first meal had gone cold when she arose to eat it. Only minutes after finishing that first meal, there was a rap at the door, and it swung open to reveal the masked man, holding a tray. Behind him, almost too small for Eileen to notice properly, was a Kobold, its tan, leathery skin exposed to the hall's light as it carried a bundle of cloth and a stool.

Aw, Hells, she thought groggily. She hadn't expected the ivory masked creep to bring an assistant.

"Greetings." Genma stepped through and a splash of pale blue light fell on him from the top of the doorframe. "Ah, a strength draining spell, locked on the door. Clever girl."

He continued forward and placed the tray on the table.

As he remained leaned close to her, Eileen tensed. "Oh, don't worry. I'm not going to hold it against you. After all, I did say that I didn't want you casting any magic, *today*. I sense that your spells were locked, yesterday.

The ivory mask had a demon's face painted on it in fine, red lines, *a fitting countenance*, Eileen thought angrily.

"Now, eat. We have things to do." Genma summoned his Kobold servant with a motion of his hand.

The Kobold was roughly the same size and body type of most of his Race, all angles and skin and bones, with a snout-like face that reminded her briefly of Lizardmen. He wore a pair of green cloth tunic pants, with no shirt, revealing a strange mark burned into his chest. The Kobold's eyes, she noted, looked slack and empty, devoid of thought. She picked at her food, stalling for time, then asked Genma, "What's wrong with him? He looks like he hasn't got a thought in his head."

"That's because he doesn't," the masked menace said flatly. "I've used my powers to seal away his spirit and free will, you see." He pointed at the mark on the Kobold's chest. "Much as I shall do to you, when all is in readiness."

She thought she could make out the hint of a smile behind those eyes, that mask and shivered despite her promise to not let this man see her afraid. The prospect of being trapped in her own body as it changed and was made into the form of Genma's late wife caused glaciers to run through her blood.

Eileen prolonged her meal as long as possible, but the masked man just stood there, watching her with infinite patience.

When finally she finished, she dabbed her mouth and stood up, thrusting her seat back to the floor, again. "All right then, you cretin! Whatever you intend to do, just do it and get it over with."

"Kobuchi, the stool please."

The Kobold set the stool next to Eileen.

"Now, my lady, if you would do us the great honor of getting undressed," Genma said, his voice positively dripping with carnal implications.

My gods, Eileen thought. "No way in all the Hells!" She backed herself to the far wall. She had kept a spell locked on her body, in the event the creep tried to have his way with her, but he had demonstrated preparedness for such tricks when he shrugged off the strength-draining spell. She tried to estimate how long it would take her to sprint out that door. It was so close, and yet it felt as though it were a million miles away, her freedom unattainable. And even if she got out of the room, who was to say that there weren't more mindless, soulless servants waiting to stop her outside the room?

"Please, dear Eileen," Genma rasped, pulling his black gloves taut, then put his hands behind his back in a gentlemanly fashion. "I have no intentions of ravishing you. We simply need to take some measurements, to make the proper adjustments when I change your body to that of my dear, lovely wife." He trying to reassure her and frighten her in the same fell swoop. "If I wanted to, I could strip you of your garments permanently, and I know this room isn't very well heated. That would only make you more uncomfortable," he said with a shrug of his shoulders, cracking his knuckles. "But, if it's that way or no way, then so be it," he said.

"Wait," Eileen shouted.

The mask shifted as Genma smiled.

Blushing like the virgin she was, Eileen undid her belt and her buckles, removing her dress and then her undergarments. She stood shivering, not with any sense of chilliness, but with shame and embarrassment. She hugged her breasts, trying to hide them, but she couldn't tell if it worked or not because she was keeping her eyes fixed on the floor. "There, are you happy?" Tears ran down her face. Before she knew it, a leather-gloved hand was up under her chin, raising her face to meet Genma's.

Those eyes, she thought, *so cold, so dead to the world.*

"Thank you for your cooperation," he breathed to her. "Now, head up, chest out, arms out to your sides, and legs slightly apart, if you please." He turned his back and walked away, picking up her fallen chair and taking a seat.

Eileen was baffled silent; he hadn't taken advantage of her, or touched her in any inappropriate way. Such a curious man, this Genma. Before relief could settle in, though, she looked down and saw the Kobold, standing on the stool, a measuring tape in his hands.

Genma had a pad of parchment on the table, a quill ready to jot down her measurements.

She stood as he had asked, letting her body be exposed.

"Kobuchi, floor to waist, please," Genma snapped.

The Kobold extended the tape measure to the floor, pressing the cold instrument to Eileen's hip.

She shivered involuntarily at the touch of it. The Kobold rattled off a number, and Genma wrote it down. On and on like this it went, with the measurements growing increasingly intimate.

"I refuse," she said evenly, keeping her breasts wrapped in her arms. "That thing is cold, for one," she said, pointing to the flexible tape. "And I'm not letting this little creep touch me there, for two."

Genma stood and gripping her wrists, holding them over her head with one large hand. She felt a strange flux of power. When he let go, her hands remained above her head. "What sorcery is this? Must be useful for perverts and freaks such as yourself." She tried to kick Genma, but the Kobold held her feet were being held fast to the floor.

Genma placed one end of the tape against the outside curve of her right breast, and used the same trick he had on her wrists to hold it in place. He walked the tape around her, keeping it pressed against her body. As he completed the circle, he nodded, walked away, and wrote down the measurement.

As Eileen sagged with relief, Genma stalked back over. Removing his gloves, he hefted her breasts in his pale, bare hands.

She gasped despite her efforts to remain calm.

His eyes rolled back and forth, and she realized that he wasn't fondling her; he was estimating the weight of her breasts. *What a freak*, she thought, poison rolling through her soul.

Genma walked away again, snapped his fingers, and a moment later, Eileen was standing there in the middle of the room, fully clothed. "How did you," she started, but stopped as he put up a hand to stay her words.

"I have Focus Sites hidden throughout the room," he said.

Eileen snapped to attention at the term Focus. She had heard that word often from her uncle Allen and her brother Jonah. It was some sort of form of Alchemy, which would make this ivory masked cretin a very skilled Alchemist. She hadn't heard from Allen in years, and had no way of knowing how to get in touch with him, but she knew that Jonah would be looking for her by now. There was hope for her yet.

A Hunter and his Prey

"You're an Alchemist. You may have mentioned that already, I don't know. My mind hasn't felt clear since I got here. Did you use Alchemy to disable the spells I locked on my body? You touched me, sir. You violated my body." She hissed, slamming her palm flat on his parchment, where he hadn't written yet. "I want an explanation, damn it!"

"I didn't violate you, miss." He barely contained the laugh in his voice. "If those were your thoughts when you locked your spells on yourself, you should be warned to be more thoughtful with your trigger condition wording. I was merely taking measurements, in order to properly adjust your body during the transformation. Your breasts are slightly larger than my wife's were, and they shall have to be reduced during the process."

His words caused Eileen to reflexively cover her chest. She had measured her progress into full womanhood with them, and was loath to be changed in any way.

"Aside from that," he continued, "and the obvious facial adjustments, you're very much like my wife. Same approximate height, same leg width, close arm width. Yes, you were the perfect choice." He rolled his parchments tightly, handing them to the Kobold. "You should feel honored. We have other information we'll be needing, but not today. For now, please rest. I'll leave this door open for you. You may roam this floor and the one below it for now. But don't try anything foolish." Fire blazed in his eye as he looked at her through the mask. "Or you shall suffer dearly."

He left without another word.

Eileen dashed for the doorway and looked out into a long, slightly sloped stone hallway.

Where was she?

Spotting a window at the far left end of the corridor, she sprinted to it, hoping to get some idea of where she'd been taken.

The news wasn't good. She was several hundred feet in the air, high in a stone hewn tower, in an area of plains she didn't recognize.

* * * *

"All right boys, it's time to wake up." Jacob Staples gave Jonah a shake and tapped Portenda on the foot.

Jonah had managed to get himself to the living room couch before he had passed out. Portenda hadn't even made it to a chair, falling on the floor in the walkway to the living room, the loss of blood and the jog back to the Staples' home draining him beyond measure.

Jonah watched the big Bounty Hunter moan and wobble as he got to his feet.

"What time is it?" Jonah rubbed his eyes.

"It's time for at least one of you gents to take a shower." Jacob curled his nose and walked out into the kitchen. "Jonah, your mother put a change of clothes out for you in the bathroom. As for you, big man," Jacob called from the kitchen, where he rummaged in the new icebox, "I don't know what to do for you."

"I've got a separate pair of pants," Portenda replied as he rubbed his eyes.

"Looks like I'm up before you for once," Jonah said, ruffling his hair. "I'm going to go take that shower. I'll get you after I'm out." He sauntered out of the living room.

Portenda felt much better than he had the previous night—at least he didn't have a ringing in his head anymore. The Simpa stalked into the kitchen, his nose twitching at the scent of freshly made lunch and preserved foods that had been kept on ice.

Jacob Staples prepared a plate and set it at the kitchen table, indicating that Portenda should take a seat and start in on his meal. As Portenda seated himself and tore into the food, the elder Staples prepared a second plate for his son.

"So, what did you two find out there?" He took a sip of some clear, fizzing liquid from a glass. It didn't smell like alcohol, as Portenda might have expected. After all, the man had been a Soldier all of his life, a good provider and loving husband. He deserved a drink now and then, so long as he didn't end up like Portenda's own father.

"I have contacts out there." Portenda tried to avoid details that might upset the man. "They were able to tell me about the rag we found in your daughter's room."

"The Tiverski brothers," Jacob Staples said.

Portenda's eyes went wide—the man knew about the Vampire trio and hadn't tried to stop Jonah and Portenda from going to meet with them. Clearly he had faith in the Bounty Hunter's abilities, and the power of the short sword he'd given Jonah.

Portenda had waited too long to put more food in his mouth, and his surprise didn't escape Jacob's notice. "Yes, I know of them, Portenda." He took another swig of his drink. "Where do you think I get this, oh, what's it called?"

"Soda," Portenda offered, his tone even and flat again. He was regaining his strength and self-awareness quickly, the rest and food just what he needed.

"Right, right, soda." Jacob hunkered down across from Portenda. "The sword wasn't for them. It was for the wraiths, although, I imagine that those things don't give you much trouble. They feed off of fear." He gave Portenda a sideways glance. "And from what I've gathered, you're not afraid of much of anything, are you boy?"

For a moment, Portenda's blood boiled; only one other person in the world still called him a boy, and he hated his father enough for the word alone to trigger a response. But he swallowed his pride, and accepted the title from Mr. Staples: the old Soldier had earned the right to call anyone he wanted 'boy', he mused.

"Contrary to popular belief, I do have a few fears." Portenda decided he could be completely candid with the Staples family. "One of them is that I'll someday turn into my father."

"And another is that you'll get attached to someone and then lose them," Jacob Staples said, more statement than question.

A Hunter and his Prey

Portenda looked the old Soldier dead in the eyes, and for a brief moment, he saw pity there.

"It's obvious in the way you carry yourself, Bounty Hunter. From what I can tell, Jonah's the only friend you've had in a long, long time. Am I right?"

Portenda said not a word, simply nodding.

Jacob lowered his eyes. "I know the feeling. Back in the day, when the War of Vandross first started, I was just a young trooper in the army of Desanadron. Our city came under assault and I found that I didn't have all the answers. My comrades were slain all around me, and I alone managed to keep alive, more concerned about defending myself and the people around me than having a high and glorious kill count. You can count your kills when the battle is over, I've always thought.

"But the longer I tried to defend myself and my friends, the more desperate the situation got. Orcs on our left, Shadowbeasts on our right, and all manner of demon and Lizardman in between. For three straight days I stood on the northern outskirts of this city and fought against them, not stopping to sleep, or eat, or take stock in the fact that I was still alive. I just did my duty, and tried not to get killed in the meantime. When Byron of Sidius arrived with his allies, we formulated a strategy as a city, and the rest, well, the rest I'm sure you've read in your recent history books. When it was all over, though," Jacob said, lowering his head again. "I searched for my friends, the men of my unit. I was the only one left, Bounty Hunter. We had all fought and died, with the exception of me. A Soldier's motto is 'fight and survive to fight again', you see. There's nothing in there about keeping your friends alive.

"I felt so alone after finding their bodies that I wanted to join them. I wanted to go out into the fields and plains and look for a battle I couldn't possibly win. But before I could get out of the city, a kind, beautiful young woman stopped me in the street, and told me the battle was over, and that I should get some food and some rest before I did something foolish. Sure enough, her name was Anna." He held his face held high, his eyes focused on the past. A moment later, he came down from his trip to memory lane, and his eyes rested squarely on Portenda's own. The Bounty Hunter hadn't eaten another bite after Jacob started to recall the events of the assault on Desanadron, so many years ago.

"Not to be rude, but what's your point?" the Bounty Hunter whispered.

"After the first three days, I would return to her home after every assignment. Every day I was put on single day duty, which was often, I would spend the evening with her in the comfort of her home. We were soul mates, Bounty Hunter. We were friends, and then lovers. Though that second part may not come true for you anytime soon, remember this: no warrior can continue to fight without something to fight for, and money is not a good enough reason to keep going on this way. Understand?" There was gruffness to Jacob Staples' voice, though it was not heartfelt. The undercurrent of concern made that much clear.

"I do." Portenda quietly finished his meal as Jonah Staples came into the kitchen in a terrycloth bathrobe and towel, rubbing his wild hair dry with one hand.

"Oh, thanks," Jonah said to his father as Jacob pulled back a chair where he'd set the meal on the table. "So, what do we do today, Portenda?"

"We take another trip today," Portenda replied, standing back from the table. "I'm going to go take my shower now. We'll talk more when I get out."

Jonah tried to collect his thoughts as he ate. He had not yet shared with the Bounty Hunter that he'd seen traces of a Focus Site embedded in the fabric of the cloak. The abductor had been an Alchemist of some considerable skill but he couldn't figure out why an Alchemist would want to abduct his sister.

"So, how'd that sword work out for you with the wraiths, son?"

Jonah stared in disbelief at his father. "How did you know about them?"

"Every adult in the city knows about the wraiths. Though, only a few of us know about the Tiverski brothers." Jacob took a sip of his soda.

Jonah stared ahead into empty space as his father said, "And you probably wonder why I still let you go, knowing what was out there."

Jonah remained silent, listening to the steady rhythm of his father's voice.

Jacob Staples smiled broadly, and clapped his son once on the shoulder. "It's because you're a grown man, Jonah. I may not know a whole lot about this, um, well, this science stuff you study," he said awkwardly. "But I do know that without it, you two most likely would have died out in those woods."

Jonah had to concede that his father was probably correct. On visits to the Tiverski brothers by himself, Portenda had most likely remained in their home until daylight in order to safely recover and remove himself from the Taiwok Forest.

The sound of the shower stopped, and Jonah finished his meal hastily, getting to his feet.

When a knock sounded at the Staples' front door. Jacob got up from the table, soda mug still in hand. "Now who could that be?"

Jonah followed his father out to the living room where Portenda already sat, his fur still standing in tufts from being damp. Jonah hadn't heard the big Bounty Hunter move from the bathroom to the living room, demonstrating once again to him just how deadly the Simpa could be: a man his size shouldn't be able to move through a house that silently. Portenda sat on the reclining chair, his reading glasses on and one of his novels opened to about the halfway point.

From his angle, Jonah couldn't see who was standing on the porch, but his father's face showed disdain and reproach. "Oh, it's you."

"Hello, Mr. Staples," he heard a familiar, feminine voice chirp. "Is Jonah here?"

Jacob Staples stood aside, and Nareena stepped through the doorway.

Jonah shot to his feet, and Portenda looked up over the rims of his reading spectacles. The crow, Talonz, just gave the big man its avian smirk.

A Hunter and his Prey

"Nareena! How did you find me?" Jonah crossed the distance between them and wrapped his arms around the Elven girl before she could respond, nearly crushing the breath out of her. He set her down and held her at arm's length. Out of the corner of his eye, though, his father's expression said, very clearly, *I don't approve, and I don't like her.*

"I have my sources," Nareena teased. "And I'll tell you, it wasn't cheap getting a Teleportation scroll to make it here. The only person who apparently had any had just given two of them to you and the Bounty Hunter." She waved at Portenda, who rolled his eyes and focused on his book. Talonz flitted through the room and perched on the back of the recliner, looking down into the book over Portenda's shoulder. Portenda reached down to turn the page, and the bird pecked him atop the head, as though indicating it wasn't done with the passages on the pages before him. *I hope she isn't overly fond of this pest,* he thought, *because I may have to choke it.*

Jacob Staples gave his son and the Elven girl a glare of disapproval, and hastily removed himself from the living room. "If your mother is looking for me, I'll be out back in the garden."

Nareena and Jonah let go of one another's arms and watched the elder Staples man exit through the back door, slamming it behind him.

"He doesn't care much for you, does he?" Portenda asked without looking away from his book.

Nareena stuck her tongue out at the Bounty Hunter, and gave Jonah a quick and easy smile, holding her hands and bobbing back and forth like a schoolgirl with a crush.

"Nope, but that doesn't matter. Somebody does."

Jonah's cheeks flushed with fresh blood. He rubbed the back of his head and laughed awkwardly, then motioned for Nareena to sit with him on the couch.

"So, where's Eileen," she asked, looking around the living room. This was the second time she had been allowed into the Staples' home, and during her first visit inside, Jonah's parents hadn't known of their rivalry. The two of them had both wound up hurling potions at one another, almost destroying the kitchen and each other. Jacob had dragged the injured Elf outside by her long hair, her hands still flying over her face in an attempt to get off poisonous powder that Jonah had blown at her. At that time, Jonah had been writhing on the kitchen floor, clutching his right hand, which had swollen to several times its normal size due to a blood flow alteration brought on by one of Nareena's violet liquids. As Jacob had tossed Nareena into the street, he'd shouted at her that if she tried to hurt his boy again, he would cut her head off.

"Eileen was kidnapped," Jonah told her.

Nareena sat stock still for a moment.

"Remember that you said it looked like my mother's handwriting on the letter envelope? Well, it was."

Jonah was about to bring her up to date, when Portenda shut his book loudly, and set it on the coffee table. He set his glasses down, got up, and dragged Jonah out into the kitchen by the wrist.

Jonah shrugged his hand off roughly, glaring at him. "What's the matter with you?"

"I don't trust her, Jonah," he replied. "Or the bird for that matter," he added, rubbing the top of his head. "Just be careful how much you tell her, understood?" Jonah shrugged and walked back out to join Nareena, who was sitting daintily, waiting for his return.

"Sorry about that," he said, and Nareena waved her hand, dismissing his need for an apology.

"So, have they sent a ransom demand yet?" she asked hesitantly.

Jonah shook his head.

"This was not an abduction for profit, miss." Portenda took his seat once again and picked up his book.

Though he didn't like to admit it, Jonah had known this to be true as well from the beginning. This kidnapping was personal, an act committed by a desperate, psychotic person.

"Therefore," Portenda continued, "there will be no ransom letter. For now, we need to pursue the evidence and leads that we have at our disposal, which isn't much." He gave Jonah a meaningful look, as if to say, *be quiet on that subject.*

Though he mentally protested keeping Nareena out of the loop, Jonah kept his silence, as requested.

"So, how can I help you guys?" Nareena asked quite seriously.

"Well, I'm not sure you can." Jonah once again rubbed the back of his head. "I get the impression that Portenda wouldn't want to have another person along."

"Actually, Jonah, if she wants to come along, she's welcome to," the Bounty Hunter replied softly. "But she'll have to look out for herself." He looked her right in the eyes.

Nareena felt as though someone had pierced her chest with a shard of ice, and her blood ran colder than the arctic regions of the northwestern mountains.

"She's not my responsibility," he continued, "and she's not your responsibility. Miss Nareena," he addressed her now not only with his dead, gray eyes, but his words as well. "Understand two things: firstly, you will not get in our way during this hunt. Secondly, if you do something to jeopardize Jonah's or my safety, I will cut you down."

Nareena nodded, conceding the point to Portenda.

Jonah and Nareena sat together and exchanged small talk while the Simpa Bounty Hunter read his book. He was halfway through Montesant's *The Grand Scheme of Things*, and wanted to finish his chapter before getting back to the business at hand. He found it difficult, however, to concentrate, with the Human and Elf woman's low chatting, as well as Talonz's constant rapping him on the head, and so he removed himself to the kitchen where, for once, nobody was preparing a meal. He sat at the fine oak table, putting his foot up on the opposing leg, and leaning back slightly. He made quick progress at first, but soon found his thoughts wandering.

Removing his reading glasses and putting them back in their hard, leather case, he marked his spot in the book and glared out the kitchen window into the back yard, where Jacob Staples was tending to the gardens he and his wife kept.

He silently admired the old Soldier as he worked tirelessly on the gardens. Jacob Staples had been able to hang up his helmet and sword in exchange for a quiet three meals a day and the company of his loving wife. Most individuals of Soldier Class stayed in service, in some capacity, until their dying day. Many died at the hands of thugs and bandits who were too young and quick for them to handle. He wondered if Jacob Staples would receive the treatment he deserved in death? Portenda hoped so.

"What's on your mind?" Jonah asked from behind him.

Portenda had heard his shallow footsteps enter the kitchen, his cautious breathing. He smelled the cold sweat that had broken out on his body: he was afraid still of interrupting Portenda's pattern of thought.

"I've just been thinking about your family, Jonah," the regal Simpa reported. "Your father has seen a lot of strife. He deserves an easy life." As he spoke, the elder Staples man grabbed his lower back and rubbed it, giving a small grimace of pain, then looking around to see if anyone had spotted his discomfort.

"He has served in wars and battles that he had nothing to personally do with. What was the highest rank he received in the Desanadron regular army?"

"Captain." Jonah also watched his father toil in the gardens. "He was a Captain when he retired. We were all very surprised when he decided to take his retirement. But he just wanted to be with us in the end. My father has a military record that some folks would consider a legacy."

"The best legacy a man can leave behind," Portenda said as he rose from his seat. "Is his children."

* * * *

Eileen Staples sat crying in the corridor by the window, her back against the stone wall. Her hopes of escape lay dashed and she could do nothing but weep.

Why did it have to be her? Why couldn't some other girl have done?

As she wiped her eyes, she had an idea occur to her that gave her a glimmer of hope. Perhaps she wasn't his only captive. There might be other people here, in the cells of the tower. If she could free them, perhaps she would have allies against this formidable foe. Even if they couldn't help her physically, perhaps they had information that could help her out of this mess.

She darted down a hallway that stretched from north to south as far as she could see, stopping at the first door she came to. A small plaque on the door read 'Focus Experiments' in bold letters, and she grasped the doorknob.

It offered no resistance as she turned it and thrust the door open.

Inside, dimly lit by a set of torches that threw more shadows than they did light, were stacks of cages, set one atop the other. Strange, guttural noises and rasps came from the other side of the threshold, and for a moment she hesitated. Gods only knew what was lurking in those cages, or how long it had been since their last feeding. But she could not just stand where she was.

She took a deep breath, held it for a moment, and exhaled slowly before stepping over the threshold and into the chamber.

Eileen Staples kept her left hand opened at her side, a Raybolt spell at the ready in case something wasn't caged properly. As she took her fifth step into room, an alien beast slammed against the door of its cage, causing her to gasp and whip her arm up, magic at the ready.

What she saw there caused her to withhold her magical attack. Instead, she turned her head and vomited.

The muzzle of a hunting dog pressed against the bars of the cage and its reptilian, lizard body poised, ready to spring. A forked tongue lolled in and out of the beast's face, sniffing at the air, its face cringing at the scent of fresh puke. An enormous scorpion stinger hovered over its back, venom dripping from the sting.

"How, how could he," Eileen whispered, worms crawling under her skin. Spasms wracked her entire body at the sheer atrocity of the poor creation. She brought herself around, however, and slowly approached it. She felt no more fear of the creature, but instead her heart sank for its miserable existence.

As she approached, something in her eyes must have caught the creature's attention, because it lowered its hackles and whined like an injured animal.

A single drop of moisture ran down Eileen's cheek as she reached out and stroked the creature's head, and it moaned under her gentle touch. "You poor thing," she cooed. The creature was no taller than her shin, and no broader than a poodle.

"You never asked for this," she said, disgusted that Alchemy had been used to create such a wretched beast. "Would you like to come out of there? I think we could both use the company."

The creature seemed to understand. It got to its mutated feet and backed away from the cage door.

There were no locks on it, simply a pair of clasps holding it shut. Eileen opened the clasps, and the creature bounded gracefully out of the cage and onto the floor, its stinger waggling like a tail.

It barked at her enthusiastically, rubbing itself against her exposed leg like an affectionate pet. "I think I'll call you Blink," she said, thinking back to the hunting dog her neighbors had once had. It looked much like this animal, at least so far as its head was concerned.

Accompanied by her new friend, Eileen felt better suited to deal with whatever other atrocities lay in wait in the deceptively large chamber. She took a few steps forward and several more monstrosities, much less friendly and far more aggressive than Blink, slammed against their cage doors.

These cages, unlike that of the beast at her side, had several locks and what appeared to be Alchemical symbols inscribed on their bars.

A Hunter and his Prey

All of them were freak aberrations, crossbreeds of animals and beasts of the world of Tamalaria. The further into the darker recesses of the chamber she walked, the more twisted and vile the creatures appeared.

Against the far wall, opposite the door, a table of some sort was visible. It was approximately fifteen feet long, and covered the distance between left and right walls almost entirely. Underneath the table, Eileen barely made out three cages. As she got even closer, she saw that ordinary animals cowering in fear in each cage.

The first of the creatures was a large house cat, a pile of feces fronting its cage and a small food and water dish back in the corner it huddled in. Eileen waited for Blink to start growling at it, but the Alchemical beast simply cocked its head sideways at the tabby cat, as if it were fascinated by it. In the middle cage rested a crow, its cage only in slightly better condition than the cat's. And on the far right, lying on its side, was the largest of the three creatures, its cage coming a couple of feet out from under the table. It was an enormous snow wolf.

"They are the Master's children," a voice echoed through the room behind her.

Eileen spun, her palm thrust out, and saw Kobuchi, the Kobold servant, standing in the doorway. Eileen kept her hand out, calling forth all of the magic she had to bear against an enemy. But something was different about the little man. His voice had an inflection to it that said he was not presently a mindless slave.

"His forgotten children," the Kobold continued, "his failures. This is the room in which he creates them, and most wind up staying here."

"Stop right there," Eileen growled as Kobuchi approached.

Blink had started to growl, and the stinger on his back end wavered back and forth threateningly.

"What are you doing here? How did you know I'd come in here?"

"The Master instructed me to keep an eye on you," the Kobold replied. "I don't think he'll care that you've decided to take project number three-three-seven-eight for a pet. He may find it amusing, even." A sad smile crossed the Kobold's rat-like face.

"I wanted the company, thanks." She kept her palm aimed squarely at Kobuchi. "It's better than being alone."

"And you'll want the company."

The Kobold took a tentative step forward and Eileen released a small blast of Raybolt at the Kobold's feet, blasting apart a small section of the stone floor.

The Kobold gave her a menacing look of disdain.

"The next one will hit your head," she threatened. This creature, though it seemed now possessed of free will, had likely been under Genma's influence so long that might enjoy its service to the masked Alchemist.

Kobuchi slithered back towards the door. His eyes narrowed in his face, and he pointed a knobby finger at the Human girl.

"You will watch what you say to me, child. The Master has taken an interest in you, and I shall do no undue harm to you. And though you are free to roam this floor and the upper levels of the keep, you may not do as you please. You were going to set those three animals free, weren't you," the Kobold accused.

It had crossed Eileen's mind the moment she saw them, three pathetic, trapped creatures, waiting for their unnatural and unholy union.

"You are to leave them be. This is one of the Master's work chambers, and you shall not interfere any further with his labors. Understood?"

Eileen said nothing, just raised her palm level to Kobuchi's head. The servant stormed away, his grumbling echoing through the hallway and to Eileen's ears. She looked down at Blink, who ceased his growling and looked up at her with interest in his eyes.

"What say we take a look around?" she asked.

Before she could move, Blink sprinted to the three cages beneath the table and used his stinger to undo the clasps.

The cat, the wolf, and the crow all made hasty escapes, their exhaustion temporarily forgotten in the face of opportunity.

"Good boy," she whispered, and Blink smiled a canine smile as they exited the chamber.

* * * *

"I'm telling you, sir, the information you've requested is not available to you," the Dwarven Sergeant repeated from his seat behind the booking desk.

Portenda, Jonah and Nareena had gone to the nearest constable station, to request a report of Eileen's abduction. The Dwarf had told them there was no such report, and though Jonah had worded the question several ways, the Dwarf's answer remained the same.

Exasperated from getting the run-around, Jonah screamed at the top of his lungs, "I'm her brother for gods' sakes! I demand to know what sort of progress you people have made. No one has been out to see my parents about the incident since I got back here—why the foot dragging, Sergeant? What's the matter with you people?" Talonz screeched aloud from Nareena's shoulder, for once helping Jonah drive his point.

As Jonah slammed his hand flat on the desk, all of the conversation in the other officers around the small department came to a stop. All eyes were fixed on the Alchemist and his companions: nobody moved, or made a sound.

The Dwarf just looked up from his pile of paperwork, his chain mail armor rattling as he shifted his position, leaning back in his chair.

"D'you want ta be arrested, young man." A wicked grin spread across the Dwarf's bearded face. "Disturbin' the peace and causing a ruckus in a constable station?"

Jonah took a hesitant step backward, shaking his head slightly.

"Good. Then bugger off, and take yer friends wif you."

Jonah shrugged his shoulders, and turned to leave, Nareena putting her arm across his shoulders as they started for the door.

A Hunter and his Prey

But Portenda the Quiet had a weapon up his sleeve, a surprise attack that the Alchemist hadn't imagined.

"According to the Desanadron Charter of 865 A.F.," Portenda said, "drafted just after the city's reinstatement of military and police forces, Chapter 6, Section 8, Article 17, all information pertaining to the victim of a crime, or to a crime itself, wherein a relative or family member has been involved, another family member is due a report on the status of the investigation, and a copy of all statements taken by witnesses upon request. Sergeant."

Jonah and Nareena turned around, eyes wider than the Dwarven Sergeant's, a spectacular feat in itself. The crow bobbed its head up and down in agreement with the Bounty Hunter. Maybe he isn't all that bad, thought Portenda.

The little man rummaged around in his desk, pulling out a red, cloth-bound book, and turned to the section that Portenda had quoted from. As his hand moved along the print, the Dwarf looked up every few words at Portenda the Quiet.

"All roit, all roit, so you've got me there," the Dwarf grumbled.

Jonah shouted excitedly, giving Nareena a quick embrace and patting Portenda hard on the back.

The Simpa didn't even blink as the Dwarf grabbed the arm of a passing Werewolf Corporal.

"Corporal, pull the reports on the Staples abduction."

The tan-furred Werewolf, his wool uniform serving as his only armor, nodded, giving the trio a toothy smile.

Newcomer, Portenda thought. They're always eager to please their superiors and the public.

The average sized Werewolf left the main office, returning a few minutes later with a manila folder in hand.

The Dwarf indicated Portenda, who reached out and gently took the reports from the Werewolf.

"Thank you very much, constable," the Simpa said to the Corporal, who positively radiated pride. "Let's sit over there," he said to Jonah and Nareena, indicating a small, circular table near the coffee station in a cubby off of the main office.

Gnomes had created a quick, compact brewing machine to make coffee, but it always came out burnt, which was why the Simpa still made his the old-fashioned way. He didn't trust most mecha, and he wasn't going to have something like the squat, white device burning his morning fix. Still, for some reason, constables and military men seemed to love the stuff burnt to a pot of sludge. 'Adds body to it,' they often said.

Portenda sat with the other two members of the party, and opened the folder.

There were several pages to the report, along with a few witness statements and secondary reports. He took the main report, handed the witness statements to Nareena, and gave the secondary reports to Jonah.

The trio read their given information several times, memorizing it as best they could, Nareena giving Portenda a look as he put his reading glasses on.

As they finished, they rotated the reports to the left, and read the new information in front of them. They continued like this, pulling new sheets from the folder a few times, until all three had reviewed the entire file.

Portenda then returned to the desk with the folder, and requested a copy of the contents, which the Dwarf was only too happy to provide. "It'll take about an hour," the Dwarf said, offering him some coffee from the machine.

"No, thanks," he said.

"Ah, but it's got body," the Dwarf replied with a smile.

"Yes, probably an arm and a few legs," Portenda muttered as he returned to the round table. "All right, Jonah. Nareena. Any thoughts?"

"Well," Nareena chimed. "They had a registry of all of the people who came into the city the day before Eileen went missing. A few names stuck out at me."

"Like who?" Jonah had also taken note of a handful of unfamiliar names. Anyone whom the constables deemed strange or a potential threat to city safety had to sign a registry upon entrance to the city. Portenda had escaped registering because he had Teleported in. Anyone with that many weapons and that bearing would be considered a potential threat to public and private safety.

"Well, like Answoir the Rebellious," Nareena said, remembering the Race as Illeck.

"Not likely," Portenda said. "His listed Class was 'undeclared,' which is classic code for 'Rogue' or 'Pickpocket'."

"Or what about Talvus Strossum," Jonah offered.

"His Race was Werebear," Nareena said, dismissing that name. "They're peaceful people, and when they do get mad, lots of people get hurt or killed. It wouldn't have been him."

"Well," Jonah said, trying to think back on the list. "What about Kobuchi? The Kobold? That got my attention." Jonah said.

Portenda rubbed his chin. The name had also caught his attention, and apparently Nareena's as well, because the Elf woman nodded, her eyes twitching back and forth. "His Class listing said 'manservant', didn't it?"

"Yes," Portenda said. "But to whom? There were several other names on that list, but to be frank, I didn't memorize them all. Just the reports." And the reports hadn't even been too enlightening. They had read like statistics projects, all names, addresses, and timetables. No motive or theory had even been listed. The officer in charge of the investigation, a Lieutenant Christopher Viper, had stated that he would be 'treating this investigation like any other major crime', which Portenda knew was the administrative way of saying, *we haven't got a clue, and aren't going to find one anytime soon.*

Jonah thought over the witness statements, which had all been rather vague except for the testimonial given by his parents. A man wearing a long, black leather cloak and a nobleman's outfit had stayed the evening with them, boarding in Jonah's old room. The man hadn't given them a name, and they couldn't see his face because he wore a pale, ivory mask with a demon face painted on.

That's it, Jonah thought, a revelation taking hold of his mind and heart. They had also mentioned that a short Kobold had helped carry the man's suitcase up to Jonah's room, and had then left.

"I know whose manservant that Kobold was. He carried my sister's kidnapper's suitcase for him, and he just left without a word!" His eyes met Portenda's, and he saw a brief grin on the Bounty Hunter's face. "We have a lead. We have a lead," he shouted, jumping up and down excitedly.

Nareena gave him a look like a teacher might give a hyperactive child in the schoolhouse, and he sat back down, his cheeks flushed.

"Very good work, Jonah," Portenda said. "I wondered when you'd make the connection."

Jonah glared at him. He'd known and he hadn't said a thing.

Portenda leaned back and the trio sat in silence until the Corporal came over with their copy of the file.

Clutching the copy, Portenda stood and shook the Werewolf's hand firmly, giving him a slight bow.

The Werewolf returned it in kind, and sprinted off to another duty.

Jonah eyeballed him for a moment. "Samurai. The katana at his hip, the way he walked, the sash around his shoulder and hip. Bowing is a sign of respect to them. Come on," he said, putting the folder in his rucksack. "Let's go see if anyone in town knows this Kobuchi."

Portenda took the lead with Jonah and Nareena, arm in arm, following behind.

Jonah had begun to enjoy Nareena's company again, like he had before Alchemy split them apart. He wondered how long it could last before their own pursuits tore them apart again.

Though Portenda claimed to only have come to this city a few times, Jonah noticed he knew an awful lot about its laws and charters, and he had quickly become acquainted with the layout of the city.

They headed into the poverty-stricken residential district, an area of the city that Jonah had hitherto avoided for fear that someone down on their luck might find him an irresistible mark. Many constables left these parts alone. After all, one or two policemen patrolling the streets versus a small mob of hungry thugs wasn't much of a match, and wasn't worth the meager four gold pieces a week of their salary.

The city's reconstruction budget had run nearly dry when this area of the city, in the northernmost region, where the damage had been heaviest during Richard Vandross's assault, was slated for repairs. As a result, most of the damaged homes and businesses had been patched up. Squatters had set up homes in condemned buildings, taking the risk of a roof collapsing on them, so long as that roof kept some rain off of their heads for a while.

As he thought of rain, a light sprinkle began to fall. Jonah squatted down for a moment and drew a Focus Site in the dirt. He pressed his palms to it, and a moment after the flash, he held an umbrella over his and Nareena's head.

"That was the art of Focus, wasn't it?" she asked.

Jonah simply smiled and nodded, having used a 'practical accessory' Site to produce the umbrella. At the moment, he didn't think of where the material had come from for the umbrella's creation.

Unbeknownst to him, a Dwarven woman in a nearby domicile wondered what had just happened to the spatula she had been using, or the rain slicker she had hung on the wall.

"Why are we here?" Nareena asked Portenda after a few more minutes.

The rain-soaked Simpa looked around at a ring of decrepit apartment buildings and condemned businesses. Only one store stood open, a general goods market manned by a rough-looking Jaft who stood outside the door and puffed on a smoke stick.

"The Kobold was listed as a manservant, correct? Most Kobolds who go into personal service live in squalor, and this place would be the perfect fit. He may have stayed here while his master abducted your sister. Kobolds are not loners, by nature. They tend to travel and stay in packs of their own kind. Someone might have seen him or hosted him during his stay." Portenda moved toward the Jaft and his store.

The blue-skinned humanoid started to take a hurried drag on his smoke stick, but Portenda put a hand up, and the Jaft finished his drag as normal.

"Wot can I do for you, gov?" the Jaft asked, exhaling smoke.

"I need no purchases right now," Portenda said as Jonah and Nareena came up behind him. "I was wondering how many Kobold customers you get in an average day."

"Oh, I get a handful of them." The Jaft took another drag. "Seven or eight of them, every day or so. Same bunch, always come in together."

"Would you recognize them?"

"Of course." He took the last drag of his smoke and tossing the butt into a puddle.

There was a slight fizzing noise, and Jonah watched the last bit of smoke plume up from the spent item.

"Nice enough little guys: always pay up front before they take their stuff. They get the same things every time."

"Has there recently been anyone new among them, maybe only stayed with them a day or so? Did they make any odd purchases?"

Portenda raised an eyebrow as the Jaft crossed his arms and rubbed his chin thoughtfully. His eyes lit up, and he held up one finger.

"Now that you mention it, they did. A few days ago, they brought a new guy in, had a weird mark on his chest, like a brand, you know? The kind they put on cows ta say, hey, this is mine, don't mess with it, you know." He spoke hurriedly. Jafts, it was well known, were not the brightest of the Races. They prided themselves, however, on having crystal clear memories for anything that wasn't black and white and written on paper. Reading tended to elude them, but they were big on picture books. "Well, this new fellah, he doesn't say a word, you know? Just sort of walks with them, but he keeps a little distance from them. The wee folk, as we calls 'em, they're usually very touchy-touchy with one another, like contact with one another, you know? Well, they all make their usual purchases, like preserved rats, couple of wheels of cheese, and a loaf of bread."

"How do they pay," Nareena asked aloud, knowing now that most of the people around here didn't have real jobs.

"Dey all got jobs, mostly cleaning constable offices after hours," the Jaft said with a smile. "Dey's a respectable bunch, them ones. I even checked on their story once, and it turns out they all clean the seventeenth precinct building at night. Dey get two gold pieces a week per person, so they can easily afford the stuff I got. I only charge a few silver fer anything I got. Not that it's not quality stuff, but I gets it pretty cheap, and folks around here ain't got a whole lotta money, you know? I don't crap where I eat, as the saying goes."

"You keep prices low in order to ensure business and customer satisfaction," Jonah said.

The Jaft smiled and nodded.

"That's very sporting of you. Most people would take advantage," Jonah remarked.

The Jaft shrugged his shoulders. "Hey, I've always been a commoner. I know life can get tough sometimes. Oh, hold on a second folks." He followed an elderly Elven man into his shop, giving the trio a smile and a tip of his feathered keppy. "Afternoon, Mr. Sola. Need the usual?"

Jonah watched the big blue man reach up to the higher shelves. *My gods,* Jonah thought, *that Elf has to be almost a thousand years old. They don't grow beards like that until they're almost near Death's door.* Once again Jonah marveled at the kindness some strangers had for others, even in a city like Desanadron.

The Jaft patted the old Elf gently on the back and sent him out of the store without payment.

The Elf smiled again at the trio, and shuffled away to the apartment building across the street.

Portenda gave the Jaft a curious look.

"What?"

"You didn't charge him."

"I never charge Mr. Sola. His wife passed on last August, so it's been real hard on him." The Jaft looked after the elderly Elf. "She used to come in here every couple of days, paid up front like the little guys, always had time for conversation. I miss her too, but not half as much as he does."

"It's good to see there's still people like you around," Nareena said with a sad smile at the Jaft.

"T'anks. Anyway," the Jaft said, turning back to Portenda. "This Kobold, he a friend of yours?"

"You could say that. We're hoping to find him," Portenda said. "We have something that he left behind. Where do the other Kobolds live?"

"Same building as Mr. Sola, in the basement apartments." The Jaft lit another smoke stick and exhaled a plume of smoke the color as Portenda's steely eyes. "They'll be home, this time of the day."

"Thank you for your time." Portenda handed the Jaft five gold pieces from his pouch.

The trio moved away, and Jonah looked back at the surprised Jaft, who gave him a quick wave good-bye. Jonah returned it as Portenda led him and Nareena to the apartment complex.

* * * *

Hunger pangs drove Eileen back to her quarters where she found a tray of food waiting for her—along with Genma.

She sat and tore into the food, handing a few strips of the meat to Blink. The animal took them gently, and hunkered down to eat. "Have you even been feeding them?"

Genma chuckled softly under his mask. "Not really. They're failures, all of them. I keep my success stories down on the fifth floor. As you can tell, it's the middle of the afternoon. You'll have a couple of days before I'm ready to take the other measurements I need,"

Eileen stopped mid-bite to glare at him. "What other measurements?" She gripped her fork like a dagger.

"Well, I couldn't use the blood sample from your home for analysis, as the drug I'd given you altered the readings," he said. "I'll need to take a fresh one, along with some other readings."

He was being purposely vague, she sensed, trying to lure her into asking questions. But she wouldn't fall for that: she knew the kind of person he was behind that mask. He wanted a person to ask him questions so that he could feel smarter than them, superior in some way. Instead, she continued to eat and give bits of her meal to Blink, who wagged his stinger.

"I can keep him, right," she asked between bites.

"By all means. I'll even have extra food sent for him, if you want," Genma said quite seriously. "In a week or so, you won't be you anymore, and I'd like to make your time left in the world to be pleasant."

Gods, she *thought, this is frustrating. He has to keep bringing that up. Does he expect me to be afraid?* Fire coursed through her veins. *I'm a Staples, and we aren't afraid of anything.*

Genma got up and headed for the door. "Wait five minutes before you go roaming again. Kobuchi shall bring your meals for a couple of days. I won't be available, except to take those measurements." Then the only sounds Eileen heard were his retreating footsteps and Blink ravaging a small, boiled carrot she'd decided she didn't want.

She looked down and patted the creature on the head, and Blink licked her hand affectionately.

A Hunter and his Prey

"Come on, Blink," she said, rising from her finished meal. "We've got a lot of rooms to explore. It's best to get acquainted with the place if we want to get out of here." She left the room, her only companion following closely behind.

There were doors everywhere on this floor, and she realized just how massive the tower must be. Most of the doors had labels: those that didn't, she dismissed as more holding cells.

As she stalked down the western corridor, a plaque on a solid steel door caught her attention. It read, 'Observation Lounge'.

She turned the knob and found herself looking at a comfortable, living room-style chamber, complete with couches, two recliners, a fireplace filled with ashes and two unspent logs. Several notebooks sat on a coffee table in the middle of the couches.

This guy isn't exactly careful about what he leaves lying around, is he, she thought to herself. *Probably no need, as nobody would likely want to read the notes or have the opportunity to relate them to anybody on the outside.*

She sat on the fluffiest couch of the three, and opened one of the notebooks to the first page.

The handwriting was elegant and almost feminine, curly and looped at every turn. The first few pages read like a journal entry, relating how the author, presumably Genma, had erected the tower with the help of several other Alchemists. A list of mountain ranges that had been altered due to the huge amount of Focus used followed the description of the process, and the author then made a note about how he had used the basement to conceal the bodies of his fellow Alchemists.

Rather grisly, she thought, but it suited the madman's style. 'This tower shall be my tribute to my family,' the journal had read. 'Nobody else can have it.'

The rest of the journal had been used to log experiments that Genma had performed, all of which had either 'success' or 'failure' written at the end. Most of the entries, even the earlier ones, were marked as successes. Only a handful were reported as failures.

The man was skilled, she had no doubt about that.

Blink jumped up on the couch next to her, circled around for a moment, and then laid down for a nap. His own entry didn't appear anywhere in the first notebook, and so she set it down, and picked up another.

Know thy enemy, she thought.

* * * *

Portenda rapped softly on the basement apartment door for a third time.

Jonah and Nareena heard a commotion on the other side of the shabby wooden door, and a moment later, a three and a half foot Kobold opened it, leaning back as he looked up at the massive Bounty Hunter. "Squeeee!"

The door slammed shut in his face as Portenda opened his mouth to speak.

"Typical," he muttered, knocking again. "I'm not going to harm you! I am not a slaver."

Their people were often kidnapped and sold as slaves on the black markets, and they had become distrustful of anyone who wore armor and had weapons.

The door opened a crack, and a small, brown-skinned snout poked out. The Kobold's eyes were wide, and he visibly trembled.

"You not hurt?" it asked.

Portenda gave him a gentle smile.

"No, I will not hurt you," he said again.

The door opened wide showing the three other Kobolds, each holding makeshift weapons. One clutched the handle of a broom, another a frying pan, and the third one had a fireplace poker in his small hands.

The Kobold at the door waved his hand down, and the others dropped their weapons to the floor.

"You come. We very sorry about mess. And speech. We not speak good Common," the Kobold leader said.

"Where are the others?" Jonah asked as he entered the tiny apartment living room, almost laughing as Portenda tried to straighten and whacked his head on the ceiling.

He knelt down, getting closer to eye-level with the Kobolds.

They seemed to relax, visibly easing up.

"They live across hall," the first Kobold said as the others went back to their strange card game. "You want lunch? We have much fried rat left."

Jonah, Portenda and Nareena all waved off the invitation.

Portenda shuffled close to the other three, who were engaged in a version of an old card game called Royal Shuffle. There appeared to be a different set of rules, however, as the jacks, instead of being of equal value to the kings and queens, held a higher value and placement on the playing field. He watched them intently for a moment before speaking.

"What is your name?" he asked, not looking across from the Kobold group's apparent leader and speaker.

"Me Upton. Upton moog Gala." The Kobold laid a jack and an ace, crossing the ace of hearts over top. "What called are you?"

"I am Portenda the Quiet," the Bounty Hunter whispered, watching the hand unfold. The smallest of the Kobolds, who could stand at perhaps two and a half feet at best, seemed to have the best field thus far.

"This is Jonah," he said, pointing vaguely at Jonah. "And this is Nareena. We've come to ask you about a visitor you may have had recently."

"Oh. Well, this Maki ex Tus," Upton said, patting the smallest one to his left. "This Roga min Vak," he said, indicating the only female in the apartment, sitting to his right. "And next to you Parag min Vak, Roga husband," he said.

The Kobold at Portenda's side beamed at him with pride. "Their Common very bad, so me do most talking," Upton explained.

"Very well." Portenda observed Upton's next move, a placement of a five of diamonds next to his jack-ace cross. "Flanking defense?"

Upton smiled and nodded vigorously. Portenda had once played Royal Shuffle in his off time with some of his tenants, meeting with them every week or so for a few hands. The game was complex and long-lasting, so he appreciated the obvious skill and intellect of the Kobolds. Commonly brushed aside as tribal and primitive, Kobolds were often viewed as foolish little creatures, good for little beyond servitude. Portenda knew better, now. He could see that they clearly made good tacticians. However, Kobolds were pacifist by nature, and so he doubted he would live to see a Kobold General in anyone's army.

"You say you looking for guest we have. What him named?" Upton asked.

"Kobuchi," Jonah offered. This was his first time watching a game of Royal Shuffle, and he had been whispering questions to Nareena about it.

She had played often when she was younger, living in the Elven Kingdom. It was the most commonly played game among both police officers and militiamen in the Elven territories, and she had developed a knack for it.

"Oh, yes. Him stay here, with us, several days ago. Him only stay one day and a half, but very memorable. Him no like be touched, which odd, because we like touch." Upton patted Maki on the shoulder after the little Kobold made a bold move of his hand.

Maki smiled at him, and then at Jonah and Nareena, giving them a shy wave, which they returned in kind.

"Him speak very good Common, very good. But, him cold, not really there. His eyes, they blank were."

Portenda sat silently for a moment, then watched Upton pull a striking maneuver to his right.

Roga discarded three of her cards from the field.

"When you say blank, what do you mean?" Nareena wrapped her arms around Jonah's right arm. She felt out of place with the little people, and clung to him for reassurance.

He understood the feeling; these people were clearly clever, and willing to fight if need be. But Portenda kept them at ease, simply sitting and watching their game, asking questions between turns.

"It, hard explain." Upton got up and moving into the kitchen, returning a moment later with a bowl of some sort of salad. He ate as he watched the playing field develop. "Eyes show us soul," he said thoughtfully, apparently searching for the correct words in the Common tongue. "*His* soul, cannot be seen. This, unusual. All souls, visible in eyes. Even his." He pointed his fork at Portenda.

The Bounty Hunter stiffened reflexively, attempting to put up a barrier of cold professionalism. "Slow, quiet rage. Anger is much in you," Upton said directly to Portenda. "But not hate. You have small hate, one person," Upton peered into the Simpa's cold, gray eyes. "Control feelings, bottle up most times," the Kobold said.

Once again Portenda had been caught off guard. This city, it seemed, was full of fascinating people. The gentle-hearted Jaft, the tough old Soldier, and now this keen, insightful Kobold.

"A good analysis," Portenda offered, clearing his throat awkwardly. "But what about this Kobuchi?"

"Him, him like, dead man walking," the Kobold said gravely. His muscles tensed under his thin flesh. "His soul, cannot see. Him talk about, duty, and a Master. Call him Master Genma." Upton finished his meal and laid down his last two cards. "Maki win again," he said jovially, patting Maki on the head. The cards were collected and shuffled as the Kobolds settled in for a new game.

"Did he tell you where he lives?" Jonah blurted, unable to control himself.

The Kobolds looked at him, confusion in their faces. "All Kobold live between earth and sky," Upton said. "Where live not matter. Who live with matter."

If his grammar hadn't been so poor, Jonah thought, this little man could be a sage.

"Him say he live with Master. But him, not like us, say direction. Him say live out east, somewhere. Near mountains," he amended as he dealt the hands. He stopped halfway between Maki and Roga, looking at Portenda. "You play?"

Portenda smiled and shook his head. "I am afraid I must decline," he offered with a friendly lilt to his voice. "We have not the time. We may visit you again, I hope?"

"Yes, again some time. But not night. We work night. Clean constable station, we do."

Without another word, the trio exited the apartment.

"Very nice little people," Jonah observed. "I'll have to come back and visit them again."

Nareena let go of his arm as they walked out onto the street.

"I'll be back," she said abruptly, moving away from the two men. "I've got to get some things from my hotel room. Where should I meet you two?"

"The Roast Cafe," Portenda replied before Jonah could decide on a meeting place. "We'll be there for a couple of hours."

The Human Alchemist gave Nareena a quick smile and wave before hustling to catch up to the Simpa Bounty Hunter, who had already moved away.

* * * *

"Someone will come looking for her," Kobuchi said to the darkness of his Master's chamber. No torch or candle illuminated the room, just a slit of light from the door that the Kobold always left slightly ajar when speaking to Genma in his personal quarters.

"I'm well aware of that, Kobuchi," a voice replied from the darkness.

The ivory mask, Kobuchi knew, would be sitting on the dresser to the right hand side of the doorway. He often felt drawn to grab the mask and whisk it away, though he wasn't sure why. Probably some sort of instinct of his Race.

"I already have certain measures in place. You know, of course, about the officers in Desanadron. But I also have another insurance policy."

Kobuchi straightened up, and kept his hands behind his back. "And what would that be?" The Kobold was always curious about his Master's machinations, again, attributing it to the natural curiosity of Kobolds as a whole.

"I have hired additional help on the matter," the voice echoed through the darkness. "A mercenary, if you will."

A Hunter and his Prey

"And what sort of man is this mercenary," Kobuchi asked politely. Always remain polite around the Master, he thought. Be polite, and you'll be rewarded for your efforts.

"A Werewolf who is posing as a militiaman. He has just sent me a report via the Focus Site in his home. A Bounty Hunter, her brother, and some young Elven woman are already trying to track the girl.

"And what are the Werewolf's orders at present," Kobuchi asked.

"To observe them and report on their progress to me," Genma said.

"You should have them slain, Master." Kobuchi kept one foot firmly planted in the slit of light, however. He knew better than to come fully into the Master's black solitude. "You should not take the chance that they will find this place."

A whip-like tentacle lashed out from somewhere, knocking Kobuchi against the door and shutting it firmly, leaving him cloaked in shadows. His heart hammered and fear, a bull elephant gone mad, rampaged through his mind.

"Do not presume to tell me what I should and should not do," The voice of his Master, slightly altered, rasped from his place in the far corner of the room. "I am the master. Do not forget your station."

"I am sorry, Master." The Kobold scrabbled for the doorknob. He opened the door a crack, and felt slightly less in danger when the light spilled over his body. The purple, scaled tentacle that had struck him slithered at the edge of the light, its pink suckers moving toward him. With a hiss of air, the tentacle disappeared.

"I shall not forget," he said. "Excuse me." Kobuchi rushed into the well-lit corridor. He would not forget his place.

Something in his mind shrieked to leave this place while he could. The symbol on his chest flared briefly, and he remembered that he could not. He belonged to Genma. Soon, the girl would too.

Chapter Six
It's Nothing Personal

Jonah watched in disgust as Portenda drained an entire pot of coffee in the span of four minutes. The Bounty Hunter had requested that the pot be left on the table, and the Half-Elf waitress had smiled and obliged.

The moment she had turned her back, Portenda began draining the pot of its contents. Jonah, meanwhile, had barely taken a sip of his own beverage, something called a 'cuppa,' whatever that meant.

Whatever it was, it tasted good, and he nursed it as the shocked waitress returned with another pot of coffee.

"How can you do that," he asked incredulously as Portenda drained the second pot. "Doesn't that burn your throat? Do you even taste it?"

"Tasting it isn't important, I find," Portenda grimaced. "I need whatever it is that's in the stuff to keep me alert."

"It's called caffeine," Jonah offered as he took another sip of his cuppa. "And it can be very addicting, which I think is half your problem."

Portenda drew out a piece of parchment and a pencil, and wrote something in very small lettering on it before sliding it across the table to Jonah.

The Human Alchemist read the words, 'We're being watched,' and almost looked around before realizing that that course of action would give them away. He wrote back, 'by who?'

'Not certain,' was the reply he got. 'A lycanthrope, I'm sure. Cuyotai or Werewolf, from the smell of it'.

Jonah made like he was cracking his back, and took a quick look around the cafe. He, Portenda, and two Dwarves were the only customers, and the staff of the cafe was all Human or Half-Elven. He looked back at Portenda as Nareena snuck up behind the Bounty Hunter.

She was half-crouched, apparently trying to surprise him, Jonah thought, and that might not be a good idea.

Before he could warn her, Nareena moved forward to put her hands over Portenda's eyes. Before she reached him, though, the Simpa grabbed her wrists and spun her round, wrapping his own thick arm around her throat.

"Hey, easy big guy," she croaked.

Portenda flexed his arm a little, and released her.

"What the Hells was that for?" She rubbed her throat, sat next to Jonah, and drained half his cup without asking.

Jonah glared at her, and she simply said, "What? I needed something after Mr. 'I'm gonna make like I'm going to kill you' over there choked me. You're awfully aggressive for a guy who doesn't talk much."

"And you're very sneaky for an Alchemist," he countered. He raised his hand to catch the waitress's attention, and she came to take his empty pot away. "A cuppa for the lady, nothing more for me, thank you."

"Humph. Half-breeds," Nareena snorted disdainfully.

"What about half-breeds," Portenda said, his voice slightly edged.

A Hunter and his Prey

Nareena suddenly felt trapped. "N-nothing. Look, I just went back to grab some things from the hotel. I've also decided to put Talonz up with a Beastmaster for a while. If we need him, I have ways of calling him back. I brought my maps as well," she offered, changing the subject quickly as she rolled out a crude map of Tamalaria. "That Kobold fellow, what's his name?"

"Upton," Jonah said, looking at the map. Nareena, while a skilled poison maker, he mused, had little in the way of artistic talent. He had seen children draw better maps. Still, he mused, it would probably serve its purpose.

"Right. Well, Upton said that this other Kobold, Kobuchi, said something about living east of here, right? Well, if we follow the main roads," she traced her finger along the map, "the nearest town is Satory. It's mostly a Lizardman encampment, but there are Dwarves and Jafts there too. They might be able to point us in the right direction."

Portenda paid the waitress the money owed, and Jonah took the last of his cuppa, asking for another one.

"Agreed," Portenda said. "Time is a factor, though, so we'll need to find some way to get there quickly. And I believe horses are out of the question," he said coldly, stopping Jonah's question in its tracks. The Alchemist hadn't enjoyed his Teleportation experience, and didn't want to have another one.

"Trust me, Jonah. Horses are quick, but we need to be there tomorrow. We have no way of knowing how long your sister's abductor will keep her alive."

Jonah's heart sank: he hadn't honestly considered the possibility that his sister might already be dead, or that she didn't have very long before she was killed.

Nareena pulled one of Jonah's Focus Site tomes from her own rucksack, and he slapped his hand on the table. "When did you take that from me," he demanded.

"Back at the Kobolds' place," she replied. "I was just, you know, looking through it back at my place. There's a Focus Site that will let us travel to anyplace we've ever been before, and I've been to Satory, so we have our quick transport. You've been a lot of places, Jonah," she said as he snatched the tome from her hands. "That Focus will come in handy."

"You barely had time enough to look through this at your place," Jonah said accusingly. "What did you do?"

"It's a talent of mine," she said, drinking from her own mug of cuppa. "I can speed read. I miss some information sometimes, but most of what's in there is fairly forgettable anyway. Like I said though, the transport will be handy. How many of those books do you have, Jonah?"

"Six or so," he replied, still fuming.

"Our transportation problem is solved," Portenda cut in, stopping the two from a potential argument. "When we're done here, we'll head to Satory. Provided the both of you have everything you'll be needing," he amended.

With these Alchemists, he'd noticed, preparation could hours while they whipped up some sort of potion or powder. Jonah opened his rucksack after knocking the clasp, and rummaged through his ingredients and supplies.

"I want to set up a few tinctures. Just in case the locals aren't friendly. Lizardmen, in my limited experience, tend not to trust folks like myself and Nareena."

"Agreed."

"Will two hours be sufficient," Portenda asked as he ordered a cuppa for himself. He hadn't tried the stuff, and now, having smelled it for a few minutes, decided he would chance it.

Both the Human and Elven Alchemists nodded.

"Good. Meet me back here in two hours' time. I probably won't move, but just in case I'm not here when you return, stay put."

Jonah closed his rucksack and headed for the door, while Nareena stayed in her seat, Portenda's heavy foot pinning her own to the floor. When Jonah was out of eyesight and earshot, she gave the Bounty Hunter a scowl.

"What was that all about," she asked.

"I feel compelled to make myself absolutely clear with you," he grumbled low in his throat. "If you do anything, and I mean anything, that might compromise this mission, including taking things from myself or Jonah without our permission, I will see to it that your grave need be no deeper than two feet. After all," he whispered, leaning forward and giving her a toothy smile as his eyes flashed wide open. "A dismembered body takes up very little space." Nareena, heart beating faster than a hummingbird's wings, thought she saw the eternal rictus of the Grim Reaper in his gray, ashen eyes. She darted out of the cafe like a streak of cloaked lightning.

The waitress approached slowly, setting his cuppa down in front of him, looking out after Nareena. "What got into her?"

"Not entirely certain." He took a sip of the sweet beverage. Beneath the scent of the mug, he could still make out the odor of a Werewolf. Whoever it was, he mused, they were going to suffer a quick case of 'where'd they go' in a couple of hours.

* * * *

As he worked in a corner of an Alchemy shop, Jonah wondered why Nareena had stayed behind. He was very careful not to cross the ingredients between his healing potion and a paralysis tincture, as that could spell disaster later on. Portenda might not require a healing potion, but he himself could very well need a handful of them by the time this business was through. And Nareena might need one or two as well.

Jonah had only a basic grasp of melee combat, and Nareena had no training whatsoever in hand-to-hand situations. She would be at risk through this ordeal.

He knew that she would prepare poisons and explosive chemicals, instead of anything defensive. Nareena's take on Alchemy again stung his heart. She was always offensive and destructive with the arts of chemicals. Her only attempt at a healing potion had sent her into a coma for a week.

Jonah had heard about it from a constable, in Palen, and had cared for her for the whole week. When she had shown signs of consciousness, he had left her in the hotel room he'd rented out for the two of them, and she still didn't know it had been him who had taken care of her. Despite their budding rivalry at that time, he cared about her.

"Do you need anything else, good customer?" the Gnome behind the counter asked.

"No, thank you," he mumbled, finishing up the potions on the table before starting on a third concoction: a powder which, when blown on, would turn into a cone of flames fifteen feet in length. These flames, unlike the tincture he had used on the half-Orc brute, would burn everything they touched. He ground rat's tail and Fairy wings with his mortar and pestle, adding small drops of salamander's blood into the mix, and grinding it into a fine paste. He then poured the contents onto the left arm of his alembic, applying a small flame from a tube attached to the device under the holding plate.

Rancid smoke filled the air around him, but he put his breather mask on and watched the paste bubble and congeal.

He was about to place the solidified muck in the calcinator when a broad Werewolf with tan fur and a single streak of black along the right side of his face entered the shop.

The lycanthrope approached the counter and whispered to the Gnome.

Jonah knew that the lighting in the shop was too dim for anyone to immediately see him. The Gnome, however, pointed a single finger in his direction, and the Werewolf smiled at the Gnome and thanked him.

Jonah returned his gaze to his work, placing the muck into the calcinator for the final step in making the flame powder.

The Werewolf sat directly across from him, and filled the background of Jonah's field of vision. He peered up from the calcinator, which was quaking slightly.

Good, he mused. *It should be done in a minute or so.*

Jonah attached a small leather pouch to the end of the shoot tube on the device, in order to catch the powder as it was spit out of the calcinator. He kept the breather mask over his face and raised an eyebrow at the Werewolf. "Something I can help you with?"

The Werewolf gave Jonah a lopsided grin, and pointed at the healing potion, which was still emitting bubbles in its tube. The green liquid, Jonah realized, might look like a poison to an uneducated individual. He realized he might need to keep that in mind with someone so clearly unfriendly.

"What's in this," the Werewolf asked as he waggled his finger once again at the healing potion.

"Tegra poison," Jonah lied smoothly, giving the vial a quick glance. "For killing snakes. Lots of folks back home need the stuff, farmers and the like." That, at least, was a half-truth, as his former employer had often sent Jonah away to gather ingredients to make tegra poison. The man hated the serpents that roamed his fields, and Jonah wasn't too keen on them himself.

"And this," the Werewolf asked, pointing to the paralysis tincture.

"Paralysis tincture," Jonah replied, watching the small pouch fill with powder. *Come on*, he thought, *come on! I might need to use that stuff right away.*

"Very good." The Werewolf got up and approached the Gnome shopkeeper again.

They exchanged whispered words, and the Gnome handed him a set of six vials.

Healing potions, Jonah thought. *Why in the world would the man buy healing potions?* Jonah watched the Werewolf open a window on the opposite side of the store and throw the vials out the window. What in the Hells is he doing? Jonah wondered. He began putting the tools away, and noticed the Werewolf slap two huge, roughly shaped coins on the counter. Ryo, Jonah thought. That's two hundred gold he just paid. Jonah's heart sank as the Gnome took the coins and ducked through a door into the back room.

Jonah had a feeling that the Werewolf hadn't just paid for the healing potions—he had paid the Gnome for silence.

Jonah ripped the breather mask off of his face but found himself pressed against the wall.

The Werewolf's long knife flashed as he drew it from its sheath. "You must understand, mister Staples. This is just business." The tan Werewolf leaned in close, his jaw next to Jonah's ear. "Nothing personal." He rammed the long knife home, squarely into Jonah's stomach.

The Human Alchemist gasped as muscle, bone and organs gave way.

The Werewolf jerked the weapon from Jonah's body, soaked in his blood.

As Jonah slumped against the wall, he watched the Werewolf wipe the blade clean and toss it to the floor. His vision blurred and quivered as the Werewolf sprinted out of the store and into the streets.

Jonah used what strength he had left to snatch his healing potion off of the table and immediately drank its contents. He flopped to the floor as the potion took hold.

The healing effect was instantaneous. Though drained, Jonah's abdomen was unscathed, except for a scar.

He grabbed the discarded knife, then got groggily to his feet, and pulled a pinch of his flame powder out of his pouch.

The werewolf was gone, but Jonah, normally a peaceful man, hungered for revenge and the traitor-Gnome would pay the price.

The Gnome shopkeeper opened the door in a rush, his own knife ready as he prepared to finish anything the werewolf left undone.

Jonah blew on the powder, sending a rampaging cone of blistering flames at his face, burning his entire upper body as he writhed on the floor behind the counter.

* * * *

The werewolf scent had drifted away a full minute after Nareena had left, and Portenda wondered about his elusive adversary. *Hired help, most likely,* he mused as he drained his cuppa.

The Bounty Hunter took another mug, and paid his tab, asking the waitress if he might seat himself on the patio outside.

"Of course," she had replied with a perky smile.

A Hunter and his Prey

Portenda hunkered down in one of the wicker chairs on the patio, and looked down the street, taking in the sights, sounds, and scents of Desanadron. He had resolved to purchase an apartment buildings here and move his tenants from Ja-Wen when he had the opportunity. He would even convince the Kobolds he had met earlier to move into the building.

"Good afternoon," said a familiar voice.

Portenda turned in shock and saw his uncle, Tiberious Amon, standing at the top of the patio steps, his wooden leg planted beside his real one, his re-attached arm extended toward his nephew. Portenda spared his relative a brief smile and took the outstretched hand, shaking it firmly.

"Please, have a seat, Uncle Amon," Portenda offered.

The hulking Khan did so.

"I'm mildly surprised that Lee isn't with you," the Bounty Hunter commented, his voice flat and emotionless. Though he liked and appreciated his uncle, he felt distant with him. His mother, after all, was the shared bond between the two men. Try though they might, their conversations almost always fell on her, and they would quickly part ways to avoid the pain of remembering.

"Yes, we're usually attached at the hip, it seems," Amon declared. "But since Bael gave me my arm back," he said, flexing his right arm. "We sometimes part ways for our own excursions. Besides, he can be rather trying sometimes. I'll be right out. I'm just going to pop in for a tea."

Portenda waited patiently and watched as an Elven girl and a Dwarven boy, children both, chased after a red ball down the middle of the street. A Lizardman boy, his short legs rushing him along, followed closely behind, despite the protestations of his father, who was wheezing terribly as he chased after.

"Children," Portenda whispered, shaking his head. "They don't know."

"They don't know what?" Amon came around in front of Portenda and took a seat across from him. He sipped at his tea and looked at the scene on the street below, howling with laughter as the elder Lizardman tripped over the Dwarf boy's outstretched foot.

The trio of children scampered away, the father of the Lizardman youth still chasing doggedly behind.

"Oh, that," Amon commented with a smile as he wiped spurted tea from his cup and his facial fur. "They'll learn," he said, taking another sip of his tea.

"But should they? Do they absolutely have to?" Portenda raised an eyebrow at his uncle. "I mean, look at us. A Khan and a Simpa, sharing a drink and conversation, perfectly at ease with one another."

Amon stopped his cup halfway to his lips, and set his drink down on its saucer.

"We're, different, Portenda. We have common ties to one another. And you're not a pure breed, so it changes things a little. But I do see your point." He watched as the trio of youths kicked the ball to one another in a triangle around the older Lizardman, who had given up trying to stop this nonsense, and decided to play monkey in the middle. He clearly wasn't trying, just letting the kids have their fun at his expense. "They're having a wonderful time, just being young and energetic. And here we sit," he said, taking a sip of his tea. "Me, a tired old veteran, and you, a relentless, restless Bounty Hunter. We've seen and done things that neither of us is very proud of. And then again, we've also both done what I'd like to think are some very noble deeds. Just remember, my boy," Amon said as he stood and adjusted his chain shirt. "With the right events, and the right people," he indicated the children with his snout, "that can become daily life for all of us."

"I just wish it could happen sooner rather than later." Portenda gave his uncle a brief smile, then quashed it. "Where are you heading now?"

The proud Khan looked back over his shoulder at his nephew.

"Wherever the wind blows me, my boy," he said. "Wherever the wind blows me." He joined the circle of children, who made way without a word to add him into the game. *How he does it, I'll never know*, Portenda thought.

He had only a moment to watch the game before an all too familiar smell came charging his way—Jonah's blood!

* * * *

Jonah Staples charged through throngs of late afternoon gatherings and merchant wagon customers, bumping and shoving when he needed to. He didn't enjoy being pushy, but he needed to get to the Bounty Hunter and warn him before he too came under attack. Together, the two of them could then track down Nareena and get out of Desanadron as quickly as possible.

Several constables, familiar with Jonah and his family, stood approximately fifty feet ahead, all joking and joshing with one another. One of them, a stalwart Jaft who had helped Jacob train Jonah in the use of a short sword, saw him barreling at the group. He took a few steps forward and stooped low, swinging his arms around Jonah and lifting him up, placing him then in the middle of the group of guards. "By the gods Jonah, are you all right," he exclaimed as he looked at Jonah's torn and bloodied shirt.

"I'm fine, really," Jonah gushed, breathing heavily. "I got myself a healing potion right after, don't worry about me," he said, trying to break free of the circle. The Elf across from him, however, put his arms out at his sides, blocking Jonah's escape. The Corporal gave him a worried look.

"Jonah, wait a minute," he said.

Jonah recognized him as Elwyn Arrans, one of the finest archers the army of Desanadron had to offer. "Who did this to you? We need to know so we can make an arrest!"

"Big fellow, Werewolf, tan fur," Jonah stammered, trying to keep his thoughts straight. He had just been stabbed, and he had to warn Portenda. He had to find Nareena, and make sure she was all right, but these guards were just getting in the way. He knew they meant well, so he tried to calm himself and tell them what he could. "He had this streak of black fur on his face, along the right side, from behind his ear to the tip of his snout."

"Sounds like one of the corporals over at the fifteenth," muttered one of the other guards.

A Hunter and his Prey

Jonah's mind went blank for a moment: he had been attacked by a constable? Impossible! But then he recalled the young corporal, the one who had gotten them the copies of the reports. Oh, gods, Jonah thought as he realized what he was dealing with.

"I've got to go." He ducked under the Elf's arms and darted away.

Five minutes later, he stood before Portenda, off of the patio fronting the cafe.

The big Bounty Hunter put his hands on Jonah's shoulders as he examined the scar. "We've got trouble," Jonah wheezed. "Do you remember that corporal who gave us the reports?"

"The Werewolf, yes, I remember him," Portenda said calmly. "He attacked you?"

"Yes." Jonah related the whole event to Portenda in detail, from the moment he had seen the Werewolf enter the shop, sans uniform, to the part where he took the healing potion. He left out the little bit where he injured the shopkeeper, already wondering how he could have handled that better.

"We have to find Nareena," he said. "She's in trouble as long as he's still out there!"

Portenda took his hands off of Jonah's shoulders, and nodded. Then he put his nose to the air, and took a couple of quick sniffs.

"That way." Hoisting Jonah on his back, like a second rucksack, Portenda charged through the streets, leaping over dazzled on-lookers as he practically flew through the city.

Jonah felt like he was about to hurl on several occasions as buildings and people flash past him in a blur of colors and vague shapes.

Portenda set Jonah wobbling on the ground, as they stood before the city's largest library. A wooden sign out front designated it the 'Byron Aixler memorial Library', and the two men went inside, Jonah rebounding off of the doorframe as stepped past it.

The building itself was vacant with the exception of three people. The librarian, a bespectacled Sidalis with four arms and four eyes, each set holding and reading a separate book, sat at his desk. At a table in the far left corner of the library Nareena had her nose buried in a red, leather-bound tome. And as Portenda rushed ahead toward her, Jonah saw, the Werewolf, broadsword in hand, poised to jump from atop a rolling ladder.

"Nareena, move," he shouted.

The Elven girl looked up just as Portenda barreled her over. The two of them crashed into a bookshelf as the Werewolf cleaved her seat and the table she had been sitting at in half.

The librarian, apparently no stranger to this sort of thing, pulled an inkwell on his desk. The desk immediately flipped over, presumably depositing him in a safe room beneath the floor.

For a moment, Jonah marveled at how cowardly some people could be, then he remembered that he himself had been that yellow at one time.

He collected his thoughts as Portenda looped around the debris of the table with Nareena in his arms. The Simpa leapt once, landing heavily next to Jonah, where he deposited the Elf girl. He spun around, teeth barred, his broadsword in hand.

The two lycanthropes glared at one another, weapons held aloft. "Jonah," Portenda whispered out of the corner of his mouth. The Alchemist stepped forward and listened intently. "Get that Focus Site readied. We can leave this puppet here, while we make good our escape."

"Um, can't you take him down," Jonah asked innocently.

"We'd wind up destroying half of the building, and he might get past me to one of you two before I kill him. We can't have that," Portenda said.

Jonah pulled out his piece of chalk and started inscribing the Transport Focus Site. He broke the chalk in half, and handed one half to Nareena, who gave a start when he pressed it into her hand.

"You have to write the name of the city in symbols," he told her. "You're the one who's been there, so you have to mark the indicated destination."

Nareena nodded, and went to work thinking through the precise words and symbols to use to get them to Satory in one piece. Both Alchemists tried to concentrate as the tan furred Werewolf charged at Portenda, screaming bloody blue murder.

The Simpa Bounty Hunter held his position as the Werewolf approached, shifting his shoulders and squatted slightly, reinforcing his posture as he easily brought his own weapon up to block the Werewolf's broadsword.

The Werewolf pressed down hard, trying to force a move out of Portenda, who glared with his gray, ashen stare.

The Werewolf shoved his face closer to Portenda's, and the Bounty Hunter spoke. "Your form is atrocious." He leveled a back leg thrust kick into the Werewolf's chest, sending him reeling.

The Werewolf's feet and his right claw tearing the floorboards as he gripped the floor for balance.

As dust flew from his heels, the Werewolf Corporal stood up from his three-point stance. A lopsided grin spread across his black marked face, and he held the sword tucked against his right shoulder. "So, the stories are true, Portenda the Quiet. You really are very good at this. But what's to stop me from striking your little friends, hmm?"

The Werewolf's hand whipped to his belt, and came flashing forward with a shining, metal object.

Before he could release the throwing knife at Jonah or Nareena, a tremendous, terrible boom filled the air, accompanied by the clash of metal on metal, and smoke filled the air around Portenda's outstretched right hand.

The Corporal stared in shock at his suddenly empty hand, and then at the Simpa. He pointed a strange, ancient mecha weapon right at his head.

His employer hadn't warned him that the Bounty Hunter had a firearm.

A Hunter and his Prey

Portenda cocked the hammer back once more, slowly, deliberately. "Your heart rate has increased. You're starting to sweat. The bones and muscles in your legs are spasming. I believe your body is telling you to leave."

The Corporal, a mercenary by the name of Wren Headsplitter, stood stock still as the Human and Elf pressed their palms to some sort of symbol they had drawn on the floor. He had been warned about their use of Alchemy, but he hadn't known what that meant.

A brilliant flash of light filled the air. When he uncovered his eyes, Wren Headsplitter saw that a white oak door, about eight feet by four feet in size, had materialized.

The boy opened it and he and Nareena rushed through. Wren stepped in their direction, but a bullet pierced his left leg, spinning him to the ground as he howled in agony.

Clutching his injured leg, he saw Portenda the Quiet approach the door, his eyes still on Wren, the firearm still aimed at him.

"This isn't over," Wren growled deep in his throat. He attempted to sound menacing, but his natural reaction was to whimper like an injured puppy, so he sounded like an awkward adolescent trying to pick a fight with the school jock. "Not by a long shot," he managed as he pressed his hands to the wound.

Why wasn't it regenerating, he fumed mentally. *Why doesn't it heal?*

"I didn't figure it was," the Bounty Hunter replied. "After all, you aren't dead yet." Without another word, the Simpa was through the door. With another flash of light only empty space remained where the door had been.

A minute later, Wren noticed that the bleeding had stopped, and the metal cylinder that the ancient mecha weapon had thrown popped out of his leg with a heavy thud. He picked the bullet up between two claws and examined it, turning it over as he got shakily to his feet. He had sorely underestimated his opponents.

He felt no ill will toward them, of course. This was simply how he made his living. Being a trooper in the Desanadron Standing Army paid well enough for the average man, but he could make a great deal more selling his unique services. Unlike Bounty Hunters, who accepted sanctioned contracts, a mercenary such as Wren often worked for one employer until they had no more need of them. In six years as a mercenary, Wren had worked under three employers. This third and latest employer had been somewhat of a mystery. The man had worn an ivory mask and a strange, black cloak that seemed almost alive.

This Mister Genma had approached him several months ago, ordering him to stay in Desanadron and carry on as a militiaman. When Genma needed to speak with him, he would contact Wren via a small mirror and give him further instructions.

When the Staples girl had been kidnapped, Wren had been contacted.

"Her family will most likely come looking for her," the masked man had said from the other side of the mirror. "She has an older brother, by the name of Jonah. He may bring help. Make certain that they never reach my abode."

It had seemed a simple task. A Human Alchemist, twenty-three years of age should be no threat. The Illusionist visual record showed the boy to be gangly and somewhat physically inept.

The Simpa had changed the equation. He had returned to the station to look for a record of any Simpa who would be that heavily armed. Only one name had caught his attention: Portenda the Quiet. Little was known about the Simpa Bounty Hunter, age unknown, origins unknown, had except a mile-long list of acquired and completed bounty contracts.

"I'll get to know you," Wren said as his wound closed. "Before I kill you." He stalked away from his pooled blood, and out onto the streets of his city. Someone had to know more about the man. He would have to find that someone.

* * * *

"It must be done," Kobuchi said flatly to Eileen, who had tucked herself into the farthest corner of her sleeping chamber, her legs pulled tight against her body.

Blink growled and waved his stinger defensively in front of her. He was protecting her from the Kobold servant, who held an oblong instrument of measurement. "There's nothing about this that should be misconstrued, Miss." Kobuchi's patience with the girl was wearing thin, and he wondered why he let the girl live. Surely the Master could find another, less capable girl than this. He had been blasted from the room by a Raybolt spell, and turned into a frog for fifteen minutes.

He inwardly prayed that the girl had run out of manna energy to cast more spells. It would certainly explain her sudden reliance on the Alchemical beast as her defender.

"You can't honestly tell me this is just another measurement," she shrieked, waving her hands in a threatening way.

Kobuchi tensed, hoping to avoid another spell. Q Magic had very quickly become his least favorite of the arcane arts, mostly because being a victim of it instead of a beneficiary of the enhancement spells, was terrible. "It's a complete invasion of my being."

"It's nothing personal." Kobuchi tried to keep his own temper in check—a monumental task. He had once been the leader of the most intelligent tribe of his peoples, and now he was reduced to this.

He thrust the cylindrical object toward her again, keeping well away from Blink. He couldn't remember if the Master had imbued that stinger with poison or not. Kobuchi kept several vials of anti-venom and poison cures around just in case, as several of the guard beasts on the lower floors were venomous, and would strike at anything except their creator, including Kobuchi himself.

"Nothing personal? How the Hells can you say that? If you ask me, it's very, very personal. Tell Genma I refuse to prod my womanhood with foreign objects! What is he, some kind of pervert?"

"He simply wants to make sure that you have the same, ah, fittings, as his late wife." Kobuchi suddenly blushed uncontrollably. This was, after all, a rather delicate subject, and he didn't truly want to read any measuring instrument that had to be inserted in any orifice on the body. "I could leave the room, and leave you to do it yourself," he offered, almost stammering over his own words.

Eileen threw her shoe at him, striking him in the ear.

"Ow! You little bitch." As he took a step forward, something sharp and raw pierced his thin left leg.

"Oh, shit!" He looked down to see Blink pull his stinger out of the Kobold's leg, a trail of vile, emerald hued fluid dribbling down his leg and off of the stinger.

Poisoned again, he thought.

Blink scrambled up onto Eileen's lap, and passed out.

Apparently the effort had worn him out, Kobuchi thought with a smile as he pulled an anti-venom out and drank it dry.

"As I said before," he continued, clearing his throat and wincing as the anti-venom took hold and fought off the poison. "You can do it yourself. I'll just, stand outside, and you can tell me the reading."

"And what if I choose to lie to you," the Human girl retorted, fury edging her voice. "Then what?"

"Then things might turn out rather uncomfortable the first time the Master beds you. I'll just pop outside." He put his back to the wall on the right hand side of the door in the hallway. Gods, he thought. This is humiliating. Forced to write down the measurements of a Human girl's, erm, how to put it? Even in the privacy of his own mind, anything to do with reproduction made him ill at ease.

He heard grumbling from the girl, and a minute later, a sharp gasp. He wanted to vomit.

"Eight," Eileen yelled from the room. She tossed the measurement device aside, feeling unclean. What she had just done constituted sin in her parents' church doctrines. And she felt personally violated in ways she hadn't thought possible.

Kobuchi scribbled the number down on a pad of paper he kept in his pants pocket, and shivered to his core.

"Thank you very much. Now you see? Was that so difficult?" He poked his head around the corner, and found that the Human girl was looming over him, the measuring device in hand. She thrust it in his face, and Kobuchi shrieked and flailed back helplessly, tripping over his own feet. "What are you doing?"

"I'm making you feel the same way I do," she shouted, and reached down with amazing strength and speed, hoisting the Kobold up and ramming the device into his mouth.

He reflexively gagged and spat it out with a fountain of vomit.

"Now get out of my sight," she howled after him as Kobuchi fled to the stairwell.

They both felt a little like laughing, and a little like crying.

Chapter Seven
Broken

When Jonah and Nareena entered the door, they found themselves flying through a tunnel flanked on all sides by shadowy creatures out of nightmare.

The black-fleshed monstrosities made no move toward them, seemingly engaged with one another in conversation or, in some instances, combat.

When an open door appeared before them again, they hurled themselves through it and landed in a heap in the center of a town square.

Jonah pushed himself up off of Nareena, who rolled out of the way as Portenda came bustling through, also airborne.

Had she not rolled away, she thought with a heave of her chest, the Simpa would have crushed her.

"Damnation." Portenda growled, rubbing his head as he stood up.

Several dozen armed Lizardmen had formed a circle around them, their spears and swords at the ready.

Jonah slowly raised his arms, as did Nareena, and the Human Alchemist smiled at the nearest guard.

"We're just passing through. It was Alchemy, that's all."

One large Lizardman, his scales shimmering in the dim sunlight the clouds above let through, broke through the ring of guards. He wore a sleeveless vest made of purple cotton, tied shut with a black sash. His pants were white and baggy, allowing for flexible movement, and his feet were bare. He bore no weapons, and as he circled the group, his tongue flicking out to smell them.

"*Nisha kim goaku*," he rasped.

The guards lowered their weapons and disbursed.

The Lizardman before Jonah stood only an inch or so taller than he, but his arms and legs were as thick as tree trunks, and his body was heavily muscled beneath the tunic. His head, Jonah noted, was not covered in scales completely. A half-moon crescent mark rested just beneath the slit of his left ear.

"*Koma ko antapibi*," he shouted at the citizens.

They all quickly returned to their activities.

The Lizardman turned to Jonah and graced him with a reptilian smile. "My apologies, young man," he said in a thick, tribal accent. "We are not accustomed to having travelers arrive in such a fashion. I was sent for when one of the guards saw a white door appear out of nowhere in the middle of our town." He gave the three of them a graceful bow. "I am Ashkadu, High Chief of Satory. And you three are?"

His manner was formal, all three noticed, but he beamed a smile at them that seemed, well, genuine. This man was clearly not the typical politician. Then again, few Lizardmen could call themselves politicians. In Lizardman society, mediation is when the leaders of two warring tribes get together and bash one another's head in with clubs until one of them passes out. That man is declared the loser of the debate.

"I am Jonah," Jonah said, returning a small bow of his own, though not nearly as graceful, he thought. "This is Portenda," he said, waving his hands at the Bounty Hunter, who bowed deeply with one arm over his chest. Ashkadu smiled broadly at the gesture. "And this young woman is Nareena."

The Elven girl curtsied as politely as she knew how.

"Ah, yes. Now that introductions are out of the way, might I ask that you review this leaflet?" Ashkadu handed them each a pamphlet. In large, italicized letters, the cover said simply, 'Laws of Satory, a guide for outsiders'.

Much to Jonah's discomfort, the pamphlet was terribly thin, and he had a sudden feeling that there weren't many rules to follow in this town. Luckily, Satory was a fraction of the size of Desanadron or Ja-Wen, and he could hoof it out of town if need be.

The Lizardman turned around and started to walk away.

"A moment, High Chief. If you will." Portenda sauntered to the Lizardman, giving the Alchemists a hand signal to wait where they were.

Jonah tried to lean forward to listen in on Portenda's whispered conversation, but Nareena took him by the arm and pulled him back.

Jonah blushed for a moment, and gave her a smile. He opened the pamphlet and started to read the very short list of laws in Satory.

"What do you require, young man," Ashkadu asked of Portenda.

"There is a man, a tan Werewolf with a black streak along the right side of his face," he whispered. "We are going to be staying here for a couple of days, nothing more. But this man may pursue us. If he arrives, make certain your guards do not attempt to engage him."

The Lizardman gave Portenda a curious glance. "My guards are more than capable," Ashkadu said.

"Your men have bronze weapons and their circle around us was not complete. Their leggings are poorly made, Human smithy work from the looks of it," Portenda said.

Ashkadu's eyes widened.

"Whoever you paid for them took you to the cleaners on them. I could have amputated all of their legs in a manner of a minute or so," Portenda reported flatly.

Ashkadu faced Portenda with rage in his slit-like, reptilian eyes.

"Do not be angry with me. I am simply giving you the facts," Portenda said.

"So it would seem," Ashkadu said. "I too was not pleased with the craftsmanship of the leggings, or the fact that the weapons were made with bronze instead of steel. I suppose you know what Class I am as well?"

"You're a Monk," Portenda whispered evenly. "The sash, the sleeveless vest, the baggy pants to allow for wide stances and swift kicking. The way in which you hold yourself, no weapons of any kind on your person," he continued. "Your men were also trembling, their muscles were tensed. None of them expected us to come flying through that door. Then again, neither did we," he added with mild irritation.

Ashkadu threw his head back and cackled. "You are amazing, Portenda. How did you observe so much about us in so little time?"

Portenda shrugged and remained silent.

"Very well. Trade secrets, I understand. I shall inform the guards that they are not to trifle with this Werewolf you speak of. It is getting late in the afternoon, however. When the sun sets, bring your friends with you to my home. It is the only red house in the town, a mark of the High Chief's residence. We shall share dinner and discuss your situation."

"What situation?" Portenda raised an eyebrow.

"People who drop out of holes or doors in midair tend to have situations, my friend," Ashkadu said in a sage manner. "One does not live so long as I have without knowing such things."

Portenda grinned at the old Lizardman's back as he walked away among his people.

"Come on, you two," he said gruffly to Jonah and Nareena. "We have questions to ask and a dinner engagement in a few hours. Let's get moving."

* * * *

Wren Headsplitter escorted the mangled Gnome shopkeeper through the streets toward the Byron Aixler Memorial Library, keeping a gentle hand on the little man while still out in the public's view. He had his uniform on and had applied the fur paint to his black streak, so that the librarian wouldn't recognize him—he hoped. If the Sidalis did, however, it would mean another body in the tally.

"It was horrible," the burned Gnome said through his bandaging.

Wren was more than a little disturbed that he hadn't killed the Human, Jonah Staples. The little puke had clearly lied to him about one of the vials, something that he took very personally. His chosen Class had been that of a Knight, and Knights were supposed to be able to catch a person in a lie. But then again, he chose not to follow the Knights' code of ethics, and had most likely lost that particular ability as a result. The gods didn't look kindly on Fallen Knights.

Not that it mattered. Like him, the trio had no idea where Genma's tower was, or how to get to it if they did find out where it was. He would hunt them down, provided the Gnome could decipher the cryptic writing around the symbol that the Human and Elf girl had drawn on the library floor.

Wren had sent a private to order the librarian to leave the mark as it was.

The great thing about being in the Desanadron Standing Army, he thought smugly, *was that the civilians tended to listen to a man armed and supported by the government.*

"I just came out of me back room, and loik, there was this fellah standin' there, waitin' fer me," the Gnome muttered through the cloth wraps.

In his own way, Wren admired Jonah Staples for what he had done: it had shown a potential for violence that the Werewolf hadn't thought Jonah had in him. It also, however, showed that the boy knew what the Hells he was doing with this Alchemy business. "And then, when I tried to talk to 'im, he just breathed fire on me, fer no reason," the Gnome lied. Wren knew this was a lie, simply because he had himself bribed the Gnome to let the Human boy be murdered in his shop, with the boy's potions and books a part of the price.

A Hunter and his Prey

"All right, we're here," Wren said gently. "Now, you say you're not an Alchemist?"

"No," the Gnome admitted. "I'm an Engineer. I just, have a thing for languages, and I wanted me own shop. I'm a pretty decent merchant, you know," he said, prodding his bandaged cheek and wincing in pain. "I'm never going to look roit again, am I?"

Wren felt badly for the little man. After all, in a way, he had caused the permanent marring of his face. Then again, the little shit should have waited a while longer before coming out of his back room, now shouldn't he?

"Well, if you have a thing for languages, perhaps you can be of some help." Wren led the Gnome inside the library.

The four-armed Sidalis was at his desk, his eyes in two separate books, as before. He didn't even look up at the men as they entered, but simply put one hand up to his lips to indicate that he wanted quiet.

Wren led the Gnome to the symbol on the floor, now cordoned off with yellow tape tied to four step stools. The private that Wren had sent, a Jaft by the name of Wilkins, stood with his body as stiff as a board, guarding the taped off area.

"Very good, Wilkins. You're dismissed," Wren said.

The Jaft popped outside and lit a smoke stick.

Dreadful things, Wren thought, wrinkling his snout.

"Is this it?" The Gnome looked up at Wren.

The Werewolf nodded and lifted the tape for the Gnome to get a closer look at the inscriptions.

The Gnome muttered to himself as he traced the lines of the Focus Site and the characters beneath it. After ten grueling minutes of this, the Gnome poked out from beneath the tape.

"Well? What does it say?"

"I believe the boy used this to travel instantly to a town called Satory," the Gnome said.

Satory, Wren thought with a mild disgust. A town full of savages and brutes. He had been there once, when he was a lad accompanying his father and older brother to do some trading with the Lizardmen. Things likely hadn't changed much in thirty years, so he shrugged his shoulders and decided that it had to be done.

"Thank you for your help in this matter." Wren stormed out of the library, leaving the Gnome behind. The stench of his burned flesh had caused Wren a great deal of discomfort, and now that he had what he needed from the little man, he would avoid him and his shop.

Satory, eh? He approximately a month's worth of leave due. He decided it was time to use it.

An hour later, after having filed the proper paperwork and trading in his uniform for the much more comfortable combat gear he favored, he strolled into the stables. He paid the Elven attendant full price for the purchase of the largest stallion he had available, and mounted.

He was charging toward Satory before the sun had even set.

* * * *

At sunset, Portenda, Jonah and Nareena had made no progress in their lines of questioning. Few of the Lizardmen spoke Common, and the Dwarves and Jafts brushed them off. They weren't openly hostile, but the message they sent the trio was quite clear: you're not from around here, and we don't trust you.

Portenda heaved a sigh as he looked to the western skyline.

"We're due at Ashkadu's home for dinner. We may as well ask him our questions."

"Here's hoping he's a bit more cooperative," Nareena chimed in. "I don't get these people at all. I practically flashed them my breasts before I asked them anything." She adjusted her dress to hide the cleavage she had tried to use as leverage.

"Well, dear heart," Jonah said, taking a last gander for himself. "These people are members of Races that don't exactly admire the Elven female form."

"Huh?" She planted her hands on her hips.

"They aren't sexually attracted to Elves," Jonah said bluntly.

Nareena looked around at the men and women of the town, most of whom had continued on with their daily routines, as though the trio had never come to town.

"Humph. Fine by me. They're not exactly lookers themselves." She grabbed Jonah's hand and walked beside him.

She leaned in close to Jonah, whispering in his ear. "So do you think he's ever had a girlfriend?"

Jonah looked at the broad, weapon-laden back of the Bounty Hunter.

"To tell you the truth, I'm not sure. I mean, who would risk it?"

Nareena cut off a chortle, and they both stopped in their tracks when Portenda looked back at them over his shoulder.

"We'll be there in a few minutes. I suggest you hurry your private little conversation," he grumbled.

Jonah leaned in and whispered to Nareena again. "I believe my point has just been demonstrated."

"I don't know." Nareena gave Portenda a quick up-and-down. "Some girls dig the strong, silent type. And some really get into the dangerous sorts. He's got both in one package."

Jonah felt himself get flustered by her attentions and double meanings.

"Are you attracted to him?" he rasped in her ear.

The Elven woman giggled. "Why Jonah, do I detect jealousy?"

Jonah gave her hand a brief squeeze. This was how it should have stayed, all that time ago. "You bet."

They wound up bumping into Portenda's back as the Bounty Hunter came to a halt before Ashkadu, who waited at the bottom of the steps to his home.

"Well met, Portenda, Jonah, and Nareena," he said with another graceful bow. "Please, follow me." The Lizardman High Chief led them through an iron door into an antechamber with a relatively low ceiling and two benches. Beneath the benches were several sets of shoes.

Jonah, feeling a tad bit awkward, removed his boots and his socks. The floor, he noted, was made entirely of steel, as were the inside walls. The whole building seemed to be made of brick and steel, with glass windows, most likely reinforced. The architectural design was reminiscent, Jonah thought, of old southland estate houses, of the variety that had several dozen acres of land to be tended by hired hands.

They went through the opposite door into an enormous and airy den/study room, where a wide fireplace and several couches, along with the addition of two recliners, had been arranged for maximum atmosphere.

Two Jaft men stood on either side of one doorway leading out of the chamber, fully dressed in tuxedoes with the little bow ties slightly askew.

Jonah almost laughed aloud at how ridiculous the pair of blue-skinned warriors looked, but the Jafts weren't meant to be elegant or even graceful by any stretch of the imagination. The tux each man wore barely contained their broad and ample musculature, and the perfume, or whatever it was that they were wearing, had the metallic odor of blood, plain and simple. The message was clear to Jonah. These are my guards. They will kill you if they have to.

As Ashkadu approached them, each bald servant gave him a brief smile and a bow, following suit when Portenda, Jonah, and Nareena passed between the two of them and into a luxurious dining room, replete with little touches of class.

Wineglasses had been set, upside down, at each of the eight seats, and some of the finest ceramic dishes to be found in the region sat untouched at the table.

Ashkadu sat at the head of the table, opposite the doorway, and indicated to the others that he would like for them to be seated as well.

Portenda remained at a distance, selecting a set two places away from Ashkadu while Jonah and Nareena took up the seats on the opposite side of the table, as close to the Lizardman as they could get.

The Bounty Hunter kept a mental log of all of the escape routes and defensible positions in the antechamber, the den, and now, here, in the dining room. The windows, while they appeared to be nothing more than glass, had a slightly shaded appearance. They were reinforced with a material, called plastic, that the Dwarves had only recently discovered how to refine. The Dwarves had been convinced, once they had produced a certain amount of the stuff, that it was one of the more useful materials in the realm of Tamalaria. Certainly the stuff was flexible, Portenda thought. He had taken down a target seven months before who had purchased an order of the material to be shaped into armor. The problem for the target had been that although the stuff was fairly durable, it still wasn't a match for the Bounty Hunter's broadsword. That, and after a few days of cooling in the mountain air, the newly shaped armor had begun to stiffen up. It is difficult to avoid decapitation when your abdomen can't bend.

But the stuff outside the windows appeared, if he had to hazard a guess, to be woven right into the glass windows themselves. He would have to punch or kick the windows out rather quickly if he were to entertain the idea of using one as an exit. But the manor's security measures didn't seem to be in place to keep anyone from getting out. They were to keep people from getting in.

"A tad bit paranoid, are we," the Simpa asked bluntly of Ashkadu, who gave him a beaming smile.

"Several assassination attempts were made on me in the last few years. I have taken the necessary precautions against further attempts," the Lizardman said. "It's all standard practice in this town." He sighed as he upturned his wineglass, letting one of the two Jaft pour him a healthy portion of drink.

The bottle was suddenly being pressed almost into Jonah's face, and the Human Alchemist realized that the Jaft was letting him observe the alcohol before deciding on it.

"Standard practice?" Jonah asked as he gave the Jaft the okay for a little pour.

He sampled the wine, found it had a good body and flavor, and let the Jaft finish pouring him a glass.

Without further pause or preamble, the Jaft left the room and returned with a different bottle, pouring some farlberry wine for Nareena.

Then, once more the Jaft left the room.

"Yes, standard practice," Ashkadu replied. "It is the manner of ascension in Satory. Lower Chiefs hire out assassins or mercenaries to dispatch the current High Chief. When the High Chief is slain, the other Chiefs hold a public election to see who the townsfolk want to take the post of High Chief. The newly elected High Chief then selects a resident of the township to move up to the empty Chief's position. It has gone on like that in Satory for the hundred and fifty years of the town's existence." Ashkadu took a long swig of his wine.

The other Jaft took his plate and bowl into a kitchen that Jonah could just make out when the narrow door swung on its hinges. They were returned a minute later, laden with food and soup and the Jaft gave a small bow.

Portenda's dishes were taken next, and the first Jaft had finally returned with a small green bottle, which he poured without question into Portenda's glass. The Simpa sniffed the mixture; it was Simpa blood wine, a blend of several sweet, fermented berries and grapes, with another ingredient added that most Simpa rather enjoyed drinking.

Khan blood.

Portenda raised a thick finger, catching the Jaft's attention, along with everyone else at the table. The Jaft leaned in close, and Portenda grabbed his privates hard with his left claw beneath the surface of the table. The blue humanoid's eyes went wide, and he turned his head slightly away, to get his ear closer to Portenda's moving lips. The others at the table couldn't hear what was being said, but it went something like this. "Use your eyes, blue man."

The Bounty Hunter flexed the muscles of his right arm, which was on the table and in clear view of the Jaft, who squinted his eyes, searching for what the trouble was.

"Notice anything, different, about my fur?"

A Hunter and his Prey

A minute passed, and suddenly the Jaft's eyes went wider than saucers.

"You have my deepest apologies," the Jaft stammered.

The Jaft was released, and he took the wineglass away in a rush.

"My my. Whatever did my attendant do to offend you?" Ashkadu asked.

Portenda's left eye twitched with closely checked rage.

"I do not imbibe traditional Simpa beverages," Portenda said evenly, his voice not so much cold as entirely devoid of feeling. "I simply had to have him take it away and replace it."

The Jaft, still rubbing his privates tenderly, returned with a glass filled with a sweetly scented Human-brewed vintage.

Portenda gave it a whiff, smiled somewhat at the blue humanoid, and took a sip of his drink before tearing into the meal before him like a savage. He hadn't eaten in a while, and sorely needed the energy.

As the other three ate in contented silence, with the Bounty Hunter asking for a second helping before they had half done with their first portions, Portenda flicked his eyes left and right. Using his keen sense of hearing and smell, he searched for any treachery against the High Chief or himself and his companions.

Nothing thus far, he thought, but that didn't mean nothing would happen.

The second Jaft, who had served the food, hadn't said a word since their arrival. He hadn't even moved to help his coworker when Portenda had grabbed the man's tender bits.

Jafts tended to be very personable with one another, standing up for a total stranger so long as the man or woman in question was a member of their noble yet savage Race. Yet this other Jaft had said nothing, done nothing to interfere on his coworker's behalf.

Ashkadu asked for a small second helping of the meal, and the Jaft Portenda had been eyeballing took the plate away without a question or comment.

Despite the light order, it took the blue-skinned humanoid a full minute and a half to return.

Portenda noticed the vein slightly bulging on the Jaft's bare forehead, the slight, slick sheen of a cold sweat. And something didn't smell quite right.

As Ashkadu picked up his fork once more, Portenda lobbed a throwing knife at the utensil, knocking it from Ashkadu's hand.

The Lizardman stared at him with both shock and menace in his reptilian features. "What is this?" he bellowed.

"Don't touch that food." Portenda stalked toward the second Jaft servant.

The fellow he had grabbed a couple of minutes before had poking his head into the room, but quickly ducked back into the kitchen as Portenda approached the head of the table.

The Jaft didn't budge, didn't flinch; either he was very good at bluffing, or the man was paralyzed. Or possibly, he was someone's puppet. In any event, the man had tried to poison the Head Chief.

Portenda grabbed Ashkadu's fork, and handed it directly to the Jaft. "Eat," he commanded. Now he saw a flicker behind those eyes: the flicker of mortal fear.

Still the Jaft said nothing, however, and made no move as Portenda held the fork at his side.

Ashkadu glared at his servant. He grabbed the big humanoid by the collar, tugging him down to eye level. "You heard the man," the Lizardman said. "Take a sample of the fine food that George has prepared. And by the way, where is Peter?"

Enough talk, Portenda decided. Time for action. With a single deft movement of his hand, he pierced a piece of crab meat from Ashkadu's plate and thrust his left hand onto the Jaft's face, ripping his jaw down, forcing his mouth open. He pushed the fork between the Jaft's parted lips as the man tried to struggle. But the Bounty Hunter was more than a match for the strength of both of the Jaft's arms. As the fork found its mark, Portenda pushed the man's mouth shut, and ripped the fork out, sans crab.

With a swift, open-palmed slap to the Jaft's belly, Portenda forced the fake servant to swallow the offending food.

After a moment, smoke plumed out of the blue humanoid's mouth and nostrils, and his body shook. A moment later, the Jaft assassin's eyeballs burst from his head. His body, already dead, fell backward like a tree.

There was no bending of the knees, or catching a glance off of any furniture. He toppled like a maple cut down for construction material.

Jonah wiped eyeball juice off of his tunic shirt, and pushed his meal aside.

Nareena sprinted into the kitchen to throw up.

"That was remarkable." Ashkadu stood and gave Portenda a deep bow. "I am surprised you helped me out of that dangerous little situation."

"Do not thank me," Portenda said brusquely. "We need both answers to our questions and the continued vigilance of your guards. I don't care what happens to you once we leave the town. But until we leave, you or anyone else who has information for us must be kept alive. Now, down to business." He took his seat as Nareena came through the kitchen door, supported in part by the other Jaft.

"Thank you very much George," Ashkadu said to the Jaft. "Where is Peter, by the way?"

"'fraid I haven't got a clue, sir," George replied, helping Nareena down into her seat as he took the plates one by one into his hands. "I thought maybe he had gone home sick, seein' as you had that other fellah here." He grabbed the dead assassin's ankles as he hauled him toward the kitchen door.

"No, I thought you brought him in," Ashkadu said to the Jaft called George.

George shook his head.

"Do us a grand favor and put him in the same area as the others," Ashkadu said.

A Hunter and his Prey

Jonah sprayed wine on his hand as he attempted to minimize the damage, choking and coughing hard enough that Nareena had to pat him roughly on the back.

"The others," Jonah asked as he gagged.

"There was a mound of fresh earth on the left hand side of the building when we were approaching. I assume from the size of it that you've been High Chief for a while now." Portenda managed a slight grin.

Ashkadu returned it in kind.

"Fifteen long years. That's about the average term of any High Chief. I intend to resign from my post in a few weeks, to tell you the truth. I will be the first High Chief in the history of Satory to resign from the post, instead of being, ah, forcibly replaced, as it were." Ashkadu took the last of his drink. "Now, you had questions for me, I believe, and I have agreed already to help you out as much as I can. So by all means, ask."

Jonah took a swig of his drink, and cleared his throat as he dabbed his lips with a finely folded napkin.

"We're looking for someone very particular," Jonah said, and began the search for information proper.

As the evening wore on, however, it became apparent that Ashkadu had never seen heard of Genma, or his servant, Kobuchi. The Lizardman High Chief offered his apologies, as well as quarters for them to rest for the night.

"If you continue east and north another day and a half from here on foot, you'll come to the trade village of Bolamar. The traders and artisans might be able to help you out more than I have," he offered as he handed a towel to his Jaft servant. "Did you find Peter?"

"Yes, m'lord. He'd been bound and gagged in his room. Apparently the assassin meant no harm to anyone but you, sire," the Jaft reported.

Ashkadu nodded, smiled once more at the trio, and stepped away.

"Make certain they get rooms of comfort," he told his servant. "That towel is for the big fellow. It's the only one in the house big enough to accommodate him."

"Of course, sire." The Jaft turned to face the trio. "Please, follow me to the west wing." George turned on his heel and exiting the dining hall.

Portenda took the lead behind the tuxedo-wearing Jaft, as he had become accustomed to. The Alchemists, he noted, tended not to be too comfortable around other people of Portenda's size, and so he had allowed them to stay at his back. In most groups, the Bounty Hunter preferred to bring up the rear, so that he could completely smell, hear and feel anything coming from behind.

They followed George for a good fifteen minutes until at last they stood in a long, gorgeously decorated hallway.

Clay busts and paintings of beautiful landscapes sat on pedestals and hung on the walls along the outer right hand wall, and along the left hand side, between the room doors, arrangements of various exotic flowers bloomed and bristled.

George sniffed a delias, a hybrid flower grown by only the most skilled of gardeners in Tamalaria. He seemed to take pride from the scent he took in, and Portenda felt his lungs fill with the mellow, relaxing odor of them.

Jonah practically drooled as he thought of the healing potions and other tinctures he could process with the petals from a single delias plant. George turned to them then, standing upright. He seemed to have remembered his place and duties as he cleared his throat and adjusted his bow tie.

"Mr. Portenda, your room." He indicated the door to his right.

The big Bounty Hunter slipped into his chambers without a word to the other two.

Jonah noticed that while standing in this hallway, he couldn't smell anything but the flowers, and suddenly felt he knew why George had grown and tended these flowers. After all, he reasoned, who else would grow them? He probably uses them to make colognes or perfumes to mask his own natural stench as a Jaft. Whatever the purpose, he knew that the Jaft was much like the shop owner in Desanadron: kind hearted and gentle beneath the gruff, warrior-like exterior.

He took Nareena by the hand once more, and the Jaft led them to another door. "Mr. Jonah, your room."

Jonah was about to let go of Nareena's hand and let her be led off to her chambers, but she followed him, still holding his hand.

"We'll be staying together," the Elven woman said.

The Jaft blushed as he rubbed the back of his bald, blue head.

"Oh, um, well then, good evening." George dashed away.

Jonah had just enough time to step through the door before his attractive companion was on him, wild and hungry in her urges. This time, Jonah Staples went with it. His resolve to resist her advances had broken like a cheaply made wall.

* * * *

At a few minutes after midnight, Wren Headsplitter felt the shaking from his cotton pants pocket.

He brought his mount to a halt atop an atoll, surveyed the surrounding landscape, and pulled the small mirror out of his cargo pocket.

Genma's ivory mask looked back at him through the mirror, but Wren could make out the slightest hint of a smile in those strange, dead eyes.

"What is it, boss," the Werewolf asked irritably. He would have to ride all night if he intended to get to Satory before the targets hightailed it out of there. With this interruption, however, he was granted the opportunity to let his mount graze and take in some water from a nearby pond.

Dismounting, he let the black stallion go on about its business.

"Are you already in pursuit of them, Wren?" The image of Genma's ivory mask flickered in and out of blurry nothingness.

"Affirmative." The tan-furred Werewolf looked around. He thought he could smell Humans in the near distance. He would have to avoid being seen by them as Humans often asked for assistance with this or that, and he felt instinctively compelled to aid them—without charge. Werewolves had come into being to protect the Human Race from the dark things that lived all over the world in the oldest days of history. Of course, back then, lycanthropes had been very few in number, and could only take their full bestial form during a full moon, or some nonsense like that. *Thank the gods I was born in this time,* Wren thought as he moved down the atoll to avoid being spotted by the Human merchant caravan heading for Desanadron.

"How long until you reach them," Genma asked through the mirror.

"Around noon tomorrow, sir," he said flatly, rubbing his eyes. He was tired, but he needed to get going again.

His mount came back toward him, refreshed and ready to continue on again.

"They used a Focus Site to get away, like I mentioned before. I need to know if there's some way to cancel that out in case they use it again. You're an Alchemist, boss, so if there's anything you can tell me, I'd appreciate it."

"There are two ways to negate their advantage of travel," Genma said calmly. "The simplest way is to follow them through the door when it appears. I know that last time you had been knocked aside by the Bounty Hunter, and didn't have time to follow. The other way is to interrupt the Focus Site."

"How do I do that," Wren asked as he swung himself up on the horse.

"Throw some sand or broken glass on the symbol when the boy draws it. It will alter the Site, and cause an adverse affect. If you go that route, keep your distance from the Site. What occurs when a Focus Site is altered is unknown." Genma said. "For all we know, a tentacle beast might come through from another dimension."

Wren stared at the ivory masked face. "Can that sort of thing really happen?"

"Of course," Genma replied. "The art of Focus is a lot like magic in that respect, Wren. Where magic deals with the spiritual energies and manna flow, Alchemy deals with the scientific laws and molecules of the universe. Magic and Alchemy are, essentially, the same. Now, I must leave you to your business. I have some of my own to attend to."

The mirror misted over, and a moment later, reflected Wren Headsplitter's own visage.

Sand, eh? He led the horse back down to the pond, opened an empty leather pouch at his waist, and poured some of the fine grains of sand from the edge of the pond into it. Wren wasn't keen on subjecting himself to any sort of magic, be it scientific or spiritual. He wouldn't follow through any weird door made out of thin air, that was for certain.

But the thought of a tentacle beast showing up out of nowhere made him chuckle a little as he hefted the sack of sand.

* * * *

It had taken a very long time, but Eileen Staples finally found a timepiece hanging on the wall of a laboratory.

Two in the morning, she thought, looking out of the single window in the room. Unlike most of the other windows she had found, this portal was devoid of bars.

Now, she thought rather glibly, *all I have to do was deal with the drop of a couple of miles to the ground below.*

The lab was filled with wooden closets, each containing an arsenal of chemicals, powders, plants, and strange organic objects suspended in some red fluid. She couldn't guess what a few of those objects were, but she knew an eyeball when she saw one.

A pair of long tables in the center of the chamber itself was laden with Alchemy instruments, and a load of handwritten notebooks littered the ends of the tables.

Her blood ran cold as she tiptoed toward a stack of notes, Blink slinking along by her left leg, silent and stealthy as the source of the creature's stinger.

Kobuchi had served Eileen's latest meal, and the Kobold had also brought a small, plastic red dish for the animal.

Blink had devoured his own meal in moments while the Human girl ate slowly, purposefully. She had wanted Kobuchi to leave, but the Kobold stood in the doorway for an additional three hours after she had finished her meal. Finally, a couple of hours ago, he had left, his eyes sagging in his face.

As soon as he was gone, Eileen had left the bedchamber to explore.

Now, she held an open notebook in her hands. She briefly scanned the notes there, noticing that the handwriting was much different from that in the animal lab she had taken Blink from. The pages were older, slightly yellowed.

There was a strange familiarity to the way the words had been written and arranged, almost poetic in style. It reminded her a little of the way Jonah went on in his own notes.

Who was this strange, ivory-masked man?

She set the notebook aside, and selected another notebook.

Again, the elegant writing style had been applied.

Eileen set the book down and turned around, selecting a notebook at random from the table closer to the back wall, and noted Genma's handwriting.

When she turned the book around, and set it next the first notebook, she noticed several similarities in the lettering. For instance, the cursive writing was broken up here and there by block lettering, and the 'o' in both notebooks, was more curly than most people wrote it. But it was the exact same character in each instance. The same man had written all of these notes, at different times in his life.

Genma, she had confirmed, had not always been Genma.

Having had enough of the lab's eerie aura of scientific discovery and experimentation, she put the books down and called Blink to follow her.

Together, they made their way to the stairwell in the western corridor.

For a moment, she contemplated what would happen if she tried to go downstairs.

Curiosity got the better of her, and she turned to descend the stairwell.

A Hunter and his Prey

The stone steps curled around the outer walls, preventing her from seeing much more than a few yards in front of her.

She had gone down several dozen steps when she froze in mid-step. Something, just out of sight down the stairs, was growling at her. Whatever it was, it was far larger than her, and several hundred times more dangerous and powerful.

Once again, her curiosity got the better of her, and she slunk down three more steps.

The creature at the bottom of those steps made her heart skip a beat.

The body and head of a golden lion faced her squarely, the wings of a small dragon spread from its back, and a stinger much akin to the one on Blink's hindquarters wavered in the air. Legs bunched with muscles and covered in scales set the creature in a crouch as it growled at her, and a soft, red light glowed deep in the manticore's mouth.

A manticore, she thought.

Creatures of legend and myth, the monsters known as manticores were created out of magic and Alchemy, entirely constructed from scratch.

At least, that had been the truth hundreds of years before. Now, methods had been found by Beastmasters of getting the beasts to mate and reproduce offspring that were even more potent than their artificial parents.

Eileen sensed no magic on this creature, other than its own innate power, which apparently it was preparing to bring to bear on her for her breach of the rules. This creature had either been created through Alchemy, a highly likely option, or purchased from someone in the outside world.

Regardless, she thought, the creature was right in front of her.

An instant later, it was below and behind her as she sprinted back up the stairs, scooping up Blink with her.

She let her momentum carry her and her pet all the way up the stairs and to the level above the one her sleeping chamber was on. An oak door stood closed on the floor's access platform, with a bronze plaque gracing its surface.

"Energy Conversion and Focus Site Reference Level," she read aloud to herself. "Well, shall we take a look see," she asked Blink, who closed his eyes and nodded.

The door swung open with some considerable effort, the hinges creaking noisily. Eileen wasn't certain if they had been ignored or purposefully left without oiling, in case Genma was within one of the labs or chambers on this floor. It would get his attention in case someone entered the floor without his permission, she thought. But he had said she could access any floor above her own, Eileen reasoned, and she stepped into another black and gray stone hallway.

Steel doors lined the hall for several scores of yards, and she saw no intersections or hallways branching off of the main one she stood in. Opposite her, fifty yards away, was the eastern stairwell.

"Pretty straightforward, eh, Blink?"

The creature on her shoulder nodded and made a strange, high-pitched croak in his throat as if to agree.

She stalked down to the first set of doors, one on her left, and one on her right. The plaque on her left read 'Manna Conversion, Internal,' and the door on her right read, 'Manna Conversion, External'.

She opted for Internal first, grabbing the oblong handle and hauling back on it, grunting with the effort it took her to pull the door open.

When she let go of the door, it didn't move to swing shut, and she entered.

Despite the torches in the hallway, the room was almost pitch black.

She fumbled along the wall to find another torch to light, but instead found something hard and strange along the wall.

A lever of some sort, she surmised, and pulled it up.

Lights glowed in the ceiling over her head, revealing a room filled with strange mecha and glass tubes, systems of them interconnecting and filled with some sort of soft, sky blue light. A black window set in a steel cabinet flashed with green, blocky lettering as she approached, and she realized that the text was in the Common tongue.

She read the information as it flashed past, but much of it was mathematical formulae, and she was at a loss to understand any of it.

She tried to find the energy source as she scanned the floor. Cords, she knew, were often attached to mecha and led to a power source of some sort, a 'generator', her brother had called them. This technology, she knew, was ancient, relic of the Age of Mecha. Yet somehow, the mad Alchemist knew how to use it all.

She soon located a single black cord leading from the right hand side of the steel cabinet to a black box made of a metal she didn't recognize. Atop the black box was a glass globe, filled with sparkling purple energy. A tube fitted to the top of the orb led to another device, which crackled with that same blue energy she had first noticed when she had entered the room.

Eileen felt herself being drained mentally, as though just looking at all of this stuff was taxing her body.

She conjured an Awaken spell, the reversal of her Sleep spell, and watched as the manna energy she invoked slipped straight from her fingers into an open-ended tube.

Her eyes widened with shock as her magical energy flowed through into the purple orb, and into the steel cabinet.

The blackened window set in the desk seemed to pulsate for a moment, and then hundreds of characters of text flew across the screen.

"I understand now," she rasped aloud. "Manna conversion, internal. He's using my magic to power his mecha."

Blink stared bug-eyed at the machinery and contraptions.

Her captor, she realized, had everything he needed to sustain himself in this tower. If someone showed up to save her, his beasts would kill them. If they employed magic, it would be siphoned through the tower's stone to this chamber, or the one across the hall.

A Hunter and his Prey

Damnation, she thought. "Hellfire, Hell and blood," she spat aloud.

She headed further down the hall, determined to find out what else the man called Genma had at his disposal. She would then figure out a way to disrupt this fortress—from within.

* * * *

Portenda couldn't sleep.

The big Simpa Bounty Hunter attributed part of his insomnia to his natural sleep cycle, which was miniscule. He attributed the other part to the moaning and thumping from the next room over.

He slammed on the wall twice, to no avail. Jonah and Nareena, apparently, were patching up their long time rivalry.

Good for them, Portenda thought vehemently, uncharacteristically bothered and annoyed by their noisy intrusion on his slumber.

"Idiots," he grumbled as he got out of his bed.

According to the timepiece by his bed, it was two in the morning, and he didn't want to have them at it all night. He wasn't certain why he couldn't ignore them, but he couldn't.

He could have torn the wall apart and knocked their heads together, but that would have been a tad bit harsh, even in his mind. Still, he smiled at the thought of bringing a harsh and screeching halt to their rutting.

Well, Jonah had earned a bit of privacy. The public records office in Ja-Wen had a file on Jonah, as he had taken up residence in the city once before in his travels. From there, Portenda had learned a lot about the boy.

When he had gone to the basement to grab a cot frame to replace the one that Jonah had transformed into the two short swords, the Bounty Hunter had opened a secret mail slot in the wall where one of his many informants left him packages. Inside of a manila folder he had found the basic facts and records concerning the Human Alchemist.

Jonah had earned continent-wide praise from the scientific community at large, and had twice been heralded a 'newfound prodigy in the arts of Alchemy', according to one article written by an Arthur P. Muddlesworth of Palen.

When Jonah was seventeen, the records indicated, he had suffered some sort of psychological incident. The Desanadron constabulary had written a report, sealed as confidential, which was copied and placed in the folder. While out shopping for his mother, two armed bandits had approached, brandishing mecha weapons known as 'shotguns.'. Jonah, the observing officer had said, had first gone slack, and then whipped into motion faster than he could see.

In a matter of seconds, the Human boy had ripped the weapons from the goons' hands, and had held one in each hand as he shot and killed both men, blowing their heads clean off of their shoulders. Jonah had passed out and been taken to the asylum for treatment and therapy.

The boy, the psyche report had stated, had no recollection of this incident.

Portenda thought now back on how Jonah had disarmed his pistol, and brooded.

Some form of brainwashing, he thought as he stalked to the door of his assigned chambers.

His leather vest had been hung on a wall hook, and he walked out into the darkened hallway, looking out of one of the reinforced windows, up at the crescent moon. Who had trained the boy in the use of the ancient firearms? How had he become well versed in a form of science that even the greatest Gnome and Dwarven minds couldn't decipher?

Jonah had started his training early on, when he had been a boy of no more than nine or ten, Portenda surmised. And his uncle, Allen, had been another accomplished practitioner. Nobody had seen Allen for years, however. Most believed he had killed himself in an experiment, and police reports from the area said that his home had exploded in a fireball several years prior. Jonah's family hadn't been informed.

And why not? Portenda turned these thoughts over in his mind one by one, trying to find some common thread, but all roads seemed to lead to dead ends.

He felt compelled to find out what the boy was all about. For the first time in many, many years, Portenda had found something he had thought he could do without.

He had found a friend.

* * * *

When the morning sun rose, a heavy knock came at Jonah and Nareena's door.

The smiling Alchemist got up out of bed, got dressed, and answered the door.

George stood there, a pair of fresh towels in his hand, along with a change of clothes well suited for Jonah's tastes—a simple, white jerkin shirt and a pair of denim pants fitted to his frame.

A velvet, green and black dress lay beneath his change of clothes.

"The master felt it appropriate that you receive these, considering the Bounty Hunter's conversation with him this morning," the Jaft said with a wide smile.

Jonah looked back over his shoulder and saw that Nareena had sat up, covering her bare breasts with their sheet. He turned back to George and blushed brightly.

"No worries, sonny," the Jaft whispered. "Good fer you." He gave Jonah a friendly punch on the arm as he handed over the clothes.

Jonah took the clothes and turned away, and then something the butler had said stuck in his mind. The Bounty Hunter's conversation. He was already up, and possibly, due to Jonah and Nareena's, erm, activities, hadn't gotten a great deal of sleep.

"So, how are you feeling, Mister Staples," Nareena cooed as Jonah changed into the fresh clothing. She took the dress he had set on the edge of the bed, slipping it on over her head, then twirled around in it, liking the feel of the material on her pale skin.

"I'm doing well, Miss Nareena," he replied, bowing to her mockingly. "But may I suggest we lose the air of levity before we run into Portenda?"

She gave him a curious look. "Why?"

"I have a feeling we may be the reason he's already awake. He might not have even gotten to sleep last night." Jonah brushed his hair back and tied the back in a ponytail. He took a long hard look at himself in the mirror on the wardrobe, memorizing that face. He might never see it again.

Without another word, the pair of Alchemists linked arms and headed to the main living room.

Portenda and Ashkadu were standing several feet apart, facing the doorway through which Jonah and Nareena entered.

Jonah noticed that Portenda's eyes were bloodshot and appeared to have bags under them.

"Portenda informs me that you two had him up for most of the night," the Lizardman said with a grin.

"Ah, well, um, sorry about that," Jonah stammered.

Portenda put a hand up to silence him. "I've been thinking, Jonah," the Simpa said quietly.

The air around Jonah suddenly seemed chilled, and his mind filled with images of glaciers.

He looked at the two men, and saw that Portenda's pistol was in Ashkadu's hand. What was going on here?

"I want you to save me now," Portenda said.

Ashkadu raised the firearm and pointed it squarely at Portenda's face.

The world turned into a blur of colors and vague shapes as Jonah moved forward. His mind reeled as information buzzed through his mind, information he was sure he hadn't acquired through normal means.

He felt like a man looking at the world through a pair of stained glass spectacles, his entire body numb.

Focus Sites blazed through his mind, and specifications data buzzed in his ears.

A voice, familiar, and yet foreign, spoke to him out of the dark recesses of his mind.

When he came to, he was holding a huge cannon of some sort. A high-pitched whining emanated from a glowing power cell under his armpit.

He had the barrel pointed at Ashkadu, the Lizardman staring at him over the steel weapon.

"What, what just happened?" Jonah asked as the weapon flashed and turned back into a pistol.

A Focus Site, drawn with the natural oils of his fingertips, was emblazoned on the pistol's grip as Portenda took the weapon from Jonah's hand.

"I see now what you were talking about," Ashkadu said.

The Simpa grinned broadly. Jonah felt fire course through his veins. "What is going on here? What was that all about Portenda?" He clutched the front of the Bounty Hunter's sleeveless leather armor vest.

"Jonah, we are going to have a very long talk sometime soon. There are things you should know about yourself." Portenda bowed to Ashkadu and moved toward the front door of the building. "Something is broken inside of you, Jonah. Before we complete this mission, we should try to fix it."

Jonah and Nareena bowed hurriedly to Ashkadu, who returned the motion in kind to their receding backs.

Out into the dim light of a cloud-covered sky the trio walked, Jonah finally catching up to Portenda.

"What do you mean, broken? Portenda, I have no idea what I just did in there. If you do, I want to know right now!"

Portenda looked at Jonah impassively, his eyes sagging slightly.

"Later, Jonah. Right now, we have something else to worry about." Portenda drew his broadsword.

Jonah felt a tingling sensation run up his spine. A tan furred Werewolf, long sword in hand, stood over a bloody heap of guards.

He, like Portenda, looked tired, but he smiled that lopsided, disturbed smile of his again.

"Get ready to take us to Palen, Jonah," Portenda said over his shoulder.

The Human Alchemist drew a Focus Site in the dirt with his fingers.

"You are persistent, aren't you," Portenda growled at the mercenary Wren Headsplitter.

"Very much so, Portenda the Quiet." Wren stepped out of the ring of bodies he had crafted with his weapon. "I have my orders, and was paid a handsome fee to deal with the three of you. I don't back out of my jobs, much as you won't back out of a contract. Oh yes, I've read your file in Desanadron. You're a very well-known man in certain circles, Portenda. You too, Jonah Staples. Now, I've spent the whole night and morning riding here."

He gestured and Portenda, Jonah and Nareena saw his horse behind him, dead from exhaustion. "I'll not be denied again. You won't escape from me this time!"

With a war cry more fit for a barbarian than a Fallen Knight, Wren dashed forward, swinging his sword with deadly speed and accuracy.

He was parried at each blow.

Citizens of Satory scattered, scrambling away from the confrontation. Even the Jafts of the town, the most capable warrior Race on the spot, wanted no part of this battle.

The loud, resounding clashes of steel weaponry echoed through the air.

Portenda tried to assemble his thoughts, get a glimpse of Wren's stance, but the mercenary kept coming at him, not allowing him time to observe his opponent before he had to make another defensive move.

Jonah, sweating now as he tried to hasten the Site, concentrated more and more on the fight between the Werewolf and the Simpa, as the fake constable drove Portenda toward him and Nareena.

The Elven Alchemist had drawn the symbols for Palen for Jonah, who finally completed the Focus Site. He clapped his palms together and pressed them to the Site. A rush of air gusted past his face as a plain white door appeared before him. He threw the door open and shoved Nareena in first, calling out to Portenda as he stepped through himself.

Portenda launched a sidekick into Wren's face and followed his friends into the Site.

The mercenary let himself fall back, reaching into the bag of sand at his hip. He got to his feet and tossed sand on the Focus Site, watching as light erupted from the symbol and the door exploded into thousands of wooden shards.

One of the splinters landed in his right arm, piercing all the way to the bone.

He cried out in pain, but smiled despite his discomfort. He didn't know what would happen to the three of them now, but he didn't care. They would most likely be killed when they reached the other side, he thought smugly. Mission accomplished.

A Lizardman opened the door on the brick and steel building before him, his body tensed and ready for battle.

"You are the Werewolf who was following them," Ashkadu said.

Easy pickings, Wren thought. I'll do this one for free. He dashed forward, his long sword splitting the air as he cut down the Lizardman. Or so, he thought. Something heavy landed on his shoulders, and he looked up in time to find the Lizardman Monk smiling down at him, his reptilian countenance almost laughing at him. "You telegraphed your action. Big mistake." Ashkadu twisted his feet, breaking Wren Headsplitter's neck and killing him on the spot.

Ashkadu landed daintily in a crouch as he jumped off of the falling body. "Portenda could have cut you down at any moment," he whispered to the dead mercenary. "He chose not to. I wonder why?" He signaled to George, who heaved a heavy sigh, and dragged the body off to bury it in the mass grave.

"George?"

"Yes, sir?"

"Make a note. Portenda the Quiet, a Simpa Bounty Hunter, is to be given free access to Satory should he ever return during my stay here."

"Why, sire? I watched the battle. He didn't make a move on this guy!"

"He was too busy protecting the other two in his care. If he had attacked, the Werewolf would have gone for the Human boy and the Elven girl. Attacking is easy, when done without concern for another's welfare. Defending is much more difficult, especially when one is not defending oneself."

* * * *

The trio from Ja-Wen tumbled in the emptiness of the void, uncertain what had gone wrong. One moment, they had been floating along toward the door that would open on Palen, the next, they were being tossed through the black space, surrounded by creatures and beings more dreadful than nightmares.

Jonah seemed to be taking it all in stride, but Nareena screamed at the top of her high-pitched lungs, and Portenda felt dizzy and ill. He wanted to vomit, but would not permit himself such a weakness, particularly when he wasn't sure he wouldn't wind up wearing it a moment later.

Finally, they straightened out and found themselves flying toward another white door. A rush of freezing wind blew in their collective faces. One behind the other, they flew out of the transfer space and into a thick, ice-crusted snow bank.

Jonah groaned as he tried to pry himself out from under Nareena and Portenda. The Bounty Hunter suddenly hauled him to his feet.

Portenda sniffed the air, and shivered slightly. He knew where they were from the scent of mountain goats, the frost in the wind, and the snow all around him.

Goats only lived in one region of Tamalaria, after all.

"Where the blazes are we?" Jonah's teeth chattered as Nareena clung to him for warmth.

Portenda looked around and then back at them.

"I'm not certain *why*, but I know *where* we are," the Bounty Hunter said. "We're in the northwestern mountains, about an hour and a half away from Traithrock, the Dwarven capital."

Jonah and Nareena shivered and looked at each other with fear in their eyes.

"Come on. If we don't move, you two will freeze to death." Portenda moved away.

Jonah realized what must have happened. The mercenary had broken his Focus Site while they were between destinations. If he lived through this, he would remember that particular vulnerability of Alchemy. That way, he would be better prepared—if he didn't freeze to death out here first.

Chapter Eight
Identity

Though he knew Nareena didn't trust of the art of Focus, Jonah knew it was the only way they'd survive the harsh environment. He couldn't use a travel Site again that day, but he created an alteration Site and stood in the center of it, pressing his palms to the Site around him. There was the scent of pudding, and a slight trace of urine, as his body was suddenly covered with bear fur. An animal howl loosed from somewhere far off in the mountains, and Jonah asked for forgiveness from the ursine he had just essentially stripped bald.

He led Nareena into a fresh Focus Site and repeated the process, watching as the white and gray fur of a timber wolf covered her.

"This is humiliating," she murmured as she pulled on the fur that was temporarily attached to her body.

Portenda looked at them with a cock-eyed glance, and sniggered.

"You see? He's laughing at us!"

"I'm laughing with you," the Bounty Hunter said as he gusted a plume of warm breath into the mountain air. "Come on. We've got to head to Traithrock. By the way, Jonah?"

The Human Alchemist looked at Portenda with his bushy eyebrow raised.

"You do look ridiculous."

Jonah shrugged, pleased that he was warm now. With a nod and his arms crossed over his chest, Jonah Staples followed Portenda the Quiet's quiet, frozen lead down the slopes and onto the mountain pass.

For nearly an hour and a half, the trio from Ja-Wen continued on the mountain paths southward and west, making a beeline for Traithrock.

Jonah knew that they were marching through dangerous territory: mountain lions, crazed bears, snow wolves, dragons, chimeras, and other monstrous creatures of the land made their home in these mountains. Though, he thought brightly, not all of the breeds of dragon were vicious. Perhaps, if they were unfortunate to meet up with a wyrm, it would be one of the more intellectual sorts, and they could avoid a conflict.

The only sounds Jonah heard as they passed on toward Traithrock were the crunch of snow and ice underfoot and the occasional call or cry from an animal. Wind whistled past his ears now and again but only in short gusts. Portenda seemed to know the best paths and branches to turn down so as to minimize the harshness of the environment. Thankfully, fur he had acquired for himself and Nareena was holding up rather well, though now he itched like all Hells and had an unusual craving for raw trout.

Finally, he heard new sounds coming from perhaps two or three hundred yards away. Through the gently falling snow, Jonah made out smoke piping up from chimneys and forges, and his heart swelled with relief.

They would be in Traithrock in ten or twenty minutes, barring any interruptions. Jonah checked himself, however, as the moment he had thoughts like that, problems tended to arise.

Portenda came to a sudden halt, and Jonah bumped into his broad back.

The Simpa had pulled a small mirror of some sort from his pocket.

"Where did you get that," the Human Alchemist inquired.

Portenda half turned to him, still looking at the mirror. "When I parried the Werewolf's third overhead strike, I snatched it from his belt. I smelled Alchemy all over it, the same scent I detect each time you prepare a Focus Site. The air fills with a sort of faint ozone scent."

Portenda watched as the mirror's surface shimmered. A moment later, an ivory masked face filled the mirror's surface, gray, dead eyes, not unlike Portenda's own, stared from the eye slots.

The eyes widened, then the man on the other side of the mirror spoke.

"You aren't Wren. What has happened? Wait, you're the Bounty Hunter."

"That's right," Portenda said coldly. "As for your mercenary, I don't think he's survived. We had been fighting in front of High Chief Ashkadu's home. The Lizardman most likely made short work of your lackey."

Genma chortled like a madman for a long minute, and then pressed his face closer to the mirror's surface.

"I hardly needed him that badly."

Jonah Staples shuddered down to his core. He recognized the voice of Genma on some primal, subconscious level. How? He couldn't remember meeting the man.

Jonah lunged forward, pressing his hairy face as close to the mirror as he could, screaming at Genma.

"Bring my sister back, you freak. So help me gods, if you've done anything to hurt her, I'll have your head put on a pike outside the gates of Desanadron."

Genma laughed again, his mirth filled with malicious intent.

"Young Jonah," Genma cooed. "Execute command seventy-three."

The surface of the mirror went blank. Jonah's mind did the same,

Portenda was about to ask Jonah what the Hells that had been all about but before he could turn, Jonah stripped his weapon and fired a single round from the Bounty Hunter's pistol into his side.

The weapon's power tossed Portenda to the snow.

Blood sprayed over Jonah's facial fur, and Nareena screamed at the top of her lungs.

Smoke billowed from the barrel of the ancient firearm, and Jonah's eyes remained blank. He turned toward Nareena, the gun still leveled at Portenda's chest height. A shot would eradicate her head.

A moment before Jonah could pull the trigger, he was pummeled from the side, bull-tackled into a snow bank twice his height and many times his density.

Portenda held Jonah's right wrist in his huge left hand, his eyes lined with fury.

"Nobody shoots me with my own gun." He twisted Jonah's wrist violently.

Jonah's eyes cleared and he screamed in agony, the bones in his wrist crushed to a fine powder.

Portenda grabbed the gun, tossed the mirror in the air, and shot it with a single bullet, shattering it over his shoulder without looking.

A Hunter and his Prey

"Jonah, what happened," he said, pistol whipping the young Human.

A tooth came loose as Jonah put his left hand up in a plea of mercy.

"I, I don't know," Jonah moaned, rolling onto his side as Portenda got up off of him. "I, I've heard that voice! I recognize him, but I don't remember why. I wouldn't have done that on my own."

Jonah thought back to the last time that he had blacked out like that, back in Satory. Portenda had forced a situation, and Jonah had reacted with a speed and course of action that he was only partially familiar with. Now, on the word of a man he couldn't be certain he recognized, he had shot his only hope of finding his sister.

The Bounty Hunter bled heavily on the snow-covered slopes.

Pain flared in Jonah's right arm, where his wrist had once been and he sat up as best he could, drawing out a healing potion and downing the entire vial in a few seconds. His arm went numb as the potion went to work repairing his shattered wrist.

The Simpa Bounty Hunter holstered his firearm and hefted Jonah to his feet.

He pulled out his auto crossbow, which he had crushed when he fell from the gunshot and tossed it into the snow, deciding that he didn't really need it anymore.

Nareena, he noted, still trembled. After all, she had been moments from death, and her lover was the one who was going to kill her. Her trepidation was understandable, but none of Portenda's concern. He felt himself withdrawing into the cold, dark space that he had carved for himself over the years as a Bounty Hunter. He felt distanced now from Jonah, because now, he felt he had to keep an eye on the Human Alchemist for more reasons than protection.

Without another word, Portenda moved back onto the road to Traithrock, his wound slowly closing as it regenerated.

His body temperature had dropped three degrees from the loss of blood and the environment. As he looked back over his shoulder at the two Alchemists, he noticed strands of animal fur falling away into the snow. Their alterations were fading away, and they had perhaps another twenty minutes before they were exposed to the elements again. Luckily, Traithrock was closer than that.

He led them on towards the gates of the Dwarven capital.

Jonah and Nareena both held themselves, shivering when they stopped before five armed Dwarf sentries.

Axes and pikes in hand, the heavily armored mountain men took defensive postures as Portenda approached, and the Simpa came to a full halt.

"Who goes there, that seeks entrance into der city of Traithrock," one of the horned helmet-wearing Dwarves asked aloud.

"I am Portenda the Quiet," the Bounty Hunter said softly, his voice and presence reaching out to the Dwarves, who suddenly felt humbled.

This man could kill them all in the blink of an eye, they thought, and they took up more relaxed stances.

147

"With me," the Simpa continued, "are Jonah Staples and Nareena. We come seeking shelter from the elements, and a place to stay for a couple of days. An accident has caused our Alchemical form of transport to malfunction." He kept his voice at a monotone the whole while. Dwarves possessed some of the keenest scientific minds of all the Races, second only to Gnomes.

The Dwarves all looked to one another and nodded. The shortest among them stepped forward, sheathing his axe as he looked past Portenda to Jonah and Nareena.

"Your Focus Site was disrupted?" he asked.

Jonah nodded in response. He didn't feel much like talking. Since his blackout, Nareena had stayed a good four or more feet away from him, as if she expected him to snap again. His heart sank to his stomach, and he felt the urge to wretch.

"Ah. Well, at least you came here before nightfall." The Dwarf straightened and looking up at Portenda, who positively towered over the bearded mountain warriors.

"Jaft raiding parties have been attacking travelers out in the open these last few weeks. They aren't like their noble kinsmen," the Dwarf said, showing his natural appreciation for the gruff blue skinned humanoids. "These attack innocent people, even Monks and Clerics. We know of you, Portenda the Quiet, and we know you are capable. But twenty Jaft warriors on one Simpa and a pair like these," the Dwarf said, indicating Jonah and Nareena with a tilt of his helmet. "Well, those aren't exactly good odds."

Portenda nodded, and the guards opened a space between them, allowing the trio to enter the city proper.

Portenda wasted no time, taking the two in his charge directly to the Hotel Outlander, a Dwarven-run establishment that serviced the members of the taller Races. It was a large structure, made entirely of stone on the outside and inside.

The city's eldest leader, Morek Rockmight, had extended a line of credit for Portenda at the inn, and he intended to use a couple of nights of it.

Today, Jonah and he would have that long talk.

He led the way to the lobby, which was blissfully heated by a series of metal shafts connected to a large, coal burning furnace down in the basement. The entire building was warmed this way, and Portenda rather enjoyed the environment whenever he stayed.

"Two rooms," Portenda said to Tograk Stonehewer, the inn's owner and manager.

Tograk was a Dwarf of nearly five hundred years. Most Dwarves died of natural causes at four hundred and fifty, at the oldest. Somehow, Tograk had held on longer.

Probably because he has nobody to inherit his estate or business, Portenda thought briefly. The man had never married, never had children, which were two things that Dwarven society treasured more than gold. Family meant a lot to the Dwarves of Tamalaria.

"No offense meant," Nareena chimed in. "But, I'll bunk by myself tonight."

A Hunter and his Prey

Jonah felt something break inside him, but he understood her feelings. He wasn't sure himself whether he posed a threat to her or Portenda.

"I had planned on that," Portenda replied, his voice filling the room with a chill so deep that Jonah thought he had been encased in frost. "Jonah, you stay with me tonight."

The Human Alchemist hung his head like a lost puppy.

"Here are your keys, Mister Portenda." Tograk smiled at the Bounty Hunter. "I must say, I'm surprised you've got company. You're always alone when I see you," the Dwarf said.

"I usually prefer it that way," the Bounty Hunter replied.

He handed one key to Nareena, and the three separated as Portenda opened the door across the hall from Nareena, and tossed Jonah inside by the shoulder.

Jonah stumbled as he tried to catch himself on a bed.

Portenda closed the door and locked it behind him, winding several inches of wire around the doorknob before connected to his spear, which he set against the wall. If someone tried to enter, they would be struck on the head by the blunt end of the weapon.

This took him only a few moments, after which he turned to face the boy, who had sat down on the bed, slumped over, his face in his hands.

"Jonah, it's all right." Portenda let a bit of concern into his voice. He had to approach this delicately, he knew. He had, essentially, a one-man hostage situation here. The day's events had rocked Jonah's confidence to the core of his being.

"No it's not," Jonah groaned through tear-wracked gulps of air. "I'm a freak. I'm a threat to myself, to you, and to Nareena. Do us all a favor and just kill me now! Then you can get my sister back for my parents on your own, without having to worry about me turning on you again."

Portenda sat down heavily next to him on the bed, his knees bunched up against his elbows.

The bed was sized for a Human or smaller creature, and Portenda almost looked ridiculous enough, hunched over as he was, to make Jonah laugh.

Almost.

Portenda put one thickly muscled arm around Jonah's shoulder in a friendly gesture, and squeezed.

This was, Jonah thought, out of character for Portenda. After all, he had shot the Simpa. He expected to be slapped around.

"Jonah, I have some things to tell you, and some things you should read for yourself." Portenda drew out the manila folder from his rucksack.

Jonah's name was emblazoned on the cover, and the Alchemist took it from Portenda's hand.

He flipped it open and began to browse through the reports and information sheets.

"Jonah, I've seen what's happened to you before, in kidnapping contracts. It's an old form of mind control, called brainwashing."

"I'm familiar with the concept," Jonah said slowly. "But I've never been abducted. Nobody's ever held me long enough to do something like this. Not that I can recall, anyway," he amended, thinking of the time when he was thirteen, and a group of Elven girls had taken them to one of their basements, to pretend he was their servant while they played silly girl games. But that didn't seem likely to have created these problems. They had been kids, just doing kid stuff. Nareena had been there, too, though she had been the oldest of the girls and was supposed to be babysitting them, not letting this sort of thing go on.

"Therein lies the problem." Portenda got off of the bed and paced across the stone floor. The carpeting was thin and offered little padding, but he didn't mind. He had always gone barefoot, even here in the blistering mountain regions. The calluses on his feet were thicker than some leather boots, and he liked it that way.

"If you were brainwashed, the one who did so to you would have used a subliminal command to clean your memory of the incident. So, as far as you or I know, you have been abducted once. Not, of course, while you were living with your parents," he added with a soft smile, looking kindly down on Jonah. "I have the feeling your father would have dealt with the villain rather harshly."

"You have no idea," Jonah said. "I remember this one time, when I was in grammar school, the principal lashed me with a belt for blowing up the science room. I had just started getting into Alchemy then, and, well, my first healing potion turned out to be somewhat explosive."

"What happened," Portenda asked, genuinely interested.

"Well, when I got home, I told my dad," Jonah said, taking a trip down memory lane. "He walked me up to the school, stormed into the principal's office, and before Mr. Macgregor could do anything, my dad took the belt from his own waist and grabbed him! He pulled him over that big oak desk of his and wailed on his back," Jonah said, making the same arm motion his father had. "It was great! My dad lashed him, must have been ten or eleven times before he let him go! And when we were leaving, he shouted at him, 'Don't you ever touch my boy again, or next time I'll have you arrested!' I think that was the moment I was most in awe of my father." He brought to mind the image of his father, toiling away in the back garden while his heart strained with worry for his children.

"We've got to get my sister back, Portenda," he said grimly. "My father and mother can't take this sort of strain too long. They'll die of worry."

"No they won't," Portenda said, sitting heavily across from Jonah. "They won't because they're strong people, Jonah, and because we're going to bring you and your sister back to them. I would suggest that when we do, you stick around for a while. Make sure things settle back to normal before you go taking off again." He got up once again, and stared down at Jonah for a long, silent minute. "Read over those files. Don't leave the room. I have something to check on."

A Hunter and his Prey

He undid the spear trap as he opened the door. "Reset this when I'm out," he said over his shoulder, leaving Jonah Staples in the hotel room by himself, to learn about his own past.

* * * *

"We understand, sir," one of the Dwarf Sergeants said as he rifled through a cabinet of files and folders.

Traithrock had peace accords with many of its nearby neighbors, and some with cities clear across the continent. Though great warriors, Dwarves preferred cooperation and group profit to war and individual victory. As a result, the main police station in Traithrock towered over the rest of the city, standing at seventeen stories in height, though they were numbered one through eighteen. The thirteenth floor had been labeled the fourteenth, due to the superstitious nature of the humble mountain folk.

Portenda had asked for all records and files concerning Jonah Staples and an Elven Alchemist, the girl, Nareena. He didn't have a last name to go by, and had simply asked that they bring him any matches they had for her. He had also inquired about anyone by the names Genma, or Kobuchi, the Kobold servant to the abductor.

His request had been a large one, and would take several hours to process, so he had been shown to a waiting lounge with comfortable sofas and a collection of books to read. One other occupant sat across the room from him, a Cuyotai youth who was filling out an application for citizenship, and another one for entry into the Traithrock police. His yellowish fur told Portenda that the youth was from one of the southeastern provinces, near the great desert known as the Desperation. Not many men or women could make a living in that wasteland, but one particular tribe of Cuyotai had been famous for surviving there. After a few generations, their offspring had begun to take on the characteristics of the desert environment, including sand-colored fur to effectively camouflage themselves. The youth smiled at him a few times, his brow breaking into a cold sweat.

"Don't be nervous," Portenda said softly. "Just answer all of the questions honestly, and shortly. Dwarves don't like reading long responses: they haven't the patience. Reading to them is impersonal. They prefer to read short responses, and hear long ones."

The young Cuyotai nodded his understanding.

Portenda, bored witless, picked up one of the books and turned to the first page. It was a Dwarven novel, written by one Alfred T. Sunstone, a Dwarven author of some note. He browsed through the first few pages, but found that the hints he had just given the Cuyotai were true also of their literature. Very short and to the point. Not a lot of description, not a lot of character development. He turned the book aside, and looked around the room.

Patience had always been one of his strong points, he thought as he mulled over his current situation. He had decided not to make another move without trying to figure a few things out. Thus far, he had come across no reports of Jonah having been abducted, and there were only a handful of times in his life when he couldn't be accounted for. Payment receipts for the few jobs he had held were on record, and most of his youth had been spent with his family. Only on a couple of occasions, the Desanadron records stated, had the minor been taken out of the city by someone other than his immediate family, and that had been by his uncle Allen. But Allen had, according to public records, died when his house near the Allenian Hills had gone up in an explosion.

His entire family had been unaccounted for, but Portenda requested all records concerning Allen Staples and his family anyway.

Tired beyond measure, he stretched out on the couch for a quick nap.

The next thing he knew, he was being shrugged awake by a Dwarven constable of the Corporal rank.

The corporal had a large stack in his left hand as he shook Portenda with his right. "Sir, the copies you requested." The Dwarf set the stack on the floor. It came up to Portenda's snout as he sat on the sofa.

"Ah, gods," he muttered, shaking his head. "How long was I asleep?"

"About two hours," The Cuyotai youth in the corner, now being fitted by another Dwarven constable for his uniform, replied. "Citizen," he added with civic pride.

"Hell's bells." Portenda rubbed his eyes. "Certainly doesn't feel like it. Thank you officer," he said to the Dwarf in front of him. "Here," he said, handing the Dwarf one of his pouches of money, with fifty gold pieces in it. Money went a long way in Traithrock, as Dwarves used gems for most of their purchases, and coin was not common here. "Put it to good use for the department." He took the first folder from the stack, and began to read more about Jonah Staples.

* * * *

Genma had broken his own mirror shortly after the connection had been severed. The incompetent boy hadn't killed either the Bounty Hunter or the girl. In a fury, Genma had punched his mirror with his bare hand, and the already mangled flesh had been lacerated badly.

A potion did the trick, but the pain was still there.

Kobuchi now stood in the doorway, a torch in his hand. The Kobold was bold to bring a source of light to his private chamber.

"Kobuchi, why do you have that torch," the Alchemist growled deep in his throat.

"No disrespect meant, sire," Kobuchi said, his voice quavering. "The manticore was rather agitated when I went to feed him, and I thought perhaps I should keep some flames around. You know, easy access," Kobuchi said.

He was an adept of Pyromancy, but his skill with the fire magic was very basic, and he preferred to have flames present if he needed to use those powers. His preferred method of magic was Aeromancy, an art he had mastered many times over. But such spells had little effect on the various guard creatures that his Master employed for defense and attack duties. Fire, though, did the trick quite nicely.

A Hunter and his Prey

Kobuchi was weaker within the tower, magically speaking, because of the Manna Converters. The girl had found them, he knew, because he had spied her opening the Interior chamber door. She would never be able to use the computation machine, but her own magical nature would surely show her what the apparatus was used for.

"Why was the manticore agitated," Genma asked out of the shadows he sat in.

"Couldn't be certain, my lordship," Kobuchi lied. He knew the girl had tried to go downstairs. "Perhaps because he hasn't had any, um, fun, in a while. You know, live food."

Genma grunted in response from the darkness. "You're probably right, Kobuchi. See to it that he gets something fresh in the next day or so, keep him on his toes. After all, I doubt the Bounty Hunter or the boy are ever going to arrive," he said. "The mercenary is dead, by the way," he rasped to Kobuchi.

"The Bounty Hunter?"

"Satory's High Chief," Genma said. "Portenda the Quiet chose just to defend the boy and the girl. He could have easily done Wren in, though. That speaks volumes to me about his character."

Genma turned in the swivel chair to look out at his Kobold servant.

"Sire, if I may speak openly?"

Genma waved his barely visible hand to Kobuchi, who sighed and relaxed a little.

"He's just a Bounty Hunter. Sure, he's good, but the boy surely can't afford his help much longer. And you and I both know they're all the way in the mountains now. Even if they use the Focus Site again, they can't know where we are."

"That, my friend, is where you're wrong. I don't believe, for starters, that the Bounty Hunter is being paid."

"That's foolish," Kobuchi said, meaning Portenda. "A Bounty Hunter *needs* to be paid. Otherwise, why bother calling yourself one? Why would he work for free?"

"I'm not entirely certain," Genma admitted. "Still, the fact remains that he is most likely doing this all *gratis*. *Pro bono*, if you will. The second point is, Jonah Staples is a terribly skilled Alchemist. He could find us if he got close to the tower. The prismatic barrier would be simple for one of his skill to break."

The masked man was referring to an illusory and force wall that was set up around the perimeter of the tower, in order to hide it from plain view. Anyone who got close enough to the force wall would set off mecha sensors that would alert the guard beasts throughout the tower that there were intruders. One by one they would attack the intruders, until they were dead. Only twice had anyone wandered onto the premises, but Genma had spared the second one. It had been a boy of no more than twelve years of age, and he and his friends had been playing a game of kickball in the fields near the barrier. After seeing the manticore, the boy had suggested, rather shakily, that they move their game far, far away.

153

"Sire, how do you know about the boy? What aren't you telling me?"

Genma said nothing, but chuckled low under his breath.

"Leave me now, Kobuchi. Keep an eye on the girl. It will only be another week before everything is in readiness. A few more adjustments on the instruments, and we shall be ready. Oh, and Kobuchi?"

"Yes?"

"You say she's named the pet?" Kobuchi nodded curtly. "Go ahead and have its name engraved on its bowl. I'll let her keep it. I owe her that much."

Kobuchi, confused beyond reason, closed the door behind him as he left. His Master was acting strangely, even more so than the girl upstairs. What could be going through his head?

Genma removed his ivory mask in the darkness, and pulled out a small mirror from one of his coat pockets. He stared at the face looking back at him. "I owe her that much," he said in a voice choked by regret.

* * * *

"That took quite a while," Jonah said as the Simpa came through the door with a stack of folders.

The spear came down, but Portenda caught it with a flick of his wrist, pulling it off of the wall.

He had discovered some disturbing facts while at the police station, and he hadn't reached the last quarter of the files. He set the stack down at the foot of his bed and tossed four folders to Jonah.

"Why do I feel more like a detective right now than a citizen?"

"Because detective work is part of my trade," Portenda snapped as he opened another folder. "Sorry. I just feel like I haven't slept in a long time."

His nap had been like blinking, and it still disturbed him that he couldn't get any rest. "I've given you Kobuchi's files and what I think will interest you the most. Your father's files." There were two thick folders for each, and Jonah opened his father's first.

His entire military profile had been condensed into shorthand on thirty sheets of parchment in each folder. His father, apparently, had been an accomplished and decorated man.

Portenda kept from Jonah the two files that he had read before coming back.

One was a rather short profile listing on a man known as Genma, a profile report taken by a constable in the Golden Empire, also known as the Fiefdom of Lemago. Not much had been written about the man, just that he had been in the area searching for Alchemical ingredients. Some side notes had been made about the man's mangled hands, and his purchase of black leather gloves. Another side note mentioned a strange black cloak that the man wore, which appeared at times to be alive. His registry signature had been copied into the file.

The second file had been lengthy, and told of the man called Allen Staples. An accomplished member of the Tamalarian Alchemists' Alliance, Allen Staples had rediscovered ancient tomes of Focus deep in a set of ruins in the western territories. He had mastered Focus Sites quickly, and became known around the realm as *the* Focus Alchemist. Several of his articles on the practical uses of Alchemy in agriculture and other fields of everyday use filled the file. But one particular item had sent a chill down his spine as he had read it in the police station.

For that reason, he didn't let Jonah see those files. As the night fell upon the city, the Human fell asleep sitting up, his face buried in Kobuchi's records. Portenda gently laid him to sleep.

"I know you now, you bastard," Portenda growled to the room in general. "I know who you are." Portenda went to the window and looked out to the darkened city. The bodies of Allen Staples' family had been discovered months after the explosion at his residence, far from the home. They had been traveling into the Allenians, the reporting officer had guessed. But Allen had never been found among them. And a medical examiner had reported that the family had been killed before the house had gone up in flames.

Using all of these facts, and one other piece of evidence, Portenda had discovered Genma's identity. The last straw had been the signatures.

Allen Staples's and Genma's signatures were essentially the same.

* * * *

The second floor above her own had revealed to Eileen the extent of Genma's power. This floor, the seventeenth of the tower, as the door leading in to the corridors had indicated, was filled with works in progress.

Two huge chambers took up the entire floor, one on the left, and one on the right hand side of a narrow corridor, much like the conversion floor below. In the left chamber, she had discovered half a dozen beasts in cages. All were inactive or incomplete, but she could tell that these creatures would become more of the guard beasts that Genma commanded.

One of the few creatures that was awake and aware appeared to be a freak crossbreed of a Jaft and a Dwarf. The man wasn't just using animal subjects; he was using people in his twisted experiments.

The baleful creature was muttering something to itself, its blue and black flesh contorting as its face twisted with rage. Its right arm, from the shoulder down, appeared to be made of some metallic material, and Eileen realized it was an artificial limb, molded directly into the Alchemical transformation.

She got closer to the cage, but stayed out of reach of the long, foreign arm.

"Kill, me," it said.

Though it pained her to do so, Eileen had thrust her left palm through the bars, pressed it flat against the abomination's forehead, and cast a Raybolt that utterly destroyed the creature.

"May you rest in peace," she whispered to the empty air.

Half an hour later, she was seated at a desk in the opposite chamber, which appeared to contain only one cage, covered in a shroud of crimson fabric. Something beneath c rattled the bars of its cage, but made no other noise.

Eileen tried to ignore it as she poured over the charts and maps that had been left on the desk in the left corner, directly parallel to the door, which she had left open.

Blink napped in her lap as she examined the maps, trying to find a hint, some clue as to where her tower prison was located.

Something in the room over her head had hummed and pulsated the entire time she had been here. She knew she had to be close to the top of the tower. Soon her explorations would become meaningless, unless she could find a way past the manticore on the fourteenth floor.

That's when she came upon something Genma had not meant for her to find: an interior map of the tower.

It was a crude design, more of a sketch work, and she realized that it might not be completely accurate. Still, it was better than nothing.

She scanned the crinkled, yellowing document, then stared in disbelief at the signature of the designer in the bottom right corner of the map.

Impossible, she thought. "That can't be." Then she shrieked as a heavy, leather glove fell to rest on her shoulder.

"Oh, but it is," Genma said. He spun her swivel chair around to make Eileen face him as he tore the ivory mask off of his face. "Now give your uncle Allen a kiss."

A banshee roar blasted from Eileen Staples' lungs, tearing the air itself with a horror more acute than glimpsing the first layer of the Hells.

Genma tapped a nerve in her neck, and Eileen slumped to the floor, unconscious.

Blink stood in a guard stance on her back. The Alchemist put his mask back over his burned countenance, and laughed derisively.

Allen Staples left his niece on the floor of the Edge's chamber to sleep it off.

* * * *

When the sun filtered light in through the chamber windows, Jonah awoke to find himself staring at sheets of information. He took Kobuchi's file off of his face and rubbed his bleary eyes. He had caught glimpses of strange creatures in his dreams, creatures that tore at his flesh and snapped crudely fashioned jaws at his throat.

As he swung his legs over the edge of the bed, he looked down at his rumpled clothes and wondered how much longer he could press on in these conditions. He was not the strongest person in terms of body, heart or mind. He needed a whole day of rest sometime soon, though that didn't seem fair now that he thought about it.

Portenda the Quiet, the Bounty Hunter of fame, sat in the window, looking out.

Jonah stood and also looked out to the city of Traithrock, watching as teams of three and four Dwarves took large shovels and cleaned the main roads of the overnight snowfall. They worked in perfect unison, clearing huge tracks of road in little time, and with little effort. "Sturdy folks, Dwarves," Jonah commented.

Portenda said nothing, just staring out the window. "So, what's on the agenda for the day?" Jonah continued.

Portenda was still taking in the fact that so little information was available on he himself. A long tally of his collected bounties was in his record folder, but little else. It was as though nobody was really interested. Constables had issued a few notes and bulletins warning others in their organizations against interfering with the Simpa's hunts, but aside from this, there was nothing. It was, in a way, depressing.

Jonah waved a hand in front of Portenda's face.

Portenda snatched Jonah's hand, stopping it and looking hard into Jonah's eyes before letting go of his wrist.

"Is something wrong," Jonah asked in a whisper. "Are you still angry with me about yesterday? Because I don't know what happened."

Portenda just shook his head as he looked out the window one more time. Without a word, he strapped his armor on and his weapons, collected his rucksack, and turned to Jonah.

The Human Alchemist, disturbed by Portenda's apparent return to form as Portenda the Quiet, stepped into the bathroom and splashed ice cold water on his face to wake up. After drying his bristly face, which would be in need of a shave soon, he too got his things ready.

The two men exited the room in silence.

The Bounty Hunter rapped on Nareena's door and the Elven girl opened it an inch, bleary eyes trying to come into focus on her companions. "Give me a few minutes," she groaned through a throat still thick with sleep.

Portenda's nostrils flared as he sniffed at the air through the crack her door was ajar. He heard the clink of equipment being packed away, and glass vials slipped into leather notches on a belt.

Portenda detected the scent of herbs and, to his interest, silver.

The rushed movement on the other side of the door pushed air over Nareena's body, breaking over extended arms and a brow that dripped with cold sweat. He could just make out the faint splash of it on the floor.

From early in his career as a Bounty Hunter, Portenda had noticed that the less he spoke, the more powerful his senses became. Today, he had resolved to do little more than observe Jonah and Nareena and try to determine what was really going on between the two of them. The Elven girl had avoided Jonah since the incident the day before, and Portenda knew more than fear of the Human Alchemist kept Nareena at bay. When Jonah had taken the pistol from Portenda's holster, he had immediately inscribed a Focus Site along the barrel, transforming the small firearm into a cannon capable of massive destruction. Portenda had spotted recognition in Nareena's eyes in that moment as she'd peering through the wolf fur. She had seen such acts from Jonah in the past, and she didn't want Jonah to know, he surmised.

The Elf woman opened the door all the way now, and Portenda and Jonah both took a step back. She wore a pair of denim pants much like Jonah's, tattered and worn and frayed at the ankles. She had strapped thick boots on her feet, and under a thick fur coat, she wore a plain, white tank top. Her ample curves were highlighted by the tight clothing, and Jonah had to suppress the urge to groan like a lust-driven idiot.

"What," she asked, looking back and forth at the two of them.

Jonah blushed, and much to his surprise, so did Portenda. The Simpa turned around and stalked slowly away.

"Look, Jonah, about yesterday, I'm sorry I freaked out." Nareena lightly touched his left forearm.

Portenda watched them out of the corner of his eye as he half turned back to them.

"It's just, whatever happened to you back there, it was kind of scary. I've never seen anything like that," she said.

Liar, Portenda thought. He took in the rapid increase in her heart rate, the secretion of the bitter-smelling acid that mixed with her sweat. Not many humanoid creatures knew it, but all humanoid Races had glands in their flesh that produced this acidic fluid. It mixed with sweat when they became nervous or tense, and this fluid, Portenda had noted over the years, was primarily secreted when nervousness or tension were brought on by lying. They hadn't even left the inn, and already one of Portenda's objectives was complete.

"It's all right, Nareena. I don't blame you." Jonah put his hand over Nareena's, kissing the back of it as he let go.

His own heart rate jumped, but Portenda discerned that this was due to his affection for the girl. Blood rushed through the boy's vessels, a good deal of it southward.

The Alchemists followed Portenda to the check in desk, where the innkeeper informed the Bounty Hunter that Morek Rockmight wanted to speak with him.

Portenda nodded wordlessly, and exited the building, Jonah and Nareena in tow.

"He hasn't said a word all morning," Portenda heard Jonah whisper in Nareena's ear. There was a hint of concern in the Human's tone, but Portenda noted more fear than concern in his voice.

The Bounty Hunter mentally chided himself for being this way with the Human and the Elf girl, but he had to do it, just for today. *Tomorrow,* he resolved, *I'll make up for it.*

"Well, he is called 'the Quiet' Jonah," Nareena said. "Maybe he already used his month's ration of speech."

Portenda heard Jonah's abdominal muscles clench as he held down a chuckle. Despite the caustic nature of the joke, Portenda had to mentally laugh as well. This did seem silly, after all. He had company. He should be taking advantage of the rare situation.

A Hunter and his Prey

The trio approached Morek Rockmight's home slowly, and Portenda listened in once again on Nareena. "Hey, if we find an inn to stay at again tonight or go back to that one, I'll make it up to you for last night," she whispered.

Portenda cursed his heightened hearing for a moment as he held a hand up for the two of them to stop.

"Is something wrong, Portenda?" Jonah asked.

The Bounty Hunter shook his head, and stalked up to the porch of Morek Rockmight's abode. He knocked on the door twice, and a minute later, the Dwarven Boxer opened the door.

The years had aged him more than Portenda had realized. He had not been to see Morek for ten years, since he had taken a contract to find his wayward son. Morek's long beard was now completely covered with gray, and his arms had shrunk a little. His muscles had not been needed much in the twenty years since the War of Vandross. His dark blue button shirt bulged, though, as he retained a very well kept frame.

"Portenda the Quiet." Morek smiled through his thick beard and mustache. "I just wanted a minute of your time. Can we talk?"

Portenda said nothing, but made a small hand signal, and Morek nodded. "I understand. Good thing I know sign language. Please, sit." He indicated a set of stone chairs a few feet away on his porch.

The Simpa and Dwarf sat down across from one another, and Morek's attendant brought him a cuppa.

"Thanks Sam," he said to the Gnome attendant, who offered Portenda one as well.

The Bounty Hunter took it and drained the cup's contents greedily. He hadn't slept much, again, and needed the extra boost.

'What's on your mind?' he signed to Morek.

He heard Nareena ask Jonah what he was doing, but the boy just shrugged his shoulders.

"There's been a lot of talk from our scouts. Seems one of them saw the boy shoot you with that firearm of yours." Morek took a slow sip of his cuppa as Sam brought Portenda a second. Without preamble he continued down off of the porch steps and offered cups to Nareena and Jonah as well, the two of them admiring the surrounding landscape of the city.

Portenda drained half of it, and set the cup and saucer down on the table. He admired the Dwarves' ability to shape stone through a force of will unique to their Race. It was much like the Elves' ability to shape wood. The mugs they were currently drinking out of were made of thinly formed rock, painted with a careful hand in shades of brown and green.

'I'm investigating the boy's powers and the disappearance of his sister,' he signed rapidly. Morek nodded and sipped his drink.

"Oh, so nothing to worry about, then," he said, signing just out of the Alchemists' sight. 'I don't trust the girl,' he signed.

'I've looked into her. She's no threat,' Portenda signed. Morek nodded. 'Why bring it up?'

"Well, I mention the incident because our miners found something interesting the other day." Morek stood and pulled down his shirt. "There was a chamber down in the ground, a shelter of some sort. We found a few mecha weapons, big stuff," he said. "Thought you might be interested."

Portenda raised an eyebrow, and signed. 'That'll have to wait.'

"We brought a couple of them up, actually," Morek said with a wide smile. "Sam, bring the long one out."

The Gnome attendant disappeared into the house for a few minutes while Portenda waited. He returned bearing a huge, metal cylinder with a wood stock handle.

Portenda recognized it immediately for what it was: a shotgun. "What do you think?"

'Not really my style,' Portenda signed. 'It's called a shotgun. Powerful in close, but no good at range.'

"Roit, roit. Sam, get the other long one, you know, with the little doodad on top," Morek said.

The Gnome heaved an impatient sigh as he stalked back inside. He returned a minute later with a similar weapon, single-barreled, with a long, rectangular tube atop the main barrel.

Portenda viewed the weapon, and found that he hadn't seen or read anything about it. But he did know what the tube atop the barrel was. It was a sort of looking glass for magnified aiming. He instinctively liked it.

'How much,' he signed.

"Consider it payment due," Morek said, and Sam handed the rifle to Portenda.

The Bounty Hunter stood and hefted the weapon. *Heavy*, he thought, *but not too heavy*. He turned out to the street, and aimed the weapon to the sky, looking through the spyglass. A bird crossed his field of vision, already enhanced by both his strange innate power, and the scope. He could make out every speck of water and sweat on the bird's body, the tension of its back muscles as it flapped its wings. When he pulled the rifle down, he found that he could barely make out the dot of the animal in the sky. He had handled rifles before, but none as large and clearly powerful as this, and certainly none with such a magnificent sight on it.

'Reminds me of the long sniper bows,' he signed with one hand. 'I'll call it a sniper rifle.' Using the leather strap as a sling, he strapped the weapon over his shoulder and across his back, letting it hang over his rucksack for easy access. 'Was there anything else you needed?' he asked with his hands.

"That's all for now. But I'll send for you if something else comes up," Morek said as he shuffled slowly towards his front door. "Oh, and Portenda?"

The Simpa turned around halfway down the steps fronting his home.

"Take care now," the Dwarven Boxer said with a serene smile.

A Hunter and his Prey

The Bounty Hunter approached the two Alchemists, drew out a pad of paper and a pen from one of his vest pockets, and scribbled something hastily. He showed his message to them, and Jonah and Nareena glared at one another for a moment.

"Are you sure? I mean, look at what happened last time," Jonah said.

Portenda scribbled furiously on the pad once more. "Okay, okay, we'll do it. You're right. I did say that the last Site was disturbed. We should do it someplace inside, though, to make certain nobody tramples it."

"Agreed," said Nareena. "Maybe the library would do."

"I'm not so certain I trust libraries anymore," Jonah said as he scrunched up his face. "I mean, that mercenary sort of ruined them for me."

"Yeah, well, I'm the one who almost got split in half, if you recall," Nareena chided him. "Besides, I think it's the only building that isn't full of Dwarves or Jafts. Let's go."

Jonah turned around and followed, with Portenda taking up the rear.

The trio walked through the crisp mountain air of the city, careful to avoid drawing unwanted attention. The miners were all heading to the shafts to work, and several of the smiths had started their labors for the day.

Near the eastern edge of town they halted before the tall brick structure of the library. Portenda listened for voices through the walls but heard nothing save for the occasional turning of pages. Not many: two or three, he thought. From the scent of the cheap aftershave, he guessed that they were Humans come through on study.

Nareena once again took the lead, and the trio entered the massive main chamber of the library.

A building consisting of one main library, a records room, and a basement filled with governmentally protected reference manuals, the library of Traithrock was not often frequented by the townsfolk. As he had predicted, Portenda saw a pair of Humans, most likely mages of some sort, scanning through tomes of black, leather-bound pages. They paid the trio no heed.

The librarian herself, a Jaft woman with a wool dress worn under an open-fronted fur coat, eyeballed them suspiciously over the top of her book. Jaft females, unlike their male counterparts, were able to grow shoulder-length hair on their heads, and did not emanate the powerful natural odor. This was due, it was theorized, to their much less powerful regenerative capabilities, as well as their slightly less muscular frames.

"Can I help you find something," she muttered over her book.

"No, actually, we need to use some floor space," Jonah said with his most winning smile. The Jaft woman was thoroughly unimpressed, and waved a hand dismissively at them.

"Do what you like, as long as you don't damage anything." She returned to her book.

Jonah cringed as he viewed the title of the book, *How to Mate With Humans, a Guide to Jaft-Human Relations*. He took out one of his last remaining sticks of chalk, and stepped forward, asking Portenda to move the chairs in his way.

As the Bounty Hunter did so, he looked around at the library; it was solid, sturdy, and there were chests with large padlocks on them scattered along the walls of the main chamber. Undoubtedly a large array of weapons was held in them, and this structure was likely a fall back point for defending the city from intruders.

Portenda took a brief look around the shelves of fiction held in the standing racks a little ways away from Jonah and Nareena. The two were working in perfect unison.

With nothing to do, Portenda examined the novels before him: a collection of mystery novels, mostly written by Gnomes and Humans.

After three minutes of searching, he found the one he had been looking for. *The Secret of Jauxis*, written by James Akado. He slid the book from its place, approached the librarian, and set ten gold pieces on the counter.

"Buying it outright, are you," the Jaft woman asked.

Portenda nodded.

"That's way more than it's worth, you know?"

Portenda said nothing, but simply clutched the book under his right arm.

"Have it your way," the woman said, taking the money off the counter and slipping it into a drawer in the wooden desk.

Portenda moved over toward the Alchemists as the flash of light revealed a white, plain door.

Jonah stepped through, then Nareena, and finally, Portenda himself.

For a moment, he lost himself in that corridor of darkness before flying out the other side onto a cobblestone street, mere inches from Jonah's retreating foot.

"Well we're here," Jonah said as he dusted himself off. The surrounding townsfolk didn't react in the slightest to their abrupt appearance in the middle of one of their city streets. Portenda stood and glanced around. They had arrived where they should have the day before, near the center of the city that all of Tamalaria referred to as the 'Magical Capital'.

"Welcome," said a friendly voice. An Elven Aquamancer dressed in light chain mail approached them with his hand thrust forward. "To Palen, city of magic."

Chapter Nine
Laws

"You don't find it strange that we just sort of popped out of nowhere?" Nareena asked the city guard.

The Elf man chuckled heartily and shook his head. "That sort of thing is standard practice around here, ma'am."

"You didn't spend much time here, did you," Jonah asked with a grin to complement the one that the guard wore.

"No, to tell the truth I didn't," she said curtly. "It was too strange for my liking, and I think I remember why," she said as a nearby toad turned suddenly into a green dog. "Too much magic, too much experimentation. I could turn into a three-eyed cat if I step in the wrong building."

Jonah was delighted. Palen was a city of magic users and scientists of all sorts, a city that relied entirely on wits and intellect, rather than brute force and combative skill. It was a city that did not just bend the rules and laws of reality: it literally shattered them, picked up the broken pieces, and said, 'well now, what shall we do with this mess today?'

A barrier made of various magics around the city allowed for all forms of life and energy to be plainly visible, or at least discernable by one sense or another. Spirit creatures stalked through the broad light of day, conversing with mortal men and women as though they had been neighbors for a very long time without realizing it. Whereas the rest of Tamalaria experienced itself on a single plane of existence, Palen did so on multiple levels within its own reality.

"Is that a specter." Nareena's voice quavered as a light yellow aura, with the head of an old man, approached the trio.

"Yes, it is," the guard said, and turned to greet the being. "Morning, Mr. Tones. How are you this fine day?"

"Bugger all and toffee for all," the disembodied head howled as it floated in front of the guard.

The Elven Aquamancer threw up his hands and waved them around in a sporadic and random fashion. Portenda screwed his eyes up, and saw that the specter had grabbed hold of the guard's wrists with its yellowish spirit, and was throwing the man's hands around. "Coffee beans and garden Gnomes fer ketchup dunking whizzakaloos," the specter grumbled.

"This doesn't make any sense," Nareena stammered, watching this obscene display unfold. "I thought specters inhabited another plane of existence? How can we see anything more than its head?"

"Because specters still exist in our reality," Jonah explained, trying to take a step closer to the spirit creature. "You see, theoretically, every dimension of being sits one atop another, and a whole collection of these is referred to as a single reality," Jonah said, slowly pulling an instrument out of his rucksack. "Also referred to by mages as a 'Realm', or by Alchemy as an 'Axis'. The barrier around the city of Palen allows all levels of being in a single reality, our reality, to be discernable by some sensory input or other."

"Okay," Nareena said slowly, still confused as all Hells. "So, can you shorten that up?"

Jonah took a small bit of floating ectoplasm and placed in one of his plastic tubes, using a stopper to close the vial before the spectral essence escaped. "Simply put, everything in our reality can be seen in this city, in some way." Jonah's smile filled with excitement. The possibilities for research in Palen were almost limitless, and he felt like a child in a candy shop.

Portenda, meanwhile, was being assailed by his combined, heightened senses. He could see, smell, hear, feel, and taste things that he never had in any other place. He might have to start speaking to bring down the sensory havoc. His head pounded, and the information he took in threatened to overload his body. But he set his teeth, and calmed himself. Still, his hands shook as he centered himself.

"Pickles and peanut butter," the specter said as it released the guard and floated away down the street.

"What've you got there?" the guard asked as Jonah held up the plastic tube with a bit of the specter's body in it.

"Ectoplasm," he whispered in a voice hushed with awe. "No telling what sort of uses I can put this stuff to." He looked at the Bounty Hunter as he regained his composure. "Are you all right, Portenda?"

The Bounty Hunter nodded gruffly, and moved slowly away. Jonah and Nareena followed immediately after.

"Enjoy your stay," the guard called after them.

Portenda followed his instincts to a low, long building made entirely of oak and pine.

Jonah glanced at the sign, and identified it as a tavern. He ducked his head under Portenda's arm, and helped the Bounty Hunter inside, then helped Portenda to a seat at a round table in the far back corner, directly opposite the door.

He and Nareena looked around them as Portenda slapped himself hard in the left cheek. There were dozens of other patrons in the tavern.

A Human dressed in a dragon-scale vest and pants tended bar, and Jonah walked up to the counter, keeping a few feet away from the creature to his right. It was a strange humanoid monster, with gunmetal gray flesh, sharp, jagged spikes protruding from all over its body. Its eyes, Jonah saw as it turned toward him, were the color of seaweed: a mixture of yellow and green.

"The fuck are you staring at, meatbag," it growled at him.

He looked hastily away, not knowing what to make of the strange being. He had heard of them only once in his travels. Rendermen, they were called, monsters that usually contained little intelligence beyond an animal level. Relentless murderers, such creatures were often used as guard beasts by wicked sorcerers and demon-lords. This one, however, sat in a tavern, in a city brimming with magic, sipping a beer and being generally hostile and belligerent.

Still, Jonah thought in the quiet, panicked recesses of his mind, *it's smart enough not to attack anyone in broad daylight.*

A Hunter and his Prey

"What can I get you?" The bartender leaned with one arm on the counter.

The Human Alchemist looked up at the gruff tavern proprietor, and asked him for a simple glass of water—make that three of them.

The bartender huffed and handed him three glasses of dark, murky water.

Jonah thanked him, and returned to the table where Portenda sat next to Nareena, staring at nothing.

"What's with him?"

The Elven woman just shrugged her shoulders.

Unbeknownst to them, Portenda was staring at the faint, ghostly outline of a humanoid woman, who appeared to him to be floating around the tavern unnoticed. He heard her humming a child's song, the sort used to put young children to sleep at night. His mind was lulled now, as he sat and smiled gently at the apparition, who turned now to face him.

"You can see me, and hear me, can't you," the ghost asked.

Portenda nodded. Nobody else in the tavern had any clue what was going on between man and spirit, he thought.

"Your heart is heavy, and you are very tired. You've been straining yourself a great deal," the spirit said, like an echo on the wind.

Portenda felt his whole body relax, and he jumped when the bartender shouted in his direction.

"Leave him alone, ma," the barkeep yelled at the apparition.

Portenda's eyes narrowed, and he snapped out of his trance.

The barkeep glared at the spirit with hate in his eyes. "No good can come of it, and you know it."

Jonah and Nareena turned their heads to look at the Human, and then back at the blank space where the ghost fluttered.

They looked to Portenda, who said nothing, but had set his jaw in a hard line. He had failed to realize that the spirit creature was trying to lull him to sleep, so that it could feed off of his subconscious thoughts. He had known that such spirits could use psychological attacks like this, but had never before encountered one. He was lucky that the spirit was apparently related to the bartender.

"Stay out of this, Henry," the spirit rasped at the Human, her white, flowing locks whipping around in the air.

Portenda stood and growled deep in his throat.

The spirit turned to face him, and Portenda saw the rotted, maggot-covered face of its true form.

"Ah, so you realize now," it said.

To Jonah and Nareena's eyes, the creature came into focus.

Several customers took their drinks and exited the tavern: apparently this was an everyday event.

Jonah looked at the wall behind him. 'Warning', a notice there read. 'The proprietor of this tavern is not liable for any accidents, including injury or death, that occur on these premises. Thank you.'

"Um, Nareena," he stammered, and the Elf girl looked at the sheet as Jonah pulled it down and handed it to her.

"Sorry sirs, ma'am," the bartender said as he put up a magical barrier around himself. "But ma needs to feed every now and then, and this was her bar. I hope you don't hold a grudge."

"Oh, of course not, none whatsoever." Jonah's voice dripped with sarcasm.

The spirit let out an unearthly cry of malice, and the entire building shook.

Jonah tried to move, as did Nareena, but both found themselves rooted in place.

Portenda slid his hand to his spear, pulling it off of his back with one hand. He waved his other hand towards himself, as if to say to the spirit, come on.

The spirit lunged at him, and Portenda rolled forward, just skirting the bottom of its ghostly dress. His body went numb for a moment, having made direct contact with a spirit creature from a far removed plane of being. He spun around, but only in time to be thrown across the building by a blast of semi-transparent, blue force hurled from the spirit's mouth.

With another air-ripping shriek, the creature flew at him, as Portenda tried to pry his jumbled limbs and body from the wreckage of the table he had landed on.

A ghastly claw raked his chest, tearing easily through the leather armor, ripping fresh wounds in his chest.

Portenda used the momentum of the blow to roll backward, and stand upright. *Screw it*, he thought. He decided to use the one weapon he had against such a spirit. Planting his feet in a wide stance, he loosed a roar of primal, animal rage.

The noise from the core of his being rang out through the air with the mixed sound of a lion's roar, and a tiger's howl. His mixed blood boiled through his body, and he launched his spear at the stunned spirit's heart.

Jonah saw the astral energy released from Portenda's jaws as he had unleashed his howl of rage, and observed that it made the spirit momentarily solid. As the spear landed on its mark, blue fluid sprayed from the hole that it tore in the spirit creature's semi-corporeal body.

The creature flailed and gibbered as it sank to the floor, the spear landing several yards away. A moment later, it ceased to move, and vanished in a cloud of smoke.

The bartender, Nareena, and Jonah all stood motionless as Portenda grasped his spear and put it back in its sheath.

He decided that he could remain silent no longer, or his stay in this city would eventually result in more of these confrontations. "What," he said aloud, breaking the spell on the three other occupants of the tavern. "You've never seen a mortal slay a ghost?"

* * * *

An untold number of miles away from the scene playing out in Palen, Eileen Staples shuddered in horror. She had been carried back to her sleeping chamber, presumably by Genma who, as she had discovered, was actually Allen Staples. Her own flesh and blood was her abductor, her captor, her villain.

Uncle Allen was an Alchemist renowned throughout the realm as the brightest scientific mind to appear in years. Eileen's family had lost touch with Allen, and hadn't been told why by any of the authorities in the region of their home. All they knew was that their family home had burned to the ground, but that nobody had been inside.

Eileen had assumed that they had simply moved to another remote location, even further out east than the Allenian Hills. Perhaps near Ja-Wen, she had thought. After all, that was where Jonah had gone. She had assumed that he was heading out to do more training with Allen in the arts of Alchemy, but now, she realized, Jonah had probably never seen Allen.

Perhaps, she thought, Allen's family had been killed. Allen, as Genma, had told her that his family had been slain by a pack of Khan in the Allenians, on their way to the free trade town that the tiger men and were-lions had allowed the other Races to settle. Anyone not traveling on the trade route were open game to the vicious Khan warriors that roamed the lands. Those fortunate to encounter a Simpa patrol were usually escorted, bound and gagged but alive, back to the trade route. They would be guarded by the Simpa who escorted them until someone else came down the road, at which point, the were-lions would simply lumber away.

Eileen tried to sit up, but found that she was dizzy and light-headed, and could hardly do more than wobble around on her feet. Something welled up in the back of her head, and when she brushed her hand against the back of her head, she felt the lump that had formed when she passed out back in the lab.

Blink rubbed against her legs as she regained some of her balance, and she bent down and scooped up the little creature from the floor.

"Hey there, little guy," she cooed, stroking his furry head. In a way, he looked a lot like the manticore guarding the floor below.

"I think I may know a way to get us out of here," she whispered to him.

The creature's head snapped to look her in the eyes. Its face was wide with hope, and she knew for certain that while Blink could not communicate back with her, he understood every word she said. "But we're going to have to move quickly, so I'll be carrying you, all right?" Blink nodded and scrambled up her arm to her shoulder, carefully planting his claws into her clothes, and not her skin.

Eileen, while shocked and afraid beyond compare, still clung to the hope that she could get out of this damned tower. If Genma had spoken the truth, there was still close to a week before he would transform her body into a duplicate of his late wife, Eileen's aunt. The mental image of her aunt came into her mind's eye, and Eileen considered just how much alike they looked, though they had only been related through marriage to Allen. There wouldn't have to be a whole lot of alteration involved when the process was started, and Eileen suddenly feared that perhaps a week wouldn't be required for whatever calculations Allen needed.

Genma, she thought vehemently, reminding herself that Allen Staples would never become such a creature. "Uncle Allen is dead," she whispered aloud. "He's dead, and in his place is a madman."

She had regained her equilibrium, and a measure of her courage as well. Somewhere in her sleep, she had discovered the way in which she could escape the clutches of the Alchemist who was master of the tower.

Sprinting to the stairwell, she raced upward, her sandals pounding down hard on the concrete steps as she passed.

Seven stories she climbed, noting that she had not looked in on any floor above the eighteenth. If this plan of hers didn't work, she wouldn't have another chance to see, or to do much of anything for that matter. If she failed, she'd be dead. After climbing all of those stairs, she found herself standing in a narrow, short passage that ended in a solid steel door. She turned the long handle and pulled, but the door wouldn't budge.

Keeping the handle turned, she hauled back with all of her meager strength and weight, but still the door didn't move.

Sweat ran down her forehead as she began to sob. "No," she moaned. "No, no, no! I've got to get out of here."

When she stopped, her hand still on the handle, Blink hopped down from her shoulder, and pushed the door easily open. Eileen felt her face flush as she put her hands on her hips and smiled with her eyes closed. "Idiot," she murmured to herself.

Seconds later she found herself at the top of the tower, outside. Overhead, thick, gray smog blocked out the natural sunlight. Yet, as she approached one of the battlements atop the tower, she saw that, perhaps a mile away in every direction, the sun beamed down gloriously on the lands of Tamalaria.

Risking a glance down to the ground, she saw that she was just over two hundred feet above the ground. She hoped in her heart of hearts that this would work.

Eileen scrambled to the lip of the tower, and concentrated all of her thoughts on a single spell at her disposal, a spell that she had thought was useless—until now. The spell was called Soft Descent, and allowed an object or person to fall from any height slowly and safely, as though they had gliding wings.

She pulled from herself the courage and reserves of manna that the spell required, and cast it on herself, scooping up Blink as soon as the swirls of blue energy wrapped around her. She cradled the creature in her arms, and threw herself forward.

She praised the gods as she slowly descended through the air, her hair flowing up over her head. "I did it, I did it! We're going to be okay, little guy."

Blink emitted a lilting, frog-like croak as he bobbed his head back and forth. Freedom was a concept that Eileen knew and loved, and she knew that Blink would be simply ecstatic.

A Hunter and his Prey

For a long time, she floated down through the air. After a full ten minutes, she saw that she was maybe twenty feet above the ground. At this point, she could safely land and take off.

Her heart full of hope, and her mind racing as she tried to decide which direction to head off in, Eileen never saw the guard beasts or the Kobold easily stalking up to where her feet would touch the ground.

As she landed, stumbling slightly, Eileen felt a rush of magical force slam into her back and toss her to the ground a dozen yards away. Screaming more from fright than pain, she landed in a heap, glaring at Kobuchi and a pair of slavering beasts that stood to either side of the Kobold.

"Impudent fool," Kobuchi growled as he held a single hand out toward her. "Did you really think you could escape? Did you not think the Master was prepared for you to try such a stunt? This tower allows us to see your every move, to record your every action! We knew you were a Q Mage before you even arrived here with the Master! Now, stand up." He kept his hand leveled at her chest.

Eileen had her left palm flat and open, facing Kobuchi. She prepared another spell and launched it at the Kobold with a howl of fury.

Kobuchi flicked his wrist skyward, and the manna of the spell was deflected over his shoulder towards the tower.

Eileen passed out as the first guard beast slammed into her from her right hand side, and did not see the dripping jaws of the monstrosity.

"Hold, hold." Kobuchi patted the beast on its square-shaped head. He hauled Eileen up and tossed her over the beast's shoulder, and looked around for the tiny creature that Eileen had been carrying.

It was nowhere to be seen, but Kobuchi shrugged his shoulders, not surprised in the least. It was free now to be slaughtered by some other monster or wanderer, so the Kobold servant cared little about what happened to it.

As Eileen Staples hung over the back of the beast, barely clinging to consciousness, she thought to herself, *good boy. Find him, Blink.*

She had realized that she might fail to escape, and had given Blink very specific instructions, whispered rapidly as they had descended.

The Alchemical creature, already nearly a mile away, looked back over its shoulder and whimpered like a lost puppy. Still, this was what his owner had wanted. Blink set off into the distance, hoping to find the boy who looked like his new friend, but had the powers of his creator.

* * * *

"Are you sure you're all right now," Jonah asked Portenda as the trio sat around a small table in a diner in Palen's famous dining district.

"I assure you, I'm fine," the Bounty Hunter replied, relieved that his heightened senses were returning to a normal Simpa's level.

The spirit creatures that had haunted his vision had faded from his sight, and now he could only sense their presence instead of knowing where they were. "It's just been a bad day. There's somebody we should speak with here.

He's an old business contact of mine, back from my early years as a Bounty Hunter. Maybe he can give us some insight."

The Alchemists nodded, and followed behind Portenda.

"But not before we get something to eat," he concluded.

"Good, because I'm starving," Jonah said. Perhaps things were returning to normal.

As the trio stepped up onto the outdoor patio of a restaurant dubbed 'The Shining Knight,' Portenda stood stiffly before the saloon-style doors.

"Jonah, could Nareena and I have a word out here? Get us a table for three, I'm paying."

Jonah eyeballed his Simpa friend with suspicion, but shrugged his shoulders and entered.

If Portenda didn't want him to hear something, there were very few ways for the Human Alchemist to force it out of him. He walked inside, and Nareena shifted uneasily on her feet as she crossed her arms defiantly.

"What do you want with me," she asked rather nervously.

Portenda took one step toward her, and shadows concentrated around his golden-furred countenance, his eyes like storm clouds that threatened to streak lightning into her body.

"You will tell me the truth," Portenda whispered as he put one heavy hand on her right shoulder.

The Elven girl felt as though her body could be crushed by that single touch, like Portenda had powers and strength she couldn't possibly grasp. And she felt compelled to give him whatever information he wanted. This was not some sort of magical or psychic attack on the part of the Bounty Hunter: he simply radiated an aura of 'lie to me and die'.

"You have seen Jonah transform before, like he did back in the mountains, haven't you?"

Nareena tried to lick her lips, but no moisture would come. Instead, she just nodded.

"Genma gave him a command through the mirror, and he obeyed so fast that even I couldn't react in time. Do you know if he ever underwent any sort of military experiments?"

"No," Nareena said, and she hung her head in despair. "But I know who brainwashed him."

Portenda glanced at the restaurant and mentally timed their conversation. Two and a half minutes thus far, he thought. She'll have to make this quick or Jonah's going to get suspicious.

"Who, and when?"

"Well," Nareena stammered, seemingly unwilling or unable to bring herself to betray Jonah's trust. "It was about four years back, when he had just left home. He and I traveled together out of Desanadron, but we separated along the road because we were rivals. We were constantly trying to one-up each other, so instead of staying away, I followed him for about a week. He would hitch rides from caravans and passers-by, so I would use speed-enhancement potions to keep up."

Three minutes, Portenda thought, checking the doorway once more. *Hurry it up, girl, get to the point.*

"After about a week and a half, this guy showed up along the side of the main trade road, and he knocked Jonah out. He had a little Kobold guy with him, and they just took him away. Before they left, I heard the big one say something to the Kobold that made my blood run cold."

"What was it?" Portenda narrowed his eyes at the Elf girl.

Though she was flushed and feeling duress, from her physical signs, she was also telling the truth. He could tell that much from what he could see in her brilliant, green eyes.

"He said, 'It's okay, friend. This one is family. He'll make a great test subject for my later needs.' Oh gods, Portenda, I've wanted to tell him, but he lost two weeks of his memory after it all happened, and I didn't see him again until I got here, and I only stayed a couple of days then. I couldn't be near him, because, well..."

"Because you abandoned him to his fate, when you could have acted on his behalf," Portenda growled, turning and stalking away from the Elven Alchemist and into the restaurant.

He never saw the tears of remorse that she shed before calming herself and joining the two men in their trio.

* * * *

Genma sat in front of another mirror in the lower levels of his tower, trying to contact another one of his agents. He had lost track of Jonah and his friends after they had left Traithrock, because they had left a note with the librarian woman asking her to erase the Focus Site upon the disappearance of the white door. Without a way to contact the boy, he couldn't issue any commands to him.

During Eileen's escape attempt, one of the guard beasts had caused some internal damage to the girl. She would have to heal naturally in order to preserve the readings he had already stored in the machine in the sub-basement level. He couldn't afford to give her any potions in his stock, and this all meant yet more delays. Not that it mattered, he thought with a grin. The boy, the Elf and the Bounty Hunter would never reach him. They would never find him, for that matter.

There was a sharp report on the chamber door, and, being that this room was lit with several torches, he put his mask back on before calling for Kobuchi to enter.

The Kobold looked like he hadn't slept in a while, his eyes puffy and his body frame wobbling slightly.

"Report," Genma said as he spun to face his assistant.

"I found very little on the girl Nareena, other than that her family name is Finch, and she has no known relatives. Her mother died in an Orc raid on the village of Festingwood seventeen years ago, and her father died back in the War of Vandross, in the field of battle. She's been alone ever since, looking for any blood relatives she may have. But according to the records, her bloodline dies out with her, sir."

"Very good work, Kobuchi," Genma said, taking a couple of lazy steps forward. "And the Bounty Hunter?"

"Well, Master," Kobuchi said, flopping down in one of the comfortable recliners in the room, into which he sank like a rock in the ocean. "There isn't much information available on him, either. I learned of one living relative, but according to our contact in the Allenians, the two of them would rather see each other dead than help one another."

"Damnation," Genma grumbled, having lost the chance for an advantage over the trio. If they had family that he could hold captive, in order to buy more time, he could complete the necessary arrangements without pause. Given enough time, despite his earlier mental boasts, the Simpa would find his way to the tower. In all probability, the guard beasts would be little more than a joke for him. Getting in touch with Jonah was now the only forward defense or offense he had against the Bounty Hunter. "So much for brotherly love," Genma groaned.

"They're not brothers, sire," Kobuchi said, catching Genma's attention once more. "It's his father."

Genma's mind reeled; he had been told that the relationship between a Simpa youth and his father was unbreakable, that they were loyal to one another in ways that the other Races could only hope to be. Yet, this Bounty Hunter, about whom he had so little information, was at odds with his own flesh and blood? How could that be?

Genma smiled gleefully. Perhaps he could use this to his advantage after all.

"Did you get the man's name? The father, I mean."

"Telroke, sire," Kobuchi said. "He is the under-leader of a clan in the Allenians. Shall I contact him?"

"Yes, immediately. Tell him I'd like to hire him for certain, ah, services." Malice dripped from Genma's voice. "I have someone else to speak to right now. You have a Teleportation spell handy?"

Kobuchi nodded, though he didn't look like he was in any shape to carry out the order right away.

"Belay that, Kobuchi. Do it after you've had some rest."

Kobuchi actually smiled for the first time in a long time.

"Oh, and before you pass out in my chair?"

"Yes, sire?"

"Did you find any trace of the animal? What did she call it again?"

"Blink, sire," Kobuchi said, his voice already trailing away. "We found nothing. It made it out of the barrier without injury."

Genma tried to think of a proper course of action, but realized that the little scamp was helpless now, alone and unaided in the wide realm of Tamalaria. He needn't concern himself with it any longer.

A Hunter and his Prey

"Never mind it," he said to the now unconscious Kobuchi. Genma turned to the mirror, and tried once again to contact one of his associates. The mirror shimmered for a moment, and then a thin, almost equine face filled the mirror's surface.

Genma now looked at a Sidalis, one of the mutants of the lands.

Though Genma had kept him on the payroll for a rather long time now, he rarely called on his services. Now, however, they would be most useful. "Good afternoon, Felix. Do you have a few minutes to chat?"

* * * *

Portenda ate his meal in studied silence, trying to think of a way of telling the two of them what he intended to do without scaring the Hells out of them. It was an ancient ritual, one he had learned of from the various ruins he had explored in his travels, and it would summon a being that few people ever wanted to see.

Everyone eventually did, but only select handfuls were ever happy about it.

Still, Portenda mused as he sucked on a crab leg, it was the best way to get the information he needed, and it was well within the laws of the cosmos.

As creatures of law, most Simpa would find what he was about to propose doing was a violation of the natural order of the universe. Yet, Portenda would reason, if it weren't within the realm of order, the ritual would not have existed, or be written down.

Nobody had ever suffered unduly after the ritual was performed, and so, he thought, that could be seen as evidence that the ritual itself was not a breach of law, natural or man-made.

Still, broaching the subject with a pair of Alchemists, whose entire field of research and abilities revolved around scientific theory, data, and mathematical laws, might prove difficult. He knit his brow as he concentrated on figuring out how to ease them into the idea.

Jonah was presently stuffing his face with more pasta than the Simpa knew he could eat, and Nareena was not exactly eating in a lady-like fashion either. She was tearing into her chicken meat and potatoes with a ravenous hunger suited to jackals, vultures, and other such carrion-feeders.

"Something's on your mind," Jonah finally said between mouthfuls.

The entire restaurant was packed now, with the typical dinner hour having arrived. Most of the customers were guards either coming off of duty, or about to go on, but there was also a healthy body of mage students and scientists taking a break from their labs and workshops.

"You've been careful to keep food in your mouth since you sat down," Jonah said, taking a sip of his ale. The stuff they served in Palen was powerful, and the Human Alchemist found that if he tried to swig it, he'd most likely ralph up his meal.

"You're right." Portenda swallowed his crabmeat. "There's a very old ritual I would like to perform. It summons someone very, well, knowledgeable, to say the least."

"So what's the problem?" Nareena asked politely. "Elves and Dwarves use ancestor-summoning rites to speak with their ancestors, so what's the big deal? We can handle that." She also sipped at her drink, a finely aged Elven wine.

Portenda took a whiff of it, and thought darkly, I shouldn't have offered to pay the tab. This isn't going to be cheap.

"Well, this isn't exactly an ancestor I will be summoning, and I'm going to need both of your help. The ritual requires at least three people, so it's a good thing you're along for the ride, Nareena." He had to play this one cool.

"So, what's the name of this ritual," Jonah asked after finishing yet another plate of pasta.

Portenda took a deep, calming breath.

"The Rite of the Honorable Guest."

Both Alchemists dropped their drinks to the floor, the glasses shattering.

"Hey, you're gonna pay for those, roit?" the Dwarven barkeep shouted.

Portenda wondered if every town had a Dwarven barkeep who kept tabs on such things as customers' glasses. He waved and nodded to the barkeep, who had a waitress bring the pair two more drinks.

"You've heard of it, I take it."

"Heard of it? We've heard of it, read of it, and I can tell you plainly, I won't have any part of it," Nareena almost screamed.

"So you'll be paying for your meal, your drinks, and your glass on your own, then," Portenda asked her coldly.

A frost giant could have frozen to death from his tone.

Nareena was about to protest that she would, when the bill was slipped onto their table. She snatched it up, and her eyes bulged out.

She passed it on to Jonah, who had a similar reaction, and Portenda smiled broadly, exposing his gleaming teeth.

"This is blackmail." Nareena shuddered at the Bounty Hunter, who shrugged his shoulders.

"I prefer to think of it as staying one move ahead of the game. When we're done here, we'll be hitting up a hotel, where we'll perform the ritual. I've always wanted to meet him, you know." Portenda's voice slowly regained its calm, neutral level. "I've sent a lot of business his way."

"Yes, well, let's hope he doesn't put us next on his list," Jonah said hurriedly. "I don't think it would be polite, after all, to interrupt the Grim Reaper in the middle of his day." *

* * * *

Death sat in silence in his study, trying to figure out where he had gone wrong. He'd had the little Gnome Pickpocket in his sights on so many occasions, and every time a new life timer would appear in his hands, the sand slowly draining once again into the bottom bulb. Lee Toren had escaped his end on far too many occasions, and the Honorable Guest, as the Gods and Goddesses called him, was certain that he was making some sort of snafu.

HOW DOES HE DO IT, he asked the study at large. There was nobody to keep him company, of course. There never had been, nor would he ever allow himself such a privilege. It would interfere with his duties, and he wouldn't have that. He was Death over many different realities, but not all, and he was limited to this one world at the moment. Still, the amount of time he had spent on one particular Lee Toren was starting to give him a headache. He pondered the idea of getting help from one of his alternate selves. THERE'S THAT ONE THAT RESIDES OVER SOME SORT OF FLAT WORLD, he mused. FLOATS AROUND ON THE BACK OF A TURTLE OR SOMETHING. BUT NO, HE GETS TOO INVOLVED, he said aloud.

Death was still trying to solve the riddle of Lee Toren when, much to his amazement, someone in that particular reality began using the ancient ritual that could force him into a meeting.

GOOD. He closed his books and stood, moving effortlessly through his desk to the doorway to retrieve his scythe. SOMEONE CLEARLY HAS SOME TALENT. IT'LL BE A NICE CHANGE OF PACE.

With a plume of smoke, Death was gone, taken from his humble cottage between Time and Space.

* * * *

The circle that Portenda had drawn crudely on the floor of the meeting hall they had rented glowed a strange orange hue, and the moans of otherworldly beings escaped into the air around him and the Alchemists.

Jonah had completed the final step of the ritual, spraying sea salt around the outside of the circle, when the light began to glow, and he now scurried back on all fours, he and Nareena clinging to one another in horror like small children. "What have we done?" he quavered aloud.

Portenda said nothing and didn't move an inch from where he stood, a mere two or three feet away from the circle's edge

As the last of the moans escaped, a tall, angular form began to take shape, dressed in a simple, tattered black cloak and hood. The figure's left hand held a scythe that came up a good foot above its own head.

The Simpa smiled from ear to ear as he bowed deeply.

"Welcome, Honorable Guest," the Bounty Hunter said, signaling back to Jonah and Nareena to stand up and do the same.

They did, but only hesitantly, not saying a word between them.

GREETINGS, Death said as he tried to take a step out of the circle.

The barrier held, though, and he chuckled quietly to himself. GOOD TO SEE YOU GOT EVERY DETAIL RIGHT. YOU KNOW THE CONSEQUENCES IF I AM TO MAKE MY OWN WAY OUT OF THIS CIRCLE, YES?

"Yes, we are subject to your judgment." Jonah was excited. He had an honest to gods chance to ask the questions he'd always wanted to ask, here and now. "But if we permit you to leave the circle, you can do nothing."

"Please, you may leave the circle freely," Portenda said hurriedly.

Death snapped his bony fingers. DAMNATION. YOU ALREADY KNEW THAT, DIDN'T YOU?

Portenda nodded slowly, and Death took a single step out of the circle. His scythe, however, remained stuck in the circle.

SO, YOU'VE GOT ME PRETTY MUCH WHERE YOU WANT ME. VERY WELL, Death said, thoroughly impressed by this trio's skill and knowledge. I SHALL ANSWER YOUR QUESTIONS, BUT ONLY ONE PER PERSON. AND I HEREBY INVOKE MY RIGHT TO ANSWER YOU INDIRECTLY, OR IN RIDDLE.

All three seemed to agree to his terms. Not that they had a choice in the matter, as the conditions only stipulated that the Honorable Guest need only answer a minimum of two questions. He was apparently feeling generous.

Portenda was about to ask his question, when Nareena ruined it for all three of them.

"Would you like a seat?"

All three felt the smile on Death's face.

YES, I WOULD, YOUNG LADY. YOU HAVE USED YOUR QUESTION.

Nareena blinked rapidly as she reached for a chair, suddenly realizing what Death had just done.

"Hey wait a minute, that's not fair," she exclaimed, and Death shrugged his shoulders.

LIFE ISN'T FAIR, GIRLY. GET OVER IT. He lowered himself towards the seat she offered.

At the last instant, Nareena, furious at her mistake and Death's unyielding attitude, pulled the chair out of the way, and Death tumbled back to the floor.

Nareena laughed for a moment—until two beams of crimson light burned inside of the abysmal hood of Death's cloak.

NO ONE DOES THAT TO ME, Death growled as he floated himself erect, spinning on Nareena. NOBODY!

But Nareena stood her ground, knowing there was nothing that the embodiment of all mortal endings could do about her transgression. "Yeah, well, there's a first time for everything, huh."

"You're all right," Jonah said, stating it as fact instead of questioning the Honorable Guest, who rubbed his spine.

OF COURSE I AM. BUT THAT DID SMART. NOW, HURRY THIS ALONG. I HAVE OTHER THINGS TO DO TODAY, JONAH STAPLES.

Jonah flushed, unable to compose himself. He pointed to Portenda, who looked deep into the shadows of that immortal hood. He could just make out the skull that served as Death's face, the eyes that looked out at him from that hood.

Despite popular belief, he realized, Death could make eyeballs appear in his empty sockets, as there were two, purple irises looking out at him. He'd never before seen such a hue in a person's eyes. Then again, this wasn't exactly a person, as far as the strictest definitions went.

A Hunter and his Prey

YOU ARE AN IMPRESSIVE PIECE OF WORK, MISTER PORTENDA, Death said, rolling his eyes out of existence. YOU CAN SEE INTO THE DARKNESS OF MY ROBE, CAN'T YOU?

Portenda said nothing, but simply nodded.

I SUPPOSE ANYTHING'S POSSIBLE WITH UNEXPECTED BEINGS SUCH AS YOURSELF.

"Unexpected," Nareena asked aloud. "What do you mean by that?"

"You're out of questions, Nareena, remember," Jonah snapped at her curtly, frustrated that she had been tricked so easily.

NO, IT'S ALL RIGHT. I'LL ANSWER THAT ONE FOR FREE. Death turned around and looking at Jonah and Nareena in turn. He picked up the folding chair that Nareena had dumped on him and sat down slowly. YOU SEE, NAREENA, THERE ARE CERTAIN LAWS IN THE UNIVERSE, AND LAWS IN THE WORLD OF MORTALS, WHICH AREN'T SUPPOSED TO BE BROKEN. WHEN ONE OF THOSE LAWS IS BROKEN, PART OF MY JOB IS TO HELP FIX IT.

"I thought your whole purpose was to usher souls to their destined ends," Portenda said quietly.

Death shook his head and laughed mirthlessly.

OH, WERE IT THAT SIMPLE. YOU SEE, A BREACH OF UNIVERSAL LAW MUST IMMEDIATELY BE DEALT WITH, BECAUSE IF THE PROBLEM ISN'T FIXED, REALITY IS TORN. THE BORDERS BETWEEN YOUR OWN REALITY AND, SAY, A NEIGHBORING REALITY, WOULD BE TORN ASSUNDER. I MUST NOT ALLOW SUCH A THING TO HAPPEN.

THE LAWS OF MORTALS, HOWEVER, DO NOT REQUIRE SUCH IMMEDIATE ACTION, THOUGH I AM OFTEN ASKED TO DO SO, Death said, looking purposefully at the Simpa Bounty Hunter. PORTENDA THE QUIET IS THE SON OF A SIMPA FATHER, OBVIOUS BY HIS GENERAL SHAPE AND PHYSIOLOGY, AND A KHAN MOTHER, AS EVIDENCED BY HIS STRIPES AND SLOWER REGENERATIVE CAPABILITIES.

This was the first that Nareena had heard on the subject, though she had suspected something was strange about the Bounty Hunter, due mainly to those stripes on his arms.

ACCORDING TO THE LAWS OF BOTH RACES, SUCH A MATING MUST NEVER HAPPEN, THOUGH IT DOES, ALL THE TIME.

THE WAY I USUALLY DEAL WITH IT IS TO ENSURE THAT NO OFFSPRING RESULTS FROM THE MATING. IN HIS CASE, HOWEVER, SOMEONE INTERVENED, Death said slowly, methodically.

He was trying to coax a question out of Portenda, so that only Jonah would be left, but the proud Bounty Hunter stood there silently.

"And so Portenda was born," Jonah said aloud. Again, he was careful to make this a statement of fact, and not an inquiry.

YES. THE BOOKS OF HISTORY HAD NO PLACE FOR HIM PREVIOUSLY, BUT UPON HIS BIRTH, THE BOOKS REWROTE THEMSELVES.

I HAVE TAKEN QUITE AN INTEREST IN YOU, PORTENDA THE QUIET, Death rumbled enigmatically. YOU BEWILDER ME AT TIMES. NOW, DO YOU OR JONAH STAPLES HAVE A QUESTION FOR ME?

"Yes, I do," Jonah said hurriedly, feeling that time was of the essence. "How can we find my sister?" Death sat silently, unmoving, for a long pause, before he turned toward the Human Alchemist and replied.

THERE SHALL COME, IN TWO DAYS' TIME, A MESSENGER. FOLLOW HIM, AND YOU SHALL FIND WHERE YOUR SISTER IS KEPT, YOUNG JONAH. NOTHING MORE SHALL I SAY.

Jonah, disappointed a little by the cryptic response, realized that he would have to settle on it.

Death then turned to Portenda the Quiet, who was going to ask that exact same question. Now, however, he would have to think of another. As those deep purple eyes turned on him, Portenda gazed into Death's face, trying to delve into his immortal soul as he had so many people. But as he felt his mind and heart brush the surface, he immediately recoiled, turning away from the Honorable Guest. He had felt, for a brief moment, the tragedy of mortality, the loneliness of Death's eternal post. And he had also felt something else there, something bordering on resentment.

DO YOU HAVE A QUESTION, PORTENDA? I'M A VERY BUSY MAN, AS YOU WELL KNOW.

Portenda looked to Nareena, and Jonah, and finally realized that he could put an end to one nagging question.

"Very well, Honorable Guest. My question is one that has pulled at me, and Jonah as well. Why is it that Jonah sometimes goes into these trance-like states, and turns on us, able to use mecha weapons and Alchemy in combination?"

Death threw his head back and laughed.

THE ANSWER TO THAT, YOU HAVE ALREADY SUSPECTED, PORTENDA THE QUIET, SON OF TELROKE! HE WAS TAKEN SEVERAL YEARS AGO, AND BRAINWASHED, SUBCONCIOUSLY TRAINED TO USE THE ANCIENT WAYS OF SCIENCE TO KILL. BUT THE TRAINING DID NOT HOLD COMPLETELY. JONAH STAPLES POSSESSES A WILL TOO POWERFUL TO BE COMPLETELY OVERTAKEN, SO HE COULD NOT BE USED AS A PUPPET, AS HIS ABDUCTOR HAD WANTED. THUS, HE WAS PRESSED BACK INTO THE REALM, WITH NO MEMORY OF WHAT HAD OCCURED. NOTHING MORE SHALL I SAY ON THE MATTER.

Death stood abruptly and moving over to the circle, taking hold of his scythe.

AND NOW, YOU SHALL ANSWER A QUESTION FOR ME, BOUNTY HUNTER. He pronounced the words as a command to a lesser being.

A Hunter and his Prey

Portenda stood straight and eyeballed that darkness beneath the hood once more.

Such lonely eyes, he thought.

"Ask your question, Honorable Guest," he said, looking over at the shocked and speechless Jonah.

AFTER SO MANY YEARS OF SOLITUDE AND SILENCE, SO MUCH TIME AS A LONER, HOW DOES IT FEEL TO HAVE COMPANY?

The question was asked quietly, without malice or contempt. Portenda tried to search his heart for the right words, but felt that the answer should be simple. After all, the exact words would never be found for how he felt about the Alchemist pair.

"It feels, warm."

Death lowered his head and thought long and hard. WARM, EH, he thought to himself. WHAT THE HELLS DOES THAT MEAN, WARM?

Portenda smiled at him, and shrugged his shoulders.

"There's no proper words for it, Honorable Guest. You'd know it when you felt it, I'm sure. If you can feel anything at all," he added as a jab at the immortal being.

Death nodded, and heaved a heavy sigh.

VERY WELL, he said to the room at large. I MUST RETURN, NOW. REMEMBER, TWO DAYS, JONAH STAPLES. TWO DAYS, AND THE MESSENGER SHALL COME.

Jonah nodded and waved good-bye as Death stood in the center of the flashing circle, and disappeared from the mortal plane.

Evening had come fully upon them, and the last vestiges of sunlight filtered through the windows of the meeting hall.

Nareena was the first to speak.

"He needs a hobby," she said sarcastically, still angry that Death had tricked her out of her question.

"What he needs," Portenda said, leaving the meeting hall. "Is a friend."

Chapter Ten
Allies

The little creature had approached the farmhouse without once stopping for a rest, and now was running for his life from a Shepherd dog the size of a small boulder.

The large canine snarled and barked at Blink as the Alchemical failure sprinted as fast as his little legs could carry it, and his animal mind raced.

Runrunrunrunrun, his mind screamed. Alchemy beasts always retained a small part of their creator's intellect, and Genma was more intelligent than most.

Up ahead, Blink saw several Humans and what he thought might be Jafts. All wore overalls and other farmhand clothing. As Blink raced ahead, he saw rows and rows of corn. The farmhands had stopped their harvesting to see what their faithful farm dog was so uppity about.

Dashing and darting between their feet and piles of cut down corn stalks, Blink disappeared into the cornfield, hoping to shake the canine in pursuit.

The pounding of doggy feet behind him slowed. *Good*, Blink thought. *Doggy needs his nose to smell me out.*

Blink used what little sense of direction he had and navigated through the maze of maize, hearing the growling and snuffling of the animal in pursuit.

It was much larger than him, and it was bringing friends, Blink realized, hearing the muffled shouts and growls of the bipeds following along.

Not much choice now, he thought, tearing ass through the cornfields straight ahead.

"There it is! Get 'im boy," one of the Humans shouted.

The barking grew more intense, and as Blink exited the fields of corn into the vast plains beyond, he chanced a look back and saw the hound closing in.

No options. Blink growled and plunged his poison-filled barb into the canine's face.

While not lethal to the huskier bipeds, the poison killed the dog almost instantly.

Blink stifled his regret—he knew the bond between human and animal better than most, but it had been is life or that of the dog. Calling up is resources, Blink was gone from sight before the Humans and Jafts could catch up. They huddled around their fallen pet and guard dog with sorrow in their hearts. "Poor Maxi," one of the Humans said, kneeling down close to the dog.

None of the farmhands could ever describe what happened next. Their brains simply couldn't accept what their eyes saw: a tall, angular figure in a black robe, carrying a scythe, approached them and the dog, swinging his weapon down through the vague blue stream that was attached to the dog's spirit. The dog's body immediately decomposed, leaving nary a trace that it had ever been alive. COME ON, MAXI, GOOD BOY, the figure in the cloak said as the skeletal remains of the canine jumped up and followed after him.

* * * *

Portenda, Jonah and Nareena sat at a round table in a little coffee shop in the dining district of Palen. 'Le Cafe Du Forte', the large wooden sign out front called it. They sat in silence, trying to cope with their recent meeting with Death.

"We haven't got two days to wait, Portenda, that's too much time," Jonah complained.

"He wouldn't have told us anything that would put your sister's life at risk." The Bounty Hunter was trying to get a fix on how Nareena had reacted to learning that he was a half-breed. He was also racking his brain, trying to figure out who would intervene on behalf of his existence. It would have to be someone who could convince Death himself to let it slide, and that seemed an impossible task. "We need to think about what we're going to do when the messenger does arrive. We need to also prepare ourselves for the possibility that this messenger will require immediate medical attention."

"Okay," Nareena said. "So Jonah makes a couple of healing potions. What else?"

The Bounty Hunter looked around the cafe, admiring the quaint setting.

Fine oak wood had been crafted to make every piece of furniture and the majority of the building's structure itself. One and a half foot thick support beams were positioned near the larger tables, with iron coat hooks placed at even intervals around them. The color scheme was soft and earthen, all greens and browns and shades of gray, lending the environment a subtle, relaxing vibe. After their meeting with Death, Portenda, Jonah and Nareena all needed that.

The seemingly random banter of the other patrons filtered through the air and mixed with their conversation, making for a comfortable background noise, and Jonah was faintly reminded of his last weeks in Desanadron, before he had moved out on his own. He had enjoyed several similar outings with his closest friends and his family, and he became momentarily nostalgic for those days.

Nareena was trying to think of a graceful way to inform Jonah that she had known about his brainwashing. It felt as though she would be confessing some great sin, and the Elven Alchemist wasn't sure he would be in the forgiving mood just now. Instead of telling him, she filled her mouth with pastries and coffee.

The trio sat in studied silence, which Jonah was beginning to feel was the most natural way for the three of them to be.

Portenda alone, among the three of them, realized that already they had trouble heading their way.

* * * *

"I've always got time to chat with a friend," the Sidalis named Felix Armstrong said through his small pocket mirror.

Although a mutant, he appeared no different than a Human, physically, so long as he kept his clothes and armor on. Genma knew, however, that beneath his tunic and chain mail shirt, the Sidalis had a gaping hole where his lower abdomen should be. His upper body was connected to his lower body only through the connection of his life force, and his clothes.

Quite a strange mutation, Genma thought. If only there were a way for him to harness it and make that useful.

All Sidalis in the realms of Tamalaria, and its sister continent, Tallowmere, possessed powers that were neither magical nor scientific, but spiritual in origin. These powers could be defended against, but each mutation was different and required a different defense. Many philosophers on the subject believed that the mutants' powers were the gods' way of trying to make up for the fact that the Sidalis Race was infinitely strange and warped. And even this theory sometimes had holes shot through it, at least in the Heavens above. After all, none of the Lesser Gods and Goddesses had any idea why the Sidalis Race was the way it was.

Genma had his own theories, but he wasn't about to get into them with an employee. After all, agents were to be used for work, not palled around with. But Felix was just, friendly, was all. For the right price.

"Very good, Felix. I have a favor I'd like you to do for me. First of all, where are you right now?"

The handsome, Human-like face in the mirror turned left and right, and Felix was grateful that nobody was around to witness this queer little conversation. A man talking to a mirror might be called a lot of things.

"I'm in Atiock, a small farming village about two days north of Waterway. That's a fishing city on the western coastline, about a day north of the Desperation."

Genma performed a quick calculation and concluded that it would take Felix five days on horseback to reach Palen.

"Do you have access to a magic shop?" Genma asked.

Felix gave him a sly grin through the mirror. "Yeah, though its nothing much to look at. Elven fellow runs the place, doesn't have a whole lot in stock aside from some scrolls."

"Good enough," Genma said. "See if he has a Teleportation scroll, and make sure it can take you to Palen. When you've done that, get back to me. Oh, and Felix?"

The Sidalis stopped his cut out of the communication, and raised an eyebrow at the ivory-masked Alchemist.

"Yeah?"

"What are you doing in a farming village?"

"I was passing through, and they needed an extra hand to help deliver some calves on one of the ranches. No biggy."

Though he was a mercenary, Genma reminded himself, and a very capable one at that, Felix Armstrong had a habit of being a nice guy. That might not play too well in Genma's designs. Then again, he had the money to pay for the Sidalis' unwilling services. Flash the right number in front of him, and he was certain that Felix would turn over his own mother.

"Very well. Get back to me in a few, when you have the scroll." Genma waved his hand in front of the new, huge vanity mirror, and watched as the image faded to a plain reflective surface.

Delays, delays, delays, he thought irritably. The girl had gone and gotten herself hurt, his first mercenary had been slain by a Lizardman Monk, and he was beginning to wonder how strong his hold over Kobuchi really was. He hadn't ordered the Kobold to prepare any recapture teams in the event that the girl got away; Genma had known that she would try something, and had prepared a little surprise for her near the edge of the tower's barrier. However, because his attendant had acted on his own accord, the girl had been injured during her retrieval. That meant at least another three days tacked on to the wait, and Kobuchi didn't seem worried by that in the slightest.

Genma stood from his leather swivel chair and formed a Focus Site on the floor with a piece of chalk that he always kept handy. Clapping his hands and pressing his palms to the border of the Site, he felt the rush of force as it wound its way through the tower and bore down on Kobuchi, the mark on his chest burning like a thousand suns as he dropped to the floor.

Though Genma did not witness it this time, he knew that wherever the Kobold was, he was suddenly in a great deal of pain, and would shortly be feeling much more compliant.

The connection between them became stronger, and for a moment, Genma could feel Kobuchi's agony. But he could also feel something else, something coming from an exterior source. What was this sensation, and what could cause such alarm in the Alchemist?

Before he could reach out for the source, his mirror shimmered back into the image of the Sidalis Felix Armstrong. "Yo," the man said, holding a scroll up for Genma to see.

"Ah, very good. Use it as soon as we are done speaking, Felix. What I need you to do is find a very specific group of people, a trio. One is a Simpa Bounty Hunter by the name of Portenda. He will be easy to identify by the gray stripes on his arms, and the fact that you'll never in your lifetime see such a heavily armed were-lion. One is Jonah Staples, a Human Alchemist. The boy is sort of gangly, a little unhealthy looking." Genma tried to be fair to his nephew. It was hard, though, because the boy never looked too sturdy. "And the third is an Elven girl, also an Alchemist. Her name is Nareena, and she probably won't ever be far from the boy."

"Okay, find them first. Then what?"

"Then, entertain them for a while, Felix," Genma said meaningfully. "There's no need to kill them. Just, keep them busy for a few days. Mislead them, misguide them. You remember where the tower is, yes?"

Felix nodded.

"Good. Keep them away from the tower at all costs. I'm not certain if they know how to get here, but just in case they find out, I want you there to keep them away, by any means necessary."

Felix smiled broadly, and set his teeth in a vicious grin. "So, what's the pay?"

Down to business, Genma thought. At least he's accepted the job.

"Normally, I'd say standard rate, my friend." Genma let it be well known that this job was different. "Thirty thousand. But the Simpa is a rough customer, and won't be easily dealt with, even for one with your, ah, unique talents," he said, emphasizing the word 'unique'. "So the pay shall be forty thousand."

The Sidalis' eyes bulged at the figure. "Rate and a half, huh?" Felix pulled awkwardly at his collar, and rubbed the back of his head with his free hand. "This Portenda guy, he's the real deal, huh?"

"Quite so," Genma said. "He has managed to get Wren killed," he said, giving no details. He liked to let his agents use their own imaginations, as their own misguided thoughts often conjured images that Genma couldn't provide with his best efforts.

Felix whistled. "Wow, Wren Headsplitter's dead huh," he said into the mirror. "Well, that's a lot of money, and I sure could use another house."

Genma rolled his eyes, heaving a mental sigh. Armstrong almost always used his money to build new homes for himself and his friends, or add on to those he already had. Considering how far a gold piece went, each job got him a sizable three-story home, materials and labor completely covered by his payments, with a little left over to help his friends move. *Charity work,* Genma thought. *Why does he bother?*

"All right, I'll do it. I'm going right now." Felix severed the link.

As the mirror went blank once more, Genma tried to feel through the tower for Kobuchi. The Kobold had returned to his normal duties.

Some things, thankfully, would never change.

* * * *

"Haaaauuuugggghhhh!" Kobuchi howled as his Master's Focus Site burned into his flesh and mind. The walls of willpower that he had been slowly building up shattered like so much blown glass, and in his mind's eye, Kobuchi saw his defenses crumble to dust. The raging dragon of Alchemical force pounded through the landscape of his soul, and scorched that ground with fiery demon's breath.

The Kobold dropped to his knees, the platter he had been carrying falling and breaking apart on the stone floor at his feet.

Eileen had heard his shouts and fits of pain, and couldn't resist helping in what small ways she could.

Ignoring her injuries, she darted from her resting chamber and found the Kobold writhing on the hallway floor, his eyes wide and glossy as his limbs thrashed.

Dashing over and kneeling next to him, Eileen tried to think of a way to help him.

"Something to bite on, something to bite on," she murmured aloud, and took the wooden saltshaker from the busted tray, setting it between Kobuchi's teeth. At least he wouldn't bite his own tongue off this way.

The symbol on Kobuchi's chest was gleaming, and Eileen feared the worst for him. She knew that he had only a limited amount of free will, thanks to her uncle's twisted practices, and she knew of only one way to help in this matter. She pulling of the sling she wore over her injured left shoulder, and placed her left hand on the mark, flooding her magic into his body. She used the Q Mage spell *Manna Shield* on him, though she wasn't entirely certain it would work against science.

In Kobuchi's mind, the Kobold had backed himself against an aging, decrepit pine tree, the needles strewn all about the ground miserably. The shadowy dragon-like beast reared up and loosed a howl of wicked delight, and charged at him. Kobuchi threw up his arms in despair, but was amazed to see the tree thrust its branches to form a dome around him.

Life ebbed back into the tree, and Kobuchi sprang up and spun about to look at it. There, in the middle of the trunk, carved out of the wood itself, was the face of the girl his Master had taken. Eileen Staples, he realized, had just spared him from becoming a total drone again.

The dragon blew away into smoke, and a moment later, Kobuchi blinked his real eyes, and found that he was looking at the Human girl through tears of pain and relief. She, too, sobbed, and he saw that she had used her injured arm to protect him.

Kobuchi sat up and felt at the symbol on his chest, which still felt hot to the touch. He couldn't bring himself to look at her. "Um, thank you, miss Staples," he mumbled, unsure of how to take this development. His Master would be furious if he took the time to notice that Kobuchi hadn't been broken.

The girl threw her good arm around him, and Kobuchi went still with surprise. *Compassion*, he thought. *For me? I'm the one who brought her back in here!*

"No living person should suffer so," she whispered in his pointy, dog-like ear.

"I agree, Miss Staples," he whispered back. He stood and helped the Human girl get her arm back in its sling. "Now you should get back in bed. I'll go get you some fresh food, and perhaps we can speak further on the matter tomorrow. For now, I don't think it wise to spend time together."

Eileen nodded and gave him a small smile, despite her own suffering. She lay back in her bed and stared at the ceiling. *Come on, boy*, she thought, picturing Blink in her mind. *Find him. Bring him to me, so I can get out of here.*

* * * *

Portenda couldn't say what exact trouble was coming, but his gut told him it would be soon. His instincts seldom deceived him, and right now, he expected trouble to come from all directions. Still, without more information, he could do little. He sat quietly, joining in the conversation with occasional grunt of agreement or disdain, not really paying full attention. He scanned the cafe, but decided that the threat wasn't here. It was close, but not one of the customers or staff.

"What do you think, Portenda?" Nareena asked the Simpa as she leaned forward on the table, her chin resting in her palm. Her bare arms were tensed slightly, and Portenda realized, as he looked at her, that she too sensed trouble. But he had also completely missed the question.

"Ah, about what again?"

Jonah rolled his eyes and chuckled.

"You were off in la-la land," Jonah said. "We were just discussing the similarities and disparities between magic and science. Nareena believes they stem from the same basic roots and sources. I don't happen to agree. What do you think?"

Portenda tried to mull the question over, but kept part of his mind free to assess the situation around him.

A handsome fellow in a chain mail shirt, tan leggings, and thick black leather boots came into the cafe, and ordered a large cuppa, seating himself in the far left corner from where the trio sat discussing magic and science. The man didn't seem very heavily armed, and appeared to be more concerned with his appearance than the actual protection that a chain shirt provided. No threat there, Portenda surmised.

"I've never had to think about it," he offered, looking once again at the Alchemists. "The only magic I bothered with is of the variety that you find in street performers, and the only sciences that interest me are biology and mecha weapon design." His tone sounded so cold, even to him, that icicles clung to the air as he spoke. The more he tried to sense the danger, the more his frosty demeanor took hold. The effect not only changed his voice and tone, but the set and bunching of his muscles as well.

Jonah slid his chair back a little from the table, ready to spring away from any danger. He had become intimately familiar with the dead, ashen look in the Bounty Hunter's eyes, and wanted to be ready to act if the need arose.

"Biology," Nareena asked, raising an eyebrow. "You're just full of surprises, aren't you," she asked. "Why biology?"

"Every target and potential opponent has weak points, due to the nature of his or her Race," Portenda reported. He stared ahead at nothing, trying to focus on where the threat he was sensing might come from. "Over the years, I have studied the biological weaknesses and strengths of the Races of Tamalaria. For instance, were you aware that Elven females have a nerve in their legs that their men do not?"

Nareena's eyes widened for a moment as Portenda tapped said nerve with one of his bare toes beneath the table.

"When struck, even lightly, on the exact point of the nerve, the woman lose all motor function from the waist down."

Nareena tried to move her legs and found that she couldn't.

Portenda tapped the nerve again, and she swung her legs experimentally.

"Likewise, when tapped again, function is restored."

"Just like the half-Orc back in Ja-Wen," Jonah said with awe. "Is there any Race that doesn't have those kinds of weaknesses?"

"No, though a few are difficult to affect with such techniques. With Lizardmen and Sidalis, for instance, the exact location of the nerves varies by person instead of by gender or age. With the Lizardmen, each tribal bloodline has their own set of weaknesses and strengths. For Sidalis, it is even more difficult, because each person of their Race has a different bodily mutation."

A Hunter and his Prey

As Portenda said this last bit, he identified the scent of the handsome newcomer to the cafe. *A Sidalis*, he thought, but didn't spare the man more than a passing observation. He hadn't sensed any malice from him. "It's getting late. We're going to find an inn now." He got up, leaving the money for the bill on the table.

Jonah and Nareena followed the Bounty Hunter out of the cafe and into the dark evening streets of Palen. The Alchemists walked arm-in-arm, while Portenda stalked ahead of them, his body tensed and ready to spring at an instant's notice.

The trio made their way to the business district, home of the city's four hotels. Each building was identical to the next—low, long buildings that stretched for a hundred yards back from their front doors.

Portenda chose one at random, and led Jonah and Nareena inside. A Human, a bored-looking teen-ager from his expression, manned the front counter.

"How many rooms? How many days?" The youth took his feet down from the counter and opened the logbook to the latest entries.

"Two rooms, two days," Portenda said flatly.

"Eight gold." The youth grabbed two of the keys from the pegboard behind him and sliding them across the counter, taking the money in return. "Room eighteen, and room twenty-two. They're across the hall from each other." The youth gave Nareena a wink.

The Elven Alchemist gave him a fake smile as she flipped him off from the waist.

"Room eighteen's the king size bed," the clerk said.

Taking their respective keys, the trio headed down the hall. Portenda took mental notes of the position of every painting, every lounge bench and bust pedestal. Their primary escape route secured, he stopped in front of the door to his room, and spun on his heel.

"No fooling around tonight you two." He gave them a fierce look. "Someone's to stay awake at all times. I'll take the first watch, then I'll wake you, Jonah."

Jonah and Nareena looked each other in the eyes, and then up at the tall Simpa.

"What's wrong? Were we followed?" Jonah asked.

"No." Portenda heaved a sigh. "But I can sense trouble. You do too, don't you?" he asked Nareena, who nodded. "Jonah, have a couple of combative Focus Sites ready for use. Nareena, coat your knives with poisons, every one you can think of. And both of you keep some healing potions on hand. You've got about an hour before I expect you both to be in bed and asleep. Plenty of time to make a couple more potions if you need to." Portenda had kept tabs on how long it took Jonah to make his most common tinctures. "Keep the paralysis vial on hand, too, Jonah. If anyone comes at us tonight or tomorrow, I want to question them. Understood?"

The Alchemists nodded their agreement.

"Good. Do what you have to and get to bed." He opened the door to his room. "And no screwing around," he added for good measure again, his voice as frosty as the Dwarven mountains. He slammed his door shut behind him, leaving the Alchemist couple to their own devices.

"Quickie?" Nareena asked, rubbing Jonah's back playfully.

He gave her a deep kiss, and the two of them disappeared into their room. They'd still have plenty of prep time, Jonah reasoned, losing all rational thought soon after.

* * * *

Blink hadn't been alive for very long, but he valued the life he had. His dog-like mind couldn't quite wrap itself around, his current problem—a river rampaging under soft moonlight.

Something wooden floated toward him over the water's surface, two figures standing on it, silhouetted in the dim glow of the moon.

The smell of soft soil filled the air as Blink took a couple of skittering steps closer to the riverbank, trying to get a better view of the creatures coming toward him.

The one in the black cloak and robes, his blue, bald head now clearly visible, smelled horribly. The Jaft's stench filled the air, and Blink had to focus hard to catch the smell of the other one.

A large cat of some sort, he decided.

Cats were for chasing, but the size of this cat, and the fact that it walked on two legs, gave Blink reason for pause.

The ferry touched the riverbank softly, and the Jaft ferryman struck the ground with his pole, holding the raft in place.

The Khan Soldier stepped off, and turned around to pay the man when he caught notice of Blink.

Before the Alchemy creature could scurry out of sight, a large, orange hand was presented to him, palm up.

Friend? Blink wondered. He took a few hesitant steps forward, and looked up into the gentle smile of Tiberious Amon. *Friend*, Blink decided, stepping fully on to his hand.

"Trying to get across, little guy?" Amon looked back at the ferryman, who appeared to be in no rush, and was also smiling—but the Jaft was also smacking his lips. "I don't think he'd taste very good, sir," Amon growled at the Jaft as he stepped back aboard the ferry raft. "Take us back across, and then bring me back here. I'll pay for all three trips at the end."

The Jaft shrugged his shoulders and pushed off from the shore. "So, have you come far?" Amon asked.

Blink nodded, surprised he was able to communicate.

Amon gave the creature a curious glance, and realized that nature couldn't have made this being. Magic of some sort had grafted several animals together into one entity.

Amon stroked Blink's furry little head, and the small animal purred in response.

A Hunter and his Prey

"You can understand what I'm saying, can't you," he whispered

Again, Blink nodded.

"Do you know where you're going?"

Blink nodded and shook his head as well.

"You've got an idea. Hmm." Amon mulling over the chance that he would encounter this strange beast. The gods, it seemed, continued to have a use for him.

As time passed, Amon held Blink and patted him on the head now and again. After a half an hour, they arrived on the opposite bank. Amon lowered Blink to the ground, and the Alchemy beast waved his stinger in the direction he intended to go.

"No, I'm sorry little guy." Amon pulled a strip of salted meat from his rucksack and set it on the ground for Blink. "I'm heading the other way. But rest assured, I've served my purpose in your task. Now go, and stay safe."

He watched as the creature devoured the meat he had left. Then, before the ferryman could push off, Blink had disappeared.

"Strange how the world works, eh?"

The Jaft said nothing in return.

* * * *

They don't seem like bad folks, Felix Armstrong thought as he watched the trio leave the cafe.

He raised a finger to catch the waitress's attention, and when the perky young Human woman flounced up, he smiled at her winningly. The girl blushed under his gaze, and he flipped his head to the side, tossing his long, beautiful blond hair back. "I'd like to trade one of my gold pieces for one that the Simpa paid with, if you don't mind." He exercised his charm.

The girl nodded and smiled at him, playing with her own hair as she fetched a coin from Portenda's table and traded it with one of Felix's.

"Thank you so very much," he said, taking a sip of his cuppa. *Good stuff,* he thought. *They really know how to make it here. Not like that backwater village.* He hadn't expected farm folks to be able to make such a beverage, but it had been awful.

"Can I get you anything else," the girl asked, captivated by his androgynous beauty.

With the proper clothes, Felix Armstrong could pass for a woman, and found that men often envied his beauty, while women wanted him because of it. His charm enhanced his Sidalis power. As an adolescent, he'd developed the ability to temporarily inhabit the body of anyone he spoke with during the previous twenty-four hours. More, he could apply this power to anyone an inhabited body spoke with. In this way, he could jump from person to person for extended periods of time, but he didn't like to be gone from his own body for too long. It left him vulnerable if he didn't have a good hiding place for his body. Mercenaries didn't last long if they left themselves open to attack.

She'll do. He paid the bill and took his leave. Upon his arrival in Palen, Felix had gone to a tavern and asked to rent out the basement, which the proprietor had been more than happy to arrange. The barkeep's mother, apparently a spirit creature, had kept him from renting out the room for a long time. A Simpa fellow, he had been told, had exorcised her earlier in the day, and Felix knew that it had been Portenda. Before he left the cafe, however, he signaled to the young waitress.

"I'm staying in town for a couple of days," he said to her, and watched as her cheeks flushed. "I might stop by tomorrow. Are you working then?"

"No, but I can meet you here," she said cheerily. "My name's Michelle."

"I'm Felix. A pleasure to meet you, Michelle." He bowed deeply and took her hand in his own. *Gets them every time*, he thought, as the girl looked away bashfully. *Might as well have a little fun while I'm in town*. He turned then and walked out into the streets.

Once out of view of the inn, he pulled out the Simpa's coin and turned it over in his fingers. He had a friend in the city who might be able to tell him more about the man by the coin he had in his hand.

Stalking through the streets as the city guards lit the street lamps, Felix Armstrong smiled and waved to passersby, maintaining his friendly demeanor before he got down to business.

After a while, he stood before a low, squat cottage, and knocked on the maple wood door.

After a series of crashing noises and some cursing, the door creaked open on hinges in sore need of an oiling.

A hunched man stood before him, his long, scruffy beard covering his entire face and neck, hanging over his plain blue tunic shirt. "Felix? Is that you?"

"Yes it is." Felix hugged the man briefly.

They held each other at arm's length, and the old man opened all three of his eyes for a moment.

"It's good to see you, my boy," the elderly Sidalis said. "Come in, come in." He pulled Felix into the disastrous home behind him.

Several inches of clothes, books, and other assorted unnecessary items created in a thick layer on the floor, covering the hardwood that might have echoed under one's boots, should they find the floor. "Can I bring you some tea, Felix?"

"No, no." Felix took a seat in one of the soft wool recliners. "I've come for business, I'm afraid."

The old man heaved a sigh.

"Don't take it badly, pops." Felix produced the gold coin that Portenda had handled. "I can always come back after this assignment."

"Humph. That's what you said last time." The three-eyed Sidalis's bristles twitched as he shook his head sadly. "Do you mean it this time?"

"Yes, Hector," Felix said. "I do. I'll have plenty of money after this one, and we can even get you a new place. Or at least hire someone to come in and clean this mess. Listen, I need to know everything you can tell me about the man who handled this before I did. I've been hired to distract him and his friends for a couple of days."

Hector gave him a curious glance.

"Define for me, distract, Felix." He took the offered gold coin.

"Oh, I don't have to kill them. Hells, I don't even have to hurt them, pops."

"But it always comes to that, doesn't it?" Felix, though he was a handsome fellow, and a nice guy to boot, had a violent streak that could run from Ja-Wen to Desanadron and back.

"It doesn't have to," Felix said softly. "Before you do your thing, I think I will take that tea. And the spare bedroom if you can offer it to me for the night," he added hastily. Although he had paid for the use of a tavern basement, his old friend's place would be more comfortable.

"Not a problem." Hector shuffled through a pile of novels about Vampires in Tamalaria.

Although any other outsider would only see a total mess throughout the cottage, Felix knew that the old Sidalis had a method of arranging his various belongings, because whenever Hector needed something, it was within arm's reach.

After a few minutes, Hector returned with a mug of tea. When he'd handed it to Felix, he sat across from him and turned the gold coin between his fingers. He closed all three of his eyes, and went perfectly still.

Felix had relied on the old man's help on several jobs, as Hector's mutant power allowed him to use an object or belonging of someone's to look into their past, their mind, and to a small degree, their very soul.

Felix had never seen the old man react like he was now.

Hector's entire body trembled.

Felix dropped his emptied mug to the floor and dashed to his friend's side. "Hector, are you all right?"

The elderly Sidalis now shook so badly that his arms thrashed, striking Felix several times across the head and shoulders before the younger mutant pried the coin from his fingers.

As soon as Felix had it, Hector slipped to the floor from his seat, his chest heaving up and down, his breathing ragged and harsh.

"Hector, talk to me!"

"Felix, listen," Hector gasped, his eyes wide. His third eye had become completely black. "You said, you don't have to even hurt these people?"

"No, no I don't." Felix wondered where the old man was going with this.

"Good. If you tried it, you'd be killed faster than you could feel the Reaper's hand on your shoulder."

Felix stared in disbelief at his long-time friend. He had been hired once to dispose of an adolescent White Dragon, and had managed the task with only a few injuries, only one of which had been major. How could this Simpa be a greater threat to him?

Hector took a heavy, calming breath, and returned to his seat.

Felix did the same, ready to hear everything the old man could tell him. "Tell me everything," he said in a hushed voice. "I have to know."

"Well, where to begin? He's about sixty or seventy years old, still young for his people." Hector eased himself into the telling. "When he was young, I saw, he lost his mother. He was very young, only nine or ten years old. I didn't get any exact images of anything that far back, but the feelings were intense. And at the same moment, he felt two greatly opposite reactions; a great loss, for he loved his mother immensely. And along side that, he burned with fury and hatred for someone similarly close. I believe it was his father."

Felix nodded. He wasn't certain he liked where this was going. "Then what?"

"Not long after, he left his homeland, to live on his own." Hector shook his head slowly. "A boy of ten years. But he took with him a short sword, and a crudely made bow, and the very same day he left his home in the Allenian Hills, he killed a man. His first violent encounter with a creature that wasn't an animal, aside from a fight with his father when he left home."

"Did he leave, or was he tossed out?" Felix asked.

"A little of both." Hector stared into space. "While walking along one of the trade roads, he was accosted by highwaymen. The first man got a leg full of teeth, and he made his way off to the horizon as quickly as he could. The second man hadn't been so lucky. Ah, such a powerful memory, I could see it all," Hector breathed. "A Jaft thug, at least twice his size. He swung a truncheon at the Simpa boy, but the Simpa had already been well trained with his sword. He blocked the attack, and cleaved the Jaft's left leg at the knee. The man begged for mercy, but there was none in the boy's heart. In that moment, a great void enveloped this boy, who would become the man you pursue! He spared the thug no mercy, cutting each of his limbs off, and then taking his head off with one clean swing. The blood sprayed everywhere, even in the boy's eyes. He didn't even blink, Felix."

"But time and experience have let him calm down, open up little by little. He has slain hundreds, perhaps even thousands, and most of it has been in the name of his profession." Hector stopped for a moment, and fetched himself some tea, and a refill for Felix.

"So, he's got a rather violent past and upbringing. What made you, you know, react like you did?"

Hector's third eye had been clearing. It now darkened again.

"Firstly, I'll tell you this. He's a very rational man, very logical. His tactical efficiency is unmatched, Felix, and his powers of perception are something that only the Gods and Goddesses should be allowed to possess. He has emotions, but they do not govern his actions and thoughts. If someone gets in his way, he'll cut them down, almost certainly ignoring any personal connections he has to them."

"And the second thing you want to tell me?" Felix felt tendrils of fear slither against his spine and heart.

A Hunter and his Prey

"Yes, that," Hector said. "Felix, I could see the source and magnitude of his strength and power, and I must tell you this, because I care about your wellbeing. When I saw the source, his soul, I knew something that few ever get to know; there are Lesser Gods who would rightly tremble before him. But don't be too afraid," Hector said reassuringly. "He doesn't yet know how to tap that vast potential yet."

"How can such power even exist in the realm of mortals?" Abruptly, Genma's payment seemed paltry rather than generous.

"At the creation of his soul and his body, he should have ceased to be. His very nature is taboo. Someone in the Heavens intervened on his behalf. Someone very influential," he concluded.

Felix Armstrong thanked his friend for his help, and shuffled off to the spare bedroom to think a while on what he had just been told. This was going to be a difficult job. Thankfully, he wouldn't have to put his own body in jeopardy. He had plenty of hosts to choose from, after all.

With such thoughts in his head, he slipped off to sleep, and in slumber, let his spirit wander towards his potential hosts.

* * * *

Portenda watched the streets through the window in his room, keeping his eyes focused and his mind clear. No external sound mixed with the inflation and deflation of his lungs as he breathed steadily, rhythmically. He still felt the twinge of caution that he had felt before, and he always trusted his instincts. But his shift was almost over, and soon he could get some precious sleep.

Which one do I wake? he wondered. He could smell faint hints of herbs, unknown liquids, and the burning scent of Alchemical tools having been put to use from across the hall. Jonah and Nareena had indeed made some preparations, after, of course, they were done rutting. They weren't exactly the quietest couple, Portenda observed, again.

The streets outside weren't deserted, but they weren't packed, either. Just before Portenda went to get Jonah out of bed, he saw the young waitress from the cafe walking down the street, looking back and forth among the people.

She seemed upset about something but a minute later, she lurched forward, like she might if she was going to vomit. A few seconds later, she looked at her hands, as though it was the first time she was seeing them.

"What an odd girl," Portenda muttered as he turned and walked out into the hallway.

Jonah was sleeping lightly, as he usually did these days. Since that first night in Portenda's apartment in Ja-Wen, he had been training his body to wake up at an instant's notice.

When the knock came at his door, he sprang from the bed and opened the door wide, his left eye twitching slightly.

Still not used to this, he thought, rubbing his eyes as he looked up at Portenda. "Let me guess," the Human Alchemist said. "My shift, right?"

"That's right," Portenda said. "How many healing potions did you manage to make?"

"Four," Jonah said, stretching and yawning. "One for each of us, and one extra. Nareena made some poisonous mist powder and a few explosive chemical tinctures. We could have made more with a little extra time."

"So in other words, if you hadn't screwed around again, despite my request not to," Portenda said evenly. "I thought I had been very specific about that."

Jonah's face flushed, and without another word the Bounty Hunter returned to his room to sleep. Jonah looked over his shoulder, and saw that Nareena had stirred for a moment, and then gone right back to sleep.

"Looks like I'm on my own," Jonah said to the empty hallway. Closing his door behind him, he strolled over to the window. The streets outside held few wandering citizens, and a number of city guards stood huddled in a circle in the cold night air, smoking pipes and smoke sticks. The waitress from the café they had enjoyed earlier that day caught his eye. She was just staring into space, looking for something out of sight.

Jonah shrugged his shoulders and started reading through the third tome of Focus knowledge, deciding to use his time productively.

For the first hour of his shift, Jonah didn't hear or see anything out of the usual. The fire in their fireplace had died down to dwindling ashes, and the soft scent of Nareena's perfume filled the room, mingling with the smell of their coupling.

Jonah smiled affectionately at her sleeping form, and looked once again out the window. Through the vaguely smeared and blurry window he saw the waitress from the cafe start to move toward their hotel and he wondered if she was meeting with someone in the late hours of the night.

Felix Armstrong had enjoyed being in this girl's body for about fifteen minutes before he realized, from sifting through her thoughts, that she was a total idiot.

Due to the nature of her occupation, Felix found that she gave him a wide array of hosts he could jump to. Because of the low amount of willpower this ditzy little Human had, Felix could take his time about selecting a host. He preferred to take them when they were asleep, because their resistance was lower. The host, most times, would simply go along with what was happening, and tell the police later, if Felix did something unlawful with their body, that they were dreaming. Any Knight that heard them speaking would know, through the nature of their honor system of belief, that the subject was telling the truth.

Nearby, through his mutant powers, he could sense another potential host, and so he moved the girl closer to the side of the building that Jonah, Nareena, and Portenda were staying in. He used his mind's eye to search, and found there the perfect host—the Elven girl.

He leapt from the waitress into the Elven Alchemist, leaving Michelle dazed and confused, asking the gathered guards nearby what had happened to her.

Felix felt a wave of resistance rise up for a moment, and then he took hold, telling Nareena's consciousness that it all just a dream. The ploy worked as usual, and Felix woke her up.

A Hunter and his Prey

At first, he almost couldn't resist feeling Nareena's body with her own hands. He looked beneath the covers to find her naked, and realized she was beautiful. The scent of her perfume, the feel of her smooth skin, and the sound of her moan as he stretched her body were magnificent.

Lost in a euphoric moment, he stared at the mirror on the vanity across the room from him/her, and saw himself smile with her face. *Wonderful*, he thought to himself. *Just wonderful!*

The Human Alchemist sat at a small table near the window, not five yards away from the bed, and Felix turned to look at him as he labored away at a book of some sort.

"Oh, you're awake," Jonah said as Nareena rolled to face him. "You may want to get your clothes on, the fire's died down." He tossed her the jeans and shirt she'd worn the previous day.

Nareena slowly got up and got dressed, taking her time about every motion she made.

Jonah had no idea that Felix Armstrong was controlling Nareena, and so he wasn't entirely prepared for her to go over to the door and prepare to leave.

"Hey, be back in a couple of hours. It'll be your shift, and I want to get some more sleep," Jonah called after her, and Nareena simply nodded her reply.

From Nareena's mind, Felix knew that the Bounty Hunter was across the hall, hopefully sleeping. Having so recently acquired this host body, the Sidalis had to wait a bit until he could make another leap.

He eased Nareena's body close to the door across the hall from where she and Jonah had been staying.

Putting her ear to the door, Felix listened for any signs of activity on the other side, but he could discern nothing, not even the soft, sound of lungs filling with air.

Ever so carefully, he gripped the handle of the door, and turned it, slowly opening the door.

What transpired next occurred so quickly that Felix couldn't even blink Nareena's eyes before it was over.

As the door reached the half-open point, the line of copper thread tied around the handle of the door pulled taut, flipping a small lever attached to the other end. A series of circular screws had kept the thread out of Portenda's way, should he awaken and decide to move about. The trigger on the other end of the thread was the release catch trigger for a large oak crossbow, which fired a single, heavy wooden bolt into Nareena's right leg.

Felix screamed through her throat in pain, and before she hit the floor, there was a huge, muscular body on top of her, hand around her throat and a long knife it its hand, tip poised to stab.

But the man's eyes went wide as he recognized her. He eased his hand off of Nareena's throat, causing her to cough and gag, and Felix knew now exactly what Hector had been telling him.

Portenda the Quiet was not to be trifled with lightly.

"Nareena, what are you doing," Portenda growled, pulling the arrow out of her leg roughly. "You know I set my room when I sleep."

Such power, such grace, Felix thought, awed beyond reason. *And to be so prepared.* This man, above all others, he would not attack outright.

But the Elf girl had other skills. So long as Felix inhabited her body, he could utilize her knowledge and Class abilities.

He pulled a small vial of green liquid from her jeans pocket, and drank the healing potion. In her left pocket, he knew, she kept two vials of a highly lethal poison, and on one of her belt loops, she kept a pouch filled with a green dust that could cause a number of altering effects in a victim.

Through these means, he could debilitate the Bounty Hunter and leave him helpless, or at least slow him down. After all, Genma hadn't hired him to kill any of these three people. He'd been hired to give them pause, nothing more, he thought with a malicious grin.

"And what's so funny," he heard Portenda say, and Felix snapped out of his mental monologue.

"Oh, nothing." Nareena rubbed the back of her head awkwardly. "I was just wandering. I don't feel right, like I'm in a daze or something."

Portenda raised an eyebrow, and turned away, tucking the long, serrated blade under his pillow.

"Possibly a spirit creature had a grip on you," Portenda mused aloud, his tone still severe and colder than ice. "You have to be more careful. Now get back to your room." Portenda forced her back out of his room with an easy hand on her shoulder. "Like I said before, no screwing around." He thrust her out of the room and closed the door again.

Felix looked around at the inn's elegant decorations. How could anyone be so cold, so devoid of feeling, and yet so deadly? A set of traps, a weapon under his pillow, and an awareness that bordered on being godly. How could Genma have expected Wren Headsplitter to kill this man?

Felix had known the Werewolf for a little while. Though the mercenary was skilled and capable, it was simply a match that couldn't be won. He wondered himself what to do, but remembered the Alchemy at his disposal. There were always ways, if he just thought hard enough on them.

Felix/Nareena returned to the room Nareena shared with Jonah, to find Jonah still engrossed in one of his tomes of Focus knowledge. Though Nareena's mind retained a little information regarding the art of Focus, Felix knew that the Elven girl knew a small fraction of the information available to the boy. With Jonah concentrating as he was, Felix would have a hard time shifting from his current host to the Human Alchemist. Besides, he mused, if he made the jump right now, they both might realize that something had taken them over, and their resistance would be too much for him. But the Simpa was probably asleep again....

Felix Armstrong closed Nareena's eyes and focused, feeling out toward Portenda the Quiet.

A Hunter and his Prey

In his mind's eye, he passed directly through the wall, into the empty hallway, through another wall, and finally, hovered over the Bounty Hunter.

As his spirit approached closely enough to lean over the slumbering form of the massive Simpa warrior, something in the air around Portenda leapt out at him—a natural defensive aura of some sort.

A barrier, he thought in shock. *A mental barrier!*

Extending his ghostly fingers like tendrils toward the vague barrier, Felix began the tedious task of working around Portenda's defenses.

This task turned out to be far more taxing than he would have imagined possible. Only Psychics had ever offered such strong mental defenses, but the Bounty Hunter was no Psychic. Though it drained him, Felix managed to create a single opening in the mental shield.

Taking his essence and forming it into a spear of energy, he dove headlong into Portenda the Quiet's mind.

"What in the name of the Heavens?" He arrived on a darkened theater stage.

The mental landscape of most individuals took on the appearance of an area or place familiar to the person, and often reflected their personality. The Elven woman's mindscape had, for example, appeared to be a large laboratory, with many different doors that led to the various realms of her mental state. Every other mind he had visited had similar doors, even if they were suspended in mid-air in a field or forest. Here, he stood alone in a spotlight upon a stage.

As he looked out into the rows of seats, however, he saw that he was not alone; out in the audience, about halfway to the back, sat Portenda the Quiet. He did not look pleased.

"Who are you?" The Bounty Hunter rose from his seat, a growl rumbling in his chest. "Identify yourself."

Felix ignored him.

The Simpa raised an ancient mecha weapon, something that Felix had once called a pistol, and trained it directly at his ethereal chest. *Oh boy,* Felix thought. *I've never had to do combat with someone mentally.*

A moments reflection dispelled his panic. *Wait a minute. I'm the one in control here; I'm the one whose power matters in the mindscape.*

"My name is of no consequence, my good sir." He bowed grandly in the spotlight. "I am a figment of your imagination, nothing more."

The Bounty Hunter cocked the hammer on the pistol.

"That can't hurt me, you know. I'm just a stray thought, a wandering image summoned up by your subconscious."

A thundering report echoed in Portenda's mind as Portenda fired a single shot into Felix's left leg.

"Haaauughh!" Felix screamed in agony as he dropped to the stage, his ethereal body suddenly very solid and bleeding all over the place.

"I was being generous." Portenda approached the stage and holstered the mecha weapon, his footfalls echoing through the theater.

Felix worried that the damage he had suffered here would appear on his physical body back at Hector's home, and realized that he had made a huge mistake in coming to this man's mindscape.

"I shot you just below the kneecap, demon," Portenda now climbed the stage stairs.

As Felix got to his wobbling feet, Portenda dashed across the stage in two leaping bounds, latching his huge right hand around Felix's throat, squeezing hard.

"I know of you Dream Stalkers." Portenda referred to the rare demons that inhabited the Dreamscape and killed their victims through their dreams. "The same rules apply to you as they do to us: if you die here, your body dies in the physical plane. Before I crush the life from you, Hell-spawn, may I ask if someone sent you?"

Before Portenda could torture an answer from his prey, Felix Armstrong pulled himself all the way back to his own body.

Shooting upright in his bed, Felix gasped for breath, and looked down at his uninjured leg with relief.

When he looked outside, the sun had begun its ascent into the skies.

* * * *

"Nareena, are you all right," Jonah was asking the Elven Alchemist as he shook her awake.

She had a headache that made her head feel as though someone had been hitting her with a soft wooden bat all night long, and she rubbed her temples as she sat up. The sun was rising outside, and she realized that she had slept through her entire shift. Yet, she was fully dressed, and lying on their bedroom floor.

Portenda also stood over her, his muscular arms crossed over his chest.

"I, I think so. Why am I out of bed," she asked, to which Jonah just smiled, giving her a hard hug.

"You were possessed, most likely by a ghost or a demon," Portenda said flatly. "In this city, it's not unheard of." He remembered how foolish Nareena had been to enter his room without heeding the traps he would inevitably have set. "The same creature tried to take me, but found I was a bit more difficult to take over. We have another day to wait for our messenger. I propose we go our separate ways for the day, meeting only for meals to discuss our day's events. Agreed?"

Jonah and Nareena smiled a little at one another, and turned back to nod at Portenda.

"Good. If you're going to have your coupling," the big man said as he turned and left the room. "Do it during daylight."

Leaving the Alchemists behind, Portenda made his way slowly out of the hotel, and into the brightening streets of Palen. *The city of magic*, he thought. Such oddities abound here.

The sounds and sights of children at play before school did a little to lift his spirits, and he ducked quickly as a soccer ball flew past his face.

A Hunter and his Prey

"Sorry mister," a Jaft youth exclaimed as he ran past.

Portenda rubbed the boy's hairless head as he passed under his massive arm, and the boy laughed and pushed off of him. *These are the moments worth remembering*, he thought with a subtle grin.

"Sorry about him," the boy's father said as he pursued in a brisk, steady walk. The Jaft's natural odor almost knocked Portenda off of his feet, but he shook his head and gave the middle-aged man the same grin.

"Boys will be boys. I understand." He noticed the way the Jaft kept glancing at his weapons. People tended to act a bit timid around the Bounty Hunter, and he realized that appearance, even in this city, wasn't very comforting to people. *Hmm*, he thought. *Perhaps I should have left the weapons behind.*

He brushed this thought aside as he continued on through the dirt roads and alleys of the city, drinking in the morning life of Palen.

Wrapped up in his morning observations of daily life, the Bounty Hunter didn't feel the eyes upon him.

* * * *

"Your guest has arrived, my lord," Kobuchi said, making certain to leave the inflection out of his voice.

Genma hadn't noticed that the Kobold now had complete control of himself, mostly because he hadn't bothered to take a close mental probe of his servant, who was giving serious thought to a change of job.

"He is in the meeting hall," Kobuchi reported in his best imitation of a soulless drone.

Genma smiled beneath his ivory mask, lifting the obscene, demonic visage a bit.

"Very good. Used a Teleportation scroll like I asked, did he?"

Kobuchi nodded without comment.

"Good. I'll go see him now. You may return to your chamber."

The Kobold moved away slowly, shuffling his feet.

Too bad these side effects last so long, Genma thought. The Alchemist formerly known as Allen Staples stalked down the darkened halls of his tower, passing by several Alchemy beasts and creatures of a nature so warped he wondered why he hadn't slated them as failures. Still, he mused, they served their purpose.

The black stone of the walls and floors stood motionless and soundless around him as he descended through the tower stairwell and stalked down the hallway of the first floor. The soft echo of his boots clacking against the hard stone met his ears and reminded him of his deep, pressing loneliness. In about a week, that feeling would recede as he remade his loving wife from his niece's body. Sure, he felt a twinge of guilt at using his own brother's daughter in such a way, but he had to have her back. There was no point to life if he had nobody to share his pain and his joy, his ups and downs. That was why, after reading the ancient texts he had saved from his home before he burned it to the ground, he kept on living. He had discovered a way to change a person's mind and body permanently, and make them a copy of another person. The creation of his tower fortress had come first, followed by the acquisition of the machinery he would use in his experiments as he awaited the right time to procure his niece. Eileen hadn't yet grown into womanhood when he first became Genma of the Black Tower, and he had been forced to occupy his time with other projects.

But he had always known that he would use Eileen for the rebirth of his lovely bride. From a young age, she had looked much like her aunt, and now, she would be her aunt in essence. But he had to put these thoughts to the back of his mind, and prepare for the meeting with Telroke. He approached the grand twin doors of red-painted steel, and thrust them open, stepping into the grand meeting hall.

He had adorned this meeting chamber with regal decorations and artifacts that he had gained possession of through the years as Genma of the Black Tower.

Seated on one of the low standing sofas was a bulky Simpa with a water skin, which Genma suspected wasn't filled with water. This man reeked of liquor.

"Perfect," he grumbled to himself, observing the sloppy way the Simpa was sprawled on the sofa, lounging like this was his own home.

"Nice digs you got here, man." Telroke gave him a drunken grin and took a swig of his water skin.

"Yes, well, they are mine. So if you would be so good as to take your foot off of the sofa."

The Simpa looked at him for a long, silent moment before pulling his left leg down off of the sofa.

"I am pleased to see that my servant's message did not go unheeded."

"He said in his letter that this had something to do with my son." The belched loudly, the raw sound of it echoing through the grand hall.

Genma squeezed his eyes shut for a moment. Such manners, he thought in disgust, but he forced a smile that Telroke couldn't see in any event. He was having a hard time keeping his emotions in check, his calm, calculating manner quickly deteriorating in this drunkard's presence. As Genma stepped closer, he smelled the stench of stale sweat, long soaked into Telroke's ragged clothes.

"So what do you want from me?"

"I want to know about your son, Mister Telroke. Everything you can tell me about him, any small detail, would be most useful. But you don't have to tell me now. This afternoon, at lunch. Arrangements have been made for you to stay here with us for a little while. May I suggest that you take a shower or a bath? I have some clothes to replace the rags you're presently wearing."

Telroke laughed, a harsh, ragged sound that tore at Genma's ears.

"Sure thing, buddy. I am startin' ta smell pretty bad, even by my standards," Telroke said. "Oh, and don't worry. I'm not gonna be sloshed the whole time I'm here." He got up from the sofa as another of Genma's servants, an ancient servant robot from the Age of Mecha, rolled on its treads up to the Simpa. "I just like to keep the edge off, you know?"

A Hunter and his Prey

"Yes, quite," Genma rasped rather more curtly than he had meant to. *Gods, this man is intolerable*, he thought. *No wonder his own flesh and blood hates him.*

"Unit F-Thirteen will show you to your quarters and get you anything you might need. My hospitality is at your disposal. Try not to abuse it too much," he added as an afterthought, storming from the meeting hall as swiftly as he could without seeming too rude.

Genma hurried to his screening chamber on the first floor, and activated the bank of monitor screens linked to the security cameras he had scattered throughout the first five floors. He watched as the Simpa followed behind the robot with a slightly drunken swagger.

"What a waste," he muttered before he sat to keep an eye on his new houseguest. "He might prove more trouble than he's worth."

* * * *

Blink had slowly become aware of his own evolving intelligence, and he now understood the Common tongue very well, though he could not respond to it in any way. As he had darted through the plains west of Palen, he had passed many merchants and bands of travelers, including a group of wagons belonging to one of the Wayfarer clans. Wayfarers were bands of tradesmen and adventurers that formed tightly knit packs that traveled the lands of Tamalaria without any permanent home. Their home, they often said, was the open road, their greatest treasure, their freedom.

Blink had landed amid one of their wagon circle encampments, and one of the children, the son of the clan leader, had scooped him up without fear. Blink knew not to harm the child, but was not very trustful of the way he was being carried in such a hurry.

The boy, a youth by the name of Billy Cole, rushed to his father's side.

The short leader of the clan, a man by the name of Steven Cole, turned as his son tugged at his chain mail shirt. "Papa, papa, look at this critter."

The Human leader of the Yellow Ribbon Clan of Wayfarers turned to look at Blink, and his mustache twitched as he grimaced at the Alchemical beast.

"Let me see that thing." The man reached out with his left hand.

A yellow ribbon fluttered about his wrist as he reached for Blink, who willingly scuttled up into his palm, and sat there looking up at Steven Cole with unwavering eyes. He was large enough to cover the man's whole hand, as Steven Cole wasn't the biggest man around. Nor was he, unbeknownst to Blink, the most capable fighter in the clan. But he had the most charisma and a knack for leadership, formerly being a Captain in the Desanadron Standing Army.

Steven smiled as he brought Blink up to eye level. "It's an Alchemical beast, son. Where's your master, little fellow?" He gently ran a finger along Blink's furry head.

Blink purred in response, and hopped around on all eight legs, gibbering unintelligibly at the Human.

"What the Hells is that thing?" one of the other clansmen asked as he approached.

The third voice came, Blink saw, from a red-furred Werewolf, a hulking brute of a man with heavy, metal gloves over his fists.

"Billy found him out by the perimeter." Steven looked Blink over. "Don't quite know what to make of him, though. I think he can understand us. Think you might be able to fetch Helena?"

The Werewolf grunted and shuffled away, and a minute later, Blink made out the sweet scent of fruit-based perfume.

A tall, elegant Elven woman came close to Steven Cole and the boy, who was jumping up and down excitedly, telling the other children of the clan about how he'd found something neat by the perimeter. Children, Blink thought, rolling his tiny eyes.

The Alchemical beast turned his attention to the Elven woman, who now stared at him, her eyes filled with a sense of wonder. An aura of power radiated from her body as she spoke very softly to him. "Speak with me," she whispered.

Blink found that he could not stop thinking about the task that his owner had set for him.

"I see," the Elven woman said after a few minutes. "He is on a mission. We cannot keep him, Billy." She patted the boy on the head.

"Aw, mom," the boy moaned.

Blink whipped his head around and saw that the boy's ears had the distinct point at their tops, revealing that he indeed had Elven blood.

"Why not?"

"Because, sweetie," the woman said, her tone more motherly now, and less otherworldly. "He has something very important he has to do. He's a messenger, and he has to be going that way." She pointed over her shoulder to the east. "And I believe he's going to need help. He's fast, Steven," she said, addressing her husband. "But I get a sense of real necessity from him. Someone's life may hang in the balance."

Steven gave a 'hrrm' of pensive consideration.

"We can spare one person," he said. "We'll send him with Raja. He's the best candidate for this sort of thing."

The Red Tribe Werewolf, grunted and darted away, grumbling something about being an errand boy. He returned with a person wrapped entirely in thick, white bandages.

Blink looked at the man in the bandaging, and shivered. He didn't know exactly what the man was, but he was instinctively afraid of him.

"Raja, I have to ask you a favor." Helena spoke softly and the creature in the bandages croaked in response. "This little fellow has to get east. I believe he'll be able to communicate to you where he wants to stop or head to. Can you do this for us?"

The creature in the bandages brought its wraith-thin arm up to the bandages around its head, moving one strap, revealing a blaring, crimson eyeball.

Blink yipped in fear, and scurried up onto Steven Cole's shoulder.

A Hunter and his Prey

"Hey now, little guy, it's all right." The Human grabbed Blink and held him out towards Raja. "He's scary, sure, but Raja won't bring you any harm. He's one of us, even if he is a Troke."

Blink, for reasons he didn't know, understood exactly what a Troke was. They were, by and large, a vicious, merciless race of shapeshifters, able to take on the form of any creature they came in direct contact with. A rare breed of spirit beast that took physical shape, they often appeared as lumbering dog-men and boar-like beasts. This one seemed to prefer the appearance of a bandaged humanoid.

"Can you take care of this one, Raja?"

There was silence from the Troke for a long pause, which it broke by itself.

"Yyyyesssss." Raja's voice was like the sound of a boulder scraping down a mountainside. He slowly reached for Blink, who hesitated at first. When he made out the hint of a smile beneath that bandaged countenance, Blink scurried onto the offered hand, which stretched to three times its normal width to accommodate the Alchemical beast.

"Whaaaat issss yourrrrr nnnnnammme?"

Blink tried to think his name at the Troke as he had the Elven woman, and it worked.

"Blink, hmmmmm? Wwwwellll, Blink, it lllooks lllike we'rrrrre going to be trrrrraveling companionsssss, for a bit." Raja set Blink down on the ground gently, and the small creature heard sudden, violent sound of bones snapping and resetting, muscle tissue tearing apart and rearranging itself. A flash of light emanated from the Troke's body as it took on the form of a great, black stallion, with white bandages about its head and face.

The bandages revealed only one eye, and it was as red and bloodshot as before. "Get on," the Troke rasped through its equine teeth.

Blink climbed up Raja's leg and onto his back, sinking down as low on his back as he could.

Steven gave Raja a playful slap in the hind flanks, and the Troke looked back at him reproachfully.

"Aw, come on, I've always wanted to do that," Steven Cole said as the Troke took off at full speed, the little messenger astride his back.

"So, this is serious, eh?" he asked his wife quietly.

"Someone's life is in danger, Steven, and he, or she, had the presence of mind to send that little fellow for help. But it was very specific help he wanted. We could do nothing more for him."

Steven Cole took this statement in, wondering how the world operated on the whole for perhaps the thousandth time that year.

* * * *

Felix Armstrong decided that his best course of action would be to come forward and admit what he had done to the Simpa. Yet as he followed him, keeping himself well concealed at every point, he remembered that powerful grip on his throat, the accuracy with which the were-lion had fired his ancient mecha weapon. The truth, it was said, could set you free. "Yeah, death is a freedom of sorts I suppose," he grumbled aloud.

The sounds of the marketplace, opening up for the day, filtered into his ears, and he tried to decide whether the money was worth the risk involved in this assignment.

Wren Headsplitter had thought about the money, too, he mused. Look at how that turned out. *No more hesitation,* he decided. He sprinted out of cover and towards the Simpa Bounty Hunter, who spun and launched a sidekick at his face, stopping just an inch shy of contact.

Felix stumbled back, falling flat on his ass. Despite not being directly connected to his upper torso, he felt the impact and rubbed his hindquarters.

"You," Portenda growled. "I should have recognized you from the cafe." He crossed the distance too fast for Felix to respond in any way, other than to try and scramble to safety.

As he turned around on his hands and knees, ready to sprint away again, Portenda hefted him up by the back of his chain mail collar.

Portenda raised an eyebrow as he looked down, and saw that he had pulled Felix's upper torso into the air, leaving his body from the waist down on the ground. "What the—,"

Felix's legs lashed out at his shin.

Pain shot through his leg and Portenda dropped the Sidalis, who levitated his upper torso over his legs, and tucked his shirt back into his pants again, putting his hands up defensively.

"Wait a minute, big guy," he said. "What say we go back to that diner and have a chat? I'll pay." His brow broke out in a cold sweat.

Portenda's left hand was on the handle of his gun, but as Felix kept his defensive posture, he relaxed his stance and glared at the Sidalis.

"I'll explain everything about last night."

Portenda nodded, waving his hand out, indicating that Felix should walk ahead of him.

"Don't trust me, huh?"

"Nope."

"Understandable, all things considered." He was away forty thousand gold pieces. Forty thousand! So much for that new house, he thought, hanging his head in shame.

"You're a handsome fellow," Portenda said as they turned down a side street, heading for the cafe. "Must come in handy, considering what you hide beneath those clothes."

"Comes with the territory," Felix said feebly as they walked up the steps fronting the coffee bar. They stepped inside, and Michelle smiled at Felix winningly.

"Oh, hello again Mister Felix," She positively beamed at him. "I went to find you last night—I think," She bounced along as she led the two warriors to a booth.

A Hunter and his Prey

They sat, Portenda glared at Felix with as much malice as he could bring to bear.

The Sidalis felt that he might scream under that piercing gaze.

Missing everything, Michelle smiled again. "What can I get for you two gentlemen?"

"Two cuppas," Portenda said out of the corner of his mouth. "No rush."

The two men waited until the waitress sauntered away.

"Explain yourself. Now," Portenda demanded.

Felix heard the hammer of his pistol cock back beneath the table.

"Whoa, easy guy." Felix gave the Simpa his most charming smile. "Last night wasn't anything personal. I'm a mercenary, see? I was hired to distract you and your little friends for a couple of days, nothing more."

"Mmm hmm. And that's why you possessed the Elf, and tried to possess me? Is that your mutant power?"

Felix nodded, his face falling in defeat.

"I figured as much. Not a common Sidalis power, that. The only reason that I haven't killed you yet," Portenda leaned across the table as far as he could without revealing his weapon, "is that I don't get the sense that you're all that bad a guy. You need the money, you're just using your skills to get a few gold here and there, right?"

Felix nodded, realizing that it wasn't yet his turn to speak.

"I understand. I'm a Bounty Hunter, after all." Portenda gave the waitress a half-hearted smile as she set his mug down in front of him.

Before she had even turned to leave the table, Portenda drained his mug, and asked for another by holding the mug up with his right hand.

"My, my. Thirsty aren't we sir?"

"You know, this stuff's no good for you," Felix offered, taking a sip of his own cuppa.

"It keeps me awake. Besides, I think I might be addicted."

"Well, there's worse things to be addicted to."

"Agreed." Portenda put the gun away and folding his hands on the table's surface. "Now, tell me everything. In order."

"Well, what's there to tell?" Felix set his mug down. "A few years back, this Alchemist with a weird mask approached me in Ja-Wen, said he needed an occasional job done for him, dangerous stuff. Mostly going into places few people go to gather plants and the like, and get books out of guarded ruins. Nothing I couldn't handle," Felix said with a measure of pride. "Anyway, he contacted me a few days ago with this." He pulled out a small mirror, setting it on the table.

Portenda snatched it up, and tucked it in his own belt.

"That's all right, I won't be needing it back anytime soon." After this fiasco, he'd never work for Genma again.

"Go on." Portenda took the second mug of cuppa from Michelle, sipping at it more slowly, in less of a rush for the caffeine.

"He offered me forty thousand gold to keep you three from getting at him," Felix said. "I only have a vague idea of where his tower is, but I know it's harder than Hells to get to."

"As would be expected." Portenda took another sip of his drink. "So why the sudden change of heart?"

"Well, to tell you the truth, I've never run into someone so, well, capable," Felix said awkwardly. "I wouldn't have expected you to have a mental barrier up in your sleep. You're not a Psychic, are you?"

Portenda shook his head. "No. I'm something, else."

Felix nodded, appreciating the need for privacy more than most.

"What's your name?" Portenda demanded.

"I'm Felix Armstrong," the Sidalis said, offering Portenda a handshake, which the Simpa took. "And I already know who you are. Well, sort of. Anyway, what do you intend to do now?"

Portenda looked out of their booth window to the streets, where children still played in their attempts to delay going to school. "Where do we go from here?"

"You stay here and pay for the drinks, and do some serious thinking about your profession of choice," Portenda said, still looking out the window. "I'm going to go play some kickball." He exited the cafe without another look back at the Sidalis.

Felix Armstrong paid for the drinks, and asked Michelle what time she got off of work. The waitress immediately asked her manager for the rest of the day off, and the two of them left the café for her home.

This is much more my speed, Felix thought, trying to think of a way to explain his odd bodily nature to the girl once things got heated.

Looking over his shoulder, he saw the ruthless Bounty Hunter playing a pick-up game of kickball with a group of children of assorted Races. *Strange*, he mused as he turned away again. *So cold, and yet, not.*

A Hunter and his Prey

Chapter Eleven
Dawn of a New Day

After finishing their romp in bed, Jonah and Nareena had gone shopping for Alchemy ingredients and other assorted items and goods. They were presently looking over the suspicious items on a traveling Gnome merchant's wagon stand. Jonah picked up a pocket watch, and tapped it with a single finger, trying to see if it would explode or fall apart, as Gnome mecha sometimes did.

Though far more advanced than Dwarven technology, Gnome inventions tended to malfunction.

But the watch was stable, and he purchased it for four silver pieces and two copper, putting it safely away in his breast pocket.

Nareena smiled at the scruffy little merchant, paying him for a carpenter's hammer. She put the handle through a belt loop at her hip, making the hammer a quickly available weapon.

The two of them continued exploring the city. When they came out of one side street, they saw something that stopped both of their hearts: Portenda was smiling, laughing, and playing kickball with a group of children.

"Is he feeling all right?" Jonah whispered.

The Elven girl listened to the Bounty Hunter's hearty laughter and realized, with a start, that it was honest and fun-filled. The children were marveling over how, despite his size, the big guy couldn't kick a home run.

"I think so," she whispered in response.

The two Alchemists watched for about five minutes, until Portenda grabbed the red ball and called the children over to him.

"All right, now, you all have to get to school. Game's over."

All ten of the children moaned, complaining that they'd rather play games.

"Hey now, you all need an education. It's very important to your parents. Why else would they send you to school?"

They all agreed, and shuffled slowly away.

Portenda tossed the ball after them, and the children took it with them towards the two-story schoolhouse.

Jonah and Nareena approached, and Jonah cleared his throat rather loudly.

Portenda spun on them, his eyes wide, but he quickly took on his cold, hard mantle.

"What?"

"It's good to see you have a heart, is all," Jonah said.

Portenda pulled out a small mirror, and handed it to Jonah.

"What's this?" the Alchemist asked.

"Genma sent another mercenary after us. I let him go, but I kept that. It's up to you what we do with that. But be careful. Genma clearly has some sort of control over you. We don't want a repeat of the last situation with one of those."

Jonah looked up at Portenda, his jaw set, then tossed the mirror over his shoulder. "We don't need to speak to him until we have him under our boots."

Portenda clapped him roughly on the shoulder. "That's my boy," he said gently. He looked at the earrings Nareena had purchased from a jewelry store. "Out on a shopping spree?"

"Yeah," she said. "Jonah picked these out for me! Aren't they great?"

Portenda leaned in close, took one look at the earrings. "They're fake."

Both Jonah and Nareena turned beet red. "I paid good money for those," Jonah said. He took Nareena by the arm, leading her back to the store.

Portenda moved away, alone once again. He took to the back alleys and dark places of Palen, the underdeveloped and less visited places. After a while, he felt a familiar presence. "What do you want? I didn't summon you."

THIS IS NO WAY TO CARRY ON, Death said. A canine skeleton, pink, fleshy tongue waggling in and out of its mouth, stood beside him.

"Why do you bother me?"

YOU KNOW WHY. I FEEL PARTIALLY RESPONSIBLE FOR YOU, AFTER ALL. Death patted Maxi on the head. WHAT DO YOU THINK OF HIM?

"I think you've lost your mind. Don't you have a job to do?" Portenda pull a piece of wood out of the wall at his back and drew a small knife for whittling.

TIME HAS NO MEANING TO ME. YOU KNOW THAT.

Portenda simply carved away at the wood.

WHAT ARE YOU GOING TO DO ONCE YOU GET THE GIRL BACK? YOU KNOW JONAH STAPLES AND NAREENA WON'T STICK AROUND. THEY'LL HEAD BACK TO DESANADRON, TO TRU LIVE OUT THEIR LIVES IN PEACE. OR SO. YOU'LL BE ALL ALONE AGAIN.

"You don't have to tell me that, Grim," Portenda muttered. "I, I haven't thought that far ahead, yet."

Portenda felt his control dissolve in the presence of Death, much as it did when he was around his father. But this was different. Instead of seething anger, he felt more of an emptiness, a fear of being forever on his own, with no one but this dark fellow for company. Gods, he thought, even Death's got a companion now!

YOU'RE A PERSONABLE ENOUGH FELLOW. I KNOW ABOUT YOUR TENANTS. YOU TAKE GOOD CARE OF THEM. Death reached into his cloak for a dog treat.

Portenda watched the treat disappear as soon as it went into the skeletal canine's mouth and listened as the animal crunched it with his sharp teeth.

ESPECIALLY THE OLD JAFT. IF YOU GAVE UP YOUR CAREER, YOU COULD ACTUALLY AFFORD TO HAVE SOME FRIENDS, YOU KNOW.

"I can't give it up," the Bounty Hunter replied flatly. "It's as much a part of who I am as my arms and legs. Besides, I've got bills to pay."

YOU'VE SAVED ALMOST EVERY COIN YOU'VE EVER MADE. YOU COULD RETIRE RIGHT NOW AND NEVER WORRY ABOUT

MONEY AGAIN. BESIDES, LANDLORDS MAKE DECENT MONEY, IF THEY PLAY THEIR CARDS RIGHT.

Maxi stalked a short way away to do his business, rather more noisily than Portenda cared for. When the pungent odor hit him, he almost vomited.

LET'S GO SOMEPLACE LESS, OFFENSIVE, Death said, his eyes blaring with crimson light as he glared at his pet, who whined in his own defense.

The three figures, two of whom nobody else could see, made their way into a darkened archway down the alley, a back door to one of the city's less popular diners.

"You never cease to amaze me," Portenda said to Death. "What made you get a pet?"

YOU'VE ALWAYS SAID I NEEDED A FRIEND. SO I SORT OF MADE ONE, AS IT WERE. HE ISN'T MUCH TO LOOK AT, BUT IT DOES FEEL GOOD TO HAVE SOMEONE TO TALK TO.

Portenda looked at the mutt, who was busily grooming his bones. He watched as Maxi took one of his own ribs off of his spinal column and started digging in the dirt to bury it.

MAXI, NO! THAT'S YOUR BONE! YOU DON'T TAKE THAT OFF AND BURY IT. Death gave Maxi a light rap on the head with the blunt end of his scythe.

The dog whined again, and returned the rib to its place, where it grafted instantly back to the spine.

STUPID DOG.

"Nobody ever said they were geniuses." Portenda finished carving his little figurine. It was a plain wooden replica of the being he was speaking with. The level of detail was minimal, but then again, there wasn't much to detail about Death. A robe, a scythe, and a skeletal hand, always visible on the shaft of the tool of his trade.

NO, AND IT'S A GOOD THING THEY DIDN'T. THE WORLD HAS ENOUGH STUPID STATEMENTS TO GO AROUND. THINK ABOUT WHAT WE TALKED ABOUT, PORTENDA. YOU NEED A FRIEND AS MUCH AS I DO. MAYBE MORE SO. Death faded from Portenda's vision.

* * * *

Blink had never been comfortable traveling on anything but his own eight feet or on Eileen's shoulders. Still, the bucking motion of the Troke beneath his body was better than swinging around in a cage in some lab of that dreadful tower.

"Don't be nervous," Raja said back to the minute Alchemy beast. "I've borne Minotaurs on my back, little one. You're perfectly safe." The Troke charged at a slower pace to put Blink at ease.

The creature relaxed his death grip on the Troke, and sighed heavily to himself. *I must be getting close. I must be!*

Blink pressed his furry head against the Troke's body, and tried to guide his thoughts into Raja through personal contact. *Where's the nearest city?*

"The nearest village is Oordek, a small farming community approximately half a day away from the city of Palen."

Something about the name of that city struck a chord down in Blink's core: that was where he had to go.

"So it's Palen, then, little one?"

Blink nodded rapidly, and Raja picked up his pace. "I'll have you there by midnight. Any idea who you're looking for?"

Once again Blink nodded.

"Good, because I don't think the citizens of Palen are ready to deal with me. When we get near the city outskirts, I'm going to let you off."

Blink thanked Raja as best he could, and settled himself in for the last leg of the long ride.

More than anything, he wanted to get back to his owner.

* * * *

Perhaps because he worried all the time, or perhaps because of the chill that had run up his spine, Jonah took Nareena by the hand and started actively searching for the Simpa Bounty Hunter. The sounds and smells of noon meals being made in the nearby diners and private homes filtered through the air, inviting him to forget his troubles, but he shrugged the sensation off and took up his search once again.

Jonah looked in all of the places he could imagine Portenda going to. First, he led Nareena to the artisans' square, where blacksmiths, armorers and artifact dealers kept their stores and booths. However, nobody he asked had seen Portenda, or anyone matching his description.

Next, they visited the café where the trio had taken coffee and cuppa, but none of the waitresses had seen him, after his meeting with the mercenary.

While Jonah tried to think of where their friend may have gone, Nareena raised her arm and pointed at the Bounty Hunter, who emerged from an alleyway nearby.

"Found him," she said.

The Bounty Hunter was scowling at nothing in particular. She remembered again why she sometimes had a real sense of dread around him.

As they stopped a few feet away, he turned his sneer on them. Slowly his facial muscles relaxed, returning him to the calm, Monk-like stare he kept at most times.

"We've been looking for you," Nareena said before Jonah could blurt out anything foolish.

Portenda the Quiet said nothing for a moment, still coming down from his strange conversation with the Grim Reaper. His mind kept turning one of Death's sentences over, trying to analyze it properly, but coming up empty. I FEEL RESPONSIBLE FOR YOU, Death had said. What did he mean by that? He decided he could review it better if he had some nourishment first.

"Come on. You two pick a new place for us to eat today," he offered, folding his broad arms across his chest. "I'll pay."

A Hunter and his Prey

"As usual." Jonah sighed with relief. Though Portenda sounded a little more aloof than usual, it seemed almost forced, as though he were restraining himself or thinking about something that he didn't want the Human Alchemist to worry about.

The stones here and there in the dirt roads skipped and skidded with the faint pit-pat they made in such towns as the trio walked along,

Jonah took the lead with Nareena a step or two back and to his left, and Portenda bringing up the rear. He sampled the air with his nostrils, and let the sweet scent of pastries and sugary confections lead him along. A light breeze blew down the streets of Palen, and the cooling gust whipped his lengthening hair across his head, taking away the beads of sweat that had been forming on his forehead.

When Jonah stopped, the other two formed up behind him.

Nareena giggled and Portenda let out a low "Hrrmm," as they looked up at the shop that Jonah had let his senses select: 'Granny Tammy's Pastries and Sweets,' the sign heralded for everyone to see.

Blood flushed Jonah's cheeks, and he turned to give his girlfriend and his ally a friendly smile.

"What can I say? I'm a twenty-three-year-old boy." He sprinted through the quaint little white door and into Granny Tammy's.

Nareena looked up into Portenda's ashen eyes, and searched for even a hint of humor. Much to her disappointment, she saw nothing but the barren wasteland that was the mystery of Portenda the Quiet. She slumped her shoulders a little, and shuffled after Jonah, sickened at heart that the Simpa could find no humor in the situation.

Portenda followed her in. Just before she went over to where Jonah was ordering a slew of teeth-rotting products, he put a hand on her shoulder gently, turning her around.

She gazed up into eyes that appeared to hint at tears.

"Forgive me," he whispered ever so softly to her. "I just have to keep myself together right now. I can't explain right now. Later, I promise."

Due to her Elvan nature, Nareena felt a powerful urge to wrap herself around him and offer her empathy. But he was resolutely holding his emotions in check, and such a gesture might break him.

How could any one man be so self-conflicted? How had he survived so long this way? she wondered. Nareena wasn't aware of how close her sentiments were to Death's.

Instead of hugging Portenda, she turned and stood next to Jonah, who was greedily piling his purchases high on a platter, and stuffing half of them in his rucksack for later.

Granny Tammy herself was running the store, and she appeared to be a kindly old Human woman, complete with white beehive hairdo and matching apron.

She's like something out of a children's picture book, Nareena thought.

The old woman smiled at Jonah, and pinched his cheek. "Now you don't eat all of those at once, young man. You'll be up past your bedtime for certain.

Oh, hello deary, how can I help you," she said to Nareena as Jonah indicated, via pantomime since he had a pastry lodged in his mouth, that he was going to get them a table.

Nareena asked for a small assortment of fruit pastries and a few doughnuts, placing them on a platter and sitting next to Jonah in a booth near one of the storefront windows.

A few minutes later, Portenda sat down across from them, his own platter heaped even higher than Jonah's.

The Human Alchemist stared at Portenda's order, then up at the lumbering Simpa as the Bounty Hunter jammed a chocolate covered doughnut in his mouth.

He mashed it around for a moment, then raised an eyebrow at the two Alchemists. "Wha," he managed through a mouthful of half-chewed food.

Jonah burst out in laughter, and Nareena joined soon after. Portenda felt a bit of an ass, but finished swallowing before he growled mockingly at them both.

"So how much longer do we have to wait for this messenger?" Nareena murmured around a doughnut.

Portenda folded his hands beneath his chin, his elbows propped on the table for support. He sat silently, chewing the last bits of a pastry, thinking on how much time had passed.

"Technically, we have to wait for another full twenty-four hours. At our audience with Death yesterday, he said two days. That means we should expect the messenger between midnight tonight and midnight tomorrow."

Jonah and Nareena looked at one another and back at Portenda, and each heaved a sigh.

"I know, it doesn't seem like we're making much progress."

"Portenda, we made more headway in Desanadron," Jonah complained. He tossed his hair, and finished his current regimen of sugar. "We should find some more files to read through, ask some questions around town, something other than drink coffee and shop."

"Or talk with Death," Nareena chimed in, taking a swig of her water.

"Uh, let's not do that again anytime soon," Jonah said.

You have that option, Portenda thought bitterly.

"Perhaps we should do some training," Portenda offered, sparking a small light in Jonah's eyes.

Nareena, while she didn't look thrilled at the prospect, seemed interested enough.

"Finish your drinks, and we'll head to a clear area. Palen surely has a training ground for their city guards. We'll ask to use it."

After hastily finishing their drinks and packing away excess pastries, the Alchemists followed the Bounty Hunter outside, and then through the busy streets of Palen, magic capital of the world.

Palen was without much in the way of criminal activity, as all of the police and constables were wielders of magic of some form. And Palen's government didn't hire amateurs, so if someone were foolish enough to break a law within the city limits, they had to be pretty good at escaping. Punishment in Palen came in several interesting forms, including being turned into a toad for a period of six years before being given to a high wizard. The sentencing was considered harsh to those who knew the tendencies of Palen wizards.

Constables had a training ground near the central administration building.

Palen, being a medium-sized city, had only four constable stations, but central was smack dab in the middle of the city, next door to the high council meeting hall. Behind the two buildings a high brick wall closed in the training area, a magically enchanted space that was several dozen times larger within the walls than it appeared to be from outside.

Time and space, through Enchantment magic, could be manipulated by a decent practitioner, and the Palen city police used this to their advantage.

Portenda had read about this feature of the city once when he had been on assignment, and decided that it would make the perfect training area for himself and the Alchemists.

A twenty-five minute walk brought them to the front of central administration.

Two Humans stood out front in uniform, puffing away on smoke sticks and laughing with one another despite their conflicting schools of magic. The gentleman on the left wore bright crimson and yellow tunics over his chain mail armor, and his hair was long and streaked with flecks of blond and black along with the bright red of his roots. The man on the right wore a similar set of tunics and sashes but in the many hues of water and ice.

An Aquamancer and a Pyromancer working side by side wasn't exactly common. Aquamancy did serious damage to a Pyromancer, after all. Gaiamancers hated being around Pyromancers for similar reasons, and Aeromancers around Gaiamancers.

"Gentlemen, may I speak with your commanding officer?" Portenda asked of the two of them.

The Pyromancer flicked his smoke into the street and smiled as he plumed out smoke.

Jonah hacked a lung, Nareena patting him on the back.

"What do you need him for?" the Pyromancer Corporal asked.

"We're involved in some rough business, and these two need to toughen up a bit," Portenda explained, giving Jonah a light shove. "We need to request permission to use the training area."

Jonah played it up and stumbled backward, falling over his own feet, and both officers sniggered.

Nareena helped Jonah up, and the Pyromancer sauntered inside of the station.

Portenda gave Jonah a little wink on the sly, and a few minutes later, the three of the them found themselves looking again at the Pyromancer, followed by a huge, heavily armored Minotaur of the rank of Major.

"Can I help you folks?" the Minotaur boomed.

Portenda sniffed, detecting a hint of Q Magic on the hulking Minotaur.

"Yes Major." Portenda tool another step forward. "We would like to borrow your training area for a short while."

The Minotaur looked Portenda up and down for a moment, and then cast his gaze over the Alchemists.

"They need it, from the looks of them. You've got as long as you need, unless my men need the ground. You'll have to record your names, though. Follow me." He ducked through the doorway, remaining ducked down all the way to his office, where the trio from Ja-Wen seated themselves.

Portenda had to stay crouched much like the Major throughout the process, and he caught the Minotaur looking him over again. Something about the way he was being watched put him ill at ease, though he couldn't explain why.

The way the Major smiled when they signed the registry sheet did nothing to ease his concerns.

"Very good," the Major said as Portenda signed the sheet. "It's nice to see you again, Bounty Hunter." Portenda finally realized why the Major made him uncomfortable. Portenda had taken a contract from him: one that had him searching for dirt on the Minotaur's commanding officer. Clearly, it had been a successful mission, because this man had been a Captain when Portenda had last seen him.

Jonah looked back and forth between the Minotaur and Simpa, feeling the tension build.

"I should never have agreed to help you," Portenda said in his usual tone of arctic chilliness.

The Minotaur threw his head back and laughed derisively.

"Ah, but the money was right, Portenda. Now, you've got what you want from me. Hells, I might even join you out there in a bit. Maybe show your little friends here what a real man is capable of in the arena."

Jonah wondered about Portenda's chances in an outright contest. The Major was larger and even more muscular than Portenda, and on top of that, he was a fighter-mage. How could the Bounty Hunter stand against him? He suspected he'd find out soon enough, and stayed close to the Bounty Hunter as the three of them made their way through the station and out the back door.

Training equipment lay strewn about the exercise field, which was roughly the size of a farm.

Portenda took off his weapons and his rucksack, setting all of his belongings, including his leather and metal vest armor, next to the door. He sauntered about thirty feet away from the Alchemists, then turned to face them.

"So, what are we going to do?" Nareena cracked her knuckles in anticipation.

Jonah had seen Portenda in combat and knew that he and Nareena would have to work together to land so much as a single blow, even with the aid of Alchemy.

A Hunter and his Prey

"Come at me. Both of you," Portenda said, inviting them to attack. "Be warned, your tricks aren't going to do you much good." He easily deflected the throwing knife that Nareena had hurled at him.

Nareena looked over to Jonah to see what he would do, but Jonah had taken off his own rucksack and had drawn the enchanted short sword his father had given him.

"Jonah, what are you doing?" Nareena rasped as Jonah took a fighting stance. "If you use Focus and I use my potions and powders, we can take him down."

Jonah just stood out in the hot sun, waiting.

Got to wait for him to make the first move, Jonah thought calmly, shifting his weight from his front leg to his back. *Any moment now.*

Unfortunately, he didn't say those words out loud. Nareena sprung forward, dashing toward Portenda with a hand full of light yellow powder.

As she neared the Simpa, Nareena swallowed the powder, letting her saliva mix with the powder to unlock its power.

The Elven Alchemist skidded to a halt five yards from Portenda, and opened her mouth wide, electrical power bursting forward like a Blue Dragon's lightning breath weapon.

The Simpa Bounty Hunter turned into a blur of gold and slightly orange motion, his fur leaving a vapor trail as he dashed backward and around to her left.

As lightning erupted from her throat, Portenda planted his feet in a wide stance, using his body motion to amplify the effect of his upward thrusting palm. His hand collided with the bottom of her lower jaw, smashing her teeth together and sending her flying end over end.

When she landed a moment later, Nareena rolled onto her sore side, spitting blood and teeth to the ground.

Jonah moved forward, trying to keep his fury in check. Nareena could grow her teeth back with a healing potion.

He tried to stay focused on the sword in his hand, and on the hulking, gray-striped Bounty Hunter.

Portenda had returned to a neutral stance, turning his back on the fallen Elf girl, and spreading his arms wide to Jonah.

A taunt, the Human Alchemist thought. *Just ignore it.*

He's being cautious, Portenda thought with a grin. *Good, he's learned something along the way. But he's waiting too long.*

Portenda reared his head back, and loosed the unearthly battle roar he had used to make the spirit creature solid in the tavern on the east end of the city.

As the unnatural sound pierced Jonah's eardrums, his entire body went numb and he watched helplessly as his father's short sword fell from his open hands. His arms and legs had gone slack and he slumped to his knees, his hands hanging uselessly at his sides.

Portenda leapt through the air, thrusting his right leg out and kicking Jonah squarely in the face, sending him sprawling, tearing through the dirt of the training area.

Flares of light burst in Jonah's field of vision, agony racing through his skull, and he thought he might have a fractured faceplate as he groaned, rolling over onto his stomach, trying to get to his hands and knees.

"All right, both of you, get up, take a healing potion, and think over what just happened," Portenda growled at the Alchemists.

Jonah hardly had the strength to move, but Nareena helped him into a sitting position, taking a potion herself and then pouring another down Jonah's throat.

He felt a whole lot better after a minute of the liquid's healing effect, and shook off his temporary daze.

Jonah raised a hand, and Portenda gave him a curious look. "What's on your mind, Jonah?"

"What was that," he asked. "That's the second time I've heard that roar of yours. I know that a Simpa roar can cause people to be afraid of them, and a Khan roar can make troopers so furious that they make stupid mistakes. But your roar," he said, being cautious with his choice of words. "It's something completely different. I was paralyzed, helpless."

Portenda grinned, but there was no mirth in it.

"How did you do that to me? What is it about you that makes that possible?"

Portenda just shrugged his shoulders.

"I haven't figured that out either. Just one of those things I can do," he explained. "Now, talk things over, and when you're ready, come at me." He once again stood in a neutral stance. "And remember, you should use everything at your disposal this time."

Jonah retrieved his short sword, sheathing it as he walked up to Nareena.

"All right," she whispered as he put his arm around her shoulder, staying close and keeping their voices low. "That didn't go well. Any suggestions, Jonah?"

The Human Alchemist tried to think over Portenda's movements, his speed and agility. As hard as he tried, he couldn't think of any weaknesses. "He's completely unarmed, but that doesn't seem to matter much, does it?"

"No, it doesn't," Jonah replied, rubbing his chin stubble thoughtfully. "If anything, it just makes him more brutal. Sometimes I get to thinking his sword and spear are for show more than anything. But, we may be able to use that to our advantage."

"How?" Nareena looked up at the Simpa, who hadn't budged.

"Well, we're out in the open, which he's comfortable with. What if that mobility and freedom of movement was suddenly cut off? I could erect stone barriers to cut off his range of movement."

"That'll cut us off too," Nareena said.

A Hunter and his Prey

"Not necessarily," Jonah said. "I could completely box him in. I'll trap him in a stone hut, leaving a small hole. You take one of your poison vapors and send it in through the hole."

Nareena smiled. "I like it. But what about the Focus Site? You'll have to take time to draw it."

He shook his head and she noticed that Jonah had been drawing a Focus Site on his hand with a pinch of his own blood.

"Nice to see you're a step ahead of me," she cooed, giving him a peck on the cheek.

"Always." He clapped his hands and let his Alchemy take over.

Portenda sensed a shifting in the ground around him, and an instant later, just as Nareena rushed toward his position, a stone hut formed around him.

Nice, he thought, *but flawed.*

Jonah had left a hole in the exterior of the stone trap, presumably so that Nareena could send a poison through, if he knew the Elven Alchemist at all.

Portenda took a deep breath, and pressed himself against the stone wall next to the hole.

Nareena grinned in triumph as she uncorked a glass tube, sticking the open end in the hole and venting the gas into the stone structure.

Portenda watched the green liquid turn to gas as it hit the ground, and the glass tube disappeared, as did the hole.

"There's no way he can get out of this one," Nareena shouted as she ran back to Jonah.

The young Alchemist couldn't help but be worried for Portenda's safety, and resolved to tear the structure apart through reverse Alchemy in five minutes' time. But a moment later, stone debris struck both he and Nareena as Portenda punched the stone barrier apart from inside.

The Simpa Bounty Hunter smiled like a man possessed.

As Jonah and Nareena broke apart, Portenda landed in a beast-like crouch in front of the Elf woman.

"Oh, ah, hi there," she stammered.

He bull-tackled her to the ground, punching her once in the right shoulder.

Nareena howled as her collarbone was shattered into broken waste.

Jonah clapped his hands together, activating one of his newly acquired Sites that he'd inscribed on his right arm.

This'll throw him for a loop, he thought as his body twisted and bent.

A moment later, he dropped to the ground, fire coursing through his veins.

Portenda was ready to leap at him, but stayed astride the Elven girl, clapping her once across the temple with one of his gnarled knuckles, rendering her unconscious. *What was Jonah doing now?*

Jonah's body contorted and expanded, and his flesh sprouted fur, his muscles exploding to several dozen times their normal size, and even his scent began to change.

"Remarkable," Portenda breathed, as a carbon copy of himself rose to its feet.

The only discernable difference was that Jonah hadn't been able to recreate the gray eyes or stripes, and patches of his skin were covered with a layer of steel.

One of the weapons racks near the central police station doors had mysteriously emptied.

Jonah marveled at the feeling so quick, so powerful. But he knew the change wouldn't last long—he had to take advantage of it now.

He took on an attacking stance, and claws sprang from his fingertips, spouting blood as they tore through the tips of his fingers. "Looks like we're pretty even now." Portenda's voice sounded almost ghastly coming from his throat.

"Not quite," Portenda said. "You've copied my body, sure. But can you copy my mind?"

Portenda sprang from his pent-up crouch, flying through the air and leveling a jump-kick at Jonah, whose right arm came up naturally in defense.

Portenda kicked off of the blocking arm, and landed in a three-point stance.

Jonah felt a rush of exhilaration as he defended himself from another chest-level kick, but the joy dissipated as Portenda followed up with an uppercut punch that laid him flat on his back.

Jonah was up almost immediately, however, his blood pumping harder than ever. He launched a hard roundhouse kick with his right leg.

Portenda parried effortlessly, but the metal plates on Jonah's artificial foot damaged Portenda's outstretched arm. The Bounty Hunter cursed himself silently for not simply evading the strike.

Jonah took to the offensive, swinging wildly with undisciplined punches and kicks as Portenda simply blocked and dodged.

Jonah was quickly losing both speed and strength, and as he half-heartedly launched a hook punch, Portenda found his opening.

He stepped forward into the strike, thrusting both hands, open palmed, into Jonah's arm, striking a nerve and the bones in his wrist hard.

The sudden impact staggered Jonah.

During that moment, Portenda backhanded him in the face as Portenda's left palm checked his chest.

Portenda drew his right hand back and punched Jonah in the stomach, still going through the motions of the self-defense technique.

As Jonah's head came down, Portenda raised his right arm and performed a heavy hammer blow on his jaw.

Jonah fell in a heap to the ground, his body quickly reverting to normal.

The entire series had taken two seconds to perform, and the sudden devastation had forced the Alchemical transformation to break apart and dissolve.

Nareena regained consciousness in time to see that she and Jonah had failed once again. Portenda was rubbing his wrist, however, a sign that Jonah had managed to hurt him a little.

Portenda lifted Jonah gingerly and carried him over to Nareena, his eyes filled with regret.

"Jonah, wake up," he urged as he laid the boy down on the dirt near Nareena.

The Elven Alchemist grabbed another healing potion, and poured it into Jonah's mouth, having already taken one herself.

A moment later, the boy was awake, and he quickly scuttled away from Portenda. His heart was filled with shame at his failed attempt to defeat the Bounty Hunter, and he felt almost useless.

"Nareena crouched down next to him, and tried to give him a comforting embrace, but Jonah shrugged her off, too ashamed to be close to anyone at the moment.

Portenda's heart sank. He, too, had once felt worthless, helpless. He stepped forward and offered his hand to Jonah, who refused it.

The boy stood up on his own, straightening his clothes.

"Jonah, don't sell yourself short. You just aren't using all of the tools at your disposal," Portenda said softly.

"Bullshit! What can we possibly do to get at you? You want to tell me that? What?"

"What about your sister," Portenda asked in a harsh tone.

Jonah's eyes went wide, and his mind came to a screaming halt.

"You still want to save her, correct? We're dealing with another Alchemist, Jonah. He's going to have soldiers, guards at his base of operations."

Nareena put her arms around Jonah's left arm, holding on tightly.

Jonah knew Portenda was right. He had to find a way.

"Take your time, and think it through. I'll be ready for you," Portenda moved away, turning to face them in his neutral stance.

"Jonah, are you okay?" Nareena gave him a quick kiss on the cheek.

"I'll be fine. It's just so frustrating! He's like the perfect warrior. I can't find a single weakness in him."

"I know of one." She pulled a silver dagger from her boot. She had kept it in a copper sheath, and she saw Portenda's eyes widen at the sight of it.

Jonah took the weapon from, tested its weight, and tried to think of how to use it to his advantage.

"About two pounds," he whispered. It was enough raw material to work with, but what could he do? If he made a different weapon out of it, he would have to use it, and Portenda could defend himself against weapons, chemicals, and traps. How could Jonah make certain that the metal touched him?

That's it, he thought excitedly.

"Sweetheart, stand right here." He moved Nareena to where he needed her, and took an inkwell from his rucksack. "This is going to seem odd, but trust me."

Dipping his finger into the inkwell and pulling Nareena's shirt out, he put his hand up under her clothes.

"Um, honey. Now doesn't seem like the right time for this."

"Portenda uses traps all the time, right? He reacts to whatever comes at him. But what about when something reacts to him? I've seen him counterattack other counterattacks, but what if the first counter isn't really an attack at all? What if it's a diversion, something to set up a chain reaction?"

Nareena thought she had an idea of where he was going with this, and Jonah darted away, keeping his distance from the Bounty Hunter. He inscribed a Site on Nareena, and one on the dagger as well.

The Simpa moved now towards Jonah, fists raised.

"Jonah," Nareena screamed.

The Human was ready for this. He ducked and rolled away from the Bounty Hunter's hard, straight-line punch.

He hadn't learned much about Portenda's fighting style, since it varied so much, but he knew the general signs of attack. He dashed in the direction that Portenda had come from, ducking down and drawing a single line in the dirt before darting away again from the attacking Bounty Hunter.

Nareena watched this odd dance for a few minutes, finally realizing that Jonah was systematically inscribing Focus Sites all over the training ground.

"Get ready," he shouted as he rolled behind Nareena, ducking down, his hands ready to clap together.

Portenda had leaped through the air, and was coming down with an overhand blow at Nareena, who leaned back as she heard Jonah's clap behind her.

The Site on her chest flared to life, and a gust of concussion force blasted the surprised Simpa as he closed to within an inch of her breastbone. That energy sent him flying, but he landed in a crouch, fist clenched and raised.

Jonah clapped his hands again.

Before Portenda could think, a pair of stone hands grabbed his ankles from the Focus Site he had landed on. Jonah's calculations were proving themselves most efficient, and Portenda was suddenly aware that he had fallen for a series of traps.

"Clever boy," he muttered, bracing his body for the impact from another Focus. A cannon had formed out of a nearby Site, and a heavy, leaden ball struck Portenda sent him sprawling.

He landed on his back near another Site, which burst with blinding light as his legs were transformed into steel weights.

"Oh shit," he murmured as he realized that his own legs had been transformed, leaving him immobilized as the silver dagger Teleported about fifty yards above him.

Just before the falling weapon slammed into Portenda's stomach, Jonah caught it.

"Got you."

Portenda's legs returned to normal, and he got up, brushing himself off.

He clapped Jonah on the shoulder as he rubbed his sore ribs. When the cannonball had struck him, it had broken two of them, and he was concentrating on his regeneration when the Major entered the arena courtyard, his heavy battle-axe over his shoulder.

A Hunter and his Prey

"I thought he was joking about coming out here," Jonah said as Nareena came toward them with their weapons and belongings in hand. He handed her the dagger, which she hastily tucked away in her boot sheath.

Portenda felt a little better as the copper sheath suppressed the silver's presence, but he didn't trust the Minotaur in the least.

"I see they managed to get you on that one, Bounty Hunter," the Major shouted across the hundred yards that separated them. "I'm not very familiar with Alchemy, but I'd say the boy is rather adept with it. It's nothing compared to real magic, though." He flexed his left hand, bringing a spark of energy to bear. "I'm surprised you bother to associate with anyone less capable than yourself, Portenda. I thought Bounty Hunters didn't keep company."

Portenda kept his face slack, but his left hand was making a fist on and off as he took his protective vest from Nareena and put it on.

"Thanks for letting us use the field." Jonah slung his rucksack over his shoulders. "I think we'll be moving along now, though."

"I don't think so, little man." The Major approached slowly, methodically swinging his battle-axe. "I'd like to pit your science against my magic, Mister Staples."

"That's not a fair fight," Portenda said as the Minotaur closed to within ten yards. The scent of dried blood wafted from his axe head, and Portenda listened to the rumble of magical force being summoned forth. The Major was going to force a confrontation, and soon, he realized. "Your magic is used to amplify your own natural physical capabilities, Major. Jonah stands no chance against you in a physical altercation, and you know it."

"Aw, what's the matter, Bounty Hunter? Afraid I might hurt your little friend?" the Major mocked.

"Yes, as a matter of fact." Portenda's voice sank to a growl. "And he *is* my friend, Major. I won't allow you to visit harm on him. Why don't you take me on instead? I don't have any magic or Alchemy to use against you, after all."

"I want the boy."

Arrogant bastard, Jonah thought as Nareena clutched him around the waist. "You can give him any weapon you want," the Major said.

An idea popped into Portenda's head. "All right."

Jonah and Nareena looked incredulously at the Bounty Hunter.

"Jonah, take this." He took his sniper rifle off of his shoulder and handed it to the boy. "Nareena, get behind me."

"Excellent," the Major said, bringing his magic to bear. "Now get ready for a real lesson, kid."

"Portenda, what are you doing?" Jonah held the sniper rifle awkwardly.

Portenda smiled broadly, his fangs gleaming in the afternoon sun. "Jonah, execute command seventy-three."

Portenda watched with satisfaction as Jonah's eyes glazed, though not nearly as much as when Genma had said those exact same words through the mirror communicator.

Portenda, Nareena, and the Major watched with fascination, and for the Major, a touch of fear, as Jonah's left hand flew over the rifle, transforming it into a sizable cannon.

The Major knocked the barrel, which had rested against his chest, aside, and moved forward, axe over his head. He swung down, but connected with nothing but air and ground, and looked to his left to find that the boy had darted around him faster than he could see.

Jonah felt adrenaline pump through his body, and he could actually see and control some of his actions as he executed the mentally programmed command. Portenda had used one of Genma's machinations as a positive course of action, and Jonah held the weapon level to the Major's head as he tossed a fire tincture at the Minotaur. It exploded against the Major, who ran around screaming, dropping his weapon as flames consumed his clothes and armor.

When they had burned away, the Major found he was undamaged, but completely naked. Jonah came down out of his trance, and the rifle became a normal mecha weapon again. The Minotaur covered his privates with his hands, and stared wide-eyed at the boy.

"You're a freak," he shouted at Jonah.

"And you're small," Nareena chided, getting a laugh out of Jonah and even a chuckle out of the Bounty Hunter. "Gods, my man there has a bigger crank than you, and he's Human."

The Major ran, cursing and shouting over his shoulder, into the constable station.

Jonah walked over to Portenda, holding out the rifle, but Portenda shook his head.

"Keep it."

Jonah positively beamed at him as he strapped the rifle to his back.

"When this is all over, it'll be useful for hunting fresh game for your mother to cook at home." Portenda's voice remained filled with good humor and spirits at the Major's expense.

As the trio left the constable station a few minutes later, Jonah pulled Portenda aside.

Nareena nodded to him, and walked a little way away, so that Jonah and Portenda could have a little privacy.

"Portenda, back there, did you mean what you told that Minotaur?"

Portenda raised an eyebrow at him, and Jonah moved his hands, feeling embarrassed about asking such a question. "Are we really your friends?"

"Certainly." He did, in fact, feel they were the best friends he'd ever had. But Death had been right: he didn't expect Jonah and Nareena to stick around once they rescued Eileen. They would most likely head back to Desanadron and settle in together. He'd be right back where he started: alone with his thoughts and his silence.

He put a companionable arm around Jonah and then Nareena, walking between them down the central road of Palen. "I say we've earned ourselves some entertainment," he said amiably to the Alchemists.

A Hunter and his Prey

"So where are we headed?" Nareena asked, surprised that Portenda was acting so chummy with both her and Jonah.

"There's a gaming house on the north end of the city. We can spend some time and money there. Who knows, maybe we'll actually win something." He doubted that they would be so lucky, but that didn't matter to him; what mattered was enjoying their company as much as he could before their messenger arrived. After that, it would be back to business.

He'd have to return to being Portenda the Quiet, instead of Portenda, friend of Jonah Staples and Nareena.

* * * *

The Master slept mostly during the day.

While Kobuchi was taking a bit of a risk, it was a calculated one.

The Kobold made his way to Eileen Staples' room, where he found her sitting at the table, picking at her lunch.

She looked up, startled to find him watching her. "What are you doing here?"

Kobuchi dashed over to her, speaking in a rush.

"There's something I need you to help me with. We'll both benefit from it, I assure you. The Master keeps a set of journals locked up two floors above us, in one of his offices. The door is hidden, so you wouldn't have noticed it, but I can get us in."

"Okay. Where do I fit in? And why do you want the journals?"

"I believe one of those journals records the process the Master used to make me his minion," Kobuchi explained. "If I can review it, I might be able to break his hold on me. But the desk drawer is sealed with Alchemy. I don't have any spells that he wouldn't notice or know of that can get me at those journals. You might. Also, you should be warned. The Master has a guest in the tower, and I'm not sure of him." He referred to Telroke, Portenda's father. "I saw him wandering around earlier, and we have to avoid him if we can."

Eileen decided that perhaps Kobuchi would be able to aid her from inside the tower when her brother came for her, as she prayed he would.

"Okay, I'll help you. When do we do this?"

"Right now." Kobuchi darted to the door, looking up and down the hallway.

Eileen gingerly raised herself from her seat, her body still stiff and sore from her injuries. She followed Kobuchi down the left of the corridor, all the way to the stairwell, and up two flights of stairs.

At the entryway to the floor, she had to stop and rest, already short of breath.

"Take your time," Kobuchi said. "I doubt that Telroke would come this far up the tower."

"Telroke?" she asked, still wheezing slightly.

"The Master's guest. He's a Simpa, a drunkard from what I can tell," Kobuchi said, glad that the offensive man had such a vice. It might make him easier to control or manipulate.

223

Steadier once again, Eileen indicated that Kobuchi could continue on.

He led her to a set of stones that didn't seem properly aligned with the rest of the wall.

Eileen felt a little foolish for not having noticed this before, but Kobuchi tapped a stone opposite the door, and it swung soundlessly open, revealing a small office with a single oak desk and a set of reference bookcases.

She followed him behind the desk, and he pointed to the top right hand drawer. "If it's opened normally, or with my magic, the Master will be alerted. I am hoping you have some other way to get into it."

He almost screamed in terror when Eileen touched the desktop.

"Be very careful," he moaned, frightened to the core that Genma would find out what he was up to, and do away with him altogether.

Eileen moved her good hand over the surface, and let a small amount of magical force carve a perfect square into the wood. She levitated the cut material up, and Kobuchi dove his hand in and withdrew two notebooks.

Eileen then floated the wood back into place, and restored the desk surface.

Kobuchi smiled broadly at her. "I'd offer you one, but I have to read them both through to make certain. Are you going to be staying in your room?"

"For a few more days," Eileen said quietly, now also afraid of what might happen if they were discovered.

"Good. I'll bring them to you with a set of notes when I'm finished." Kobuchi poked his head out into the hallway. When he saw all was clear, he led Eileen Staples back to her room and helped her into her bed, pulling the covers up over her.

She smiled and thanked him before nodding off to sleep. She really was a very pretty girl, and sweet to boot, he thought.

He had to help her escape the Master.

* * * *

Genma was not, in point of fact, asleep at the time. He was quite awake, but distracted by his visitor, the Simpa Telroke.

The man had done considerable damage to his provided quarters, and was trying to explain what had happened to Genma, but the ivory masked Alchemist finally held up a hand to stop him.

"Enough of this. I have some questions I'd like you to answer. Tell me about your son."

"What d'you wanna know?" Telroke managed halfway decent speech, seeing as Genma had cut him off after two bottles of his finest Shiraz.

"First off, what's he capable of?" Genma crossed his legs and folded his hands in his lap.

The entire room smelled like sweat, liquor, and freshly washed fur.

At least the man had taken a bath and changed his clothes, Genma thought as calmly as he could. Just being around this man flustered him.

"Well, you've got an impressive little army of beasties," Telroke said with a sloppy smile, waving his hands around for emphasis as drunks often do. "He'll be able to rip through most of them without a sweat, though. He'sh really good, at fighting, ya know?"

Genma had to restrain himself from yelling that he wanted specifics, statistics, something of more value than a vague statement like, 'he's good at fighting'.

"Why is it that you don't get along with him?" he asked, taking a different tack. "He's your own flesh and blood, after all. I would imagine you should be quite close."

"He's a little freak." Telroke's face turned into a familiar scowl. "If I didn't have to, I wouldn't even admit to being related to the boy. Besides, we've never been close."

Genma realized Telroke wasn't wholly in the room with the Alchemist, and wondered how this Simpa had become the drunken, angry soul before him.

"I suppose you have your suspicions about what he is," Telroke said quietly, his eyes drooping slightly. "His mother was a Khan woman."

"Ah, I see," Genma said. He had only caught a glimpse of the Bounty Hunter through the mirror communication with Jonah, but he had noted the odd gray stripes on his forearms. "So he's a half-breed, then? I thought Simpa and Khan were, incompatible. How did he come to be?"

Telroke spat on the floor, causing Genma to twitch slightly as the saliva struck the royal blue rug.

Have to remember to wash it or replace it, he thought.

Telroke shrugged. "I'm not certain. It's highly taboo what I did in the first place. And as far as I know, there's never been a child born from such a mating."

"Mating?" Genma asked, twisting the word meaningfully. "You took her by force, didn't you?"

Telroke looked away and growled deep in his throat. His mane stood on end, and he bared his teeth ever so slightly.

"I see. So how about it? Tell me what happened." Genma activated a Focus Site he had marked under the Simpa's seat.

Telroke's eyes glazed over for a moment, and he began speaking without willing it.

"Me and four of my tribesmen were patrolling the Hills around our village. We came upon three Khan, presumably collecting reconnaissance on the area. We hadn't been prepared to find anything out of the ordinary, but these Khan weren't even carrying weapons. That seemed a tad strange to us, so instead of outright assaulting them, we stayed back and observed from behind an outcropping of rocks. There were two men and a young woman, far more beautiful than the women of my tribe, even for a Khan. The men were muttering to themselves in some strange language I had never heard before. As they chanted, an orb of black energy began to form between them.

"Then the woman stretched out her arm, and a white light streamed from her palm into the orb. A wave of concussion force threw my allies and myself to the ground. The Khan men heard us, and they came at us, launching kicks and claw swipes that were clearly martial arts of some sort. But we were highly trained Soldiers, and our weapons were at the ready. The four of us hacked them apart in less than a minute. The woman tried to run, but I chased her down and had my way with her." There was the gleam of rapture in Telroke's eyes as he relived the sexual violence.

What a repugnant creature, Genma thought. *Then again, I have similar designs for my niece.*

"Any idea what they were trying to accomplish," Genma asked, letting the Focus Site's effect gradually wear off.

"No, and I didn't care." Telroke realized that something peculiar had been done to him. "And before you tell me what in the seven Hells you just did to me, I'd just like to add that my actions that day have led me to this place, speaking to you about my son. Strange, don't you think?"

"No, not really. And I just used Alchemy to help this little conversation along," Genma said slyly, crossing his legs as he spoke.

"Alchemy," Telroke said, raising an eyebrow. "Some new sort of sorcery, is that?"

"No, but science can get very close to magic." Genma smiled beneath his ivory mask. "Often times, I find, it's even better than magic. Now, please, continue Telroke."

The alcoholic Simpa scanned the room for any liquor bottles he hadn't emptied, and spotted one on the dresser behind Genma. He stalked around the masked Alchemist and opened the bottle with an echoing pop as returned to his seat. He took a long pull on the brandy, and wiped his mouth.

"After I was done with the girl, I punched her once in the forehead. I knocked her out." The quick drink had steadied his voice.

It appeared to Genma that without alcohol, Telroke could no longer function properly.

"My men admonished me for what I had done, yelling at me about the laws of nature that I had broken. I explained that I was leaving a clear sign to our hated enemies that we owned the Allenians, and that we owned *them* if we so chose. I bound the girl with some rope I kept in my pack, and hauled her back to the village with me.

"The elders didn't like it, but they approved from the viewpoint of conquest." Telroke took another swig as he smiled at the memory. "They declared that I could keep her as a trophy of war, use her however I wanted. But they tried to let the men that had been with me take turns with her, which I argued against. They agreed after a while, and I took her to my tent."

Genma had been listening intently when he had an odd chill race up his spine. Something strange was happening in his tower keep. Deciding to investigate later, he turned his attention back to the Simpa. "I assume she didn't go along peacefully."

"Not exactly. But after a few beatings, she stopped resisting. I took her every night for a month. Then one night, she told me that I couldn't. I asked her why not, and she told me that she was with child. My child." Telroke's eyes glazed over once more as he took down the last of the bottle's contents. "I would have told her that was impossible, except that Khan are known for their instincts for such things. In their society, a man cannot lay with his woman when she is one month along in her pregnancy. Instead, the man is then allowed to choose one of his wife's available sisters or friends, and take them when they have the urge."

"That's rather unusual," Genma said, genuinely surprised to learn something new about the world and its cultures from this drunkard. "I would imagine that leads to a lot of jealousy and broken marriages," he said.

"In Khan culture, I have learned, the bearing of a child is the most powerful statement of love between a man and woman. They will not risk the child's welfare by having relations, so the men are allowed an outlet for their more, primal urges." Telroke gave a sloppy grin. "No such standards exist in my people's society. However, I didn't wish to force the situation because I never expected her to carry to full term. After all, it had never happened before."

"I see." Genma, folded his hands in front of his chin. "But she did carry to full term. Were you there?"

"No," Telroke said flatly. "I was with most of the rest of my tribe, engaged with a small Khan village on the outskirts of our patrolling borders. As it turned out, it had been her village, her tribe.

We were entrenched outside of their village for six days. We made several attacks each day, slaying more and more of them each time we struck." Telroke swung the emptied bottle of brandy in the air like a weapon, reliving his glorious moments of sobriety, when battle was all that mattered, when victory measured one's worth. "We lost a few of our own, too, though. It is the nature of war that there is no such thing as victory without a price.

"Upon our return back to our own village, which we could now expand a bit since we had no immediate threats around, I noticed that a large group of women and the elders had gathered around my tent. 'She has delivered a child,' one of the elders told me.

I remember the anger in his voice, the hatred he felt for what I had helped create. A freak of nature." Telroke heaved the bottle at a side wall, smashing it into tiny pieces.

Genma grimaced at the sound of the impact, the explosion of glass against the concrete wall.

"But the elders did not bother me so much as the other one who stood there."

"The other one? Who do you mean?" Genma asked him, curious now that things had taken a turn in the tale.

"I swear that I saw the Grim Reaper looking in at the child." Telroke's voice said his mind dwelled in a faraway memory. "But he turned and stalked away when I spotted him, not once looking back at me or those gathered around my tent. The boy was born looking almost completely like a Simpa, one of our proud people. But the stripes of gray hue, and his eyes of the same ashen color, gave him away for what he was. A boy," Telroke said, tears threatening to escape from his eyes. "My boy. His mother named him Portenda, which in the Khan tongue means 'he who defies the laws'."

"Rather fitting, really," Genma said. "So, you let the boy live, raised him as your own. What of his mother?"

Telroke stood, tensing his muscles. "Well, for starters, the boy grew far more quickly than anyone expected. For the first year of his life, his bitch of a mother wouldn't let him out of her sight. By the time his first birthday came around, he was running, wearing a boy's clothes, and speaking the rough tones of the Khan tongue. He appeared to be a boy of five or six years of age when he turned just a year old, and many of the tribesmen started distancing themselves from me and my family, if that's what one could call them.

"He was a freak, but Gods damn it, he was my son." Telroke clenched his fists in rage. "I took the boy from the tent while his mother slept, and asked him if he could understand my words.

"'Of course I can,' the boy had responded to my disbelief. He knew both the language of the Khan and of the Simpa, and he was barely thirteen months of age."

"Remarkable," Genma rasped, now completely lost in Telroke's tale. "Please, continue."

"His mother and I spent much time apart, and I had started to take an interest in some of the other available women of the tribe. But the elders warned me that I could have no other woman. I had a child with the Khan who was my trophy, and as punishment for my violation of ancient taboo, I could take no other wife. I was furious. Now I was as much of an outsider as my own son and the woman I had brought to the village. I began accepting assignments from the elders that took me further and further from the village, for longer periods of time.

"I lost track of time. I started drinking," he waved a hand dismally towards the broken brandy bottle. "For eight years I was lost in a fog of alcohol and blood, but I didn't care. One day, when I came home, I found the boy was armed and training with weaponry. One of the young Hunters of the village told me as I approached my own flesh and blood that the boy had almost killed him in a sparring session. He was good, too good to be real. When I approached him, he dropped the weapons, and rushed up to me. He, he hugged me around the waist. 'Daddy, you're home,' he said to me."

A single tear streaked the fur on Telroke's face.

"But I knew what he was, and I knew that I had to do something to make myself free of him and his bitch mother. He was so fond of her, so close to her. Yet she never spoke to me, not a word in years. Not even to resist what I did to her. She never tried to escape, spent most of her time in the tent or the fields, working to harvest what few crops we grew in the Hills.

"I told the boy, Portenda, why don't you go a little further south of the village and train. The terrain is rough, and will be perfect for training your balance and strength. The boy was gone before I could blink, Genma. He's always been terribly fast." Telroke waved a finger at the mad Alchemist. "Don't be fooled by his size! Your guard creatures won't be able to so much as clear their throat before he blasts through them."

Genma figured that the man was blowing smoke, being drunk and not wanting to remember everything clearly. "I'm not worried too much," Genma said confidently. "Please, finish your story. I sense it's coming to an end."

Telroke grumbled and nodded, for he was indeed almost done.

"I took out my broadsword and stalked to my tent. Several of my tribesmen must have sensed what was going to happen, and they fetched two or three of the elders to bear witness. I entered my tent, and she was just sitting there, praying. She opened her eyes, and I her mute acceptance. 'I've come to kill you, you know,' I told her.

"And then, finally, she spoke to me. What she said haunts me to this day, Genma. She said, 'I died the day our child was born. My purpose in this life is served.' I used a single blow and took off her head. When I carried it over my shoulder outside, the whole village cheered for me. They welcomed me back as one of their own, but one voice cried out in agony. The boy charged through the crowd, swinging his own sword at me.

"I easily blocked him, kicked him away like so much trash.

"The village turned on him, all together once more. The boy turned and ran, and I followed after, leaving his mother's head behind on the ground. I caught up with him almost twenty minutes later, and he came at me, hard. I was actually being beaten back by a boy only half my size, a boy nine years of age. But his fury made him sloppy, and I disarmed him. I would have finished him off, but he invoked the Rite of Exile, a sacred tradition among our people. I could do him no harm, and he had to remove himself from the Allenian Hills. If ever he returns, both Races will target him. The elders of my village were willing to take him back recently, but he refused their offer. He will not stand against the Khan nation of the Allenian Hills. All because of some misbegotten allegiance to his dead mother." Telroke f moved over to the bed, slumping down onto it after a moment. "We're done for now, Genma. I assume I've given you what you want."

"For now." He got to his feet, still taking in everything that the Simpa had told him. *It was true, then*, he thought. Nine years old and on his own in a very harsh world. Yet, that boy had survived, and become the Bounty Hunter that threatened to ruin his plans.

He left Telroke to his thoughts and rest, and stalked the long corridors of his tower keep. He would have to speak with Kobuchi, make certain that the guard beasts were up to snuff. After hearing the Simpa's tale, he knew that Portenda the Quiet was as dangerous as he had suspected, perhaps more so. He also sensed that the confrontation between son and father hadn't gone exactly as Telroke had described it. He would have to take every precaution in the event Portenda found the tower before Eileen's transformation.

In the guest chambers, Telroke broke down and wept for the many sins of his life.

* * * *

Night had fallen on the city of Palen, and Jonah, Nareena, and Portenda had each blown roughly one hundred gold pieces on the gaming tables in the gambling hall of the city. As the three companions made their way out into the darkened streets of Palen, they looked around at the dimly lit buildings and the torch lamps that illuminated the streets.

"Come on, we should get to a hotel. A new one tonight," Portenda said.

Jonah and Nareena walked hand in hand behind him, following all the way to the western district where they entered a humble inn and got themselves rooms to bed down in for the night.

When at last Portenda closed the door behind him, he heaved a sigh. He had enjoyed spending time with the Alchemists, but soon he would have to pick up on the trail of Eileen Staples and her abductor: the man formerly called Allen Staples.

"Genma," he whispered, stalking over to the window in his unlit room.

He peered out into the night sky, watching as clouds rolled in overhead, and listened to the skittering of the rodents in the walls and between the floorboards of the inn room. His nostrils flared as he took a deep, centering breath. "Why have you taken your niece? What have you become?"

He removed the leather and metal protector vest from his torso, hanging it on a hook in the wall next to his bed, setting his weapons around and underneath the bed for quick access.

Portenda's mind touched here and there on what he knew about the facts of this quest. "A quest, not a job," he muttered to himself. "I'm not getting paid for this, after all." He opened his rucksack and withdrew a single folder. The file contained all of the relevant information that Portenda had on Genma, Kobuchi, and Eileen Staples.

The Bounty Hunter reached in and drew out a second folder, containing the few scribbled notes he had taken down concerning the connections and motives of the subjects involved in this mission. He had as yet not found the connection between Genma and Eileen, other than their blood relationship as uncle and niece. The Bounty Hunter had long ago learned how to make the ties between individuals involved in his contracts. The art of detective work was tricky business for most, but his own enhanced powers of perception had always given him an edge.

Portenda had also gained first-hand knowledge of Alchemy through watching Jonah use the Focus Sites. Nareena's potions and tinctures, in addition to the Human boy's, could have dozens of various effects, many of them as yet unknown to the Simpa. Until he had an idea of why Genma held his niece captive, Portenda couldn't gauge how long he had to find the girl.

If it took him a week, Portenda would draw out the torture that Genma deserved for doing such a thing to good people.

The beast came to a screeching halt, stone and scrub grass kicking up and flying into the otherwise still and unbroken air, the harsh echo of its stampeding hooves through the night now an abrupt explosion of stopping energy. The soft and easy scent of fresh loam filled the air around Raja as he stood, neighing, perhaps twenty yards away from the western gate of Palen, Blink still clutching to his morphing flesh like a creature in its final death throes.

Night birds swirled overhead, occasionally letting out brief caws that Blink's increasingly limber mind interpreted as 'hey, how's your wife doing?' The responding croaks from other black feathered avian animals loosely related as, 'oh, she's fine. You know, sitting on the eggs.'

Momentarily distracted by this exchange, Blink hadn't noticed that his path was clear into the city. No guards kept watch over the western gates of Palen. No shouts came from anyone demanding to know identity or business in the city. Instead the balmy rasping of an evening wind told of secrets overheard during the daylight hours. The Alchemical beast descended Raja's flank, dropping to the ground easily as he got to the Troke's underbelly. The sound and sight of dark flesh moving and sliding into a new shape rent the air, and the sensation of impending departure filled the little beast's heart. Though they hadn't spoken much, he was immensely grateful to the Troke for his help in this matter.

"Well, little one, this is where we say good-bye." Raja took the form of a huge, obsidian raven with a bandaged head and beak. A single eye poked through the bandages, giving him an obscene countenance, like an animal partially treated by half-assed medical techniques and released, permanently scarred, into the wild. "I trust that what you're looking for is here."

Blink nodded his furry little head, and gave his thanks by emitting a wave of energy towards the Troke; Raja felt a cooling sensation brush over him from Blink's body, and he smiled to himself. "Perhaps some day we shall meet again, little one. For now, though, I wish you the best of luck." He took flight into the night sky, appearing to be a lone bird, charting its own course.

As time had passed throughout the day, Blink had formed an increasingly solid mental image of the person he had been sent to find. As an Alchemical beast, his intellect and memories were highly affected by the knowledge of his creator, who happened to be related to his quarry by blood. Blink had gained a sort of genetic memory from Genma, who had used a few drops of his own blood to merge three separate animals, creating from them, this creature now known as Blink.

His eight scorpion-like legs carried him through Palen's open gates and into an environment that smelled of magic and science in high potency and concentration. The only other occupants of the streets, it appeared to the Alchemy beast, were a few town guardsmen and rats that had escaped from the labs they had been kept in.

A couple of them, Blink knew, weren't rats at all, but Wererats, using their animal form to remain unseen as they looked for places to rob or loot. Wererats were natural thieves, and most of them were very professional about it—even in a city like Palen, the natural order of things seemed to march on.

There. Blink's nostrils flaring like a canine hunting animal's might when it sniffs a doe. Someone close by smells like the girl, like my owner. Dashing over dirt and cobblestone streets, Blink made his way to the solid oak door of a hotel.

He looked up at the door in dismay. He wasn't strong enough to push the portal open and step through, and he might have to wait until someone entered or exited, risking being stepped on.

Perhaps, he surmised, someone on the first floor would be up at this late hour. If he could get their attention, they might open a window and grant him access inside.

A few minutes later, Blink found himself in luck. He dropped down on an exterior window ledge, and looked up at a huge lion-like creature: a Simpa, if he remembered correctly. More information filtered through his mind as Genma's knowledge of the world seeped into his brain.

The huge lycanthrope was well muscled and had lit a few candles on a nightstand near the chair he sat in as he read over some papers through his thin, elegantly crafted spectacles. Gray stripes lined his arms and tree trunk chest, light in color but definitely there, nonetheless.

But the Simpa wasn't looking at the window. Blink had to get his attention. While he sensed that the man on the other side of the glass was dangerous, not a man to be trifled with, Blink also got the feeling that he could trust his safety to the Despite the Simpa's size and obvious power, the Alchemical beast he would be gentle and kind to such an unfortunate creature as himself.

Portenda pored over his information once more, looking over at the timepiece next to his bed and noting the late hour. "One in the morning," he muttered to himself. "I should get some sleep."

As he set the folder on the nightstand, he heard a light tapping of something hard and sharp against his window.

He removed his reading glasses, and found himself looking at a creature that appeared to be a mixture of a small dog, a scorpion, and some third, unknown animal. "What in the Seven Hells?" He got up out of his chair, which groaned appreciatively to be free of his massive weight, and approached the window slowly, so as not to frighten off the Alchemical beast. Portenda unfastened the latch, and slid the window open with care, allowing the creature some space.

"Hello there, little man," he said calmly, reassuringly. "Can I help you?"

Blink leaped through the air, landing on the Bounty Hunter's shoulder and lowering himself close against his fur and flesh. The image of a young woman rushed from Blink's mind into his own Simpa brain.

"Eileen," he whispered in shock. "Eileen Staples sent you, didn't she?"

The little beast nodded its head vigorously, and Portenda smiled like a demon that has just been offered the purest soul. "Well, it would appear that our messenger has arrived. My name is Portenda, little one." The Simpa patted Blink appreciatively on the head. "And sleep can wait for now."

Chapter Twelve
Back to Business

Their sheets mercifully covered Jonah and Nareena when Portenda's foot thrust open the door to their hotel room.

Jonah shot up in bed like a bolt of lightning, and he clapped his hands together, setting off the Focus Site he had put up over the doorframe before finally going to sleep.

Portenda narrowly dodged the sledgehammer that swung down at his face, tucking and rolling carefully, keeping Blink in his left hand. As he got to his feet, he gave the naked Alchemist an approving smile as he looked back at the spent Focus Site.

"Good, you're learning."

The little Alchemical beast squeaked and jumped from Portenda's hand to the floor, skittering up to Jonah's foot and waggling his stinger like a puppy who has found a new owner.

"What the Hells is this thing?" Jonah pulled on a pair of trousers.

Nareena rolled over, looking at Portenda and quickly pulling up the sheets to cover an exposed breast.

Portenda smiled broadly once more.

"That *thing*, as you put it, is our messenger." Portenda kept an eye on the Alchemical beast as Jonah finished dressing.

Nareena had wrapped herself in their bedsheet and dashed to the bathroom to take a shower and get dressed while Portenda shook his head. "Or had you forgotten we were getting one when you and she hit the sheets?"

Jonah blushed a brilliant shade of crimson, unable to hide his embarrassment or his pride in being Nareena's bedmate.

"How do you know it's the right creature?"

The Alchemical beast raced up his right arm and settled onto his shoulder, using the same communication technique it had now used successfully on Raja and Portenda.

Jonah marveled as he saw the mental image of his sister issue from Blink's body into his own mind. "Oh my Gods." He plucked Blink from his shoulder, and held him in his left hand as he patted him on the furry little head. "You've done a good job. Do you want to be free now, um, what's your name anyway?"

Blink, he heard whispered into his mind. *That is the name my savior gave me.*

"Blink, eh? Do you want to go free now?"

No, Jonah heard in his mind in a high-pitched, boyish voice. It reminded him of his own voice when he was five or six years old. *I want to return to her, make sure she's okay. I'll ride with the big fellow.*

Jonah watched as Blink launched himself through the air and landed on top of Portenda's head.

"Jonah, would you be so kind as to grab one of those pastries you've been saving from Granny's place."

Blink moved off of the Simpa's head and onto his left shoulder, a natural perch for the Alchemical beast it seemed while Jonah rummaged through his packages, and produced a Danish for the little creature, who took it with his front forelegs and nibbled appreciatively on the offered food.

Nareena came out of the bathroom, dressed once again jeans and a cardigan sweater over a plain white tank top.

"Is this what we've been waiting for?" Nareena brushed her hair hurriedly, checking through her own rucksack to make sure she was properly packed to leave.

"Indeed, it is," replied Portenda flatly, regaining his professional demeanor. "Meet me out front in ten minutes. I have to get my things, and we'll head out on foot. Blink will guide us. Correct, little one?"

Portenda's eyes grew ashen and glossy as his calm, icy persona resurfaced after so many days of being set aside.

The Alchemy beast could detect that this was the big man's usual state of being, and he decided not to interfere with the transition, though he could have. It might be best to let the Simpa do what he had to in order to save his liberator.

Blink nodded, and pressed his underbelly against Portenda's skin.

I shall give you directions. In his head, Portenda heard a voice like a young Human boy.

"Ten minutes," he repeated to the Alchemists, who were already busying themselves with final preparations.

Jonah tossed Nareena the first two tomes on Focus.

The Elven beauty gave him a questioning glare. "I've already memorized them," Jonah explained, shoving the rest of his equipment into the appropriate pocket, thinking on his spare clothing and tapping the snap on the enchanted rucksack. He stuffed the three towels from the hotel room's bathroom into the spare clothing, smiling slightly to himself.

"Jonah, why do you need those towels?"

"You never know when you'll need one," Jonah said, quoting his mother. "Now come on, we've got the break we've been waiting for."

Nareena didn't move for a moment though, and her face had a crestfallen look about it.

"Honey, what's wrong," Jonah asked, moving slowly to her side.

She put her hand over top of his on her shoulder, and gave him a wan smile.

"He's never going to be the same, is he?" she asked.

Jonah knew exactly what she meant. He lowered his chin, and shook his head. "No, he isn't. Actually, to be fair, he hasn't been himself since we arrived in Palen. This city did something to him, made him a little more relaxed. And we've all become close, as people often do in times of stress. What's important, though, is that when we get Eileen back, we make sure he doesn't just dash off into the horizon. He has the capacity to be friendly, even warm at times. You've seen that."

"Yes, I have, Jonah." Nareena followed him to the door, giving him a peck on the cheek as the entered the hallway. "But I've also seen how cold he can be, how distant. And I want you to know that I fully expect him to take off once we have Eileen back safe."

The young man looked heartbroken at the idea, but he nodded, accepting that it was most likely the truth of the matter.

"Come on." He looked at his wrist timepiece. "We've only got a couple of minutes to check out and get out there. You know how much he hates being late."

* * * *

Kobuchi had copied the entirety of the journals after reading through them, and his tiny Kobold heart swelled with hope as he thought about his eventual freedom from this oppressive tower and its twisted master. Kobuchi had even managed to stop using that term mentally with a capital 'm', deciding that he had to disagree with Genma's methods at last. Genma's Alchemy had manipulated, controlled him for several years, it seemed. One of the handwritten journals had described the exact process through which Genma had selected Kobuchi and ensured his devotion.

Kobuchi had been traveling with his family pack of Kobolds, a group that called themselves the Orga Family. The pack numbered six, and was comprised by some of the most intelligent and educated Kobolds in all of Tamalaria.

Reading through the notes that Genma had kept on them, Kobuchi remembered his friends, his traveling companions for nearly eight years. All of them had been skilled mages, studying several schools of magic instead of dedicating themselves entirely to one school or other. One of the members, the youngest of the group, he recalled now, had been an Engineer, using the ancient sciences to craft mecha devices to aid the group in their travels and studies.

Genma had selected Kobuchi because, according to the research he had written down and copied out in the journal, Kobuchi showed the most promise as a wielder of multiple magics.

As the group had traveled through the vast desert in the southeast known as the Desperation to study a set of ancient ruins, Genma had come upon the family. He had offered them water skins that were enchanted to not run dry, and the pack had eagerly purchased them. After another day of traveling, they had all fallen asleep hard after taking some of the water from their 'enchanted' skins.

"'The gullible little saps fell for it, hard,'" Kobuchi read aloud once again, anger seething out from his heart. He had to regain control of himself, though. He had been in his personal quarters, which had one wall of video monitors connected to several of the surveillance cameras throughout the tower. Genma was stalking the halls at this late hour, and would most likely visit him soon.

Kobuchi hid the journals and his own notes in his dresser, and lay on the bed, getting under the covers and pretending to be fast asleep.

The master of the tower would likely be checking in on him soon.

A few minutes later, Kobuchi heard the door to his room creak open.

Genma peered in at his servant, and noted the slow, deep rise and fall of the bed sheets. *Hmm,* he thought. *Asleep.* He'd hoped that the Kobold would be awake and able to provide him a little bit of company. The ivory-masked Alchemist couldn't himself get any rest at the moment. Though the conversation with Telroke had been taxing, he felt wide awake now, especially knowing just how much of a threat the Bounty Hunter posed if he should find his way to the tower.

Genma had been able to take a little comfort in one of Telroke's statements, though. Portenda had named himself an exile from the Allenian Hills. He would place himself at risk by coming to the tower, which fronted the Allenian Hills on the eastern border of the region. Should Portenda be spotted near the tower, he would be in breach of his exile, and could come under attack from any number of Khan or Simpa tribes. If what Telroke had told Genma were true, then perhaps the Bounty Hunter could be dealt with before even getting inside of the perimeter of the tower.

Genma already intended to use the Bounty Hunter's father against him, pitting the old drunkard against his son in mortal combat. If a few more lycanthropes from the Allenians wanted to join in, all the better. He would speak to Telroke about it in the morning. He felt assured that the man's hatred for his own flesh and blood would win him over, and he would agree quickly to the idea of fighting Portenda.

He had fought the boy once and survived. But that had been many years ago, when Portenda had been a whelp. Now, the Bounty Hunter had years of training and experience. Adding a few more Simpa to the mix could even the odds. Perhaps the tiger-men could be convinced to help their hated enemies if the exiled freak of nature showed up.

Genma heaved a heavy sigh, though. He understood why the boy had chosen exile—he hadn't wanted to kill his own father. Genma knew that part of Telroke's story had been inaccurate, though the older Simpa had himself thoroughly convinced. But Genma had seen the truth of that battle in his own mind; it had been Portenda who had disarmed his father, and it had been Telroke who had used the law of exile to save his own life.

But the old man had years of watching his son from afar. And clearly he had some sort of power that might cause Portenda the Quiet to falter. If Telroke could shatter Genma's calm so easily, then surely the freak was no exception, right?

The ivory-masked Alchemist realized finally that he had been so lost in thought that he had unwittingly descended down his private stairwell into the basement of the tower. Why, he wondered, did he always wind up down here when his mind wandered and he lost track of himself?

Painted portraits of his family hung about the dingy basement chamber, and the tables, makeshift creations at best, were littered with his old personal affects. Stacks of research papers, reviews of his latest theories in Alchemy written by other scientists, lay strewn about the tables and floor. Genma felt his heart slow to a near stop when he looked across the room to the single device that he had placed down here once he had left the life of Allen Staples behind.

A Hunter and his Prey

The machine stood like a silent, permanent accusation, its levers all pointed at Genma like the fingers of disapproval.

Genma looked away from the device and sprinted from the basement, away from the machine he had used in an attempt to brainwash his nephew. The machine had failed near the end, unable to deal with the boy's free will as it had been designed to do. It was another in a long line of failed experiments.

A failure, he thought, that might lead to his demise. After all, the boy and the Bounty Hunter were partners in their mission to retrieve Eileen Staples. And between the two of them, they had enough power and skill to stop Genma in his tracks, save the girl, and destroy the tower.

"They have the power to make the Gods tremble," Genma whispered to himself as he returned to his personal chambers, and lay down to sleep.

Though he hadn't meant to, Kobuchi, two floors above, had also nodded off.

* * * *

SO YOU'RE SAYING THAT NOBODY HERE REPRESENTS HIM? Death asked of the astral being known only as Fate.

Fate took the form of a man in a blue cloak and robes, wearing a flat, plain mask of gold, in which a thin slit had been crafted to grant him a field of vision. Shioten, the God-Father, had given up omnipotence and the Great Book of Histories, claiming that no being should have such knowledge, lest they be parted from emotion and judgment.

Fate could not judge, and for the most part, could not feel. Even as an astral being created by the hand of the Almighty, he had limits on how much he could interfere or intervene in the mortal realm. And he shared his knowledge with only three other beings; Shioten, Truth, and Death.

"No, Honorable Guest." Fate's booming voice echoed through the Halls of Eternity.

The home of the Holy Triad, Fate, Truth, and Power, the Halls of Eternity served as the holding place of the Great Book of Histories. It also played host to conversations between the astral beings that currently stalked its marble hallways. "No single God or Goddess lays claim to him. You know full well why that is," Fate added matter-of-factly.

WE AGREED NOT TO TALK ABOUT THAT, Death rasped.

"And why not?" Fate asked as they approached Fate's personal quarters. The Heavens have their own dimensions, though most are ethereal and have no meaning. To the astral beings themselves, however, a certain degree of solidity was reassuring. They had that much in common with their mortal counterparts. "Haven't you ever questioned our judgment, our decision? I am not supposed to intervene, but that once, I did. And so did you."

Death gripped the shaft of his scythe hard, leaving a slight imprint on it.

Maxi barked happily as he followed behind the astral beings, and Death produced a dog treat, tossing over his shoulder to silence his pet.

Fate opened the door to his room, waving his hand in front of it. No knob or handle was present to grip, and as his hand finished its motion, the door swung open.

WHY DO YOU NOT PUT A DOORKNOB ON THERE?

"It's mostly so nobody but you or I can enter without my permission. Nobody else is supposed to see the Histories, though I occasionally relate their contents to Truth," Fate said flatly.

I SEE NOW WHERE HE GETS IT, Death mused, referring to Portenda's cold demeanor.

"He gets it from you too, you know," Fate said bluntly as he and Death entered his private chambers. "Now, let us discuss why you've come to visit me."

WILL TRUTH BE JOINING US?

"Yes, in a few minutes. She is presently taking council with a few of the Lesser Gods. Apparently, one of them has only three believers left, and they are slated to die of a local disease soon. He's petitioning for more faithful, so that you won't have to collect."

Death grinned deep in his hood. He enjoyed it dearly when one of the self-righteous Lesser Gods lost their believers. They put up one hell of a struggle and it was always fun to stomp them flat in front of the other Gods and Goddesses, to remind them of who alone had that power among them.

A rap came on the door a minute later, and Fate waved his hand to allow a white winged woman into the room.

Her golden skin reflected the astral light in the room, almost blinding both her brother Fate, and Death, despite his lack of eyes to blind.

"I am here, brother, Honorable Guest," she said, giving them a brief curtsy.

Death bowed deeply. Truth's beauty affected even him to some degree.

THANK YOU FOR COMING, TRUTH. WE DO NOT MEAN TO KEEP YOU FROM YOUR OTHER AFFAIRS.

"What is that thing?" Truth pointed to Maxi.

OH, YES. I MADE HIM. TO HAVE SOME COMPANY. Death patted the skeletal hound on the head, which set his tail flapping.

"It is good to see you've finally come to your senses about having a friend," Truth said. "As always, your actions outside of your duty elude my eyes and ears. Now, I understand that you have some questions for me, Grim. As do you, brother. I do not understand why you are so reluctant to simply look up any question you have in the Histories."

"The Histories relate facts alone, sister," Fate said. "And our questions, I fear, are not covered by them."

Truth gave Fate a skeptical look through her vibrant, ocean-blue eyes. "I have checked," the golden-masked entity admitted.

"This must be a grave matter. Does Father know of our meeting here?"

I INFORMED HIM MYSELF. Death patted his cloak front, gripping Maxi's front paws and walking with him a few feet on his hind legs. He set his pet down and retrieved his scythe, which he had set against the wall. HE HAS

APPROVED, SO DO NOT WORRY. I WISH TO ASK YOU THE FIRST QUESTION, Death said, looking to Fate for his approval.

Fate nodded, and so Death continued, his hood shifting back towards Truth. THERE IS A MAN IN THE REALITY OVER WHICH YOU PRESIDE. Death wasn't sure what Truth looked like in the other realities, because he seldom visited the Heavens in the other realities that he watched over. The Gods and Goddesses were all different, depending on which reality one crossed over in to. This one happened to be Death's favorite, and was the only one in which he had ever become very personally involved.

"There are millions of men in this reality," Truth said. "To which do you refer?"

PORTENDA THE QUIET, Death said flatly. Irritation at Truth's mockery tainted Death's tone. DOES HE HAVE A SOUL?

Truth stood still, the light from her flesh shining brighter for a moment as she crossed her arms over her chest, touching her hands to their opposing shoulders, and tucked her chin down, accessing her wealth of information. After a minute of this activity, she looked up at her brother and Death.

"Yes, he does. Why do you ask? Does he not have a timer, like all other mortals?"

NO, HE DOESN'T, Death said irritably. I HAVE SEARCHED MY ENTIRE INVENTORY, AND I CAN'T FIND A THING. Death shifted his weight onto one foot, uneasy at having to admit that he couldn't find the timer for a mortal under his watch. Especially considering his connection to the man.

"That is most unusual," was Truth's reply to this fact. "Now, brother, what was *your* question?"

Fate stepped forward, standing next to his closest contact, Death. "Does he know why he exists? Does he know why he was allowed to be born?"

Truth raised an inquisitive eyebrow again at her brother, but said nothing, instead going through the motions of her use of power again.

"No, he does not," she said. "Though, he has his suspicions, and they are close to the truth." She looked from her brother to Death and back again. "I know that the two of you are responsible for his birth."

Fate and Death looked away, ashamed by the tone Truth took with them. "Father does not know, does he?"

Fate shook his head miserably, and Truth crossed her arms.

NOT THAT WE ARE AWARE OF, IN ANY EVENT, Death said, pointing to the floor for Maxi to sit.

The skeletal canine did as he was silently asked, and waggled his tongue up and down, panting despite not having any lungs.

IT IS DIFFICULT TO TELL JUST WHAT YOUR FATHER IS AWARE OF. AFTER ALL, HE DOES HAVE CONNECTIONS TO YOU TWO AND YOUR OTHER BROTHER, Death waved his hand vaguely. HE COULD BE WATCHING THIS CONVERSATION THROUGH YOUR EYES AND LISTENING THROUGH FATE'S EARS FOR ALL WE KNOW.

"We would be aware of any such connection being made," Fate offered. "Father's touch can't be missed. We would know if He were watching, and trust me, we wouldn't be having this pleasant conversation."

SO, WHAT DO WE DO FROM HERE? HE'S BOUND TO NOTICE WHEN THE HISTORIES ARE ALTERED.

"Well, you don't have to worry much about it, do you," Truth fairly hissed at Death. "He can't touch you, after all, though none of us knows why." None of the Gods, Goddesses, or Triad members knew that this incarnation of Death resided over more than their own reality. And being a force outside of the Triad's influence allowed Death to keep this fact a secret, even from Truth and Fate, his only regular contacts in the Heavens.

AND HOPEFULLY, YOU NEVER WILL, Death countered. The scent of jasmine incense filled the air, and Death shifted his stance, pointing one bone finger at Truth. DON'T EVEN TRY YOUR TRICKS ON ME, TRUTH! THEY WON'T WORK, AND I'M A LITTLE OFFENDED THAT YOU WOULD TRY!

Truth used the scent to pry information from the Lesser Gods, and even the Greater Gods when they resisted her attempts to collect information on their faithful. It always worked on them, so she reasoned that it would work on Death. She gasped as Death ignored her charm technique, and the scent of jasmine left as quickly as it had cropped up.

Furious, she stormed from her brother's chambers, letting herself out as normally as if the door were made of common wood and iron hinges.

"That could have gone better," Fate said, shaking his head and rubbing the mask where his temples should have been.

LET US HOPE SHE DOESN'T RUN TO YOUR FATHER, Death hissed as the crimson lights in his hood dimmed down. DESPITE WHAT SHE THINKS, SHIOTEN CAN HAVE A VERY PROFOUND EFFECT ON MY WORK. LIKE MAKING A LOT MORE OF IT. I DON'T CARE FOR THAT POSSIBILITY.

Death swiped at the air with his scythe, and Maxi bound through the tear and disappeared from Fate's room.

"So, he has a soul, but no timer. He has no Gods or Goddesses willing to claim him. Why?"

MOST LIKELY BECAUSE THEY AREN'T AWARE OF HIM. OR, THEY'RE AFRAID OF WHAT HE REPRESENTS. SURELY YOUR SISTER'S CLOSEST FRIENDS AMONG THE GODS WILL SOON BE MADE AWARE OF HIS NATURE—AND WHERE HE COMES FROM.

"And then we'll both be sitting in front of a panel." Fate sighed heavily. "I don't want to deal with that. Perhaps we should find that timer and undo him."

Death's eyes flared and he wheeled on Fate, his scythe raised to hip-level, held ready to strike.

I WILL NOT TAKE SOMEONE WHOSE TIME HAS NOT COME, FRIEND. IF WE MUST ANSWER FOR OUR ACTIONS THOSE MANY YEARS AGO, SO BE IT! BUT I WILL NOT SIMPLY GIVE UP ON HIM!

A Hunter and his Prey

CHECK THOSE HISTORIES AGAIN, FATE. I GUARANTEE HE'LL BE SHOWING UP SOON. Death lowered his scythe, and he passed through the rift in the Heavens, disappearing as Maxi had a minute earlier.

Fate tried to stop his trembling legs, but he found that he was rooted in place. He and Death had together decided to see what might become of such a creature, a crossbreed of two Races that were never meant to bear children. They had imposed their wills on reality, bending it around the mother's womb and the child itself.

Portenda the Quiet had been that child.

* * * *

Portenda led the way with Blink on his shoulder. The trio from Ja-Wen made their way out of Palen and into the high grasslands due west of the city. The moon was in its full phase, providing plenty of lunar light by which to navigate, and Jonah and Nareena had little trouble keeping pace, spurred on by Blink's arrival and what that meant.

The Simpa did not seem to be in much of a hurry, it seemed to Jonah. *Perhaps he's distracted, or perhaps he's just communicating with the Alchemical beast.*

This was a correct assumption, as Portenda listened to Blink through their mental communication. Blink had one scorpion leg pressed against Portenda's neck, as the protector vest didn't allow Blink to hunker down against his flesh to maintain contact. Portenda had learned a great deal about Blink and Eileen's situation through the mental communication. Thanks to Blink's gradual retrieval of Genma's memories, Blink was able to inform Portenda of his intentions for Eileen.

Portenda had never felt such immense disgust at an idea, but this one nearly made him step aside to vomit. Allen Staples intended to transform his own niece, through Alchemy and other sciences, into his late wife. The Gods should not have permitted such acts, but sometimes, he realized, the Gods and Goddesses could do little to influence the mortal realm.

Portenda considered how to tell Jonah what he had learned from the beast. The boy would panic and then he would start asking questions. Questions that Portenda didn't want to answer. He decided to remain silent, and further his observations. He had no idea what sort of traps or pitfalls lie ahead of him, but he had an idea of where they were heading.

He didn't like the idea, but he would have to pass dangerously close to the Allenian Hills. Exiled from the Hills by his father, he would be subject to attack from both Simpa and Khan. He would have to protect both himself and the Alchemists, though they had already proven themselves capable of the task.

"So, how long are we going to go tonight?" Nareena's body was still sluggish from lack of sleep.

"Only a couple of hours," Portenda said. "But we need to make the trip without using any Teleportation techniques or scrolls. If we can find mounts to carry the two of you, I can take on my animal form and run with them,. There's a village not far from Palen, and I think they may have a stable that can provide."

"We could have got horses back in Palen," Jonah said.

"Those were all taken," Portenda said. "I checked on that the first day we were there. We can make it to the village in a couple of hours. We'll camp outside of their borders, and in the morning, we'll purchase a couple of mounts for the two of you. That way we'll be able to make good time to Genma's tower," he said.

"How do you know it's a tower," Jonah asked suspiciously.

"This little guy is speaking to me through my mind." Portenda pointed a furry finger to the Alchemical beast on his shoulder. "He's told me everything he knows. We're heading towards the Allenians."

Jonah felt his heart sink. The Allenians were no place for a Human to wander, even if he was in Portenda's company. Patrols of Khan and Simpa warriors would crush anyone who intruded on their territory flatter than an insect.

"Towards them, but not into them, right?" Jonah asked squeamishly.

"I hope not," Portenda said quietly. "After all, I'm an exile. Exiles are allowed no quarter. From anybody."

As the night sky shone lunar light across the open plains, the trio from Ja-Wen marched along at a steady clip, careful not to travel too slowly or too quickly.

As they passed through fields and meadows, their feet springing lightly off of the soft soil of the region, a sense of unity came over Jonah, who found that the silence between them had grown comfortable. It reminded him a little of the quiet dinners he had shared with his parents and his sister in the weeks before his departure from home.

But with night travel came the risks of highwaymen, nocturnal predators, and creatures that showed themselves only to feed. The northeastern flatlands of Tamalaria were well known for harboring hermit Necromancers, who resided in ramshackle dwellings of primitive design, made with little thought to permanency. They would raise undead minions from the surrounding area, and lurk near the roadways, waiting for victims to have slaughtered and turned into more minions. Jonah had no desire to see any such individuals.

After an hour of walking, Portenda slowed to nearly half of his set pace, and Jonah and Nareena almost walked into his broad, weapon-riddled back.

Portenda held an open hand up, swiveling his head slightly to the left. His eye was barely visible to the Alchemists, but Jonah could see the gleam of anticipation in that gray orb.

"Stand very still," Portenda whispered.

Blink scurried from Portenda's back to the ground, where he curled up into a defensive ball, his stinger poised to strike anything that came too close for his comfort.

Jonah listened for any sounds that might be out of the ordinary, but his own Human senses weren't as well developed as the Simpa's. Nor did he have

Portenda's gifts of observation. His limitations frustrated him, but before he could mull the problem over, he finally heard something moving.

Nothing came into view as Jonah looked straight ahead.

Portenda hadn't moved since raising his hand, but in the span of a split second, the Simpa Bounty Hunter leapt into the air, drew his broadsword and swung it down in a flash of steel, the arc of lunar light reflecting brightly as it slashed through the body of a translucent creature.

A primal roar of fury and agony erupted from the throat of a long, black-furred beast, its body appearing to be that of a wolf with several snake-like protrusions flailing about its bleeding body.

Portenda landed in a three-point stance several yards on the beast's left flank, his muscles bulging and tensed for further combat.

"A rashum," Jonah breathed as the supernatural creature turned its blood-soaked body towards the Bounty Hunter. Rashums were a mix of spirit beast and flesh-and-bone creatures created when both came into existence in the same general location, though on two separate planes of existence. Their semi-magical abilities often reflected the nature of the spirit beast, while their physical behavior was governed by whatever animal they had merged with during birth. With so many such creatures lurking the lands of Tamalaria, scholars had agreed on an umbrella term for these beasts: rashums. This creature had approached the trio wrapped in an aura of near-invisibility, but Portenda had noticed it: either by sound alone, or, as Jonah suspected, by smell.

Thick arterial blood spewed from the long gash across its back, and the Alchemist felt certain that the danger the rashum presented had decreased by degrees. The two combatants stayed their position, however, neither making a move.

Portenda realized he had been quicker than the creature by only a fraction of a second, jumping out of the way of one of its flesh whips a moment before impact. His strike had made its mark, but skill alone hadn't given him the first strike—an element of surprise and luck lent a hand.

Even bleeding as this rashum was, Portenda knew that it could still deliver a lethal attack. It retained enough intelligence to stay where it was, to wait on him to make a move. *Perhaps it'll bleed to death*, the Bounty Hunter thought hopefully.

But that option washed away like debris in a flood as the wound on the creature's back healed at a rate of regeneration not even heard of in Jafts. Blood dripped through its thick fur and over its carapace, leaking onto the ground, but no new fluid joined it.

The rashum bared its teeth at the Simpa and growled, the fur of its back standing on end.

This could be a problem. As Portenda readied himself for a fresh onslaught, a crack of thunder tore the air and the rashum's head exploded in a shower of soft brain and magma-colored blood.

Portenda turned his gaze over to Jonah and Nareena and saw smoke billowing from the end of the sniper rifle's barrel, with Jonah in a crouched aiming position. The boy had a smile on his face that could have stretched into the stars themselves.

"Very good shot, Jonah." Portenda sheathed his broadsword. "Aim a little more to the right next time, though." He wiped gray matter off of his proud, feline snout. "That way you might not spray blood and brain on me."

Jonah blushed a bit and then slung the rifle back in place across his back.

Portenda stepped around the area, sniffing the air to test it for signs of other, more material hostile forces, catching himself in time to sidestep Blink as the Alchemical beast skittered up his leg and onto his back, moving immediately to his right shoulder.

"Hmm. I think we should get moving again. Won't take us long to reach the village." Once again, his tone was flat and devoid of inflection.

As the trio from Ja-Wen made their way through the night, they noticed traces of natural animals having passed through the area.

Here and there, the smaller, less fortunate among them lay in pools of their own blood, having been broken in the powerful jaws of the rashum.

Their necks had been snapped, and their stomachs torn open, their innards taken as nourishment for the half spirit creature.

Nareena gripped Jonah's arm, her natural Elven empathy towards such victimized creatures hitting her hard.

After another hour, Portenda called a halt to their march. They had come to the crest of a hill overlooking the low grassy plain on which the village rested. "I'll keep the first watch," the Bounty Hunter proclaimed. "I'll wake you up in a few hours, Nareena. Jonah's been taking most of my opposite shifts."

The Alchemists prepared their bedroll, tucked themselves inside, and were asleep before Portenda could ask them if they wanted anything to eat before knocking off.

The lumbering Simpa Bounty Hunter stalked around the perimeter in a slow, cautious circle, keeping his senses on end.

He wondered what could be making him feel so cold despite his fur when he realized that the sensation was coming from behind him. VERY HANDY LITTLE TRICK OF MINE, Death said.

"So, *you* put them to sleep," Portenda said evenly.

DO YOU THINK ANYONE COULD FALL ASLEEP THAT QUICKLY WITHOUT A GOOD DEAL OF PHYSICAL ACTIVITY?

"Bark Bark," came another nearby voice.

Portenda turned and saw Death standing beside his new pet, Maxi.

"What brings you around, again," Portenda asked, walking around the perimeter once more.

WE NEED TO TALK. Death took a seat on a nearby felled log. I FIGURED WE SHOULD GET SOME THINGS OUT OF THE WAY. YOU PROBABLY WONDER SOMETIMES WHY I SHOW UP SO OFTEN AROUND YOU.

To Portenda's surprise, he hadn't been thinking about it until the astral being mentioned it. He stopped midway through his route, turned and faced Death.

"I never really thought too much about it, until you just mentioned it now." Portenda took one last look around him, and realized that in the presence of the Honorable Guest, he probably didn't have to worry too much about Jonah and Nareena's welfare. He shuffled towards the embodiment of most mortals' fears, and sat down, cross-legged, in front of him. "So, start explaining."

STRAIGHT TO THE POINT, EH? Death raised an impossible eyebrow. I USED TO BE IMPATIENT LIKE THAT TOO, ONCE UPON A TIME. WHEN I WAS YOUNGER.

"Younger? Does that concept even apply to you?"

Death scratched his head with a single finger of bone. WELL, NOT REALLY. TIME ITSELF HAS LITTLE OR NO HOLD OVER ME. IT'S A CONCEPT THAT CAME INTO BEING AFTER ME, I THINK. I CAN'T REALLY RECALL.

"Sort of like which came first, the chicken or the egg," Portenda muttered, shifting his weight to make himself more comfortable for what he was becoming aware was going to be a rather momentous conversation.

THAT'S SIMPLE. I WAS THERE FOR THAT.

"So, which was it?"

I REALLY SHOULDN'T TELL YOU. Death grinned. IT'S ONE OF THOSE THINGS THAT SHOULD JUST BE LEFT ALONE. LOOK, WE HAVE TO DISCUSS SOMETHING FAR MORE IMPORTANT THAN THAT. PORTENDA, YOU ARE AWARE THAT YOU ARE A HALF-BREED, CORRECT?

"I know what I am, Grim." Portenda instinctively looked around the area one more time.

DON'T WORRY. I WON'T LET ANYTHING HAPPEN TO YOUR FRIENDS—FOR NOW. Death pulled a small, hard biscuit from his robes and tossed it over his shoulder.

Maxi barked his strange bark as he darted off after the doggy treat, dust kicking up into the air around him.

BESIDES, THEY'VE BOTH GOT PLENTY OF TIME LEFT. Death drew two sand timers from his robes. Nareena's, being as she was an Elf, was much larger than Jonah's, and her sand flowed more slowly. For a Human, though, Jonah had a great deal of sand left.

Portenda smiled to himself softly, and looked over at his companions.

BUT DON'T FORGET THAT THESE TIMERS CAN BE MADE TO FLOW MUCH FASTER, GIVEN EXIGENT CIRCUMSTANCES.

"What do you mean?" Portenda stretched his arms and legs.

IF THEY ARE SET UPON BY OUTSIDE FORCES, THE SAND MAY MOVE TO THE BOTTOM FASTER THAN EVEN YOU COULD SEE, Death intoned meaningfully. YOU LEAD THEM INTO DANGER, PORTENDA. BUT I UNDERSTAND WHY YOU MUST DO IT.

ANOTHER LIFE HANGS IN THE BALANCE. YOU MORTALS HIGHLY VALUE EACH OTHER. NOT AT ALL LIKE SOME OF THE COMPANY I KEEP. The Gods tended to get on his nerves, or would, if he had any.

"So you've mentioned before. Look, this isn't what you wanted to tell me." Portenda stared up at the moon. "You're stalling. You don't really want to tell me what you came here to tell me, do you?"

Death rubbed Maxi's head as the skeletal canine wagged its bone tail.

"You don't think I can handle it."

Death got to his own feet, and tore a rift in the air with his scythe.

IT'S ABOUT YOUR TIMER, PORTENDA. Death faced the rift, his back to the Bounty Hunter, who was now looking at him with keen interest. I DON'T KNOW HOW TO TELL YOU THIS. Death put one foot through the portal. He looked back at Portenda, his eyes flashing in his eternal skull. For a fraction of time, their eyes met, and Portenda saw a sense of duty so immense, so vast, that he felt overwhelmed and lost. No mortal ever could hope to take on such responsibilities as Death's. But there was also a personal connection there, something unspoken between them.

"So, just spill it." Unable to maintain the eye contact any further, Portenda looked away. It was the only time in his many years that he had broken eye contact first.

I CAN'T FIND IT, PORTENDA. IN ESSENCE, YOU DON'T HAVE A TIMER.

Portenda's entire body went stiff at these words, because they could mean any number of things to him.

BUT REMEMBER, YOU WERE NEVER EVEN SUPPOSED TO COME INTO BEING. I SUPPOSE YOU CAN BLAME BOTH OF THOSE FACTS ON ME, Death offered as he stepped through the rift.

Portenda spent the remainder of his shift turning these words over in his mind and his heart. Even after he awoke the Elven Alchemist to take her shift, he lay staring at the night sky, unable to fully deal with what he had just been told.

"What am I," he asked the night sky as he slipped off into slumber land.

* * * *

When morning came, Portenda decided to leave behind his thoughts of the night before. If he kept brooding about his encounter with Death, he might never get the energy up to continue forward.

Nareena had used a long stick to poke the Bounty Hunter in the foot several times, until he shot upright like a bolt of lightning, snatching the stick away and bit it in half before getting groggily to his feet.

The fresh scent of morning dew clung to everything, from the grass to his bedroll. It wasn't an unpleasant smell, but it came, it seemed, far too early in the morning.

With his eyes still half closed, Portenda opened his water skin and poured a small portion on his face. "Hrprrrrbbbbb! Gah," he muttered as he rubbed his eyes, clearing his vision for another day's work.

A Hunter and his Prey

"Good morning to you too," Jonah called, stretching his own limbs for the long day ahead. "Hey, where's the little guy?"

Portenda sniffed the air, and detected the sulfuric scent of the Alchemical beast's flesh.

"He's around."

The trio watched as Blink skittered from a nearby shrub, a field mouse in his mouth.

First, he dropped it in front of Portenda and Jonah, while Nareena shrugged away from the sight.

Blink smiled happily and wagged his stinger like a dog seeking approval from his master.

"Go ahead, little one," Portenda said, crouching down and patting Blink on the head as the little beast tore into the field mouse. "Good boy, eat up."

He hitched up his rucksack. "All right, let's go people."

Moments later, the village came into sight.

A long, low building at the outskirts of the village indicated to the Bounty Hunter that this was the stable, as did the scent of horse manure and the braying of stallions inside.

The sun shone brilliantly in a sky devoid of cloud cover, and Portenda's Khan blood surged with the power its pure rays lent him. Khan took strength from the sunlight, and in higher elevations, a single hour standing in the light could easily grant a full day's energy.

Portenda, however, was only half-Khan, and was walking across lowlands in Tamalaria's countryside. He didn't take the same strength from the day's light as his uncle Amon might, but it was nourishing nonetheless.

Before the company even reached the side of the stable, he felt fully renewed, ready to take on the day proper.

Piles of hay surrounded the stable building and crunched loudly underfoot as Portenda, Jonah and Nareena trampled to the front of the building.

As the Bounty Hunter cleared the side of the building, he almost stepped right on an Elven male attendant's foot.

At the last second, Portenda shuffled to his left, and avoided crushing the poor little man.

The Elf looked up at Portenda's proud face and half-hearted smile, complete with teeth.

The Simpa didn't like using intimidation tactics, but sometimes, in his experience, Elves had a hard time selling their mounts, even if they were for sale. A little show of potential force might hurry things along.

"Can I, ah, help you folks," the Elf squeaked.

"Actually, yes." Jonah stepped between the giant warrior and the diminutive horsekeeper. "My lady friend and I need to acquire a pair of horses. Moderate size, we're not that big."

"And, ah, your big friend," the Elf asked, taking a step backward, into the stable proper.

Portenda shook his head.

"Well, come inside and I'll show you what we have, folks. The name's Jean-Vierre." The Elf extended a hand to Jonah, who shook amiably. The horse tender gave Nareena a familiar smile, one he probably reserved for members of his Race.

The trio followed him into the dimly lit stable, taking in the overpowering smells of horse manure and sweat, and listened to the braying, neighing, and the compliments that the Elven and Human attendants showered the animals with.

Portenda raised an eyebrow when his eyes fell on a single Lizardman in beige robes holding one horse's head in its hands.

The reptilian humanoid pressed his forehead gently against the animal's, clearly communicating with it in the manner of a Beastmaster.

Strange, Portenda thought as Jean-Vierre lead them to a stall near the back of the stable. Only this particular Class of Lizardman didn't engage in the arts of warfare. With their kinsmen, they had little in common.

"This is Buck," the Elven attendant said.

Jonah looked up into the middle-aged face of a bronco that easily stood six and a half feet high at the back.

"Buck's been around for a while." Jean-Vierre opened the stall door and stepping inside, stroking the horse with a sense of familiarity. "He used to be a racing animal, even won a few big events in Desanadron." He grabbed a brush from a nearby shelf and ran it over the black bronco's coat. "He's still got plenty of stamina, and understands the basic commands of a rider. Perfect for you, sir," he indicated Jonah, who had taken a step closer to pat the side of the creature's neck.

Buck seemed to take to Jonah immediately, and even nudged him with his big head.

"I'll take him," Jonah said, patting the bronco and offering him an apple from a closed bucket inside the stall. The horse took the fruit whole into its mouth, and began crunching.

"Very good! I'll leave you to get acquainted." Jean-Vierre led Nareena away from the stall with Buck and Jonah.

"Say, where's your big friend?" the Elven attendant asked the Alchemist, who looked around the stable.

Nareena couldn't see Portenda anywhere, and worried that the attendant might ask her or Jonah for the money to pay for the animals. But as Jean-Vierre led her to a smaller horse with a shimmering bronze coat, she spotted Portenda standing by another Elven man, this one so old that he had actually begun to grow a beard.

Elves couldn't grow facial hair until they passed their one-thousandth year of age, which made the stable owner an experienced dealer of animals.

"This is Elhaym." Jean-Vierre regained Nareena's attention as he opened the door to the bronze female horse's stall. He stroked and brushed this horse much as he had Buck, with a familiar set of motions that Elhaym moved in sync with. "She's been a strong runner her whole life, and was mostly used back home as a labor animal on the farms near Palen. She hasn't gone very far from this region in all of her short life." He knew these strangers would be going far away, and that Elhaym might be scared when she left familiar grounds.

Elves were very in tune with animals and nature, and Nareena envied this man his empathy. Her courses of study were almost purely scientific and fact-based, so her own innate Elven senses had dulled over time. She couldn't tell much about Elhaym's mood, despite the fact that the horse had brushed against her with its face.

"She likes you. A very good fit," Jean-Vierre said as he moved away to let them get acquainted.

Meanwhile, Portenda had been speaking with the stable owner, an aged Elven man with a slew of years of experience training and tending to horses.

"I'm sorry, mister Portenda, but you'll have to pay for these horses now, in full. I know about your little escapades, boy," the elderly Elf said, waggling a long, bony finger at the Simpa. "I'm grateful you were able to help us with those Orcs a few years back, but you were paid for that and I need to be paid for these."

Portenda reached into one of his vest pockets, and withdrew a yellow pad of paper, flipping back through the pages one by one, scanning the notes he had jotted down there.

"Ah, here we are," he said after a minute, handing the pad over to the old man, who scanned the writing there. "I believe that's your signature at the bottom, mister Horton," he said, grinning broadly.

The old Elf, Eric Horton, looked at what Portenda had written and he had signed off on. It read as follows:

For the ensured safety and return of my stock, I, Eric Horton, do agree to pay the sum of five thousand gold pieces, as well as agree to one favor, to be collected on at a later, unspecified time. –Eric Horton

The old Elf gnashed his teeth together, furious that he could have forgotten something like this after only a few years. He remembered so much: eleven hundred years of memories. How could he forget an unspecified favor to a Bounty Hunter like Portenda the Quiet? He had to know, even then, that it might cost him dearly. Then again, the Orcs had stolen all of his beasts, and had even kidnapped Jean-Vierre, who had described Portenda's slaughter of his Orc captors with vivid detail.

"All right, Bounty Hunter," Horton fairly groaned. "You can take the horses and the equipment you'll need for them. But now you can tear that paper apart."

Portenda slowly, agonizingly ripped the paper free from the pad, meaningfully tearing it apart and scattering the pieces on the hay-covered floor.

"Good. Now take your little cohorts, the horses, and get out of my stable."

Portenda marched over to Jonah, who had the saddle attached to Buck and was already preparing to mount up. But the horse was still far too tall for him to get up on, and the Human Alchemist had little experience with equine creatures.

Portenda crept up behind him unnoticed, and hefted Jonah up on the horse's back.

The boy gasped in shock as the Bounty Hunter's huge hands thrust up under his arms and planted him on Buck's back, but when he looked down, he gave Portenda a smile and a nod of thanks.

"Well, shall we be off, then," Nareena asked from Elhaym's back.

Portenda looked up at her astride the bronze nag, and nodded.

Blink was on his shoulder, and he set the Alchemical beast on the floor as he straightened his back and began to change his shape.

Muscles tore free of his bones, which also rearranged themselves in his body. A flash of light from the center of his chest shone brilliantly as his equipment disappeared into a spiritual space. A primal roar ripped through the air of the stable and the village outside, and in the small, one room schoolhouse in the center of town, the Human teacher nearly lost control of his bladder as he ducked under his oak desk.

Jonah and Nareena were amazed that the horses maintained their composure. A tiger-striped lion, too massive to be real, stood before them.

Portenda the Quiet, in his animal form, padded out of the stable and into the light of morning. Nareena and Jonah followed, and Blink hopped up on Portenda's back, clutching a few tufts of fur to keep himself securely on the Bounty Hunter's animal back.

Without a word, since he couldn't speak in this form, Portenda darted off at a modest pace.

Nareena and Jonah looked at one another for a moment before shrugging their shoulders and following into the west.

* * * *

"You didn't exactly tell him," the gold-masked being said as Death came into his chambers through the rift in space-time.

NOT EXACTLY. Death searched the room for Maxi, who had arrived before him and was currently snoozing on Fate's unused bed.

Fate never slept, never even rested for a moment. A waste of time, he had said.

BUT TRUST ME, I GOT THE PROPER WHEELS TURNING IN HIS HEAD. HE'LL THINK IT THROUGH, WHEN HE'S GOT THE CHANCE. I THINK HE'S A BIT BUSY RIGHT NOW, THOUGH. Death moved to Fate's bed and took a seat next to his pet.

"Indeed." Fate looked in on the world through a sphere on one of his desks. "He's a strange one, that's for certain. His mixed nature is highly apparent in his animal form."

Far below, Portenda the Quiet ran along on all fours over the plains of northeastern Tamalaria towards the Allenian Hills.

DID YOU HAVE ANY LUCK FINDING HIM IN THE HISTORIES?

"Actually, yes." Fate looked away from the sphere and at the door that closed off the Chamber of Histories. "While you were gone, I perused through them again. He has begun to appear. The Histories are changing again. But now they hold not just his life, Death." Fate looked at the Grim Reaper as he ran a skeletal hand along Maxi's spine.

The dead dog wagged its tail affectionately as it slept in response to the attention.

"They tell now of how he came into being."

Death stopped his stroking, and got to his ethereal feet.

THEN, IF TRUTH ASKS AGAIN, YOU'LL HAVE TO ANSWER HER, Death intoned. I MUST RETURN TO MY DUTY FOR A WHILE. I'LL VISIT AGAIN, FRIEND. BUT BEFORE I DO, I'M GOING TO MAKE SURE HE SEES THROUGH WHAT HE'S DOING. THEN WE'LL HAVE A LONG TALK, ALL THREE OF US.

"You know he can't come here," said Fate. "And I'm loath to go down there, you know."

SOMETIMES THE RIGHT THING TO DO ISN'T THE THING WE WANT TO DO, Death said. I BELIEVE I'M QUOTING YOU ON THAT ONE. He tore a rift in space-time and carried Maxi and himself through.

"You have me there," Fate said to the empty room.

* * * *

"So, you're healing up nicely," Kobuchi said as Eileen removed her arm from the sling.

"Yes I am, thank you." She wiggled her fingers and winced slightly. "Not completely up to par, but I think I can manage. I've read through the journals."

Eileen took the teacup from its saucer and sipped a little of the relaxing liquid. "I can't believe he did that to you and your family. I know that Kobold family packs are very close-knit. I'm very sorry, Kobuchi." She patted his hand across the table.

"Thank you, Eileen. It's not your fault, though. In a way, it isn't his, either." He slid off of his seat. "I was foolish, and didn't see the trap for what it was. Had I been a bit more careful, I could have avoided this mess." He waved his arms to indicate the entire tower and its inhabitants. "Well, I must be going. When last I checked on him, he was asleep but Genma doesn't rest for very long. Neither do I, of course.

"Well, I've got to check on him. If he's still asleep, or he's busy, I'll get started on getting myself free of this, this curse." He touched the scar-seal on his bare chest. "Maybe even put on a shirt," he added to Eileen's amusement before leaving her to her thoughts.

Eileen had felt confident that Jonah would come for her, and this confidence had been bolstered by a dream the night before. In her dream, she and Jonah had watched the tower crumble from within while seated on the back of a black steed. She sometimes had premonitions, her mother had called them. Since her fifteenth birthday, she had experienced four of them, and each had come true. With past experience to guide her hopes, she waited patiently for her brother and whatever help he brought with him to arrive.

She didn't hear or notice the drunken Simpa enter her chambers.

* * * *

Drown it out, Telroke thought. *Drown the pain, drown the sorrow, drown the regrets. That's the only way.* He drained yet another bottle of brandy, his stomach and head both on fire with alcohol.

Genma's forced conversation had surfaced memories he preferred to keep suppressed, locked away behind a barrier of liquid courage.

"Rapist," he had muttered, tossing the bottle against a far wall and listening with rapt satisfaction to the sound of glass shattering. "That's all I was. Brute. Ravager." The images had become a part of his nervous system, and he could once again feel the flailing of the Khan girl's limbs against him, her claws raking through his back to try and pry him off. He felt the impact of his closed fist against the side of her head, the way her body went limp and offered no more resistance. The smell of sweat and blood as he tore into her with animal ferocity and hunger, with unnatural need.

And finally, the straw that broke his will's spine, he saw the empty, vacant look in the girl's eyes as he finished with her. She had, in the end, given in to him. She had given birth to his only child months later, a freak of nature that should have never been. He had defied the will and laws of the Gods and Goddesses by allowing the child to live.

"Raping her was not the worst of my sins," he said as he opened the last bottle of booze in his chambers. "And I'll rectify that last one. I'll fix that right," he slurred, emptying the bottle and throwing it too against the wall.

His judgment was thoroughly clouded, and his thoughts turned to the good points of his heinous acts. In his stupor, he memory of pure physical pleasure was among the best feelings he had ever experienced. He wanted it again. Of course, he had been sober when he had done it. In his current state, he might not be able to deal with a fighter.

But the girl upstairs, higher in the tower, was no fighter.

Genma had warned him about going near her, sure, but plenty of people had warned him against courses of action that he took anyway. Why not one more, for old times' sake?

Telroke smiled his slovenly smile, his breath reeking of liquor and his shuffling gait showing anyone who might be watching that he wasn't to be interrupted.

At the foot of the stairs, a large Alchemical beast stood guard. Telroke's mind was a blur, but his eyes were still working just fine. The creature had the body of a wolf, the head of a hawk, and the wings of a giant bat. It stood at eye-level to Telroke, but the mass of its body must have outweighed him by at least three hundred pounds.

"You can go no farther," the creature said, moving its beak open and closed with a sort of animated gesture that resembled Human lips. "The Master does not want you going upstairs if you are in your, er, current state of mind."

That voice, Telroke thought, annoyed by the grating tone of superiority it held.

"Please, turn around and return to your chambers."

"I don't think so, bub." Telroke launched a balled fist into the Alchemical beast's face.

Despite his drunken state, Telroke's strength allowed his fist to pass through the creature's fragile, avian skull.

Shards of bone tore through Telroke's arm as he drew his arm back through the dying beast's head.

His wounds closed over almost immediately, and thick, black clouds of smoke poured from the Alchemy beast's open head as it dissolved in a flash of steam and bubbling fluids.

"Pathetic," Telroke murmured as he made his way into the stairwell.

Upward he climbed, his footsteps uneasy and loud as he used the outer wall to balance himself.

He approached the floor on which the Human girl was being kept, and stepped out into the hallway.

Looking up and down the hall, he thought for a moment that he could make out an unfamiliar scent, but decided that it wasn't unfamiliar at all. It was simply that he hadn't met an owner of that smell for long. He'd found a female.

"Heh, this should be easy," he stammered, thinking of a new piece of ass after so long a drought.

Teetering slightly, he made his way towards Eileen Staples' room.

He slipped into her room almost completely unnoticed.

Almost, he realized, wasn't enough as the Q Mage spun in her seat and leveled a Raybolt spell at his chest.

The force of the magical strike hurled him out into the hall and against the opposing wall of stone, slamming the air out of his lungs.

He sat in a heap against the wall, rubbing his scorched pectoral muscles and growling deep in his throat. Crimson hatred blurred his vision, and his lips twisted into a wicked grin as he thought of the ways in which he would violate this little witch.

"Bad move, girl." He pushed away from the wall.

Eileen backed against the far wall of her room.

"When I'm done with you, you'll wish I had just killed you instead," he shouted. He had taken two steps forward when a raging fireball slammed into his left side.

He was thrown down the hall, his fur and clothing set ablaze by Kobuchi spell.

The Kobold had checked in on his master, who had in fact been in the basement, staring absently at the device he kept stored down there. Genma had told Kobuchi that he needed some time to think, and sent him away without another thought.

Kobuchi had then gone to the viewing room and witnessed Telroke destroy the Alchemical beast guarding the stairwell. The Kobold had made a mad dash to catch up with the Simpa and ensure Eileen's safety.

He was taking a monumental risk, because if Genma took himself away from the basement, he would surely notice Kobuchi's magic and question his control over the Kobold. But he'd had to do it. He owed the Human girl for her help, and taking this risk was as nothing compared to the hope she had given him.

Telroke's wails of flaming agony reverberated through the hall, and Kobuchi flexed his magical energy, taking the flames away from Telroke's smoking body. "You're the one who's made a mistake, fool," the Kobold rasped as he darted to the doorway of Eileen's room. She had slumped down against the floor to rest herself. "Eileen, are you okay?"

"I'm fine," she breathed, her voice barely audible. "I, didn't have the spell properly prepared." She stayed on the floor to conserve her strength.

Kobuchi moved towards Telroke, who had gotten to his hands and knees.

He raised his lion-like head, and glared at the Kobold with murder in his eyes.

"You! I'll rip you apart with my bare hands." He set himself into a three-point stance, ready to charge Kobuchi.

The Kobold held his left hand out, palm forward, chanting in an indecipherable tongue.

Telroke took off, dashing forward with his shoulder aimed squarely at Kobuchi's head.

The bull-like tackle would have crushed his skull had Kobuchi not put up a PhysBarrier spell to protect himself.

As it was, the Simpa bounced off of the barrier and fell flat on his back, growling at his inability to take down such a small nuisance.

He sat up like a bolt of lightning, much as his son did when woken from a light sleep. He grinned menacingly at the Kobold, and cracked his neck with the help of his hand under his chin.

"You will cease this foolishness at once," Kobuchi proclaimed, puffing out his chest proudly. "The master didn't want you up here when you've been drinking," he said, taking a whiff of the air. "Clearly, you have come anyway, intoxicated. I'll let this barrier down, but I'm going to put it in the girl's doorway. Try anything further and I shall destroy you, regardless of the master's intentions." He moved the PhysBarrier over the doorframe to Eileen's quarters.

Growling and cursing, Telroke strode right past Kobuchi, towards the stairwell.

"I won't soon forget this, little man," the Simpa called over his shoulder. "When you least expect it, I'll have my claws in your eye sockets."

Kobuchi waited a few minutes before letting the barrier down. He crossed the chamber to Eileen, who smiled at him fondly.

"Thank you," she said, throwing her arms around the Kobold, who stood stiff, flabbergasted.

"Um, ah, you're welcome." He put his hand on her back and patted her awkwardly. "Um, you're crushing me."

"Perhaps I should get going," he said when Eileen let him go. He walked out of the chamber. "I'll try to get a Mage's Eye set on your brother so you can see where he is, at least."

A Hunter and his Prey

"I already know where he is," Eileen said, moving toward her bed. "He's on his way."

* * * *

The trio moved over the fields and towards a small woodland, staying their course. As the sun came down from its noon position of an hour earlier, Portenda transformed himself back into his man-beast form.

He stood silently, looking into the wood line with interest. The long morning hours spent in silence had honed his senses to a high degree, and he could hear the distant clack-clack-clack of a large spider climbing a tree about fifty yards away. There were many forms of life lingering in the woods, both natural and otherwise.

His eyes narrowed as he peered into the woods, and he heard Jonah and Nareena both drop to the ground behind him, dismounting and taking their horses by the reins.

"What are you looking for?" Jonah asked as he approached.

Portenda held up a single finger to quiet him, and Nareena rummaged through her bag for something.

Jonah looked over at his lover as she produced a pad of paper and a quill pen she had purchased in Palen. It never ran dry, and she thought it would be much more reliable than those Gnome contraptions called 'ball-point pens.'

Jonah took them from her, gave her a peck on the cheek, and walked around in front of Portenda, pushing the pad and quill to the Bounty Hunter.

The Simpa nodded, took them, and jotted something hastily.

"He says he's scanning for trouble," Jonah read Portenda's written message.

Portenda narrowed his eyes again, searching for any signs that they might encounter hostility once inside the woodland. Here and there were traces of yellow ectoplasm, presumably left behind by spirit creatures of some sort. But the ectoplasm was dried, and barely visible even to his heightened sense of sight. Whatever had left the trails and drops was nocturnal by nature, and they would be through these woods before nightfall.

"What's he saying now?" Nareena asked as Portenda scribbled something more on the pad.

"Pretty obvious, isn't it?" The Alchemists took their horses' reins and fell into step behind Portenda, who led them single-file into the woodland.

The sounds of animal life flourished around them, the calls of birds to one another, the chittering of squirrels accusing one another of stealing from their stash of nuts and berries flowing seamlessly.

Nareena felt at home here within the confines of the woods, more so than she had in any city thus far. She could almost understand what the plants and animals were saying to one another, but years of exposure to science and hard fact, to city life, blocked her ears from effectively translating the nature speech.

Portenda could understand every little cheep and chirp, however. The trees stood like silent sentries all around them, but their message was clear as he led the Alchemists through the forest; 'Beware,' they were saying.

Portenda sniffed the air once more, and caught a whiff of something far off, to the south, on their left. Whatever it was, it was approaching slowly, stealthily.

Why can't I ever go anywhere without a fight, he thought miserably to himself.

Whatever it was, it was large and nearly silent despite its size.

The Bounty Hunter mentally shuffled through the mental images of creatures he had encountered in this region over the years but came up empty. He generally stayed out of wooded areas and forests, because he could not be in the sunlight during the cloudless days. Though it only gave him a small boost of power, his Khan blood gave him an extra advantage in the direct sunlight.

He halted in the middle of the path, and held up his fist.

Jonah and Nareena stopped dead behind him and watched the Bounty Hunter write something on the pad.

He tossed the pad over his shoulder without a backward glance, the pages fluttering like a bird of stationary.

Jonah caught the pad, thinking, *hmm, he's always accurate*. He hadn't had to adjust to catch the pad, which he now read.

Portenda had only written two words down; 'Ride, NOW'.

Jonah glared wide-eyed at Nareena and she seemed to get the message as he tucked the pad away and leaped with super-human agility atop his mount. Panic did wonders for the adrenaline flow, he thought as Nareena mounted her own horse.

Trees began falling to their left as the creature that had been stalking them realized that they were aware of its presence. But the Alchemists couldn't prepare themselves, or their panicking horses, for the sight of the monstrosity that emerged from the woods.

Two huge, blue-scaled hands gripped the trees on the immediate left of the path, then tossed them aside with no apparent effort, the wooden sentinels completely uprooted.

The creature's face extended on a neck far too muscular to be natural. It reminded Jonah of a frog he had once dissected for its organs, each used in a different potion.

Round, bulbous eyes spiraled around on the sides of the monster's face, focusing on nothing. A fat, fleshy body, spherical but slightly obscured by the huge, flaring nostrils of a nose on the chest, appeared as it stepped onto the path. The monster towered over Portenda and the horses, standing at least thirteen feet in height. Jonah's mind reeled in the presence of such a monster.

Had Portenda not moved as quickly as he had, he might have been crushed underfoot by the amphibian biped. But as the creature stepped down, the Simpa dashed backward with a single leap, his pistol held loosely in his right hand, his spear in his left.

A froggrip, he thought, finally recognizing this creature. He had encountered one before, in the marshlands of the southwestern regions, but it had been smaller, less aggressive. He certainly hadn't had to kill it, as he most likely would have to with this adult of the species.

A Hunter and his Prey

The creature brought a club-like arm down towards the Bounty Hunter, who rolled through the nearby high brush to avoid being crushed.

Jonah and Nareena tried to calm their mounts before they were thrown from their backs, and managed to get them lucid enough to scamper away from the battle between monster and mortal.

As Portenda shot himself upright, he fired a single round at the froggrip.

The concussion of the impact turned the large blue amphibian to the right as brackish fluid sprayed from its wounded right arm.

Portenda holstered the ancient mecha firearm, and gripped his spear with both hands, crouching in preparation for a defensive maneuver.

The froggrip shambled a few hulking steps back, bringing its webbed hands to its sides. Despite the bullet wound, the creature threw its unnatural force into a single thunderclap as it slammed its hands together towards the Bounty Hunter.

Ripples of shock wave force tore through the air, throwing Portenda nearly three dozen yards away, his body twisting in mid-air.

He landed against a tree trunk, his feet touching the bark as his legs bent at the knees to help him bear the brunt of the attack. He hadn't been ready for such a strike from the froggrip, but he knew what was coming when the blue amphibian brought its hands together.

With superior agility, he sprang from the tree and rolled end over end, landing on his feet as he hurled the spear at the froggrip.

The creature dodged to the side as its tongue flailed out of its mouth, knocking the weapon out of the air and to the ground, useless. Jonah and Nareena watched from a hundred yards away, spyglasses up to Jonah's eyes. "This doesn't look good," he said aloud, though he hadn't meant to.

"Let me see those." Nareena snatched the spyglasses from Jonah's hands. "Why not just pull out that firearm of yours?"

"Because Portenda only got enough ammo to fill the clip. I don't want to use it all up too fast. Who knows when we might need it again?"

The Human Alchemist began rifling through his rucksack for a particular potion or powder, but realized that he hadn't prepared any of the smog-producing liquid or its powder form. He had to do something to help the Simpa, but when he took the spyglasses away again from his Elven mate, he saw that Portenda had things pretty well in hand.

The Bounty Hunter had dashed forward, avoiding yet another crushing blow by the froggrip. Closing into melee range, Portenda hacked at the froggrip with his bare claws, tearing open the flesh and muscle tissue beneath as the monstrous amphibian screamed a high-pitched whine.

"Look out," Jonah shouted, too late.

The blue-scaled creature wrapped its muscular arms around Portenda's body and hauled him upward, pressing the Simpa's body against its torn and gashed torso.

Portenda felt his muscles and bones press out against the crushing force being applied to his body, which now seemed more frail than he recalled. He clamped his eyes shut and planted his hands against the creature's chest and tried to push away, but the froggrip's strength was immense. Pressure built in his back as the creature grabbed its own forearms for support, applying all of its strength to its attempt to crush the life from Portenda's body.

Only on a few occasions had the Bounty Hunter been so imperiled. His vision, he realized, was growing dark around the edges. Like Jonah, he was afraid that he might be in serious danger.

His consciousness wavering, Portenda felt an unknown force building behind his eyes, a force with its origin in his very soul.

The froggrip smiled devilishly, thinking that he already had secured a meal for a week, when the Simpa's claws sank into its shoulders.

Its face fell to dust as Portenda smiled from ear to ear, his eyes gleaming with a strange, crimson light. TIME TO DIE, Portenda said in an otherworldly tone.

The Bounty Hunter opened his mouth wide, and the terrible roar he had used to solidify the specter in Palen issued forth from his throat.

Waves of force tore through the froggrip and it dropped Portenda and tried to cover its ears.

The force dropped it to its knees, flailing its head around as it tried to block out the noise.

It managed to bring its head up and look at Portenda just as the Simpa regained his senses.

That was too close, he thought. And what had happened to his voice back there in the grip of the monstrous amphibian?

Portenda charged the fallen froggrip. Bringing forth a flurry of martial arts hook kicks and hard-line punches, he battering the monster backward.

The froggrip tried to shield its head from the crushing blows, but its arms had been broken by the first few kicks. Portenda easily knocked them aside as he punched the froggrip in the chest, knocking it to its back.

The Bounty Hunter jumped on the fallen froggrip's stomach, reaching down and grabbing the creature by the right arm. He hauled on the appendage, and listened with a madman's delight as the muscles and bone snapped and tore, the arm pulling free of the froggrip's body, blood and bile gushing from its open shoulder.

Still, the creature thrashed about, swiping at Portenda, who ducked, dodged and crouched to avoid the monster's attempts to displace him.

With a Godly effort, Portenda wrenched the creature's mouth open and stuffed its own arm down its throat, choking it on its own detached limb.

The Bounty Hunter back-flipped away from the dying behemoth, landing in his classic three-point stance.

The froggrip flailed, thrashing its final death throes as Jonah and Nareena watched with mixed triumph and horror.

Portenda had proven to be far more deadly than they had even previously known. Sure, they had seen him destroy other mortal men of the known, civilized Races, but sometimes, the creatures of the land proved far more dangerous, as this creature nearly had.

As Portenda retrieved his spear from the ground, he grinned at them.

"Not a problem," he said as he stalked past their stunned mounts. "Barely broke a sweat," he added.

Jonah laughed.

Nareena looked at him with a queer expression as he continued to chuckle.

"Hey, I'm just glad he's okay and back to normal," he said, urging his horse onward.

As they continued through the woods, the Alchemists kept a slightly larger distance between themselves and their lycanthrope companion.

"Did you notice his voice, back there?" Jonah asked Nareena, who had very clearly noted the momentary change in the Simpa Bounty Hunter, both in his voice and his presence. For a moment, he had become something entirely out of this realm.

"No," she lied, carrying on behind Jonah.

But Jonah heard the hesitation in her voice, and saw through her deception. Only Portenda, it seemed remained unaware of what had happened.

Ahead of them on the beaten trail, Portenda shuddered inwardly. He had a feeling he knew what had happened to him in that moment. He would ask about it after his mission was over.

He would have some answers, because he was afraid of what his own heart was suggesting. For now, it was back to business.

Chapter Thirteen
Family Ties

Telroke hadn't slept well after taking a beating from, of all things, a creature less than a quarter of his total mass.

Genma hadn't warned him that some of the servant staff was less than cooperative and he had paid for it with a series of burns and scrapes. The impact from running into Kobuchi's magical barrier had also dislocated his shoulder. All in all, the Simpa was not having a good time.

He decided it was time to ask the ivory mask-wearing Alchemist why he was here.

After a short nap, which he took mostly in order to regenerate his burns and his shoulder, the alcoholic Simpa got up, changed his clothes so as not to let Genma know there had been trouble, and set off to find the Alchemist.

The hallways of the lower floors of Genma's tower were draped in a veil of silence as he made his way through, scouring the tower in search of the Alchemist.

Finally, he saw an oak door cracked slightly open, with flashes of light from within.

Too curious to help himself, Telroke pushed the door open, and was immediately shocked to find the Alchemist seated in a lush, leather swivel chair, watching several shimmering, flat objects. "They're called monitors," the Alchemist said without turning to see that he had a visitor.

As soon as Telroke had crossed the threshold, a thin wire had been pulled, which had been attached to a small metal box in front of Genma. A dim green light flared to life, telling Genma that the Simpa had arrived.

Without any monitor cameras on the first three floors, Genma wanted to ensure that he could remain prepared, and so he had set up several such devices in the rooms he most frequented. Without another moment of hesitation, he turned in his swivel chair, facing the Simpa with his hands folded together. "They're mecha, Telroke, nothing you'd be very interested in."

"No, I'm probably not." Telroke crossed his arms over his barrel-like chest. He had always been a large specimen, though he knew he wasn't as capable as his own son. In terms of pure strength, he felt certain he could outlast the boy; but Portenda was faster than any being he knew and possessed a keen level of intelligence and perception that the older, pureblood Simpa simply couldn't meet. On the field of battle, Portenda had the advantage.

"But that isn't why I'm here, Genma. I want to know what your intentions are for me. I want to know why you brought me here, aside from learning what little I can tell you about, uh, Portenda."

"That's simple, really," Genma said, smiling behind his ivory mask. "I want you to kill him when he gets here." The Alchemist had sadly given up on the hope that his nephew and the Bounty Hunter might not reach his tower.

He'd had no further contact with the Sidalis in his employ, so he assumed the mutant had been found out and destroyed.

Telroke stared at the Alchemist, as if the man had sprouted two extra heads.

A Hunter and his Prey

"How the Hells exactly do you suppose I'm going to pull that off? Maybe you haven't noticed, or bothered to do your research, but that little freak can't be stopped."

Genma got to his feet and stalked towards Telroke, brushing past him with his long, black leather cloak. His cloaks, he mused for a moment, had been brilliantly constructed, made to perform various offensive and defensive duties. The one he currently employed was among the best. When the cloak brushed against a sentient being, it tore away at the mental and physical barriers in place. Telroke found himself following after Genma without question, without pause.

The overall effect wore off as soon as he passed over the threshold of yet another strangely equipped laboratory.

Mecha devices glimmered and buzzed all around him in the small lab, the walls lined with tables upon which large sheets of paper were spat from softly humming apparatus. "What is all of this," he asked in a low whisper, impressed by the ancient technology.

"This is the chamber of recollection." Genma walked to a sturdy metal chair bolted into the far wall. Several straps had been attached to its arms and legs, and an orb of vibrant emerald had been fashioned and set into a sort of headset. "I sometimes use it to gain information from the guests I keep here, Telroke. Surely in your long years apart from your, son," he emphasized this word in order to get a rise out of the alcoholic Simpa. "You have bumped into him on occasion. I'd like to use the chair here to delve into your memory, see if perhaps you have some hidden knowledge of the boy's weaknesses."

Telroke shrugged his shoulders noncommittally, not agreeing, disagreeing, nor understanding a word of what he was being asked to do.

"So, how does it work, exactly?"

"You'll sit in the chair, and I'll just operate a few levers and switches, here," Genma said, waving his hand over a set of controls for the chair.

Telroke had an instant dislike, and more importantly, distrust of the apparatus.

"It'll be painless, I assure you," Genma cooed, playing on the Simpa's pride and ego.

It worked. "A little discomfort never killed anybody." He seated himself in Genma's device.

The Alchemist touched a button, and the straps secured themselves around Telroke's wrists and ankles, holding him fast to the chair.

Almost without a care, Genma lowered the helmet segment onto the Simpa's head, throwing another switch as he returned to the panel of controls.

A blank monitor screen fizzed into view, revealing a soft, white fog.

As soon as Genma turned on the main control, Telroke wondered how wise he'd been to scoff at pain. Fissures of nerves opened throughout his body, making the very circulation of air in the room over his flesh feel like a thousand razor blades whirring and buzzing just beneath the surface of his skin.

Hunched over the monitor screen, snickering like a little boy who has just deposited a frog in his sister's hair, Genma watched Telroke's life flash before his eyes.

* * * *

By the time the trio from Ja-Wen made their way out of the woods, evening was swooping down over the land, a jet-black raven that hunted the light of the day until it scurried beneath the horizon. The raven's wings were a deep gray, forming overhead clouds that shielded the lands of Tamalaria from lunar light.

Portenda felt the sun's naturally lent strength leave his body, but he was good enough to deal with this dreary nocturnal environment.

Regardless of his self-confidence, he knew the woods had been a harrowing experience for the Alchemists. Monsters like the froggrip didn't usually show themselves in broad daylight, but the canopy of the treetops had seemed good enough to the slain amphibian beast. It had been a judgment call that the monster wouldn't have the opportunity to foul up again.

"Let's set up camp for the night." Portenda stopped in his tracks when the company had moved perhaps a hundred yards away from the woods.

Neither Jonah nor Nareena put up any complaint, letting the horses go to a nearby stream to water themselves, and flopping on the ground soon after setting out their bedrolls. Without a word to each other or Portenda, they both quaffed some strange, sky blue liquid from a pair of Jonah's vials, and fell instantly asleep.

Portenda leaned over and plucked one of the vials from the ground, giving it a good sniff. "Hmm," he said to himself. "Sleeping potion."

Blink had remained fairly quiet since their encounter in the woods, not even giving Portenda directions to follow. On his way out, the Alchemical beast had made his way through the woods without incident. Now he couldn't cope with the fact that such a monster had been there the whole time he had scuttled through.

Sometimes, Blink thought, *it pays to be small.*

"You've got that right," Portenda said aloud, and Blink gave the Bounty Hunter a small, canine smile.

Sorry, it thought to Portenda. *Didn't mean for you to hear that.*

"Hard not to." He plucked Blink from his perch and set him on the ground. "That should make things a bit easier for your privacy."

Blink darted off towards the stream.

Alone with his thoughts, as usual, Portenda heaved a heavy sigh.

Jonah and Nareena had grown quite close since the company joined together, but he had grown slightly apart from the boy. He enjoyed their company, as he rarely had any of his own. What was this feeling he had toward the Elven girl? Jealousy, he thought in response to his own question. The ethereal wings of night withdrew slightly, letting some little precious moonlight onto the fields and plains around the company. They hadn't lit a fire for warmth, because their bedrolls had been altered by Jonah's Alchemy, using the power of Focus to retain heat. With no light other than what was available,

A Hunter and his Prey

Portenda sat down near his companions, took out a small piece of wood, and began carving.

He rarely thought about what he was going to carve out in the pieces of wood. Most times he wound up making animals and creatures that he had seen in his travels of Tamalaria. But on occasion, he couldn't identify, readily at least, the end product. In a few instances, he wound up carving replicas of his contract targets. They always had that deer-in-headlights look of panic, a look their faces actually gained when they discovered that they couldn't get away from the Simpa Bounty Hunter. He didn't intend for their faces to have that horrified or confused expression, but it was always the first thing that stuck in his mind when he thought back on the jobs.

Tamalaria's plains, forests, mountains and hills were dangerous when one didn't follow the main trade routes. With no patrols or guards around, many pilgrims succumbed to the creatures and thugs that inhabited the less traveled regions. But Portenda had long realized that few of the things he came in contact with in the wild were much of a threat to him. It was difficult for anyone in his line of work to stay on government-regulated roads. Checkpoint guards tended to like making a lot of paperwork and jailing 'suspicious sorts' overnight. And his targets tended to stay well clear.

Having traveled mostly away from such routes, it came as a bit of a surprise when Portenda looked up from his finished miniature, a Desanadron military guard of the Elven Race, to see a group of torches heading in the company's general direction. *A patrol?* he wondered. *Out here?*

Portenda rose, but opted not to awaken the Alchemists: they had enough on their plates to deal with as it was.

As the torches drew closer, Portenda made out the scents of each of the four armored silhouettes. A Human, likely male, in steel plate armor. An Elf, also male, dressed in light mythril chain mail. He took a deeper sniff of the air—probably a mage of some sort. The third and forth forms, large and lumbering, were Minotaurs, wearing thick, steel, full plate armor.

The Human stood at the front of the group as they came to a hesitant halt twenty feet away. He held his torch aloft, his face concealed by the close-faced helmet on his head. "Who be there?"

The Bounty Hunter sighed once more. He put his hands out at his sides and took a few steps forward.

Although his posture was both defensive and cooperative, the Minotaurs drew war axes from their backs and crouched in preparation for combat.

"I am Portenda, and with me are Jonah Staples and the Elven girl Nareena," he said loudly to the Human, clearly the leader of this patrol.

The head of the patrol made a few whispered remarks to his companions, which Portenda opted not to hone in on with his sense of hearing.

"I am Brian Force," said the Human, opening the visor of his helmet and revealing a face that surely might have once been handsome. Over the years it had accumulated so many broken bones, cuts, scrapes and bruises, that it looked more like a mound of healed flesh than a face, per se. "We are with the Order of Hegrate, citizen," said Brian Force. "Are you familiar with us?"

"Indeed, I am." Portenda relaxed a bit. The Order of Hegrate was a guild of Soldiers, Knights, Paladins and elemental mages that roamed the dangerous regions of Tamalaria, protecting those who needed protection against the dangers of the wild and bandits. "While I thank you for your services and concern, we are hardly in need of protection."

Brian Force returned Portenda's smile, but only barely.

"Are you certain, citizen?" He gave his men a hand signal to stay their position and keep an eye out. "These regions are home to creatures that few can handle on their own, and your companions," Force said, pointing around the Bounty Hunter to the slumbering forms of the Alchemists. "Well, they don't look like they could handle much of anything." His lackeys laughed viciously behind him.

Portenda's eyes narrowed as he tried to figure out the Human's intentions. Members of the Order of Hegrate were known for being a tad, fanatical. They may even resort to extortion, he thought. None of these men was a Knight, he realized, taking in their behavior and Mr. Force's attitude.

"Believe me, Brian Force, you'd be surprised what they're capable of." Portenda took a few defensive steps back. "We don't want any trouble with your guild, so if you'd be so kind as to report back to the nearest Knight in command of your patrol, we'd appreciate it."

Brian Force seemed to consider this as rubbed his chin; Portenda really didn't want a confrontation with these men although he knew he could trounce them without much effort. At least, he would trash the Minotaurs and the Elven mage. Force had the air of an experienced veteran about him, and he might provide a few minutes' entertainment.

"If you're capable, then you won't mind giving us some assurance of that." Force signaled his men to draw their weapons.

Undisciplined Soldiers, Portenda thought as he drew his spear, are the worst kind.

"This isn't necessary, or wise," Portenda said, strafing around Force and his men as they regrouped and prepared for combat.

"Aren't you going to wake up your little friends, Mister, Portenda, was it," growled one of the Minotaurs with a grin. The others in the group chuckled in response.

As the second Minotaur dashed forward, weapon at his side, Portenda ducked and rolled under the sword swipe, throwing his elbow into the Minotaur's abdomen.

A sound like a balloon deflating wheezed out of the Minotaur Soldier as he dropped to the ground, clutching his side.

Portenda brought his spear up over his head, blocking the downward hack from behind him.

The second Minotaur stuttered in shock as his attack was thrust aside, and Portenda spun about, bringing the blunt end of his spear hard against the side of the Minotaur's head. The lumbering Soldier was down for the count before he hit the ground.

Brian Force took a few cautious steps towards the sleeping Alchemists. If he could get a hold of one of them, he could force a standoff with the Simpa. Force had been with the Order of Hegrate for seven years, and had forced dozens of travelers to accept his unit's aid. Someone like this Simpa rarely came across his path, and he knew that he couldn't handle Portenda even if his Minotaurs hadn't been disabled.

He turned away as Palco, the Elven Aquamancer, began casting defensive spells to protect himself from the skill and wrath of the Bounty Hunter.

When he looked back to the Alchemists, he found that the boy had just drawn an occult symbol in the dirt.

"What the Hells--"

Thorny vines lashed out from the ground around him as the boy pressed his palms to the symbol. They whipped around his ankles to hold him in place, and several of them squirmed their way into the connection spaces in his armor. Thorns no larger than his fingernails scraped at his exposed flesh beneath the armor, and Force could feel his lifeblood drain away.

"Jonah, don't kill him," he heard the Bounty Hunter say.

Portenda stepped up next to him, dragging the unconscious Aquamancer by his ankle. The Simpa faced Brain Force as Jonah cancelled out his Focus Site, his teeth bared and glinting in the pale moonlight. "

I tried to tell you, Mr. Force, that we are hardly in need of protection. Rest assured that as soon as I have the opportunity, I am going to report your activities to your nearest guild Commander."

Force broke out in a cold sweat. His commanding officers in the Order had been so impressed by his record of service that they hadn't bothered to find out how he got so many purchases of service. If word got back to a Commander, he was in for a good deal of suspension, and perhaps incarceration.

"Look, perhaps we can work something out here." Force feigned a smile as he bled on himself slowly. The wounds weren't terribly serious, and would clot soon, but he was presently at the trio's mercy. Though the Elf girl hadn't moved the whole time, the Simpa was clearly a threat to his life, and the boy hadn't proven to be so vulnerable. His strange magic had been able to immobilize and wound the Human Soldier with relative ease, a task few mages in his travels had managed.

"We're listening," Portenda growled, sheathing his spear on his back next to his broadsword. "What's your offer?"

"Well, you folks let me collect up my chums, provided you haven't, er," Brian Force stammered.

"Do not worry," Portenda said flatly, his tone arctic, and his cold, professional aura spreading through the air around him.

Force almost lost control of his nerves in the sudden chill, but he held on.

"I do not kill when it is not necessary. But they are heavily concussed," Portenda added.

Force heard one of the Minotaurs groan as it got to its feet.

"Ah, very good, then," said the Human Soldier. "Well, if you let us go on about our business, we'll give you some coin. What do you say?"

Portenda looked back to Jonah.

The Human Alchemist shook his head, and came up to the Bounty Hunter, whispering something in his ear.

"Are you sure about that," Portenda whispered back, but Jonah smiled and nodded.

Portenda turned his frosted gaze back to Brian, who had taken a few defensive steps back towards his comrades. "My friends are Alchemists, Mr. Force. Jonah would like some samples for use in his experiments from you and your friends," he said flatly.

"Samples?" Brian Force had only a moment to think it over before Jonah Staples had a pair of scissors and a straight razor in his hands, along with a few sample collection dishes and vials.

Jonah pressed one open dish against Force's forehead, collecting some of the blood that dripped down. He closed the dish and tucked it away, producing another as he clipped part of Force's bangs into it. "Oh, I see! He's one of those Scientist types, eh?"

Force was feeling better about this arrangement already. It wouldn't cost him a single coin, and he wouldn't be reported to command. All in all, a moral victory, since physical victory was clearly not an option with these three.

Jonah moved to each of the Soldier's allies in turn, collecting samples of hair, blood, and in the case of the unconscious Minotaur, a tooth. He had used a pair of pliers to remove the offending incisor, but the Minotaur hadn't budged, despite the cringing of Force and the conscious Minotaur. As the skinny Alchemist returned to Portenda, smiling broadly at the tooth in its vial, he nodded to the Bounty Hunter and moved over towards his bedroll.

Portenda moved in close to Force, his snout almost touching against Force's forehead. "Your other little friends will be waking up soon. As soon as they do, get yourselves together and get your gold bricking, extorting asses out of my sight."

Five minutes later, the trio from Ja-Wen was alone again, enjoying the crisp night air.

"That could have gone better," Jonah said from his bedroll, trying to roll over and get back to sleep.

"Yes," Portenda said evenly, his tone like the Void. "He could have tried something stupid. Then we could have just killed them all."

* * * *

Genma sat in a thick leather chair in the chamber of recollection, musing over the images he had seen on the mental monitor device on the right hand wall.

He had watched a capsulated review of every major moment or event that Telroke shared in common with his son, Portenda the Quiet.

A Hunter and his Prey

Telroke himself was asleep in his personal quarters, taken there by one of the Focus Sites Genma had committed to memory.

After the chair device had extracted the necessary information from the Simpa, Telroke had slumped forward as the harnesses loosed themselves and the helmet unit swung back into its original position.

Now, the ivory-masked Alchemist watched the video feed for a third time, enhancing the audio playback as much as possible. The equipment was ancient and, although he took very good care of it, he wasn't as familiar with it as an Engineer or Tinker might be. Gnome Tinkers and Dwarven Engineers tended to be the best acquainted and suited for working with the mecha of the old world. But Genma viewed such Races with disdain and a trace of the sort of superiority that the very rich usually reserve for those who paid rent a month behind schedule.

But the equipment was simple enough to operate that he could control the feed, and watch the displayed imagery in slower or faster motion. He watched yet another time as Telroke's memory of a hunt in the Allenians played itself over on the screen that hung down from the ceiling. From the vantage of Telroke's eyes, he saw the Simpa aim an arrow on a small deer about a hundred yards away. The scene turned out of focus, except for the tip of the arrow and the intended target, both as clear as crystal light.

But then the boy was there. Young Portenda dropped down out of a tree near the deer and landing silently next to it. The Simpa half-breed lunged upward, his claws tearing effortlessly through the deer's throat as the arrow was released in shock.

"No," Genma heard Telroke's voice rasp.

The boy flicked his right hand, and came stalking back toward his father with the arrow in one hand, and the deer being dragged in the other.

Portenda held the arrow up to his father, a half smile curling his lips.

Telroke stared at the arrow and then proceeded to strike the boy about the head with his open hand, calling him a "little freak," and an "interloping little bastard."

But that single word, that utterance of 'no' had shown Genma that Telroke hadn't always hated Portenda. As the years passed and the boy grew even more capable and deadly, Telroke had distanced himself and let the hatred brew.

The final straw had come when Telroke had taken his son to the fields outside of the village, intent on destroying the abomination. Telroke had been bested by a child, and had used the law of exile to save himself and banish the boy from his life.

Despite his avowed hatred, Telroke had repeatedly visited his son, starting when Portenda had just moved out of adolescence, when he had been a Bounty Hunter for only a few years.

Telroke had found him through a series of contacts in the major cities, and found the boy living in the Port of Arcade, a thug-infested port city on the northeastern shore of Tamalaria.

Portenda had been squatting in an abandoned apartment building when Telroke found him. The boy had become a man, and a rather large and quiet one at that.

Genma found this scene the most intriguing, because it certainly cemented the sort of relationship that father and son now harbored. He decided to watch it again.

* * * *

835 A.F., the Port of Arcade. The city was overrun by gangs, as usual. Packs of marauding bandits scoured the streets by day and night, but none of these thugs bothered the city's only Simpa resident. They have seen what he is capable of, and none of them wished to be torn limb from limb. Besides, the man was a known Bounty Hunter, and many of the streetwise goons who inhabit the city had rather large price tags on their heads. Some joined Lord Viper's military forces to avoid detection, but only as a last resort.

Telroke took in the scene and realized that he was being left alone, because the thugs feared his sons Many of Portenda's physical features aped his own father's, and most of the townsfolk of Arcade suspected that there was a connection between the two. They gave Telroke a wide berth, which he enjoyed as he asked the few brave souls willing to pass close by where his son was staying.

All of them pointed him in the right direction, and finally, he stood in the muddy streets as rain washed over him, looking up at an apartment building that appeared to be in shambles.

A sign out front stated that the building was condemned, but the boy was an abomination, Telroke thought, his thoughts transmitted clearly through Genma's audio apparatus. He's likely to stay anywhere he can.

Telroke moved up to the front of the building, tearing the restricting boards off of the front door. Nobody tried to stop him as he ripped the boards away and tossed them aside, working steadily to gain access to the inside.

As the last of the boards came away, he threw the doors open, and was immediately slammed in the chest by a short log attached to several swing arms, set to spring when the doors were opened.

Telroke's view of the world turned into a blurring spiral as he flailed through the air, landing in a heap in the street.

Thick, derisive laughter was cut short by the presence of Portenda, who leaped out of the building and onto his father's limp, recovering body.

A long knife was braced against his throat as he heard the boy's voice, no longer a boy's, but a man's. "What in the name of the Heavens above are you doing here?"

"Just came to see my son," Telroke growled.

The knife and body lifted away. Telroke got steadily to his feet, his long years of alcohol consumption already begun. He brushed himself off, and followed Portenda inside.

A Hunter and his Prey

Telroke's eyes focused on the metallic object on his son's left hip, but he largely ignored it in favor of noting the arrangement of other weaponry strapped to the Bounty Hunter.

Inside the front door, Portenda closed the building off, and Telroke took a seat in the lobby of the old apartment building.

Portenda reset the trap, and whirled on his father. "I want to know what you're doing here, father." His mastery over his own emotions was still a fragile art that he had not yet honed. And in his father's presence, all pretense of having that control was gone. "Perhaps you've decided to let me finish what I started all that time ago." The Bounty Hunter's right hand moved slowly towards the hilt of his broadsword.

"That's not why I've come," Telroke said with a grin of his own. "Besides, so long as you are under my exile by me, you cannot personally harm me, unless I attempt to harm you first. Those are the rules of our people, you know."

The long knife that had been pressed against his throat flew through the space between himself and his son in the blink of an eye, jamming itself firmly in the couch just between his legs.

"*Your* people," Portenda said. Disdain stained his voice darker than a moonless night. "I abide by the rules of Mother, which in the case of exile alone are the same as yours. What have you come for?"

"Well," Telroke said, his mind almost blanking out for a moment in pure rage as the boy referred to his mother. "Your old dad's having a bit of hard luck, lately." He swallowed a good amount of pride in preparation for what he was about to ask, and propose. "Some deals have been made lately among our tribe, as a result of a sudden increase in population. I need someplace to stay for a few days while things get sorted out. And I'll need some money for expenses while I'm in town."

"For booze, from the smell of you." Portenda could not, even now, deny his father's wishes. Among the Khan tribes, even an exile must respect the wishes of his or her parents, and must aid them in any way they can. Simpa, on the other hand, owed their tribe nothing whatsoever, not even their parents, if they were in exile. However, they too could not raise a hand against the one who exiled them, except in self-defense. He was screwed in every instance.

None of these emotions or explanations were conveyed to the Alchemist as he watched the strange scene play itself out. Telroke stayed with his son for three days, and the time slipped away mostly in a haze of drunken blurs. Genma could access only small amounts of that time, but what he saw wasn't so important as how he could analyze Telroke's thoughts and observations and the Bounty Hunter's mannerisms. On the third day that was played back, Genma watched as Telroke's vision cleared for a couple of minutes.

This, Genma realized, was important.

The point of view, as always, was Telroke's. However, the surroundings were different. Instead of being drunk at Portenda's place, Telroke had decided to visit a bar.

Apparently, someone had tried to threaten Portenda, because the boy moved almost faster than Telroke's eyes could register.

Blood sprayed in all directions, splashing on the wooden tavern floor like gutters that were previously clogged suddenly bursting open. Bodies flew, cut, broken and bruised in unlikely fashions.

Gradually Genma realized that Telroke's alcohol-induced state of blurred vision wasn't the only thing hampering observation of the fight: Portenda was simply moving too fast. "By the Gods," Genma breathed under his mask.

The playback fizzled, and Telroke's memories faded away. Genma, still sitting alone in the chamber of recollection, sipped at his tea and began the playback one final time, this time starting from the beginning of the fight. Something still bothered him, something that was nearly off screen every time, but just barely noticeable.

He watched in standard playtime, and again saw the small, grayish blip in the upper right-hand edge of the screen.

He used a dial to rewind the imagery, and played it again. Once more, the little blip appeared, as Portenda gouged a half-Orc's eyes out of his face.

Genma used the dial, rewound, and this time, played the imagery back one half second at a time.

As soon as the gray blip solidified, he stopped the playback, and used a number of other buttons and levers to enhance the blip's image.

After a full minute of silent, stunned observation, Genma was struck with the sensation that his time rather rapidly sprinted away from him now.

"To Hells with the precautions," he muttered to himself, setting the control device down and blanking out the monitor. He had only until the Bounty Hunter arrived to do what he had to with the girl and get as far away from the tower as possible. A tarantula named Mortal Fear had scuttled across his heart and laid eggs, sinking its venomous fangs in to let the Alchemist's will become soft and edible for its soon-to-come children, often referred to as Dread, Loathing, and a host of other such titles.

The gray blip had been a creature dressed in a long, black cloak, looking intently at the Bounty Hunter. A creature holding a scythe.

* * * *

Jonah stood watch for the second shift of the night, rubbing his eyes clear of crusty mucous. Next to him, Nareena continued to sleep peacefully while Jonah used his calcinator as a coffee brewer, heating himself up a nice fresh cup of steaming sludge.

He never could manage to make coffee that didn't have to be chewed near the bottom of the pot, he thought.

An hour into his shift, Jonah set his coffee down and took the sight scope off of the rifle, using it separately to scan the surrounding area for anything that might be amiss.

He saw nothing out of the ordinary, but heard a high-pitched whine from somewhere off to his right. When he turned his scope that way, he saw no likely source of the noise.

A Hunter and his Prey

When he spun fully around, pulling the scope down and resetting it on the rifle, the sound got louder, and seemed to be coming from both sides of him. "Oh, no," he muttered, clutching the sides of his head.

Another headache, he thought as his head swelled and pulsed with the onset of more waves of high frequency screeching.

When they had first started, a few years back, they had been almost crippling, and occurred almost every day. Now, these episodes were more spaced out, and of a much lesser severity. This one seemed almost as powerful as the old ones. Now, however, he had a feeling he knew what caused the headaches—the procedure that his uncle, no, that Genma, had put him through. The mad Alchemist had tried to program him, and the whole operation had ended in overall failure. But traces of it still remained, such as the commands that he could execute without a second's thought.

Perhaps, he thought to himself as the whining decreased in volume and intensity, that's why I'm so good with Focus Sites. He had only read through each of the tomes, and could remember their entire contents without much effort. Only one of the six volumes remained unopened, but he had a pretty good idea of what its text would entail. Had Genma already taught him Focus during the brainwashing treatments? It was possible, certainly, though even Genma couldn't have taught him everything.

The whining passed completely, leaving Jonah sitting in the middle of the company with his coffee cooling on the ground, and his companions softly snoring on either side of him.

He quickly looked around: no intruders, he thought with a mental sigh of relief. It would have been very bad for him had anything happened in his temporary absence of mind. The only other thing stirring nearby was the Alchemical beast, Blink.

The arachnid hybrid stared at him, its canine eyes wide open and its stinger waggling back and forth like a tail.

"Sorry, little guy," Jonah whispered to the eight-legged creature as he sipped at his coffee again. "I'm not much of a conversationalist at times like this."

The Alchemical beast scurried over faster than the wind. It crawled up onto Jonah's lap, and in his mind, Jonah heard a response. *It's okay,* the voice in his mind said. *Can't be much worse than the big guy.*

"How, how do you do that? How come I can hear you in my mind, little Blink?"

The contact, Blink thought directly into Jonah's mind. *So long as I maintain contact, I can talk to anyone this way.*

"Were you created with intelligence, or did it rub off from your creator?"

Mostly from my Creator, Blink thought. Jonah noticed the emphasis on the word 'creator', and mentally capitalized it. Or perhaps Blink sent the word that way. He couldn't be entirely certain. *Your sister is waiting for you, you know?* Blink said.

"I know, Portenda told me so." Jonah sighed. "Any idea how much time we have left to get there and stop Genma?"

I'm not entirely sure, Blink said. *The Creator, Genma, as you call him, works in strange ways. He'll be expecting you, I'm sure, and will have ramped up the timetable for his project.*

"His project," Jonah said, softly. "What project, exactly," he asked Blink. "And how is my sister involved?"

I'm not supposed to say, Blink replied nervously.

"And why not," Jonah asked, reaching for the Alchemical beast, who was poised to spring away.

The big guy said not to say anything, Blink said as he bound away from Jonah's grasp.

Damnation, Jonah thought. *So that's how it is.* Portenda knew something, and clearly wanted to keep it from Jonah. More and more he disliked the Bounty Hunter's secretive nature, but he respected the Simpa a great deal, and chose not to question his judgment. He would find out everything soon enough. He had many questions, and he would wring them out of Genma's throat when the time came.

For now, he would simply have to settle for watching the scenery.

* * * *

Death, it should be said, is a very patient man. He had memories that stretched back before Time had been honed and instated in the first Reality. He remembered just about everything, because Time had no meaning for him. In all of the span of his unique existence, he had never been so confused and infuriated.

The crimson lights in his cowl were mostly directed at himself as he scoured through his home in the time-space vortex.

GRRRRAAAAAAAAUUGGHHH! The unearthly scream of rage echoed through every Reality over which this particular Death reigned.

Small earthquakes, tsunamis, and thunderstorms broke out as a result, and Death's entire body went stiff as he realized the amount of work he might have just created for himself.

He heaved a deep sigh, and Maxi tried to nuzzle up to him nervously.

NOT NOW, MAXI, Death said as he stood.

He had been reaching under his bed, looking for Portenda's timer, because it was one of the last places he thought to look. Surely the man had a timer, because everyone, even the Gods and Goddesses, with four exceptions, had a timer. I APPRECIATE THE GESTURE, BUT I HAVEN'T GOT TIME TO PLAY WITH YOU.

Death stalked out of his bedroom, leaving the bed he never used behind him.

THE CELLAR, he said to himself. I HAVEN'T CHECKED THE CELLAR.

Death made his way as calmly as he could to the center of the bedroom he hardly used, and grabbed the iron ring in the middle of the floor. He hauled up on it, and revealed a set of aging wooden steps that creaked as he descended.

A Hunter and his Prey

They didn't have to creak—it was a minor detail he'd had put in a long time ago. Now, it merely got on his nerves instead of creating atmosphere.

At the bottom of the steps, Death stood before a long, low-ceilinged cellar with a few wine racks against the wall behind the steps themselves, and many, many sets of wooden shelving units and bookcases lining the walls for hundreds of yards in front of him. Everything he'd ever gotten from mortals during his existence, and a few things he had simply acquired as the eons passed, rested on the sets of shelves. Back in the earliest ages of mortal kind, some of the smaller clans of primitive species worshipped him. He had known then what the Histories said they would become, and on a lark decided to keep many of the offerings they brought to their fire circles.

He kept most of the animal organs in jars and tanks filled with formaldehyde, and the crudely made crafts and pieces of art he kept in chronological order from oldest closer to the stairs, to the most recent further along the hall that was the cellar. These shelves only pertained to the gifts he had received in Portenda's Reality. This was, admittedly, due mostly to the fact that none of the other Realities much cared for him, at any time in their Histories.

Death stalked down the cellar towards the end opposite the stairs. Against the far wall, at the other end of the cellar, there stood a single set of white tiles, which rather stood out from the all-black tiling in the rest of the cellar.

No doorknob or handle of any sort was on it, but Death knew it was a door because he had put it in himself. It was much like the door to Fate's room: if Death didn't want you going back there, you'd never find a way in.

Death approached the white tiles and tapped them with the end of his right index finger. A brilliant flash of whitest light poured from the right hand side of the door.

Without a sound, the door swung open, and Death gazed into a perfectly organized office. Only a few items sat on shelves on opposite sides of the perfectly polished white wooden desk.

IT HAS BEEN A WHILE, he said to no one in particular.

The objects on the shelves here, in the corners, and in the desk, had mostly been his own, personal creations. Those that he had created were the only things he had ever made that worked or made any sort of sense to outside observers. If anyone had ever observed them.

Death set his scythe against the wall next to the open door, and swung himself into a large, comfortable swivel chair given to him by Truth, the sister of the Holy Trio.

It had been made of real leather, actual cow's hide, unlike the chair he had made for himself in his primary office upstairs, in the main house. It had a sense of former life to it, even in the metal springs, because metals came from ores, which came from the earth, which was, itself, a living entity.

The chair had essence, which put Death at ease. He almost forgot what he was doing here, because he became thoroughly relaxed in the chair.

RIGHT, he said, shaking his skull and opening one of the ivory drawers. Inside of the first one he checked was a handful of maps and papers, each map depicting the main continents of his primary charges, or worlds he presided over. Seven Realities he watched over, and all of the most densely populated continents were mapped out in that drawer, but he wasn't looking for a map. He closed this drawer, and opened the one below it.

In this one, there was a small collection of children's toys.

If Death could weep, he would have at the memory of these trinkets' collections. He didn't care much for taking children, because for the most part, they were innocent and devoid of blame for what had happened to them. It pained him to have to cut an entry in the Histories so short, especially when they had so much potential, but it was part of the job. A job he was really beginning to hate.

Finally, on the other side of the desk, in the bottom drawer, he found them, in the one locked drawer of the desk.

Two sand timers rested inside this drawer, almost identical in design. Thick, black iron frames, hewed with strange, occult designs, held in them the glass sand receptacles. However, one had no sand at all, and was labeled on the little brass plaque at the bottom, 'Death'. This one he left where it was. The other one, nearly the same, had more sand in it than many of the Gods' own timers. It had a single name on it as well.

'Portenda'.

* * * *

Two Alchemists rode on great steeds while a lion with gray stripes along its body ran just ahead of them.

Blink rode with Jonah that morning, enjoying the shifting, changing appearance of the sky above.

Thick, gray and black storm clouds loomed overhead, and Jonah was afraid that the company wouldn't make much progress before the rains and thunder hit.

His fears were confirmed when, at perhaps nine o'clock in the morning, the first crack of lightning lit the sky and land with yellow, electric flares, and the first drops of rain splashed down on his head.

"Jonah, when do you think he'll have us stop?" Nareena shouted as rolling thunder cracked and rumbled through the atmosphere.

Jonah looked ahead to Portenda, who seemed to be leading the way on pure instinct or, perhaps, directions already given to him by Blink. He was taking them more directly west now, according to Jonah's compass, straight at the Allenian Hills. They would reach the outskirts of the region by nightfall, if they were somehow able to continue throughout the storm.

"I'm not certain, but I hope it's soon," Jonah replied. The rain began coming down in earnest, obscuring his view ahead. "I don't think it would be any good for the horses to keep on in this weather!"

"Or for us," Nareena responded with a wry smile.

Jonah returned the gesture, and looked ahead once again.

A Hunter and his Prey

The streamlined Simpa had taken another turn, and they followed him towards a small hill.

In the side of the hill, stood a wooden door.

As he got to within fifty yards of it, Portenda changed to his man-beast state, and finished the jaunt on foot.

Jonah and Nareena dismounted a few feet away as Portenda pounded on the door, his fur already matted to his body, revealing the scars on his body more prominently than before.

There are so many of them, Jonah thought.

After another round of hard pounding on the door, a small, bandana-wearing head popped out, and a Human of a rather scruffy appearance eyeballed the trio and their horses. He smiled up at Portenda, revealing a mouth of teeth that had seen better days. "Oi there Portenda," the man said cheerily. "'ave them take the 'orses round the back," the head said before disappearing again.

"Around what back," Nareena asked as she looked around, rain spattering against her. Without a proper rain slicker, she was already soaked to the bone, her thin clothes so wet that her figure and measurements were revealed to anyone who bothered to look for more than a few seconds.

Portenda led them around the side of the hill, and pointed to where three more men, all dressed like pirates, stood waiting for them.

"You can trust them," Portenda said calmly.

Jonah and Nareena shrugged their shoulders at one another before taking the horses to the trio on the hill.

The men said nothing, simply taking the reins and guiding the horses swiftly away.

The trio from Ja-Wen returned to the door in the front of the hill, and the same ratty looking man poked his head out.

"The horses are taken care of, Leonard. Now let us in," Portenda said, his tone still cold and flat, but with a hint of familiarity.

"Roit you are then, mate." The man named Leonard swung the door wide open, revealing an earthen tunnel that led down into the ground. "Mind yerself this time, Portenda," the Human Rogue said. "No more of that stuff that went on last toim, or big boss'll have a conniption fit, roit?"

Portenda gave the little man a brief, unsettling smile, and Jonah and Nareena walked in behind him out of the rain, staying close and holding hands.

As the trio passed, they heard from behind them, "Wot's this then? Escorting a couple of lovers now, are you? Getting hard up for work or what, mate?"

Portenda stopped dead in his tracks, his shoulders were bunched, tense. He spun on his heels and brushed past Jonah and Nareena, hauling the Rogue up by the front of his white sailor's shirt.

"Why I'm with these two is my business, Leonard," he growled at the man, snout to nose with him.

Leonard's entire world became those strange, alien gray eyes. Somewhere in that tiny world, the potential for high volumes of pain pressed its way in.

"You leave questions for big boss, right?"

Leonard squirmed, but nodded feverishly.

Jonah squeezed Nareena's hand for a moment. "Glad we're with him and not against him."

"No kidding," she whispered back, giving him a quick peck on the cheek as Portenda unhanded Leonard and led the way down into the stronghold.

After a minute of descent, their way lit by torches evenly spaced down the tunnel, Jonah had to ask the question forming in his mind.

"Portenda? Who are these people?"

"Oh, these men and women are the Assembly of Jaded Hunters. Sort of a gang of Bounty Hunters that are mostly out of work," Portenda said.

Jonah realized why Leonard had seemed so smug. It appeared that Portenda had a contract, and Leonard probably hadn't had an assignment in years. "They take odd job contracts whenever they can, and resort to highway robbery when they're too low on funds. They don't have a code of ethics," Portenda grumbled with clear disdain. "They're wholly unprofessional."

"Then why are we here?" Jonah felt a bit nervous now. Animosity stirred in the air around them as they passed by a handful of guards, until at last they stood before a steel door.

"Because," Portenda said with a wicked grin. "I send them money every year to ensure that I have a place to crash when I'm this close to the Allenians. Someplace where there are few questions of a legal nature, and where few will think to look for me in case I don't want any work. Believe it or not," he said, throwing the door open and blocking a kick that came his way with a deft sweep block, throwing the attacker to the floor. "I do like to take some time off."

Jonah and Nareena stared as three armed Werewolves of various fur colors attacked Portenda and Portenda, unarmed, defended himself and knocked each of them aside and away.

"Stop," shouted a rough, grating voice from within the huge meeting hall the trio now stepped into.

A Red Draconus, one of the Dragon-men that had descended from the Dragons' collective fascination with Humans, sat on a high-backed wicker chair, smiling rather wickedly. "There's no need to be hostile towards one of our own, gentlemen."

Portenda gave him a brief smile.

Tattoos covered almost all of the visible portions of his body, as the Draconus wore simple jeans cut off at the knees and an adamantite protector vest with no sleeves, much like Portenda's, but made of a much more durable and expensive material. "Good to see you again, my friend," the Draconus said, standing and walking towards the Bounty Hunter through a pack of Bounty Hunters who had parted like the Red Sea for his passage.

"It's good to see you too, Colin." Portenda grasped the offered red claw and shook it hard. The previous air of animosity quickly evaporated, and most of the men and women present wore grins and laughed at one another.

Jonah and Nareena both felt their hearts slow back down to normal, and Portenda shrugged his shoulders at them. "Sorry, you two. We do this whenever someone brings a newcomer into the hovel.

Colin, the Red Draconus Bounty Hunter, clapped him on the shoulder roughly. Jonah almost collapsed to see that someone could actually move Portenda with such a friendly strike.

"Come on in, folks, tell me what's on your minds. By the way," he said, extending that horrible, gnarled claw to Jonah in greeting. "Colin Caulkins, former Bounty Hunter."

"Former?" Jonah asked as he shook the offered claw. Caulkins had a firm, but not overpowering grip.

"Yes," Caulkins said as he gave Nareena a gentlemanly kiss on the back of her hand. "I'm a Monk by trade, little man. A martial artist." He walked towards a table on which several containers of refreshments sat, most of them completely drained and in need of refilling. "I'm out of the bounty business, but I take odd-jobs now and again, until I've got enough of my own money to start an academy for martial arts instruction. You look like you could use some training yourself."

"Thanks no, I'll stick with my science." Jonah used a Focus Site on his arm to make his forearm completely steel.

"Ah, the path of the scholar." Colin Caulkins nodded as he took a sip of his coffee. "Please, have some Portenda," he said to the hulking Simpa. "You and I are the only ones who drink the stuff anymore."

"What about your brother, Newt?" Portenda asked in a familiar tone.

He had clearly spent a good amount of time with the Draconus, Jonah thought, because here they were, talking as if they had lived together for years.

"Ah, he was never very big into it. Besides, he's moved to Flagstone, down south. Taken a job writing scripts for those Gnome 'moving pictures' he loves so much." Colin smiled that reptilian smile that Jonah and Nareena had come to associate with Lizardmen, but this was far different in that there was little malice or menace behind it: just a smile. "He's doing really well with it. Good pay, he gets to flex that creative mind of his, and he doesn't have any complaints."

"Or a girlfriend, if I recall correctly," Portenda said flatly, to which Colin spurted out his coffee.

Jonah and Nareena were offered drinks, which they took, and seats, which again they accepted. These folks didn't really seem so bad, now that they had taken down the facade of tension. *So, it was all a practical joke,* Jonah thought. *Good to see that the big guy knows what one of those is.*

"What about your younger brother," Portenda asked. "What was his name?"

"Oh, yeah, him." Colin looked down into his coffee. "Nobody's heard from him in a long time. Must be, six months now."

He and Portenda moved away from the Alchemists, who had started talking about the events that would probably take place in the next few days.

"He was looking for something on the Isle of the Unknown," Colin whispered to Portenda. "That was the last we knew, anyway. He'd written a letter to mom and dad, you know how they worry, even though they don't say as much."

The big Simpa nodded. "What exactly was he looking for?"

"Some sort of doorway, he said." Colin looked around at the former Bounty Hunters gathering. Many of them had become little more than mercenaries and assassins now, but the money came in, and nobody asked questions so long as one man's business didn't cross with another's. "A way to get to another Reality. He went on and on about that sort of thing for as far back as I can remember. Always wanted to see what else is out there." Colin took a long pull of his drink. "Space case," he muttered. "Anyway, what brings you around again?"

"I've got an assignment, Colin. I'm taking this one sort of personal." Portenda took a pull on his own coffee.

"Personal? You? That's a bit of a surprise and a relief." Colin smiled. "You've always been sort of clean, clinical about the business, Portenda. A lot of the guys still don't like that you're so, distant. It's like you don't feel anything."

Colin Caulkins gazed over at the Alchemists sitting in the far corner of the room, being slightly lovey-dovey. "So, which one of them did it for you?"

"Did what?" Portenda let his defenses down for a little while longer. It felt good to unwind and unload, and he was glad he had someone like Colin to talk to about the business he was currently involved in.

"Which one of them managed to get through that wall you're always putting up?" Colin's Dragon-inherited tail flickered back and forth on the floor behind the chair, and he brought it up around the chair and into his lap, where he kept it pinned with one hand. "Damn thing has a mind of its own, I swear."

"To tell you the truth, it was a combination of things, mostly the boy and his folks. His sister's been abducted, and—," Portenda cut off when he noticed the shifting in the plates on Colin's face. "What?"

"What's that thing on your shoulder?"

Portenda hadn't even noticed Blink climbing up along his back, settling in for a nice nap on his shoulder.

"Oh, this is Blink," Portenda said in introduction. "He's an Alchemical beast. Not created by Jonah or Nareena, though. He was created by the man who took Jonah's sister."

"How do you know that for certain, Portenda? That thing could have come from anywhere, and it doesn't look much like it can talk."

"He speaks through one's mind." The Bounty Hunter explained that the Alchemical beast could communicate only with a person he made physical contact with.

A Hunter and his Prey

The Draconus Monk sat in studied silence for a short while, occasionally glancing over at the Alchemists.

"Jonah, have you thought any more about what's going to happen to him when we get your sister back?" Nareena asked her lover in a low whisper. The Simpa was checking them on, and they didn't want him to overhear their conversation, which wasn't difficult to ensure. After all, they were whispering, and all around them men and women of different Races and, now, different trades, were being half drunk and rowdy around them.

"Well, he did seem interested in buying the apartment building in Desanadron where those Kobolds were staying," Jonah said, pulling the sixth and final volume of Focus Art knowledge from his rucksack. "But that's just wishful thinking. He's very rooted in Ja-Wen, after all. I don't think he could just up and leave those people behind."

Jonah didn't like where Nareena was taking this conversation; at first, she had simply been after him about nipping off to a dark storage closet somewhere in this group's hideout. Jonah had flushed, but was more than happy to entertain the idea. Now, however, she was being serious, and right at the moment, he only had room in his heart for the business of saving his sister. Her time, he knew somehow, was about to run out.

"No, he probably couldn't," the Elven Alchemist said, holding his hand tightly. "But maybe he could keep both."

"I don't think so, Nareena." Jonah sighed as he opened the Alchemy book. "Desanadron and Ja-Wen are at almost complete opposite ends of the continent. He'd have to keep himself in good supply with Teleportation Scrolls, and I don't think he cares much for that form of transportation. Besides," he added, somewhat mournfully. "I don't think he's going to want to see much of us after this mission. He isn't making a copper piece off of this job, and I'm sure he's thought of that. He is a businessman, after all."

"Maybe so," Nareena said with a smile. She gave Jonah a quick peck on the cheek. "But thanks to him, we're closer than we ever were before."

Jonah looked longingly into those deep, sea green eyes of hers. Gods he was in love with her, Jonah thought. He had always been, but things had blinded him to that fact: things that shouldn't have stopped them.

"That's true. I suppose we owe him something, but that's just the problem. We haven't got nearly enough money to pay him for everything he's done for us, and still has yet to. So, when the job's done, that he'll most likely just up and take off. He's a Bounty Hunter, and in case you haven't noticed. He's not prone to bouts of emotional judgment."

"We'll see, dear. We'll see." Nareena stroked Jonah's hair distractedly. The big Simpa approached them, ducking and dodging through the bodies around him as someone struck up a chord on their guitar. "What's up?" she asked as he stood before them.

"We're going to rest up here until the rain ceases," Portenda said, mostly to Jonah. "Come with me, I'll show you two to a room. They've always got a few unoccupied guest chambers, and Colin has a couple of men checking on the weather for us. We've got at least a couple of hours. You two could use some time alone, I think." He didn't have time for any further comment as Nareena dragged Jonah by the wrist towards the only other open door in the large meeting hall.

They were gone from sight before Portenda could even reach the corridor that held the sleeping chambers. "Ah, to be young again," Portenda said, moving off down the hall for a quick catnap. "Lucky dog," he whispered as he passed by the door through which the Alchemists were already making primal noises of mating. "Hope Jonah's up to a lot of this in the coming years."

Portenda found one of the other free rooms after a few tries, apologizing a couple of times to folks who were playing cards, charting maps, and on the next to last try, ducking out of the occupied room before the other romantic couple present knew he'd seen them.

He shuddered violently. "Werewolves," he muttered as he made his way into a free room. Well, mostly free: a black robe with an opaque cowl sat on the edge of the only bed in the room. Despite the darkness under the hood, Portenda felt Death's cold smile.

HELLO, PORTENDA. Death patted the bed next to him. COME, HAVE A SEAT.

"I'll stand, thank you Grim." Portenda closed the door behind him.

Blink hadn't moved from his spot on the Bounty Hunter's shoulder, but now Portenda felt all eight legs grapple for a better purchase on his fur.

"You can see him, can't you little one?" He patted Blink on the head.

Blink couldn't even answer: he just clutched at Portenda for comfort and protection.

"You're not here for the little one, are you Grim?"

Death shook his head, an imperceptible motion, if not for the opening in the hood. Twinkling blue lights flared to life in the darkness of his robe.

NO, I'M NOT HERE TO COLLECT ANYONE. I JUST WANTED TO LET YOU KNOW THAT I FOUND THIS. Death produced Portenda's life timer. YOU DO KNOW WHAT THIS IS, RIGHT?

Portenda said nothing, just nodding as he continued to pat Blink on the head.

Death put the timer in his robe, tucking it away in the infinite space therein. VERY GOOD. MOST FOLKS DON'T CARE MUCH FOR SEEING HOW MUCH TIME THEY HAVE LEFT, BUT AS YOU SAW, YOU HAVE LITTLE NEED TO WORRY.

"Not entirely true, Grim. You told me that certain events can cause the sand to flow much faster, or the timer to shatter entirely," Portenda said. "Why else are you here? It couldn't be that simple."

YOU'RE RIGHT. Death stood. AS YOU USUALLY ARE. LOOK, SOMEONE HAS BEEN NAGGING ME TO TELL YOU ABOUT YOURSELF, AND I'M SURE YOU'VE HAD A FEELING THAT YOU AREN'T EXACTLY, WELL, NORMAL.

A Hunter and his Prey

"Of course I'm not normal," Portenda fairly shouted. "I'm not even supposed to be alive, according to the rules of nature." He walked past Death and sat heavily on the edge of the bed. "I should never have been conceived, much less carried to full term."

ATTEMPTS WERE MADE TO KEEP THINGS NICE AND ORDERLY, Death said cryptically.

Portenda wasn't sure he liked where this conversation was heading.

BUT A PAIR OF INTERLOPERS, ONE IN PARTICULAR, WERE VERY FASCINATED BY THE IDEA. ONE MORE THAN THE OTHER, MAINLY BECAUSE HE HAD NEVER HAD A PART IN HELPING A LIFE ALONG.

"It was you, wasn't it?" Portenda said suddenly, cutting Death off at the pass.

If Death had a heart, it would have skipped a beat, because here the boy had figured him out. NOW THAT I THINK ABOUT IT, I WASN'T BEING ENTIRELY CLEVER ABOUT MY CHOICE OF WORDS, WAS I?

"Not really. So, you and someone else took a hand in letting me come into being. I imagine the Gods weren't exactly pleased with the idea."

TO TELL THE TRUTH, FOR THE MOST PART THEY DIDN'T KNOW WHAT WAS GOING ON. MYSELF AND MY ACCOMPLICE MADE CERTAIN THAT THEY WERE KEPT BLIND TO WHAT WE WERE DOING. OF COURSE, AFTER YOUR BIRTH, QUESTIONS WERE ASKED, BUT THEY LEARNED NOTHING. THEY STILL HAVE NO IDEA.

"But someone suspects, I assume. So, who else was involved? I imagine it was Fate, wasn't it?" Portenda hazarded a guess based on his prior conversations with the Grim Reaper.

Death nodded, remaining silent.

"You're worried the Gods will try to put a stop to me when they find out, aren't you?"

FATE AND I ARE TRYING TO HOLD THEM OFF UNTIL YOU APPEAR IN THE HISTORIES. ONCE YOU'RE IN THE PAGES, NOT EVEN THE GODS ARE ALLOWED TO DIRECTLY INTERFERE WITH YOU, UNLESS YOU DO SOMETHING TO WARRANT THEIR WRATH.

Portenda's fears and suspicions were now confirmed. He was the son of a drunken Simpa, a harmless Khan, and two astral beings who had never before, that he knew of, anyway, directly involved themselves in mortal affairs.

"I just have one more question for you, Grim," Portenda said quietly.

Death turned his attention to the Simpa as he tore a rift in time-space with his scythe, having done what he set out to do after leaving Fate's chambers.

SURE THING. I SUPPOSE I OWE YOU THAT MUCH, AFTER ALL THESE YEARS OF KEEPING SECRETS FROM YOU. FIRE AWAY/ Death kept his tone level despite the strange feeling he was experiencing. He thought mortals referred to it as, regret. Yes, that was the word, regret.

"Why did you do it? My whole life, I haven't felt quite right. I've been different, more capable. My senses enhance with more time spent in silence, and my roar has the ability to damage spirit creatures, or at least solidify them, pull them into the material plane. And that, I realize now, is because of the nature of my birth."

Death slowly nodded. YOUR STATEMENTS ARE ASTUTE, AND CORRECT. WITHIN YOU RESIDES SOME OF MY AND FATE'S ASTRAL POWERS. FATE PERCEIVES EVERYTHING, YOU SEE. HE CAN SEE, HEAR, TASTE, SMELL, AND FEEL ANYTHING, ANYWHERE. IT'S JUST PART OF WHO HE IS. HE DOES, AFTER ALL, HAVE TO MAINTAIN THE ACCURACY OF THE HISTORIES. Death put one skeletal foot through the rift to keep it open. AS FOR YOUR PROFICIENCY IN COMBAT AND THAT ROAR OF YOURS, YOU GET THOSE FROM ME.

"Funny, I wouldn't imagine you as much of a fighter," Portenda chided. "Being a robe with bones inside, you know."

YOU'D BE SURPRISED HOW MANY SOULS TRY TO PUT UP A FIGHT WHEN I COME TO COLLECT, MY BOY, Death said. AND FOR THE MOST PART, THEY'RE ALLOWED TO STRUGGLE. THEIR POWERS ARE SIMILAR IN THE AFTERLIFE TO THOSE THEY HAD IN LIFE, AND SOME OF THEM PUT UP ONE HELL OF A FIGHT. I'VE BEEN DEALING WITH IT SINCE THE DAWN OF TIME.

"Don't you have to collect the Gods that lose their followers," Portenda asked, suddenly aware of just how much of a fight Death must have had on his hands at times.

YES. AND TRUST ME, *THEY* DON'T GO QUIETLY. NOW, AS FOR YOUR ACTUAL QUESTION, PORTENDA. WHY DID I DO IT?

Death waved his hands noncommittally, sort of a shrug. MORTALS, OVER TIME, HAVE GROWN ON ME. I FEEL AS THOUGH YOU FOLKS SOMETIMES DON'T GET A FAIR SHAKE, YOU KNOW?

Portenda shook his head, and patted Blink, who had loosened his grip on him.

BASICALLY, I WAS CURIOUS. AND, WELL, Death said, rubbing the back of his hood awkwardly, a gesture Portenda had come to associate deeply with Jonah, who was constantly doing this.

I'VE GROWN A LITTLE TIRED OF ALWAYS BEING THERE AT THE END OF ONE'S LIFE. FOR ONCE, JUST ONCE, I WANTED TO HAVE A HAND IN THE CREATION OF A LIFE. THANKFULLY, Death said with what could have been called a grin, if his face weren't a flat skull. YOU'VE DONE ME PROUD, THUS FAR. KEEP UP THE GOOD WORK.

With that said, Death disappeared through the rift.

"You too, old man." Portenda set Blink down on a pillow on the floor. "You too," he said again, laying down for that nap on the simple bed before him.

A Hunter and his Prey

Chapter Fourteen
Arrival

"You're not fooling me, Kobuchi," Genma said to the Kobold as they stood together in the main greeting hall. Genma had set the machine to its final stage of preparation, and in three days' time, his niece would be transformed into his bride. He had grown bored, however, since the machine took care of itself now, and with Telroke outside of the tower, making final adjustments to his battle plan for his son, he had nobody left to talk to. As a result, he had called for his Kobold servant to play a game of chess with him, but the Kobold was acting rather out of character.

When fully in Genma's grip, Kobuchi played brilliant and aggressive strategies that always failed in the end. Here, however, he was being slightly conservative. Although he was left a few opportunities to the Alchemist, they were clearly left on purpose.

"The Site is losing potency again, more rapidly than before," Genma said, much to Kobuchi's relief.

He hadn't been found out just yet. The ivory mask wearing man hadn't figured out that Kobuchi had had help resisting the effects of the controlling Focus Site burned into his chest. For that, he was wholly grateful.

"How did you know," he said, making a move on the board.

"Firstly, the way you're playing. Secondly, you forgot to iron my cloak," Genma said, though this second bit only annoyed him slightly, not really an issue of importance. "You're speaking somewhat more fluidly than you do in full control. But I must admit," Genma said as he made a defensive play. "You're better company when you've got a measure of your free will. Perhaps I shall leave you where you're at right now. You're more intellectually stimulating this way."

Kobuchi's blood boiled, rampaging through his body with a rush of adrenaline as he felt a newfound resentment for this cretin who had stripped him of his good life.

"I could be downright fascinating if you hadn't done this to me at all," Kobuchi shouted as he made his move. "Checkmate," he hollered, getting to his feet and flipping the chess board to the floor, scattering the pieces everywhere.

Genma sat in shocked silence, appalled at Kobuchi's outburst as much as he was surprised.

"Kobuchi, you forget yourself," he squeaked as the Kobold hurled a bolt of magical lightning past his head, blowing apart a section of stone in the wall behind Genma. "Take the rest of the day off, Kobuchi," Genma said, adjusting his ruffled white shirt, particularly the collar. "Get your head on straight, and we'll discuss what to do about your, erm, outburst, later."

"Go sod yourself," Kobuchi grumbled under his breath as he left the room.

Genma's spine iced over as he realized the potential damage that Kobuchi could have wrought upon him. The Kobold was very willful, and a very powerful magic user. The tower's magical energy conversion equipment couldn't handle the high-power spells that the Kobold used.

Genma felt he had suddenly trod on very dangerous ground: only traps set for tigers in the jungle consisted of such rough soil.

His panic quickly faded and before long, Genma felt a bit of a fool. He had managed to get the Kobold under his control in the first place, and Alchemy's power was far greater than anything that Kobuchi could throw at him. All he had to do was find his reference manual for the use of control Sites again in one of his libraries, and reapply the power to the Kobold.

Resetting the pieces on his board, Genma drifted out of the meeting hall and up several stories into one of the packed libraries.

Literally hundreds of volumes of reference material sat on the shelves, many of them retrieved from libraries and private owners throughout Tamalaria who either couldn't read them, or had no idea how valuable they were to the proper reader. Most of them were ancient texts that referred to the art of Focus, and many of them were guides to the old world's technologies. A handful of tomes were cultural studies of the peoples who had lived in the time before the Fall of Mecha. They apparently marked their time by centuries, as did some of the ancient texts, the ones falling apart mostly, had clearly marked dates. Many read something like, 'Second Age of the Empire, Century of the Sword, Fifteenth Year,' or other similar date marks.

Genma spent a good half an hour looking for the specific volume he needed, which he found on a low shelf. It appeared to have been taken off of the shelf recently, he thought, because it was not back in its proper place. It was supposed to be on the left of 'Accelerated Mutation in Alchemical Compounds,' not the right of it. Who else had access to his libraries?

He had insisted that the Alchemical beast he had named Foxtrot cease reading his books because the fox-bull-lion hybrid could get the books down, but couldn't manage getting any back up. Although he only read the history books, it still had annoyed Genma to constantly clean up after Foxtrot.

The only other people in the tower, then, who had access, were Telroke, who didn't seem the bookish type, and Kobuchi.

Had the Kobold been so bold because he knew how to stop the effects of the Focus Site burned into his chest? Genma wondered worriedly.

No, that couldn't be it. Kobuchi couldn't use Alchemy, because his power was derived from magic and spiritual energies, not the pure power of science. Mages of lesser knowledge or power could use Alchemy because they didn't fully comprehend the power of magic. Such wisdom generally made the use of science impossible, because mages had the insane notion that not everything had a scientific and concrete explanation.

Fools, Genma thought. Everything can be explained with science. At least, he hoped so, because if he was wrong, there were an awful lot of Gods and Goddesses who'd want a shot at him when he died.

Genma rifled through the pages of the tome as he took a seat on one of the comfortable leather recliners in the library, searching for the exact Focus Site he had used on Kobuchi.

He found it mostly because the entry was dog-eared.

A Hunter and his Prey

Strange, he thought, I don't remember marking the page. I use bookmarks. Clearly Kobuchi had been reading through the book, but thankfully the Kobold hadn't destroyed the entry. He had, in point of fact, highlighted and underlined a number of passages.

"How helpful," Genma remarked as he re-read the entry.

Nothing seemed too out of place, and the noted passages that Kobuchi had marked seemed to be the most essential bits. Near the end of the section, however, Genma got a cold chill in his spine again, much as he had back in the meeting hall. It leeched into his brain after a few minutes, and he realized as he read the last marked passage what had gotten into him. 'The most essential thing to remember is that this particular Focus Site has a tenuous hold on any magic-using creatures,' the entry read. 'Although one of the more powerful Sites known to us Alchemists, a magic wielding individual can break the Site's hold on them with a highly concentrated expenditure of magic directed at the Site. This is why it is recommended that the Site be somehow permanently marked into their flesh, so that the use of magic on the Site may result in injury or incapacitation, including death, of the target. Again, this Focus art should only be used in times of war, and only as a last result. We Alchemists do not condone the abuse of science's power', it read in the final passage.

Although allowing Kobuchi to kill himself with his own magic was tempting, Genma knew that he would live through anything he threw at himself, and for good reason. Genma had many hundreds of artifacts scattered throughout the tower, many of which could keep Kobuchi alive if he blasted himself with even his most powerful spell. And if he used *that* spell, he might destroy a good amount of the tower itself. Genma had to stop him, and that was that.

He tossed the tome aside hastily, and gave Foxtrot, who was peering around the doorway of the library, a withering glare. "Look, I've got a good excuse," he rumbled at the Alchemy beast, who raised his eyebrows. "Out of the way you damned idiot," Genma shouted as Foxtrot blocked the door with his massive frame. "Oh, fine! Go ahead and read to your heart's content, I'll deal with it later."

"My thanks," the creature said as it pushed its way past the Alchemist.

Genma rushed through the halls of his tower, seeking out the Kobold. Everything was now flying out of control. The girl had hurt herself, delaying the recreation of his wife. Telroke hadn't recalled any weakness in the Bounty Hunter who was most likely on his way to the tower at this very moment. His nephew hadn't been completely brainwashed and hadn't killed his companions when Genma gave him the order through the mirror. The mercenary Wren had been slain. The Sidalis hadn't reported back. And now, his most dependable servant, the only thing he had always been so sure of, was about to go and break the hold he had on him. What else could go wrong today? he mentally shouted at himself.

This was when the cloak got caught under his foot, and he tumbled to the floor in a heap. "Grrrauuuugggghhh!"

* * * *

It was always something, Portenda thought as someone nudged him out of his slumber. He rolled over, and found himself looking through sleep-blurred eyes at Jonah and Nareena. "What?" he growled, his teeth barred.

"The rain's stopped." Jonah took a step away from the bed. "We thought you'd want to know, so we can head out."

Portenda swung his legs over the side of the bed, and rubbed the sleep from his eyes.

"Sorry about the attitude," Portenda mumbled. "I feel like I haven't had a good night's sleep in the longest time," he said, which was mostly true. He hadn't had a full night's rest since before Jonah had run into him at the Flaming Tongue. Or rather, since the Human Alchemist had run into trouble with a half-Orc.

Portenda sprang from the bed to his feet, strapping his weapons back in place. "There'll be plenty of time for rest when this job's done."

He opted not to comment on the subtle change that swept through Jonah's eyes. "So, Jonah, when this is all said and done, do you still want to be a Bounty Hunter?"

Jonah guffawed. "After seeing what you put up with, no, not really."

He put an arm around Nareena's shoulders, and the Elven girl blushed brightly. "I've got everything I want waiting for me in Desanadron. Present girlfriend excluded," he said.

"Duly noted and thoroughly envious," Portenda grumbled as he led the way out of the sleeping chamber.

Colin Caulkins waited by the entrance as they made their way up the tunnel staircase and outside. Blink rode shotgun on Portenda's shoulder, ready for the shape change that Portenda would go through when they were all prepared to leave.

"Colin, it was good seeing you again."

"Likewise." The Draconus made a complicated bowing gesture with his hands and some footwork. At least, it appeared complicated to Jonah and Nareena. Colin looked from Portenda to the Alchemists, and then back at the steeds. "The warrior and the scholar," he said quietly, the fresh sunlight illuminating his tattoos brilliantly. One of them, Jonah noted, was a yin-yang on his leg, with two red arrows around it. On his bare left foot, flames had been inked onto the thick, protective scales. There were almost a dozen other tattoos visible, but those two caught Jonah's attention the most. They must have hurt like Hells.

"Indeed. Jonah is a fine scholar, as is Miss Nareena," Portenda said.

"A good thing, too, because you clearly fill the only warrior position." Colin laughed at his own good humor. "Well, until next time. Take care of yourself."

"We will." Portenda reared his head up as his body began the morphing process.

Minutes later, the trio from Ja-Wen was once again speeding across the land, now heading almost directly north, but still skirting the Allenian Hills.

A Hunter and his Prey

They sped on this way until well past noon, encountering only wild animals here and there, and avoiding the other traveling parties they spotted well before they were spotted in return.

Portenda's sleek, animal form raced on ahead of the Alchemists and their mounts, the fresh sunlight giving him an extra measure of vitality.

As mid-afternoon approached, the trio came to a halt to take a brief, late lunch.

Portenda kept his wits about him, and his nose twitched continuously.

"What's the matter," Nareena asked, since Jonah's mouth was presently full of dried strips of beef.

Portenda simply held his hand up, indicating to them what they already suspected: he was keeping his senses sharp, in case they got too close to the Allenians. They were, technically, in the region, but not yet up in the hills themselves. A mere fifteen minute ride would bring them into the hills proper, but both Alchemists knew that Portenda had to avoid doing so, even if it would have shaved time off of their travel. They couldn't risk being ambushed by a patrol of Khan or, worse for Portenda, Simpa.

As the trio cleaned up their temporary campsite, Portenda's ears stood on end, and his nostrils flared wide. "Hellfire," he muttered, drawing his pistol from its holster and taking aim to the west. "Get ready."

"We should get out of here," Jonah shouted, moving towards his mount.

The horse, however, had other ideas. It reared away from him, as did Elhaym from Nareena. They trotted a short way to the east, and remained where they stood. They weren't abandoning their owners, it seemed, but if their owners became corpses, they would be prepared to save themselves from the same fate.

"We haven't got time in any case," Portenda growled as Simpa warriors popped out of hiding on all sides of the party. "They were wearing Soga powder," Portenda said quietly. "It masks anyone's scent temporarily. They must have taken advantage of our distraction. Lunch, that is."

Three Simpa on each side of them approached with weapons raised.

Portenda aimed his pistol directly towards the sky, and pulled the trigger, just once.

The resounding echo of the mecha weapon filled the area, and all of the patrolmen stopped dead in their tracks. Eyes wide with recognition and fear, they took two or three more hesitant steps forward.

One of them, clearly the leader of the patrol, approached to within a few yards of the trio, who now stood in a ring.

Jonah was preparing Focus Sites over his arms and torso, and a few on Nareena. She, in turn, was handing him pouches of powder that would turn into a poisonous mist when blown on.

The leader of the patrol was a lumbering fellow, even larger than the Bounty Hunter exile. He was a strapping creature, wearing a brace of short swords that had been sharpened rather recently, from the gleam of them.

"You are Portenda, the Exiled One, aren't you," the Simpa rumbled, his deep, earthen voice causing ripples in the air.

"I am," Portenda replied, his voice colder than the breath of an Ice Dragon.

"Then you know the penalty for entering the Allenian Hills." The patrol leader's voice held a hint of a tremble.

Was the man afraid, Jonah wondered, even with all of this backup? Then again, the patrol leader stood within striking distance of the Bounty Hunter, while everyone else was being careful not to get too close.

"I am aware of the penalty. If, in fact, we were in the hills, which, you may note, Karsh, we are not," Portenda said flatly.

The larger Simpa took a step back.

"Firstly, exile, how do you know my name? And secondly, you *are* in the Allenian Hills." A short sword appeared almost without hesitation in the leader's left hand, but it quavered slightly.

"You are Karsh Anasi of the Folard Tribe," Portenda replied, his tone still flat and emotionless as he leveled the barrel of his pistol at Karsh's forehead. "Your people were my neighbors before my, unfortunate incident with my father," he said, fairly spitting the word 'father'. "You were the Folard Tribe's patrolling second-in-command. I assume you have gained a promotion. The challenge was honorable, I assume?"

Karsh Anasi growled deep in his throat, insulted that a filthy exile would question his honor.

"Yes, I thought it was. Your family is heralded for its honor. Despite how I personally feel about you, you are an honorable man. As for the second part of your statement, we are not, in fact, in the hills themselves. You are out of your patrol jurisdiction. I believe we are still in the eastern flats, by way of there being no hill under our feet."

Much to Jonah's relief, Karsh Anasi put his weapon away and smiled the smile of the damned.

"Your argument is persuasive, Exiled One." Karsh made a hand motion for the others to stand down and return to their duties.

They walked past the trio, keeping well away on either side.

"You know," Karsh said, "I understand your Tribe held a council recently. Last I had heard, they had decided to extend a welcome hand to you, to lift your exile. But they hadn't heard back from your father yet. What was your response?"

"I refused." Portenda lowered his gun and holstering it. "I will not aid in your pointless war against the Khan Tribes."

"No, of course you wouldn't," Karsh said with overwhelming disapproval. "Still, even refusal grants you a single request. You can make it to me, I'll make it official among the councils. What is your request, in lieu of returning to your people?"

Portenda didn't need to think about this question at all. He already knew his response.

"You know of the Khan Soldier, Tiberious Amon?" Karsh nodded, though he raised an eyebrow. "He is my uncle. He wants nothing to do with your war. You and the tribes shall allow him free passage, if you should spot him."

"And how exactly are we to know if it's him we spot? Accidents and misjudged identification tend to happen, after all."

"You'll know it's him. He has a wooden leg. Never saw a priest to regenerate the one he lost many years ago, in the War of Vandross. You are to leave him be, understood?"

Karsh seemed to mull this idea over, but at last he nodded his agreement.

"Very well. But mind your footsteps, Exiled One," Karsh said, pointing at Portenda's chest. "If and when you do next step on our sacred hills, you will be slain on the spot."

"You're very welcome to try," Portenda said with a smile.

Karsh Anasi made his way back towards the Allenians proper.

Portenda, Jonah and Nareena waited for all of the Simpa patrolmen to disappear from view, and then set out again to the north. The horses had returned to them when they sensed that there was no more immediate threat to their well-being, and Jonah and Nareena were quick to remount. Portenda shifted back to his animal form and led the way once again, making certain to stay a little ways to the east of the hills.

The trio from Ja-Wen traveled in this fashion until early evening, when they had begun to turn their course westward again. They had gone north of the Allenian Hills, and would soon be at their final destination. *At least*, Portenda thought, *according to the little one we will be. But I still don't see any sign of a tower, anywhere.*

As the Alchemists dismounted once more to prepare a camp for the night, Portenda prowled the area in his animal form, keeping a sharp eye and nose out for anything out of the ordinary.

For a short while, he didn't think he would come across anything. As he shifted from his animal form to his man-beast shape, his armor and the rest of his equipment returning through the spirit realm to his body, he noted something that seemed, well, out of place.

The big Bounty Hunter looked over his shoulder to check on Jonah and Nareena, who were in the process of setting up the campsite and a fire for preparation of their meal. Perhaps two hundred yards away, north and west of his current position, the air shimmered in a high and wide sheet. It was a barely perceivable disturbance in the air, and would have surely gone unnoticed, had he not been silent in his animal form for so many hours. However, thanks to his inability to communicate while in lion form, his powers of perception were many times amplified, and he could just make out the waves of disturbance energy.

Portenda undid the button on his holster, drawing the ancient mecha weapon slowly as he approached the wall of energy. The closer he got, the higher pitched the whine of energy got in his ears—again, something that few others would have noticed.

When he got to within ten feet of the wall, he thought he could vaguely smell something, familiar, on the other side.

"Hey, Portenda," he heard from behind him. Jonah was hailing him, and Portenda put his weapon away as he turned to look at the Alchemist.

"We've got the fire going and we're ready to make dinner over here," Jonah called.

Portenda returned to the camp, and looked once more over his shoulder.

Blink had told him everything he needed to know when he had caught that sniff near the wall of force.

They had found Genma's tower.

* * * *

Telroke was still assigning patrols to the Alchemy beasts on the outer perimeter of the tower when he felt a disturbance near the wall of force hiding the tower. He tried to look to the wall itself, but unfortunately, the barrier concealed the outside world from view just as much as it did the tower from the outside world.

But something had come close: he could smell it. It was unsettlingly familiar, and sent a chill racing up his spine faster than a light chases cockroaches into hiding.

Still, without leaving the area around the tower, he couldn't be absolutely certain what lay in wait outside of the barrier. It likely wasn't an animal of any sort, or any normal patrol of guild members or lawmen; they wouldn't have noticed the wall of force, and would have stumbled directly into harm's way.

The nearly two dozen Alchemical beasts on guard outside of the tower could tear anything that came within reach apart, and a few of them had been created with Semdragons, miniature Dragon-like creatures that had the same potency of magic and breath weapon attacks as their larger progenitors.

With these Alchemical creations around, few men or women that might be likely to pass through the area would ever be heard from again.

"But they aren't the boy," Telroke muttered to himself. No, of course he didn't expect any of these monstrosities to kill his son, Portenda the Quiet.

They might wound him, but none of them could kill him, even if the entire assembly of them attacked at one time.

The Alchemists, the ones that Genma had mentioned, might be wounded by the Alchemy beasts; perhaps, if the ivory-masked man was lucky, they would be killed. For some reason, Genma was more worried about those two than he was about the Bounty Hunter. Why? Portenda was the one with the big metal weapons, the firearm, and the skills to use them.

Telroke decided that he couldn't concern himself with what was going on outside at the moment. He had to get inside the tower because Genma had some plans that apparently needed Telroke's help to execute. There would be, he was certain, a level of physical work involved, which he was not strictly looking forward to. However, it would kill time, and he needed something to occupy his time since the strange Alchemist had cut off his liquor supply.

A Hunter and his Prey

When Telroke had been preparing to go out and assign the Alchemical beasts their patrols and duties, he had scoured his entire chambers, and many other rooms, of the floor he was staying on.

Genma left a note under his pillow, where Telroke had been keeping his personal flask—the flask hadn't, of course, been there. Just a snide little note, stating that the Simpa had to be 'at the top of his game', lest Portenda prove too much for him upon his arrival.

Now, heading back into the tower for Genma's task, he wondered if perhaps the boy wouldn't come at all. After all, how would he find out where the tower was? It wasn't as if they had anything to use as a form of reference. And even if they did, they couldn't possibly find the tower before Genma completed whatever dark ritual it was he intended to perform. Yet still, something primal, dark, vicious and brooding clung to his heart. The boy would come, and the boy would not lift a finger, unless Telroke did first.

Seeing as he wanted to, and this was a once in a lifetime chance to get the boy while he was weakened by the guard beasts. He would attack Portenda. There would be no hesitation, no questions asked, and no quarter given. Father or son would be slain.

Telroke shortly bumped his forehead against the wall of the entry room as he walked into it, completely lost in his own thoughts of the battle to come. He hadn't even noticed that Genma was standing in the antechamber, staring at him through the eye slits in that horrible little mask of his.

"Everything all right, Telroke," Genma asked derisively.

"Fine, just thinking about the boy," Telroke offered feebly as he rubbed his forehead. "So, what is it you need me to do for you right this second?"

Genma rubbed his hands together and giggled softly, neither of which Telroke regarded as a good sign of things to come.

"I need you to aid me with some, ah, final calibrations to my equipment. There are a few adjustments that I have to make, and the devices are a tad on the heavy side. I'd normally just create a golem for the task, but I am afraid that too much energy would be expended in the effort. I have a great deal of work to do before the night is over. I want to be able to relax tomorrow, for it shall be the eve of a great and final process. I shall even grant you access to my alcohol reserves again if you do this for me," he added.

Telroke's heart skipped a beat. "Lead the way." His blood churned at the chance to absorb more of what he had come to rely on for so much of his daily living. Somewhere back in the dark recesses of his mind, his sense of self rebelled. *How did we come to this?* it bellowed from the darkness. *Are we really such slaves to our own feeble desires?* But he couldn't argue the point, even with himself; his own physical, chemical dependence now ruled him, and he would do just about anything for a drink. He had gone almost an entire day without, and his hands had begun to shake.

He followed Genma up through the tower. The Alchemist didn't so much walk as lurk now, his own thoughts twisted up into mental images of what he would do with his newly reborn bride. Ah, there would be such sweet times, such rapture and pleasure.

But one mustn't celebrate too soon, Genma thought, bringing himself under control. If one, slight error were to be made, all could end for him in defeat and loss. The girl could wind up disfigured, maimed, or worse still, dead, as the result of a single element of the process going wrong. That was why he needed the help of the Simpa so desperately.

The chamber device in which Eileen Staples would be secured and enclosed had three individual levers, each controlling the influx of certain elements that would be used in her rebirth as Genma's late wife. Primary among these elements were water, oxygen, and liquid calcium. The three largest levers on the device were massive indeed and Genma hadn't thought about how he was going to get them moved without a golem. He truly didn't want to use the energy that would be necessary for such a creation. It would severely drain the energy stored in the tower's collection tanks and hoarded for the transformation. *Might as well make the drunkard earn his keep while he's here.*

Genma led the way, while Telroke struggled with his temporary sobriety.

* * * *

In many places, in many Realities, on the stroke of midnight, a sacred time is noted in the hearts of mortal men and women everywhere: it is commonly referred to as, the 'witching hour'. This phrase, however, loses a great deal of meaning when the only two magic wielding creatures within a ten-mile radius are completely unconscious.

Nevertheless, a sort of magic ebbed and flowed along Portenda the Quiet's aura as he prepared himself for the night's watch. His own connection to the occult had been, until very recently, uncertain. Questions about his strange powers of perception and the ability to sense and affect the spiritual beings around him had risen and fallen in swelling tides. However, upon learning that he had a third side to his family, one which only went back a single generation, things had begun to clear. Even the unending loneliness had an explanation, though knowing the why didn't make him feel any better.

His ears twitched, and his nostrils flared as something moved a ways off, behind that shimmering rift in the air he had detected earlier.

With Jonah Staples and Nareena both asleep, he had nobody to talk to, no reason to be distracted. More importantly, he wasn't prone to speaking to himself. His senses had become highly sharpened through three hours of dead silence. He hadn't so much as cleared his throat, which he did now, risking the loss of a fraction of his power.

Much to his delight, there was no apparent loss in his hearing, sight, smell, taste or touch. Everything fairly hummed to a slow, dense vibration around him: even colors appeared more crisply, and possessed their own unique scent just barely noticeable to his keen nose.

When something moved in his vicinity, like the grasshopper that just flew past, he took notice. The barrier merely dampened, his perceptions.

A Hunter and his Prey

Patience, he told himself. In another half an hour or so, and his senses would be so highly tuned they could be played like a harp.

Blink slept atop Nareena's softly rising and falling chest, his stinger occasionally waggling on its own accord. Portenda smiled to himself: nice little critter, he thought. Maybe I'll ask to keep him when everything's said and done. Well, *done*, in any event, he amended.

A small breeze blew through the Allenian Hills to the west, flowing eastward over Portenda and his companions, who took little notice in their slumber.

Shadows pooled around the edges of the campsite, despite there not being any fire to throw light and cast shadows other than those created by the lunar light upon the land. Images of violence flashed through Portenda's mind, blades and claws flying, cones of flame and frost eating through the air like it was fuel for the destructive force streaming at him.

These images, he gathered, spoke not of experiences past, but rather, of trials soon to be faced. There would be carnage: that much was certain. But the imagery flashed through his mind's eye so fast that he could not clearly discern one moment of conflict from the next. He couldn't say for certain who or what would be slain or injured, mauled or spared.

The images continued on through his mind's eye, spinning faster and faster before his mental view. After a solid twenty minutes of this torture, his head ached terribly, as though several very small Fairy-folk had decided to take turns smashing his temples with stake-driving mallets.

Portenda focused himself, purging his mind and heart of all images, of all emotions, as he had trained himself to do many years ago. He sat upon the grass, his legs crossed over one another, his palms pressed together in a silent prayer. Finally, his mind cleared, and the long series of moving, flashing images ceased. All Portenda could sense now was movement: movement from beyond the barrier.

The assorted scents of various animals, including foxes, bulls, horses, and other such wild creatures mixed together in a strange mesh.

More Alchemical beasts, he thought silently to himself. Keeping his eyes shut, Portenda pricked up his ears, and tried to listen in for any more clues he might gather.

Growls, unnatural and unfriendly to say the least, echoed through the vast silence.

Must be twenty or so of them, Portenda thought, moving closer to the barrier. He took one more look over his shoulder, and saw that the Alchemist couple remained silently asleep.

The Bounty Hunter decided to risk a closer look at the barrier, perhaps even passing partly through it for a quick glance at the waiting threat.

Portenda the Quiet drew his broadsword, keeping it at the ready in case he had to pass completely through the barrier for any period of time. He would most certainly be set upon if he found himself amongst the Alchemical beasts standing guard, and at least one of them would be willing to pursue him beyond the barrier's walls.

He drew to within ten yards of the shimmering wall of force.

His nostrils flared at the strange scent of the animals beyond the wall, and the barrier itself, at this proximity, smelled of blood and brimstone. It was almost a familiar scent: at least, the blood was.

No more time to hesitate. He brought the broadsword to his side, then Portenda stepped into, and, a moment later, through, the barrier.

On the other side, close to two dozen creatures milled about, their obscene bodies moving somewhat sluggishly until one or two of them let out a hissing growl at the sight of him.

Great, Portenda thought, bringing the blade up in front of him and taking a defensive posture. *More of them than I had thought.*

Despite the fact that he was about to be set upon, the scent and presence of the Alchemical beasts was not foremost in his mind. His father's scent clung to the air, like an offensive body gesture, prodding at his nose.

Before any of the guard creatures could attack him, Portenda back-flipped through the barrier, landing in a crouch on the other side.

Though nothing came through after him, Portenda had stirred quite a ruckus from within the tower's perimeter.

* * * *

Genma stared, wide-eyed and silent, at the monitor screen. The Bounty Hunter had come through for just a few moments, sniffed the air, and disappeared rather acrobatically before any of the guard creatures could move on him. *They were already here!*

The ivory-masked menace stormed out of the screening room at full tilt, speeding through the hallways to where he knew Telroke would be.

As suspected, Telroke was in the dining hall, a rather large collection of emptied bottles on the table before him. His eyes were so blood-shot they were almost entirely red.

He faced the Alchemist, who stood not five feet away now, rifling through one of the various compartments on his belt.

Genma produced a slim gray pill from one of the pouches and dropped it into Telroke's current victim, a long-necked, glass specimen of a green tint. This particular breed was known as 'drunkus maximus,' not because of its contents, but because it would be victim number fifteen.

"Wha' chyou think yer doin, buddy," Telroke slurred as he grabbed Genma by the wrist.

"I'm just helping bring out the full flavor of your beverage," Genma lied, slipping out of the Simpa's grasp. "Trust me, and drink."

Telroke smiled and gave a harsh bark that might have passed for a laugh, and then tipped the bottle back, draining it in its entirety.

He shook his head, and a moment later, stared wild-eyed at Genma with clear eyes.

"Yes, I lied," Genma admitted, trying to convey his sense of urgency. "But trust me, we both need you sober right now. Your boy has just been spotted breaching the perimeter."

Chemical sobriety aside, knowing that the boy was so close to his position brought Telroke around like nothing else could.

"He's here? Already?"

"He popped in to take a look around at the level of security." Genma led the fuming Simpa through the hallways.

"Did any of the beasts give pursuit?"

"Of course not," Genma said, as if this was obvious. "They're programmed not to leave my sphere of influence, which only extends to the barrier of force."

"Programmed?" Telroke raised an eyebrow as he ducked into his personal chambers to retrieve the battle-axe that Genma had made for him to use against his son.

"They were created with certain, restrictions," Genma said in explanation as the Simpa returned to the hallway. "If they roam outside of the barrier, they will cease to function properly. It's something I do with all of my successful experiments, except for a few items or creatures of interest," he said, hinting at Telroke's weapon. "Now, you have your battle plan to execute, I'm sure. Be certain they do not gain access to the upper tower levels, Telroke," he said, moving into the doorway of a stairwell.

"Where's your servant?" Telroke asked, looking around as he tested the weight of the axe.

The Alchemist had neglected to tell him what was so special about it, and Telroke had no knowledge of weapon enchantments of any sort. A weapon made with Alchemy might have any number of special qualities, none of which he could readily identify. Telroke grumbled mentally as he thought, *I like to know about my weaponry.*

"Kobuchi cannot be counted on to aid us any further," Genma said flatly, furling his cloak around him. "I believe he may have found a way to break my control over him. If this is so, I have to work quickly. And you need to keep an eye out," Genma said. "I didn't just see your memories of your son when I had you in the chamber of recollections. I know you had a hostile encounter with our Kobold friend. I also know you didn't come out on top of things." He was irritated that Kobuchi would soon be free from him. Still, if he had to deal with the Kobold himself, Kobuchi wouldn't stand a chance.

Up the stairwell he went, haste propelling him faster than he had gone in some long time. He *had* to take the girl to the transformation device now, before the Bounty Hunter and his nephew had a chance to get into the tower.

He had created a weapon for Telroke to use on his son with the aid of several Focus Sites, but he knew it would only give him a marginal edge on Portenda the Quiet. It would lend Telroke more strength and speed the longer he held it, but Telroke was now stone sober, and Genma wondered if he would be a better fighter for such a condition.

The axe couldn't be broken, or removed from his grasp unless he dropped it himself. In addition to these traits, the weapon was made with mythril, and so was extremely lightweight. Telroke may have been a drunkard, but he was a pack leader, and an accomplished warrior. He could handle himself in a fight, and the axe would aid him in his battle with his son and the Alchemist couple. But Telroke's fate was the least of Genma's worries at the moment.

Genma made his way steadily toward his niece, who he would soon transform into his bride. He hated to rush things, because doing so brought with it risks of failure. Then again, if he didn't hurry, he might not be alive to try later on. After the transformation, he would use a Teleportation Site to take himself and his newly reborn wife to a safe location, far from the tower. He didn't care for the idea of abandoning his abode, but he could build another if he survived.

Finally, he arrived at his destination, the floor on which his quarry was most likely resting.

Genma took a single step into the hallway, and was nearly flattened by a fireball coming from the left of the intersecting corridor.

He had sensed the searing heat coming at him, a high velocity ball of fire intended to wound or kill the target, who had been him. Because he ducked, bits of stone showered him as the wall exploded.

His cloak pulled before him, stiffer than slate rock, Genma peered over the edge at Kobuchi. The Kobold had his hands before him, his fingers hooked as he prepared another spell.

"How dare you, you ungrateful little shit," Genma howled as he slowly and stealthily reached into his belt, his movements shielded by his hardened cloak. "I own you. I have kept you fed and sheltered for years."

"Yes," Kobuchi said, fairly growling as he shifted his feet into a wide, splay-legged stance. "You have kept me fed and sheltered. And under your total control. Well, I shall be your slave no more.

"*Vakras durodenum*," he shouted.

A swirl of air surrounded his out thrust hands, tinting the air a vague shade of green, like old grass. A whirlwind of magic flowed around his hands, and he pressed them forward further, firing a cone of white wind at the ivory-masked Alchemist.

The force slammed into Genma's cloak, forcing him back across the stone floor and down the corridor.

After the whirlwind dissipated, Genma found himself standing twenty or so yards away from the intersection of the corridors on this floor. The stairwell doorway on his left side of the hallway stood at the center of the intersection, and if Kobuchi hadn't interfered, he would have had a straight shot to Eileen's chamber.

Genma had hoped that Kobuchi would wind up being Telroke's problem, not his own. If he used too much of his Focus art power, he would be left unable to complete the transformation process on Eileen. But Kobuchi was already preparing another spell, and potions, tinctures, powders and poisoned throwing darts weren't enough to bring the Kobold mage down.

But he would have to use them for now, until he knew for certain a Focus could be used to secure victory in one fell swoop.

"Hrrauugh," Genma screamed as he tossed a vial at Kobuchi.

The blue liquid inside shimmered as the vial shattered against the floor at Kobuchi's feet, spraying him with sharpened shards of ice.

Lacerations bled on the Kobold's arms and legs, but the wounds were rather insignificant.

The vial bought Genma time, however, and he dashed forward, drawing out a dart and tossing it at Kobuchi, who rolled to his left into the wall to avoid being struck.

"*Makarus esta*," Kobuchi muttered, pointing a single finger on his left hand in Genma's direction.

The air sizzled with crackling ozone, and the scent filled Genma's lungs, cramping his chest as a thin ray of lightning struck him squarely in the chest.

He was thrown far down the hallway, landing in a heap and writhing in agony as electrical power surged through his already maimed body. But the spell had been cast in haste, and thankfully for Genma, wasn't lethal. It did, however, hurt like all Hells, and left him temporarily stunned.

He heard Kobuchi approaching, and managed to get one of his powders out of a pouch at his hip and into his hand.

As Kobuchi took a new stance, his body low to the ground, Genma sat up and blew the powder at him.

The powdery cloud turned into a wave of water that slammed into the Kobold and washed him all the way down the corridor to its opposite end, striking him against the far wall.

Genma smiled to himself as Kobuchi slumped against the wall, incapacitated.

"That takes care of that," he whispered to himself. He thought for a moment of making certain that his former slave was dead, but he didn't have the luxury of time. He had to get to the girl, and now.

Genma made his way to the intersection, and turned right, heading for Eileen Staples. Her door hung open, and he saw that she was sitting at the simple table, eating a small meal and smiling faintly to herself.

She looked up at him, and her smile broadened.

"What are you smiling at, girl," he rasped, suspicious of her.

"Oh, nothing much," she said, holding up one of his journals. "Fascinating stuff in here, uncle Allen."

Genma's hands clenched into fists of rage.

"Especially the parts about how you trapped Kobuchi into your service. Oh, and I don't think he's too happy about that part."

"It doesn't matter what he's happy about, Eileen," Genma said, taking a step forward and rebounding off a barrier spell. "What the Hells is this? This spell isn't in your arsenal, girl."

"But it is in his," Eileen said with a wicked smile as a disk of stone slammed into Genma's side, breaking several ribs as it threw him aside.

Once more he landed in a heap, this time on his stomach, clutching his broken side. He rolled onto his uninjured side, and looked through the eye slits in his mask at the Kobold, who was on his knees down the corridor.

"We're not finished yet, Genma," Kobuchi said, wheezing still from the impact of the water rush. "Not by, a long shot!"

* * * *

"What is it," Jonah mumbled as he was roughly shoved awake.

Portenda said nothing, simply hovering over him as he reached across Jonah and shoved Nareena roughly.

Both Alchemists woke groggily, climbing up out of their shared bedroll.

The Bounty Hunter shoved piece of yellow paper under Jonah's nose, and he took, quickly reading the hasty scrawl.

'We're here' was written on the page.

Jonah came wide-awake very suddenly, scanning the area with his bleary eyes. "I don't see anything," he said while Nareena set about packing up the camp as quickly as possible.

Portenda wrote something more on another piece of paper, and thrust this under Jonah's nose.

"Could you not do that," the Human Alchemist complained as he snatched the sheet away.

'You aren't supposed to', it said. 'Follow me' was written just beneath this.

Portenda, still silent as the shadow of Death led Jonah and Nareena to the barrier, which now flickering strangely.

Even Jonah could see the barrier as it rippled.

"An Alchemical barrier of force," Nareena said in awe. "It's huge. This sort of thing requires a whole lot of Focus Sites, evenly placed around a building or area."

Jonah eyeballed her.

"What? It's in your forth volume, you know," she said in her own defense.

Portenda drew his broadsword once again, and led the way for the trio straight through the barrier.

Jonah and Nareena stopped dead in their tracks when they saw the dozens of guard beasts gathered around the perimeter of the tower that loomed high overhead.

Like a fist upraised against the Gods, the stone structure stood solid in the plains, and its guardians were milling about now, ready and fully aware that intruders had come into their territory. Even those three or four that had no apparent eyes on their faces were pointed toward the trio.

Jonah was mesmerized by the horror of the creatures for only a moment before his hands started flying around him.

He drew Focus Sites hastily into the dirt, onto his clothes, and he withdrew a few prepared Sites on pieces of parchment from his trouser pockets.

A Hunter and his Prey

"Haah!" Jonah shouted as he activated the Focus on the ground in front of him.

Portenda dashed ahead of the Alchemists, his sword catching the moonlight, glinting as he began his assault.

Jonah had constructed a full sized golem with his first Site, and the stone giant grumbled from an ill-shaped mouth as Jonah prepared its first command. "Golem, defend Nareena and your master!"

Nareena had prepared a single Focus Site on a parchment, her first Focus Art attempt. She clapped her hands together with the sheet in her hands, and kept her hands together on the parchment as the flash of light took hold.

A moment later, she held a short sword that glimmered along its edge. She stood her position as a griffin-like creature approached her and Jonah, her posture firm and defensive, ready to strike back.

The beast began a head-first charge at them, but came up short as the golem raised its hands over its crudely-shaped head, and brought them down in a double axe handle smash along the creature's spine.

There was a sharp snap, followed immediately by a death throe and a howl of agony as the Alchemical beast spewed blood from its beak and twitched on the ground, dying almost instantly.

Jonah kept track of the positions of the guard beasts, and noted that Portenda had already cut down nearly half a dozen of the creatures.

But he was now using his spear to keep a pair of them at bay, dodging and ducking away from cones of frost and black smog.

His assailants' heads appeared to be almost exactly like those of Dragons, but Jonah knew that Dragons couldn't be manipulated by the Alchemical process of Beast Fusion. Their smaller, lesser cousins, however, were often used in such experiments. The spear gave Portenda the reach he needed to strike at them and keep himself at a safe distance from their short-distance breath weapons.

However, Jonah saw that he wasn't making much progress against them, because the creatures had the low, sleek bodies of a lynx, and their movements kept them well out of harm's way from the Bounty Hunter.

More attackers were preparing to take Portenda from the sides.

Jonah activated another Focus Site, this one summoning up a set of spear launching tubes.

He ran behind the launchers and fired two of the five spears, which hit their marks in the breath-weapon-bearing creatures' sides.

The minor injuries were enough to take them off balance, allowing Portenda to stab them each through the heart two times a piece before whirling on his new assailants and tearing them apart with his long handled weapon with ease.

Nareena took a few steps back as a hulking, bipedal bull-like beast crashed through Jonah's golem as though it were so much dry clay.

The golem shattered into small fragments as the beast got to within a few yards of the Elven Alchemist.

Oh Gods, she thought, panic setting in.

"I hope this sword can handle this," she muttered to herself. The specifications of the weapon she had created included the crippling of whatever it struck.

As the guard beast raised its right hand to smash her apart, she stabbed forward into its leg.

The end result wasn't quite what she had been expecting.

The blade of her weapon shook and glowed, and her target quivered uncontrollably as she drew the bloodied tip out of the creature's leg.

The stab wound began to split and widen, reaching up the leg and onto its hairy abdomen. Blood sprayed from the fresh wounds, and a hundred small incisions erupted all over the creature's body. Crimson arterial blood showered Nareena as the bull-beast was torn apart from the inside.

It unleashed a primal roar of pain and rage as bits and pieces of its body fell to the ground.

Weapons, Focus Sites and Nareena's poisonous powders flew about the battlefield. Together, Nareena, Jonah, and Portenda destroyed the guard beasts, one after the other

After about twenty minutes, the trio stood in pools of blood.

Portenda had taken only a few minor blows, his ribs bruised slightly and a fresh gash across his left leg, bleeding slowly. Jonah had taken the full brunt of a creature's barbed tail across the chest, and was in a half-seated position, Nareena applying one of her healing salves to the wound.

"Not exactly as quick as a potion, but you know I've never been good with healing potions," she said he grimaced at the burning sensation of the gooey syrup entered his wounds and began its slow but steady work.

"Don't celebrate yet," a low, rumbling voice called out from the direction of the tower.

Jonah and Nareena looked over at a Simpa with a large battle-axe, a sloppy grin on his face, and a striking resemblance to Portenda, who growling a ferocious, malice-tainted sound low in his throat.

"Who is he?" Jonah wheezed, though he was fairly certain he knew the answer already.

"It's my father," Portenda rumbled, the first words he had spoken since the sun was still in the sky. "You two get into that tower and get Eileen away from Genma." Portenda put his spear away and set an offensive martial arts stance. "I'll deal with this vagabond."

He barred his teeth at his birth father.

Telroke swung his axe lazily up to his shoulder, setting it to rest against his collarbone.

Nareena helped Jonah to his feet, but neither made a move toward the tower.

"Oh, by all means, go ahead," Telroke said with a wicked smile. It was the sort of expression that says, very quietly, you can do what you like. I'll come for you when I'm done here.

A Hunter and his Prey

Jonah shivered to his core, but felt obligated to stay and help the Bounty Hunter in any way he could.

"I'm not going to stop you," the older Simpa said. "My business is with my boy, here, anyway. Genma said nothing about dealing with you two, aside from what the guards could manage." He looked at the dozens of slain creatures. "Which apparently wasn't much. Besides, I'm sure he'll have more surprises for you two inside."

Though he didn't want to, Jonah started to move away, side stepping around Telroke.

"Portenda," he said, starting to apologize.

"Don't," the burly Bounty Hunter said, his voice still as cold as ice. "We'll meet up after I'm done here. But understand me, Jonah," Portenda set his legs slightly farther apart in readiness. "I have to deal with this on my own. I've got you this far, haven't I? Just trust me and leave this to me."

Telroke barked out harsh laughter. "What's so goddamned funny?"

Portenda's question was rife with malice and contempt, a strange loss of temper for the Simpa Bounty Hunter.

"Oh, nothing, dear boy," Telroke said, wiping his eyes clear. "I'm just amazed and a little surprised that you care about anything other than money. Or are these your contractors?"

Telroke set himself into a fighting stance with his axe. "I thought you didn't bring clients along, Bounty Hunter? Ha ha ha ha haaaa."

"They aren't my clients," Portenda grumbled, struggling to keep his composure. "They, are my friends."

Once more Telroke burst into laughter.

Nareena and Jonah started towards the tower, looking over their shoulders as they went.

"Did he just say—?" Nareena began as they hurried along into the tower itself.

"Yes, he did." Jonah smiled the most genuine smile he'd had in a long time. "Yes he did."

* * * *

Magical and scientific energy collided in a flash of opposing forces. Harsh crackling noises ripped through the air as the combined arts pressed incessantly against one another.

The sound nearly deafening Eileen, who watched, filled with tension and apprehension from her chamber doorway. It had been quite a gamble on her and Kobuchi's part, but they had agreed that something was up when Kobuchi saw that the guard beasts were almost all taken from the tower and set around the perimeter of the inside of the barrier.

They knew that Genma's powers were vast, and most likely amplified by the equipment in the higher levels of the tower. In order to counteract this, Kobuchi had destroyed the magical energy converter with a concentrated blast of lightning from his palm. Genma had been distracted, and hadn't bothered to check the equipment that wasn't essential to the operation of the transformation machine.

But this part of the plan had been more loosely assembled. Kobuchi had said that he would distract the ivory-masked Alchemist while she kept herself safe and ready to escape. It had turned into more than a distraction; Kobuchi was going for the kill. And she could do nothing to help Kobuchi so long as he kept the barrier erected in her doorway; the only way to get through it would be for the Kobold to be incapacitated or for Eileen to use a spell to dissipate the barrier.

If she did that, however, she would be in the middle of the conflict, and she might very well be more of a hindrance to Kobuchi than help.

The Kobold mage tucked and rolled out of the way of a blast from Genma's out thrust palm.

A single stream of Focus-created lightning crashed into the stone wall, throwing splinters around the hall.

Kobuchi countered with a swift wave of rippling air currents, sweeping Genma down the hall away from him. *Just hold out for time,* Kobuchi thought. *Focus arts take more energy out of him than magic does out of me. If I just continue to use distraction spells, make him expend all of his energy before I run out, I can go for the kill. No more controls, no more commands.*

"Baraka Duzava." He waved his hands up and down, creating a series of ripples and waves in the stone floor.

The entire tower trembled as the floor raised up and slammed down in a wave that struck full force into a thin barrier the Alchemist erected at the last second.

The barrier was the only thing that kept him from being crushed against the back wall of the corridor. The force of the blow still managed to completely throw his concentration, as well as damage something in his leg.

"Face it, Genma," Kobuchi screamed as he summoned up more manna for use. "You can't beat me in a head-on battle! Your Focus arts are as nothing compared to true magic."

Beneath the ivory mask, the man formerly known as Allen Staples smiled broadly. He had expected the Kobold to be good, though admittedly, he had underestimated his talent. Still, he had the overall advantage, because Kobuchi wasn't entirely out of his control.

"Oh, aren't they? Alchemy is about more than just Focus arts, my friend." Genma straighten up and deepened his voice. "Kobuchi, execute command number thirty-five."

Kobuchi felt his left hand clench involuntarily in response to the Alchemist's words. His hand balled into a fist and he punched himself squarely in the jaw, throwing himself to the floor in a firestorm of pain.

"What the Hells have you done to me," Kobuchi screamed as he pulled himself up off of the floor. The blow had disrupted the flow of his manna, and he had to square himself away before attempting another spell.

A Hunter and his Prey

Genma laughed derisively, the sound of it echoing strangely off of the walls like a death knell.

"It was all part of your first few weeks with me in the tower, Kobuchi," Genma said as he took a few steps back in the direction of the Kobold. "Kobuchi, execute command number twenty-four."

Kobuchi tried to stop himself, but the ivory-masked Alchemist's brainwashing methods too thorough to resist. He moved his hands up and down in front of himself, and tried to stop the words from coming.

"*Magara Musdaga*," he croaked, trying to clamp his jaws shut.

A sheet of fire, stretching from the floor to the ceiling of the corridor, glimmered radiantly before him, and washed over his own body, burning him horribly and setting his clothes on fire.

Screaming and thrashing around uncontrollably, Kobuchi tried to stop the progress of the spell, but couldn't utter the counter-spell for it.

Bastard! Total freak, maimed, pathetic freak, Kobuchi thought as he tried to get to his feet for one last stand against the man who had enslaved him for so long.

"You couldn't possibly resist the order commands right now," Genma said, moving confidently down the corridor toward the Kobold mage, both men's breath starting to rattle in their chests. "You probably don't have much manna left, either, do you? It's all being collected by the converters, so you're having to put an awful lot of effort into your spells, hmm?"

So smug, Kobuchi thought, as he got up on one knee and one foot, his hands pressed hard on his raised knee so that he might get up for one or two more shots of magic. Come on, he screamed at his own body. Get up.

"And without your magic," Genma continued, "you are nothing, Kobuchi. Nothing but a scrawny, mangy, half-naked Kobold with none of your precious free will. Ha ha ha ha haaaa!"

Genma threw his arms back and cackled like a demon, waves of malice pouring from him like a geyser's final, and fatal, eruption.

When he brought his head back down, the ivory mask reflected a hint of moonlight through one of the large, open windows in the corridor wall. Scar tissue revealed itself around the maddened orbs in his eye sockets, a visage that Kobuchi had gazed upon twice in his entire time under Genma's control.

Timing, Kobuchi thought, *it's all about timing*. The girl will be okay, as long as I'm alive and Genma can't figure out a way around the barrier. It's time for plan 'b'.

"This ends now, Kobuchi," the mad Alchemist said, his voice barely more than a whisper. "Kobuchi, execute command num—"

"*Veras, Silencio!*" Kobuchi cut off Genma's words with a spell.

A flash of blinding light flared up from the air around Genma.

He shielded his eyes with his cloak, throwing it wide open to finish giving the compulsion order to Kobuchi. But when he tried to speak, no words came from him. He clutched at his throat, felt the vibration of the air and words passing out of his lungs and into his mouth, where they were inexplicably stopped short. What had the Kobold done to him?

303

Enraged, the Alchemist drew one of the daggers from his back, but too late. Kobuchi used a non-verbal spell on himself, crouched on a window ledge. *No time*, he thought, *no time*. As he released the knife in Kobuchi's direction, the Kobold waved and fell forward out of the window, into the world beyond the tower.

A Silence spell, Genma thought as he sagged against the stone wall next to the window. He peered out and watching the Kobold drift easily towards the earth below. A damned Silence spell saved the little ingrate. His conversion devices had been keyed to absorb the entirety of such spells cast in the tower, so how had he managed it?

Then Genma realized, as he let loose the quietest roar a man could, that he hadn't checked the equipment. Kobuchi's betrayal had included quite a lot of sabotage. If it took until the end of days, Genma would have his revenge on the Kobold.

For Genma, things had not gone from bad to worse. They had actually gone from bad to potentially fatal.

* * * *

Air rushed past Portenda's head as Telroke swung the enhanced battle-axe, missing over and over again.

The Bounty Hunter worried because the consistently missing swings were getting closer every time his father brought the weapon around at him. Soon enough, Portenda would actually have to block the attacks with his own broadsword, which had rested idle in his hand since Jonah and Nareena had raced into the tower beyond his present confrontation.

"Come on, boy! Attack me why don't you?" Sweat soaked through Telroke's thick golden fur. His mane was completely matted to his neck and head, but he felt more powerful, more alive, with each hack and slash he attempted.

The ivory-masked freak had spoken truly to him of the axe's special properties. He had merely to attack, and keep on the offensive. In time, even his accursed offspring would fall to the onslaught he brought.

"You've been waiting for this opportunity for years," he said, emphasizing the word 'years' as he spun round to his left, swinging at Portenda's right flank.

Too fast, Portenda thought as the tip of the axe head left a thin, bloody mark on his body. It cut through his protector vest without effort, giving him a small laceration. *Nothing major*. He squared himself to his father's movements. *Just have to focus, predict the next attack*.

He had barely finished this thought when Telroke swung again. When Portenda brought his sword up to block the attack, Telroke launched a vicious sidekick into Portenda's chest, sending him skidding, heels tearing up the ground.

Flashes of pain blurred Portenda's vision for a moment after the blow, and he tucked and rolled to his right out of sheer instinct when he heard a breakage of air around a massive body; his father landed several feet away, where Portenda had been standing. The axe was embedded to the second head in the dirt, but Telroke smiled sideways at Portenda, pulling the weapon out without effort.

Wait a minute, Portenda thought, pricking up his ears. *Something, there, rhythmic, over and over.* He hadn't spared many words for Jonah and Nareena, or for his father, and his heightened senses continued to report to him regularly. The rapid, earthen beating noise, as on a tribal drum, continued and accelerated a little more.

Finally, he recognized the source of the sound as he avoided another heavy blow from Telroke—it was the older Simpa's heart. If it continued to accelerate on its present course, it would soon explode.

"What's the matter with you, boy," Telroke screamed as he set himself in a defensive posture. "Why don't you come at me? Afraid of your old man, eh?"

Telroke held the axe up to his face. "It's only natural, you know. Sons are supposed to fear their fathers." He paced in a circle, matching footsteps with his son. "Sure, they can love them, even respect them, but there's always and forever that trace of primal fear."

He took a moment to study Portenda's movements.

The boy wasn't going to attack him, he realized. He was waiting for something, the perfect moment to counterattack, Telroke thought. *When I attack, I can't let up, not for anything.* "I can smell it on you, Portenda. The fear is calling out to me, from your very soul!"

Timing, Portenda thought. *The world is based almost entirely on timing.* The slow and steady increase of blood production in his father's body as the battle continued had introduced a problem unique to his Race. When in the heat of battle, Simpa produce a chemical most notably present in Humans, called adrenaline. Portenda had studied up on this, and found that almost all of the Races of Tamalaria had a gland in their body that produced this chemical, usually in correlation to outward stress, such as combat.

In Simpa, the overproduction of this chemical makes them extremely strong and fast, but makes them inaccurate and somewhat clumsy as well. *And predictable,* Portenda thought lastly, bringing his head down and parrying the axe blow with the long spear on his back.

Using his own balanced body weight, Portenda shifted the attack to the side, and dashed forward, holding his own broadsword out at his side. The tip of the blade tore a streak through Telroke's lower abdomen, spewing thick, crimson blood all over the grass.

Not a fatal blow, Portenda thought as he spun round to face his wounded father, *but it will hurt, and slow him down.*

Telroke himself had gone wide-eyed the moment his son had ducked his head and come forward, into the blow. *Madness,* he thought, *sheer madness! How had he been so easily turned aside?*

More troubling than this was the sharp sting in his stomach, and the sight of his own blood all over the ground. He turned slowly, holding his hand up to show him his own blood, and faced Portenda the Quiet.

I've brought this fate on myself, he thought.

"How? How could you do this? I have an enchanted weapon! Years of fighting experience." He took a stumbling step forward.

Too much blood loss, he thought. *Have to stall, buy some time for my regeneration to kick in.*

"Throw down the weapon," Portenda said, his tone as frosted as ocean-bound icebergs. "It's causing your heart to accelerate dangerously, Telroke. In a few minutes, you will have a heart attack, and you will be beyond my aid. I don't know enough about medicine to help you if that happens."

No inflection, show no emotion, he thought.

This time, in the face of the man he had grown to so loathe, he had mastery of himself. Perhaps the current circumstances helped him in this respect, he thought.

"Help me? You, help me," Telroke asked. "Oh, that's rich! Like you would even consider the idea."

"I would," Portenda said, his tone the same as before. "You are not my target. You are just an inconvenient obstacle. If you can be neutralized without coming to lethal harm, I shall endeavor to do so. A Bounty Hunter does not waste life unnecessarily. That is, unprofessional."

"Ha! Unprofessional you say," Telroke said, mocking his son. "Fine! Be unprofessional then! I have no qualms with that."

He growled as he struck at Portenda again. The blows flew fast and hard, but Portenda read every one of Telroke's motions, blocked and dodged, rolled away and lashed back with martial arts kicks and punches, keeping Telroke at bay.

After a few minutes of this, going back and forth, Telroke began to feel a cramping in his chest. When he brought the axe up for one more strike, he collapsed to his knees, one hand on his chest, one on the ground, supporting his weight and holding the axe.

"I tried to warn you," Telroke heard Portenda say, as fire burned through his chest. It felt like a Phoenix had been born inside of his ribcage, and presently stretched its legendary wings around inside of his body, pressing for free space.

His vision blurred, and sweat, salty and slick, stung his eyes as it flowed into his face.

Telroke felt his left arm going numb: *ye Gods*, he thought, *the boy was right! I'm going to die if I don't let go of this axe! But also, it's the only thing I have to use against him.*

"Not much good to you if you're dead." Portenda knelt next to his father.

"What, are you a Psychic now too?"

"I can read your face, even from a lower vantage and from the profile," Portenda said flatly. "I also know that my blocks and counterstrikes should have dislodged the axe from your grasp. It's locked onto your palm, isn't it? You have to let go of it for yourself, Telroke." A hint of compassion snaked into his voice. "Just let it go, and I shall let you leave here, alive."

A Hunter and his Prey

Telroke heard the soft click of the hammer on Portenda's ancient mecha weapon as it drew back. The cold steel of the muzzle pressed gently against his temple. "Try to swing that thing at me one more time, though, and you'll either have a heart attack, or I'll spread your brains all over the dirt and rocks. Your choice."

Telroke didn't dare so much as turn his head to look the boy in the eyes, try to make out whether or not Portenda was just bluffing. He relinquished his grip on the axe, slowly, carefully, and dropped immediately to the ground, huffing and wheezing.

He lay on his back, staring up at his own flesh and blood as Portenda holstered the pistol.

Portenda stepped gingerly over him, planted his left heel down on Telroke's wrist, and reached down for the axe. When he had it in hand, he stepped off of his father's arm, twirled about a few rotations, and hurled the axe into the air.

It quickly became little more than a speck on the horizon, thanks to the barrier's visual illusions.

"When you manage to get up, go home," Portenda glared down at his father with eyes boiling over with hatred. As he turned his back on Telroke to stalk away, the older Simpa clutched at his ankle weakly.

"Wait! I have one question for you," Telroke said, his heart now heavy not with labor, but with guilt and self-pity. "I know we've never gotten on very well, and I know I'm partially to blame for that."

"Entirely," Portenda retorted hotly. *So much for that self-control,* he thought.

"All right, I'll give you that one," Telroke wheezed, knowing full well that he would soon be passing out. "Just, tell me something. Why don't you ever just call me, dad?"

Portenda had been waiting for this question each and every time the two men met, and he finally had the opportunity to tell the bastard why he felt the way he did. And now, he had a better understanding of why. Portenda the Quiet turned back to his father, knelt down next to him, and sighed heavily.

"Because, Telroke, that moniker would denote affection, love, and a connection that, well, we don't have, you and I," he said, gesturing vaguely with his hands. "You aren't my dad. You're barely my father," he said, leaning in close, his breath filling Telroke's tiny, private little world. "You just happened to be there when I was conceived."

On this note, Portenda bared his teeth, exposing a full set of ready-to-kill daggers in his mouth. "If you ever come at me like that again, I won't hesitate, I won't be so nice. I've spared you out of familial duty. And because she wouldn't have wanted me to do it." He stood and once again turning his back on his father. "Go home, Telroke of the Allenian Hills. Go home, and never again cross my path."

With these words ringing in his head, Telroke passed out of consciousness, and into the sweet release of dreams.

Dreams haunted by the image of a gun barrel pressed against his head.

Chapter Fifteen
Staples Family Reunion

Jonah and Nareena had expected a little resistance when they threw open the stone doors of the tower's base floor. They hadn't expected a battle with two fire-breathing Gorgons—which had been exactly what awaited them in the main hall.

Nareena tossed an explosive vial of chemicals down one Gorgon's throat, completely on accident, though, she thought upon reflection, it had been a very happy accident. The serpent-like beast had exploded into countless chunks of bloody gore, and Jonah had used Focus to pin the other Gorgon to the floor with the very stone all around them.

Running like a man possessed, the Human Alchemist had sprinted alongside the pinned beast and straddled its neck, pulling one of his spare belts out of his rucksack and using it to clamp the beast's mouth shut.

Overall, the encounter had taken them less than a minute, and both felt that they owed their reactions and timing to the Bounty Hunter. Just from watching the Simpa they had learned better how to think on their feet, and just react instead of thinking everything through. From training with him, they'd learned even more.

But now they stood at one of the four doorways in the main hall, the one behind them still open from their entrance into the tower.

Jonah felt hopelessly small and daunted by the sheer size of the tower. How was he going to know where to find Eileen?

"Upstairs," Nareena said behind him, and he turned to find her sprinting to one of the other oak board doors, Blink on her shoulder.

"Lucky guess, then," he asked rather sarcastically.

As the two pounded up the stone stairwell, she gave him a light tap on the arm. "I'm never that lucky," she said.

"I don't know, that vial certainly went down that Gorgon's throat on a slim chance," he replied.

Nareena laughed nervously, thanking the Gods for their brief smile on her.

"Yeah, well, you know how it is," she said. "Besides, the little guy is giving me directions. He wanted to stay with Portenda, but he thought he'd be too much of a nuisance. You know how the big fellah worries."

"Yes, as a matter of fact, I do." Jonah worried himself for Portenda. When he had glanced over his shoulder in front of that other door in the main hall, Portenda had been struck in the side with a rather wicked looking axe. He prayed for the Bounty Hunter's safety but couldn't take time to do more.

They came to a landing, where the stairwell suddenly stopped.

"Great. Where to now?"

"This way." Nareena poked her head out into the corridor of the sixth floor. She took a quick look left and right, and listened intently to Blink's mental directions. "Come on." She grabbed Jonah's hand and led him out into the hall. "Blink says there's a defense system that's going to hold us up for a while. Are you any good with mecha?"

"Good? I'm one of the best," A cold sweat broke out on his brow. "Why? Do I have to be?"

Nareena smiled at him as she opened the door to a rather strange looking room, filled with ancient mecha equipment.

"Well then, this shouldn't give you any trouble, now should it?"

* * * *

"Damn it all straight to the seven Hells!" Genma had been laboring on the magic barrier in Eileen Staples' doorway for a solid ten minutes, and none of his tinctures, powders or tools worked against it. The process could have been interesting, perhaps even noteworthy for later study, if the girl hadn't stood there making faces at him the whole while. "When I do get through this barrier, the first thing I'm going to do is put a sack over your head, girl." He couldn't concentrate properly, not with such an audacious display before him.

Genma drew out a thin vial of a thick green fluid, and drew his arm back to toss it into the barrier.

The vial slipped from his grasp when Eileen, in one of her more inspired moments of distraction, pulled up her blouse, exposing her bare breasts to him.

"Gaauugh! Holy Hells," he shouted as the vial burst open at his feet, poisonous smog drifting into the air.

Genma darted down the hall, away from the smog, and wrapped a cloth around his mask. "Damn fool girl," he rasped.

Genma rarely got so flustered, and he slammed his fist against the floor as he cursed himself for being so easily distracted. Had he been a few seconds slower, he might very well be dead. But the smog didn't permeate the barrier, he saw from down the hallway. If the barrier relied on Kobuchi's concentration and life force, he may be here for hours trying to get through it. Time he didn't have.

Eileen, on the safe side of the barrier, laughed heartily as she watched the Alchemist dart away. She never did such things back home, that much was certain.

"What an idiot," she said between giggles to herself. But a very real possibility cropped up in her mind—what if Genma did something to the wall on either side of the doorway? He couldn't get past the barrier in the doorway, but what about making another doorway into the room? Surely his precious Alchemy could make a new portal, even if it involved using something as basic as a vial of explosive acid.

No, she thought, that would put her at risk for injury, and he couldn't have his puppet damaged in any way. That simply wouldn't be acceptable. But that gave her an idea.

She had been handling Genma quite improperly. The time for sitting behind her security wall was over: now she would put the Alchemist on the defensive.

"Sorry uncle Allen," she whispered.

Genma appeared in front of the barrier once again, madness in his wide eyes, clearly visible in the mask. "You, have been a thorn in my side at every opportunity, young lady," he rasped. "I have tried to be kind. I have provided reasonable hospitality. And I have left you, for the most part, unharmed. Now just come through this barrier, right now, like a good girl." He spoke to her in the same tone of voice he had used to scold his own children, and her as well, when he visited from time to time.

Eileen smiled winningly at him, and produced a wooden shank at her own face level.

Genma's heart skipped a beat, and he looked from the rather deranged sight of his niece holding a splintered fragment of wood to her face. "Back off, jack off," she growled at Genma. "Try to take me by force, and you'll never get your perfect little doll." Genma straightened and started to chuckle low in his throat. His laughter quickly erupted into an uproar, and he found himself quite unable to stop. The volume and pitch of it fed off of one another, and in a minute, he sounded like a jackal that had most recently lost its genitals and found it hilarious despite the pain.

"Go ahead! Maim yourself, child! Do you think I can't fix you, can't take you away to some other place until I can return for my equipment? Have you not realized that your fate is sealed? You cannot hope to stay me from my course, Eileen Staples."

Genma took a pinch of powder from his hip and inscribing something hastily on the palm of his left glove.

Once finished, he pressed his right index finger against the Focus Site, and Eileen watched in horror as her earlier fear came to fruition; Genma pressed his palm flat against the stone wall next to the doorway, creating a new opening into her chamber.

As Genma pressed into the room, Eileen changed her grasp on the shank, swinging it wildly at the Alchemist's ivory mask as he stepped through the new doorway.

His hand appeared instantly, though, holding her by her frail wrist, twisting her arm until it snapped at the point of contact.

Eileen let out a hoarse cry of pain, and her makeshift weapon clattered uselessly to the floor.

"I am the master of this tower, Eileen. I am the master of Alchemy. What I seek, I shall have. And nothing shall stand in my way!"

Behind him, out in the corridor where he had engaged Kobuchi in mortal combat, he barely made out the sound of approaching footsteps, coming at a full tilt run. There came two sets of them, and Genma sensed that one of those sets belonged to Jonah Staples.

No matter, he thought as he struck Eileen over the head with a leather sap, rendering her unconscious. *I have a solution to the boy.* The ivory-masked Alchemist stepped back through his self-made doorway and faced the stairwell.

A moment later, his newest guests arrived.

Jonah he skidded to a halt several dozen yards away from Genma, Nareena bracing herself next to him.

He sensed something familiar about this masked menace.

A Hunter and his Prey

The man stood there, his arms folded over his chest, like an idol of power. Alchemical power crackled around his body, reacting to the sudden presence of Jonah's Focus energy.

Nareena drew two vials from her hip, one in each hand, ready to hurl them at high speed at Genma's masked face.

"Where's my sister?" Jonah asked as he drew a sheet of scrap parchment from his inner pocket in his tunic shirt.

He had roughly a dozen more of these Focus Sites prepared for use—all he had to do was choose one and draw it out, activating it with a clap of his hands.

"She is right in there, dear boy." Genma waved his right arm vaguely at Eileen's limp body. "If you would like to retrieve her, you are more than welcome to try. You need only get past me."

Genma shifted his stance to match Nareena's.

"Oh, and it's so good to see you taking an interest in a girl," he said, smiling behind his mask. "Your father and I had become so worried you'd wind up married to your work."

Jonah's mind raced through memories he'd long since thought buried. The voice, it was so familiar! And how could this masked man know what his father had voiced so many times to him? He didn't think anybody had been around when Jacob Staples had pulled him aside to discuss his future. There had been, a few times, but uncle Allen was dead.

"Just be quiet and get away from Eileen," Jonah shouted. "There doesn't have to be a fight here. Your guard beasts are probably all dead, this tower can be easily brought down, and it's two on one right now. You can't stand against both of us, Genma."

"You know, you're right," Genma said, folding his arms once again over his chest and turning sideways to the Human and Elven couple. "It is two on one, isn't it, young Jonah?"

Genma thrust an accusing finger at Jonah. "Jonah, execute command twenty-five!"

Oh Gods, the boy thought as his vision blurred and his thoughts began to dull. *Not again. Have to resist, have to do something.*

Jonah's hands flew to the sides of his head, and he dropped to the stone floor, screaming as he fought against his programming.

"Ha ha ha haaa! Why resist?! You know it is futile, Jonah Staples! You cannot disobey my commands. I have ensured it!"

"Hey, asshole," Nareena shouted, gaining the ivory masked man's attention. "Did you forget about me?"

He hadn't forgotten the Elf woman, he had simply expected Jonah to respond instantly to the command.

The Elven Alchemist hurled a light green tincture at Genma, shattering it against his upturned cloak and forming a thick, dark green mist.

Genma inhaled the toxic vapors for a second, gagging and shuffling away from the smog, once again cursing his slow responses. Had he been a few years younger, or perhaps not been burned so badly in the fire that incinerated his home, he might have been able to take care of all of this without any issues. As it was, he was at a disadvantage, at least until he got Jonah under his control again.

Nareena drew a rough sketch of a Focus Site on the stone floor with one of Jonah's pieces of chalk as the boy got back on his feet. Unsure of Jonah's present alliances, however, she kept a safe distance behind him.

"Jonah, how are we doing?" she asked, her voice trembling.

Genma was already preparing a Focus Site of his own, and her own Focus would only create a defensive wall. Genma had years more experience, and his Focus power would surely be able to destroy anything she put in his way.

Then again, he had breathed in some of the toxic gas, hadn't he? She had to try something, though, and before Jonah could give her a response to her question, she clapped her hands together, and activated her Focus.

The hallway trembled once more as a sheet of the stone floor came upright, locking off the hallway entirely. Jonah shook his head, and turned to face her. "I, I think I'm going to be all right," he breathed.

Nareena threw herself at him, but he thrust her away quickly. "Good job on the wall, but there's just one problem with it."

"What's that," Nareena said. "We're on this side, he's on the other. What's the problem?"

"Eileen's on the other side too," Jonah said.

Nareena shook her head as she turned back to the wall, feeling quite the fool.

"Right, right. Didn't think about that much. Um, I'll just go ahead, aaaand —" she said.

"Just tear it down," Jonah said, clapping his hands together. The parchment in his hand flashed brightly, and a moment later his entire right arm lifted toward the ceiling, metallic plates glimmering in the artificial light of the hallway. A set of whirring blades, sharpened to razor edges, spun on the mounted arm and shoulder harness that covered his right upper body. One of the nearby labs, once filled with equipment, now had shreds and scraps of metal lying in heaped, smoking piles of ruined mecha.

Nareena concentrated all of her efforts into dispersing the molecular energy she had used to move the stone of the floor into a wall.

On the other side of the wall, as Nareena and Jonah were preparing to take the fight to Genma, the ivory masked man was readying his own Focus Site. "It's a rush job," he said to himself. "But it'll do nicely, for now." As Nareena tore down her wall of stone, Genma activated his Site.

Before him stood a golem made of stone.

Jonah, he saw, had come up with some strange sort of weapon, attached to his arm. It appeared to be a working mecha, complete with a small motor that oscillated the blades on the end of the mount.

But that's impossible, Genma thought. *How could he use Focus to craft a motor?*

The equipment in the lab down the hall blew through the doorway and into the tunnel in a shower of sparks and scraps.

A Hunter and his Prey

"My machines!"

"Oh, were those yours?" Jonah crouched, setting himself in a wide stance. The mecha he had crafted through the Focus Site was heavy, but it would prove an effective weapon. At least, against Genma's flesh and blood. The golem that stood stock still in front of the ivory masked Alchemist was made entirely of stone, however. Jonah couldn't be certain that the metal of his blades would cut through the stone guardian. Then again, he won't know if he didn't make a move.

"Sorry about that, Genma, but I needed them more than you at the moment. Now give me back Eileen, and this doesn't have to go any further!"

"Oh, but I think it does." Genma thrust his finger once again at Jonah. "You may have shrugged off my command before, but only when your concentration wasn't muddled by impending death at the hands of my servant. Golem," he said, addressing the guardian. "Crush Jonah Staples."

Without a word or a sign of understanding, the nearly one ton of solid stone began its slow, unstoppable march toward Jonah and Nareena.

"Jonah," Nareena said.

"Yeah?" Jonah's free left hand flew about a set of switches that came along with the arm attachment. He had no idea what any of them did, and he panicked for a moment when the second switch turned out to be the one that turned the motor on and off. "What is it?"

"I don't suppose you have a backup plan? I mean, the blades are nice, but are they going to cut through that thing?"

The golem stalked closer, now only twenty yards away.

"We're going to have to wait and see." Jonah located a switch that caused the blades to spin at an even higher speed.

Hollering like a barbarian warrior, which made him feel a little out of place, Jonah Staples stampeded toward the golem, blades flying.

Genma chuckled to himself, and turned to retrieve his captive, only to find another magical barrier in his path.

"What the," he managed before Eileen Staples stepped right up to the barrier's opposite side. Genma took a few stumbling steps back, and found himself pressed against the opposite wall. "How? I knocked you out!"

"Not before I used an Awakening spell on myself," she said, smiling as she rubbed the sore spot on the back of her head. "I couldn't keep myself from being rendered unconscious, but it did shorten the time I was out. You'd know that, if you studied magic."

"Why you little wench," he growled. "When I get to you, you will be in great pain."

A buzzing and screaming of metal on stone rose in the air to his left, and Genma turned, smiling, expecting to see his nephew being bore to the ground. However, the situation turned out to be quite reversed. Jonah crouched atop the golem, his strange mecha weapon tearing slowly, but easily, through the stone arms that the golem held before its poorly hewn face.

"Give up, Genma," Nareena called to the mad man. "When the golem's toast, Jonah will come for you."

"Why not do it yourself, girl," Genma said.

His mocking tone twisted in Nareena's mind; how dare this, this Human, challenge her?

But she quickly remembered. Genma wielded the art of Focus like a surgeon does his scalpel. She wielded Focus like a toddler does his toys. The comparison, she felt, was quite fitting, and too much for her to try to work against.

"Well, because I can't," she said, feeling lame. "I at least can admit that I'm not up to the task, though! Look around you Genma! Your guard beasts are all dead, your mecha have become fodder for Jonah's Focus creation."

Jonah's blades appeared to have been damaged in their task, and thick, sulfurous smoke poured from the motor, but Nareena smiled wickedly at the ivory masked Alchemist.

Though he panted from the effort, Jonah came away from his encounter with the stone sentinel unscathed.

He used another Site, much like the previous one, to summon a steel suit of mobile armor around his body. "You see what I mean? Surely more of your precious equipment is now in tatters."

"Yes, balance of energies and molecules," Genma said, an edge to his tone. "But the efforts involved have left him weakened, Elf girl. Jonah! Execute command twenty-four!"

Nareena whirled around, but far too late.

Jonah's his empty hand, coated in metal armor, came hard across Nareena's face, breaking her jaw and sending her spiraling to the ground.

She looked up as her hands came up in front of her face defensively, and she saw the same glaze in his eyes that she had seen in the northwestern mountains, outside of Traithrock.

His mind lay dormant, his willpower broken by the brainwashing techniques created years before by his own uncle. It would take a physical shock or a mental one of great magnitude to bring him around this time, because the command had been given in person, not through some enchanted mirror. He would remain under the mad man's control unless something was done, and soon. He might even kill her in this state of mind.

"I believe this is where you admit defeat, little girl," Genma said as he laughed aloud.

His words had been aimed more at Eileen than Nareena, but both young women felt trapped, defeated. Without the aid of her brother and his Elf friend, the Q Mage girl was practically helpless.

The use of the Awakening spell, and the erection of a barrier and its maintenance drained her reserves of manna.

The three of them needed help, and fast, or Genma would have his victory.

"Now, Eileen, drop this barrier and come to me," he said. "We have little time now to make our escape."

A Hunter and his Prey

"I'd rather jump out the window." She moved to the makeshift portal she had created in one side of her room with an altered Raybolt spell. When she looked down on the field around the tower, she saw the dozens of slain guard beasts that had caused her own escape days before to fail. They hadn't just died; they'd been massacred.

That's right, she thought. Hadn't there been someone else the Ivory Alchemist was worried about? A Bounty Hunter, she thought. But where was the guy?

"I don't think so." Genma smiled so hugely that his mask shifted on his face. "That would lead to a rather gruesome death, my dear. The fall wouldn't kill you, mind you."

"You just said it would lead to a gruesome death though," she said.

"I know. The fall wouldn't kill you. Generally speaking, it never does," Genma said. "It's the sharp, sudden impact that does the trick. Now, please be reasonable. Life as my bride is surely better than being dead, isn't it?"

But Eileen wasn't listening to Genma at all. She had returned to the barrier, keeping it close and thus requiring less of her quickly draining magic reserves. But when she had walked up to it, her eyes had wandered down the hall to the stairwell, where a huge, hulking Simpa stood, covered in blood and grime.

His stance remained neutral, a spear in his left hand, planted against the floor. In his right hand, an ancient mecha weapon rested idle, the tip also pointed downward.

"The Bounty Hunter," she whispered.

Her words hadn't been intended for Genma, but the ivory Alchemist's eyes spread wide open.

He whirled so quickly to face Portenda the Quiet that his cloak came in brief contact with the barrier, causing a crackle of energy to run up the fabric and into his shoulders and arms. There was a brief numbness, which quickly disappeared, but his body now trembled for different reasons.

The Bounty Hunter was massive, he saw now that he was so close to him. Even at around fifty yards away, Genma could see that no amount of Alchemy created equipment was going to help him. He didn't have enough time to construct a complex Site, because he recognized the pistol for what it was. Portenda could fire a single round into his chest or face and kill him! He had to stall for more time, and he had the perfect way to do so.

"Jonah, execute command thirty-nine. Now."

The boy cocked his head up at Portenda, who remained perfectly still and silent.

Jonah lunged at the Simpa, his motorized blade arm jumping into motion as he swung it in a deadly arc at the Bounty Hunter.

Portenda took a single step to the side, evading the lethal blow with ease. He rammed his right elbow hard into Jonah's ribs, sending the boy sprawling. In the same motion, to conserve energy and effort, Portenda hurled the spear down the hall, landing it in the stone floor a few feet away from Genma.

Humph, he thought, *a slight miscalculation in angle.*

315

No time to think about it, because Jonah sprang at him from the floor.

A hard, straight punch with his metal-coated left fist glanced off of Portenda's blocking arm, and the Bounty Hunter slid his free hand forward, palming the boy's face. With his right arm, he took aim and fired a single shot at Genma, whose cloak had already come up over him in his defense.

The bullet crumpled harmlessly against the enchanted material.

One of the whirring blades managed to cut into Portenda's side, but the Bounty Hunter holstered his pistol and grasped the mounted device, tearing it free from Jonah's shoulder and arm and tossing it aside like so much scrap.

There was no help for it, he thought. He couldn't afford to harm the boy at the moment, because Genma was stirring up something with several Focus Sites at that precise moment.

Portenda, while he felt more than capable, admitted to himself that he knew little about the nature of Alchemy and its scientific powers. That many Focus Sites could only create something troublesome. He needed Jonah's knowledge now more than any firearm, or weapon.

"Jonah, listen to me very carefully. I have to tell you something important," Portenda said as Jonah flailed against his grasp. Had the situation not been so grave, he might have laughed at the sight of it. After all, the two of them looked like fighting siblings, the older one holding the little one by the forehead to keep from any blows being landed.

"Jonah, Genma is Allen Staples. He is your uncle."

* * * *

Darkness, pure and complete, surrounded Jonah in a warm blanket of nothingness. He knew full well that something had been done to him to lock away his mind, but he felt no urgent need to escape the darkness. It was, well, comfortable. He had no worries here, trapped in his own mind. He heard nothing, saw nothing, felt nothing. He didn't even know where he was at the moment. He just knew his body was moving out there, in the real world, doing whatever needed to be done.

But a voice called out to him. A voice that he recognized, and both feared and respected. It spoke to him of great strength of body and mind, of potential. It was a voice not unlike what he remembered in Death's own speech. Why was it so familiar? Why did it reach him here, where only one other voice had managed to reach before?

Once more, the voice spoke, but louder this time. A shaft of light burrowed through his personal darkness, bringing him back to reality. The voice spoke again. "JONAH STAPLES, YOU WILL HEAR ME," it said. "GENMA IS IN TRUTH ALLEN STAPLES. HE IS YOUR UNCLE."

Jonah Staples came screaming back to reality.

* * * *

The boy had one Hell of a set of lungs on him, Portenda thought as his voice returned to normal.

Genma continued to work on his Focus Sites, several of which were already producing strange, hybrid creatures of mechanical and biological design.

A Hunter and his Prey

The tower quavered terribly as the equipment and raw materials of the structure evaporated into the null space of Focus transformation to create these new guardian creatures.

Jonah continued to scream, unable to cope with what Portenda told him. The brainwashing, his sister's abduction, the plan to transform her into another person, all the product of his Uncle Allen's mind?

He hadn't even believed Allen Staples to be alive, much less turned into this mask-wearing freak. How could this have happened? How could he not have seen it coming? And how did Portenda know?

He sensed the truth of the Bounty Hunter's words, mostly because that strange tone of voice didn't seem capable of telling lies.

Now, though, faced with the truth, what could he do? He had fully intended to kill Genma if necessary to retrieve his sister. But that meant killing a family member, the very man who had introduced him to Alchemy so many years ago.

"Jonah, we've got a bit of a problem here," Portenda said to him.

Jonah looked to his right, and saw several low, sleek creatures approaching, scuttling forth on many legs of metal and dripping organic material.

Genma drew upon everything available in the tower, from the scorpions and mantis-like creatures to the ruined machinery now serving as Jonah's weaponry.

The first of the metallic monstrosities leaped at the young Alchemist, a scream of mixed misery and killer instinct erupting from its plated throat.

Jonah manipulated a Focus Site preset on his wrist to reattach the device to his shoulder and arm, and brought the whirring blades on his arm down hard on the beast.

He shredded it to pieces, but in return he was struck by shrapnel in the chest and shoulder.

He avoided the most grievous injury by turning his head as a scrap piece of metal flew past his eye, nearly blinding him.

Portenda danced past him, his claws tearing through the servants with the ease of a skilled ballet dancer doing a pirouette. His movements flowed like water, soft and rhythmic between blows, harsh and crashing at the precise moment of impact.

Jonah found himself once again in awe of the Bounty Hunter, but this temporary spell was broken when Genma rolled a vial of crimson liquid across Portenda's path of progress.

As Portenda landed on the vial, it erupted in an inferno of brightest flames, and the Bounty Hunter was genuinely caught off guard.

His fur caught quickly, and Portenda squeezed his eyes shut against the pain.

The best meditative techniques, those he had learned in his time with a sect of Monks in the north-central mountain ranges, offered him no solace here; something in the tincture struck at his very nerves, disrupting his concentration.

Being careful to avoid the boy, Portenda leaped backward through the tunnel, praying that Nareena would have something on hand to quench the fires.

His forearm muscles had caught fire, the flesh covering the outer forearm completely burned away now, the chemical flames working on him slowly and painfully.

The Elven Alchemist, familiar with this sort of situation, pulled a powder out of a pouch on her hip, and sprinkled it over the flames. In the presence of the high heat, the powder turned into ice water, and Portenda went swiftly from burning to death to soaked and slightly chilled.

"You're running low on tricks, Genma." Jonah kept a watchful eye on the remaining half a dozen metallic servants.

Something in the frame support of his arm device snapped, and once again it fell off of him. No matter, he thought. I've got other tools at my disposal.

"And your toy has failed, nephew," Genma replied.

"Don't you dare call me that, filth! You are not my uncle! You are a sick freak with a mask."

Jonah drew the sniper rifle off of his back and sett himself in a kneeling position.

Without a moment's hesitation, he cocked the hammer and fired on the foremost of the servant creatures, shattering it into scraps of metal. Two shots, three, four, five, and finally the sixth and final creature died.

Genma, who chuckled under his breath, took no defensive posture, no evasive action.

"What's so funny, freak?"

"That's a sniper rifle, correct," Genma asked.

"That's right."

"Familiar with it?"

"I know how to use it." Jonah took aim directly at the ivory countenance.

"Then you know that there's a small slit in the cartridge clip," Genma said matter-of-factly.

Jonah wasn't going to fall for any feints at this juncture, however. He steadied the sight, and pulled the trigger.

And listened as the hammer struck, followed not by the air-rendering kaboom of the rifle fire, but by studied silence, punctuated by Nareena coughing nervously.

"And anyone close enough to see it, can count the number of rounds left in the weapon." Genma whipped a throwing knife at Jonah Staples.

The triangular blade imbedded itself in his left shoulder, and Jonah spun around and dropped the rifle on the floor.

Blood sprayed freely from the wound.

As he grasped the throwing handle to remove the projectile, the blade already spread wider and tore more inner tissues apart.

Jonah howled, but managed to get to one knee as he pulled again at the offending weapon.

A Hunter and his Prey

Nareena came forward, a healing potion in hand, and gave it to Jonah as he tore the weapon free, tossing it limply aside. He would have used one of her tinctures as a projectile at Genma, but it appeared that Genma had erected a sort of barrier in front of him to repel any such attempts. Jonah's vision was slightly blurred: he couldn't tell for certain if the barrier had a weak point, but he continued to look through hazy vision at the shimmering wall of force.

Genma spoke once more before either the Human or Elven Alchemist could do anything. "Jonah, execute command number eleven."

Jonah didn't even feel a compulsion. Portenda's words had broken the hold the ivory masked menace had on his nephew.

"No matter." Genma took a step backward. "You can't get at me right now in any event."

As Genma turned, he came face to face with Eileen Staples, her slender fingers pressed lightly against his chest.

His eyes went wide with fright, the image of Eileen's beauty shattered by the cruel, twisted smile that stretched across her face.

"*Hyagu van*, Raybolt!"

Her spell words echoed through the cavernous hallway as pure magical energy exploded against Genma's chest, sending him hurtling like a siege weapon missile through the air. Through his own barrier, over the heads of Jonah, Nareena and Portenda, and almost down the stairwell to his demise.

At his present velocity, going down the stairs would have broken every bone in his body.

But even damaged and injured, Genma had the presence of mind to adjust his weight in mid-flight. He crashed in a heap against the wall to the left of the stairwell.

"Eileen, are you all right?" Jonah wheezed as he sprinted to his sister's side.

"I'm, fine," she panted in response. Their eyes met for the first time in months, and both Staples children knew what had to be done. "You know he won't stop unless you finish him off." Eileen drooped from her extreme usage of magic.

Jonah nodded, and drew a single piece of paper from his rucksack.

Genma was finally getting to his feet after taking a healing potion of his own.

Portenda appeared to still be having problems moving around with his weapon. What Jonah didn't know, and Nareena had forgotten, was that a couple of her healing potions and powders had spoiled over time. Portenda now knew, and his system was trying not to go into toxic shock as a result. His regenerative powers worked overtime to keep him from being sick all over the place.

Genma pulled a piece of chalk from his hip pocket, and roughly inscribed a Site at his feet. He stood in the center of it, and as the familiar light flashed, a dome of stone covered him and the doorway.

Jonah finished his own inscription, and drew his father's short sword, using it to cleave the symbol on the paper in half. Another flash of light, but Portenda saw no visible difference in the weapon Jonah held.

"When it comes down to it, sometimes the old ways are best," Jonah whispered. He charged toward the protective dome over Genma, the ivory Alchemist.

With a barbarian war cry, Jonah brought his father's short sword over his head, and leaped skyward, bringing the weapon crashing down on the stone dome.

Portenda expected the sword to shatter apart, or the dome to explode outward. Neither occurred.

There was a glint of metallic light, a sound like flesh being torn from the bone, and then a muffled curse.

The stench of freshly spilled blood washed over Portenda's nose like a tsunami.

The stone dome split cleanly open in two halves, revealing Genma on his knees, his hands up over his face.

A line of thick, coppery-scented blood flowed down the exact center of his body for a moment before his body, like the dome, split cleanly in half. The sounds of a wet sack of animal entrails smacking against concrete rose up from the impact of the two body halves hitting the floor.

"Jonah," Nareena whispered, stepping forward and putting a consoling hand on his shoulder.

Jonah just stood there, unable to move, to speak, even to feel anything. Had he had done the right thing? He couldn't tell, and a minute later, it didn't matter. The tower trembled so badly that it leaned slightly, causing the trio from Ja-Wen and Eileen to catch their footing.

"Jonah," Nareena said. "We've got to get out of here. Portenda, is there a way to collect what's left of Allen?"

"No," Jonah looked back at Eileen as he picked up one half of the ivory mask. He kicked Eileen the other half with his foot, and she took it in hand, gazing at it for a moment. "There's no need for that, Nareena. We have this to remind us." He pocketed his half of the ivory mask. "We won't soon forget him in any case. Not as Uncle Allen, but as Genma."

"Pretty words, Jonah," Portenda groused, clutching his stomach as he gave Nareena a glare full of daggers. "But we haven't the time to appreciate them. This tower's creator is dead and the whole place is starting to come down around our ears! We have to get out of here. The only way is out a window if we want to get out in time."

"In case you haven't noticed, spoil-sport, we don't have wings," Nareena said, aware now of Portenda's glare. "We'll have to use the stairs, and we'll have to go now. That's all there is to it."

So the trio from Ja-Wen, with Blink on Jonah and Eileen Staples lashed to Portenda's back, started down the stairs as Genma's tower began its final stages of self-destruction.

A Hunter and his Prey

* * * *

"They'll never make it, you know," the golden masked entity said to the only person he called friend.

YES, THEY WILL, Death said, watching through the orb in Fate's bedchamber. AND WE DON'T EVEN NEED TO INTERFERE.

"How can you be so certain without checking into the Histories?"

Death, it should be noted, believes in being a man of action, for it speaks louder than words ever could. He said nothing to Fate, choosing instead to pull Portenda's timer out of his cloak. Fate gasped as he looked at it, turning his head this way and that for a better look. "That's his timer?"

INDEED, MY FRIEND. AND I BELIEVE YOUR NEXT QUESTION WILL BE ALONG THE LINES OF, IS IT THAT WAY BECAUSE OF OUR PART IN HIS CREATION? THE ANSWER, AGAIN, IS YES.

"But how will he get out of it this time? He has spoken, thus breaking the flow of his power. There's no sunlight in the tower, so his Khan blood cannot charge off of that. How, Grim, is he going to survive the toppling of the tower he's in?"

KEEP WATCHING. I DON'T THINK HE'S GOING TO BE IN THE TOWER MUCH LONGER, FATE. AND DON'T TELL ME YOU DIDN'T ALREADY KNOW THAT.

Death's eye sockets flaring brilliant sky blue as he watched the orb before him.

YOU KNOW WHEN THE HISTORIES ARE ALTERED. YOU CAN SENSE IT. AND I CAN SENSE THE MOMENT OF TENSION IN YOU. Death looked up at Fate. YOU'RE EXPECTING SOMETHING, BECAUSE THE HISTORIES ARE SPEAKING TO YOU AGAIN, AREN'T THEY?

"You are right," Fate said, his shoulders sagging slightly. "The last time they did that, the world of mortals shifted greatly."

THE FALL OF MECHA, AS THEY CALL IT, Death said. THIS IS DIFFERENT. NOT QUITE AS EXPANSIVE IN ITS AREA OF EFFECT, BUT DEFINITELY IMPORTANT. TOO BAD I DON'T GET TO SEE IT ALL THE WAY THROUGH.

"Why not?"

BECAUSE, I HAVE A JOB TO DO. ALLEN STAPLES MUST BE ESCORTED TO HIS FINAL DESTINATION, AND NO ONE CAN DO IT BUT ME.

MAXI, he called, and the skeletal hound got up off of Fate's bed.

Death tore a portal in the air, the other side of which led to his timeless home.

YOU CAN'T COME WITH ME, BOY. AND DON'T GIVE ME THAT LOOK. He prodded the sulking animal in the hindquarters with the blunt end of his scythe.

As the rift closed, sealing Maxi in Death's domain, the Grim Reaper tore a new rift, which opened into the trembling, disintegrating upper halls of Genma's tower.

321

He stepped into the hallway, watching with the same detached curiosity he always did when the soul separates from the fleshly host.

In this case, as sometimes happened, it appeared that Allen Staples, who had named himself Genma, wasn't aware that he had been slain.

His soul, which appeared mostly as it had before Jonah Staples' Alchemy-enhanced sword cleaved him cleanly in half, stood with its arms thrust upward, bracing.

Death cleared his throat as politely as he could, but the resulting noise sounded like a beast trying to laugh.

Allen Staples looked up at him, his eyes filled with dread apprehension.

"What's going on here? What happened to my barrier? And," he said, his left hand moving slowly to touch his face. "Where is my mask?"

YOU WON'T BE NEEDING IT ANYMORE, ALLEN STAPLES, Death said.

"My name is Genma." Allen Staples took a few brash steps forward before he saw the skeletal countenance beneath that eternally black hood. "You, you're —"

YES. YES I AM. Death moved a little closer to Allen Staples, feeling a little sorry for him. Especially considering what he was facing.

"How? How did it happen?" Allen turned to find that the spot he had been standing in was occupied by rubble. At the opposite end of the corridor, he watched as Jonah, his kind and genius nephew, took one last, long look down the hallway at where his body should have been.

JONAH USED A FOCUS SITE TO SHARPEN HIS FATHER'S SHORT SWORD. ALMOST GOT IT AS SHARP AS MY FRIEND HERE, Death said, moving the scythe slightly around. CUT RIGHT THROUGH THAT BARRIER OF YOURS, TO SAY NOTHING OF YOUR MASK AND BODY.

"He, he cut me in half?" Suddenly, the prospect of seeing his body one last time didn't appeal to him any more. "All right," he said, straightening himself up. "Let's get this over with. To tell you the truth," he said, following Death as he opened a rift in the air. "I never really believed you'd appear like this."

LIKE WHAT, Death asked, slightly perplexed. THE ROBE? THE BONES?

"No, I mean, well, I never really believed in angels and demons and, well, things like you. I've always assumed there was a scientific explanation for everything. I always assumed when I died, there'd just be, well, you know."

NO, I DON'T, Death led Allen Staples' soul into his domain.

"I didn't think there would be anything," Allen said. "I assumed the lights would go out, and then, well, nothing. My body would deteriorate, turn into nutrients in the soil, help grass grow, that sort of thing."

AH, I SEE. WELL, YES, ALLEN STAPLES, THAT WILL HAPPEN TO YOUR BODY IN THE LONG RUN. AS FOR YOU YOURSELF, WELL, YOU ARE CURRENTLY IN YOUR NATURAL STATE.

"Meaning, I'm, my soul?"

CORRECT. YOU ARE ALLEN STAPLES. THE BEING KNOWN AS GENMA WAS NEVER REAL. IT WAS JUST A TITLE YOU APPLIED TO YOURSELF FOR A WHILE.

Death lead Allen through the fields of his home, over grasses that felt and looked and smelled more real than anything he had ever observed in the mortal realm.

"So, what happens to me now," Allen asked, slightly nervous now. "I mean, I'm pretty much a heretic, right? I never believed in any of the Gods, never prayed a day of my life! Oh lord," he said, clutching desperately at Death's robes. "What's going to happen to me?"

CALM DOWN. Death pried Allen's hands from his robes.

YOU HAVEN'T DENOUNCED ANY GODS EITHER, NOW HAVE YOU?

Allen Staples shook his head, his eyes fixed on nothing, his thoughts churning.

HAVEN'T STARTED WORSHIPPING ANY DARK GODS OR DEMONS? ANY OF THE ARCHDUKES OF THE HELLS?

Again, a silent shake of the head.

VERY GOOD. THEN THE ARRANGEMENTS THAT HAVE BEEN MADE WILL PROVE SUITABLE. FOLLOW ME.

In the middle of one of the fields, Death set his scythe on his back, and moved his hands before him in a circle.

Waves of black energy rippled around his left sleeve and skeletal hand, white energy around the right. The two waves slithered off of his fingers, merging into a single, golden orb that pulsated a few feet away.

As the energy pulsed and formed together, the orb became a swirling pool of golden light, with a single point of pure white in its center. Finally, Death stood straight, and reclaimed his scythe from his back.

"What is it," Allen asked, completely awed.

IT IS A DOORWAY, ALLEN STAPLES. *YOUR* DOORWAY, TO BE PRECISE. I HAVE ONLY HAD TO ERECT IT A FEW TIMES. IT IS FOR THOSE WHO HAVE NO GOD OR GODDESS TO SPEAK FOR THEM, BUT ARE NOT BOUND FOR THE LAKE OF FIRE, EITHER.

"So, it's a sort of void?" Death sighed heavily.

NOT EXACTLY. IT'S DIFFERENT FOR EVERYONE WHO GOES IN. IT'S A SPACE WHERE YOU CAN DETERMINE YOUR OWN DESTINY, BY YOUR OWN MEANS. ONE OF THE HEAVENS OR THE HELLS AWAITS YOU WHEN YOU ARE FINISHED.

WELL, Death said, positioning himself behind Allen Staples' soul.

He lifted his skeletal foot up, and gave the Alchemist a swift thrust in the rear end, thrusting him toward the portal.

BEST OF LUCK WITH THAT!

Death felt eyes upon him, and looked up at the black sky of his domain. He knew Fate was watching.

AND YOU ALWAYS TELL ME I'VE NO SENSE OF HUMOR.

* * * *

Portenda led the charge down the stairs, carrying Eileen Staples on his back like an invalid child. Jonah followed with Nareena just ahead of him, both of them streaming sweat like ribbons.

"We need a miracle," Nareena shouted over the din of the tower caving in on itself.

"Or just a helping hand," Kobuchi shouted in through a window port on the landing as he glided in through the window itself. He handed each of the stunned members of the party from Ja-Wen a strange, pure white feather.

Jonah's hand clenched slightly around the object, because the deep, pure chill radiating off of it made him feel as though his bones were freezing in place. "I've had lots of time to make things like this," Kobuchi said hastily.

"You've thought about this before, haven't you?" Jonah grasped the feather in one hand and the window ledge in the other.

"Escaping? A great deal, actually," the Kobold mage said as he turned around to prepare for his flight. "Every time I got my free will back, just before Genma stripped me of it again. Come on! This place is coming apart!"

With that, Kobuchi took flight, and Jonah, Nareena, and Portenda each leapt out themselves, their bodies surrounded by swirling white winds coming from the feathers they held.

Portenda held Eileen Staples over his left shoulder as he descended, dropping rather faster than the others of the company. Jonah worried that he would hit with too much speed, stumble and perhaps hurt himself or his sister.

"Why is he dropping so fast," he shouted to Kobuchi, who looked down to see that Portenda and Eileen had already drifted well away from the tower, but also much closer to the ground than the others and himself.

"I never thought to adjust the power of the spell for weight," Kobuchi shouted back. "He's too heavy by himself as it is, and he's carrying Eileen with him to boot. Don't worry, though! He'll be fine," Kobuchi said as he watched Portenda adjust his legs. "He's a professional, I can tell."

"Yes, he is," Jonah said, mostly to himself. "Yes he is."

A Hunter and his Prey

Chapter Sixteen
Home Again

The group sat around the campfire, looking at the ruins of Genma's tower.

Blink rested peacefully in Portenda's lap, where he had taken up residence since the Simpa Bounty Hunter sat down in front of the fire that Jonah provided with a pinch of one of his powders.

"So," Jonah muttered, "Uncle Allen just kind of, lost it, I guess."

"He couldn't handle the stress of it, Jonah, that's all." Nareena put her arm around his waist.

Eileen remembered the Elven girl and gave her the iciest stare she had available.

"He lost everything in the blink of an eye. All he had left was his science," Nareena said.

"He could have come to us." Eileen was still too disgusted with her uncle's actions as Genma to feel any measure of pity. "He didn't have to put Jonah through that brainwashing, or me through my ordeal. He didn't have to make Kobuchi a slave."

Silence followed her fury, a void of conversation broken only when Portenda stood up and moved toward the tower's rubble.

"In his own way, he did come to you," the hulking Bounty Hunter said, his back still to the rest of the party. "He knew the extent of Jonah's ability. He therefore knew that Jonah could handle the brainwashing, and be completely efficient. And he came to you, Eileen, because he knew your home, from the interior layout, to the daily routines everyone had. He already knew you were a near perfect match for your aunt. Only his family could provide him with what he needed. In the end," Portenda said, his voice dropping a few audible levels. "Isn't that what family is?"

Each member of the company spent the remainder of the evening and night relating the events of the last few weeks to one another from their own point of view.

Jonah had intended to hire the Bounty Hunter to train him in his art; he hadn't assumed he would have to ask Portenda for his services, or fight alongside him.

Eileen and Kobuchi's stories gave Portenda, Jonah and Nareena a better sense at what it was like being Genma's captors. Portenda conveniently left out the parts involving his father.

Jonah understood: not all family affairs should be aired out in the open.

The company went peacefully to sleep, assured that Portenda's keen senses would keep them safe from ambush through the night. They would be on their way to Desanadron come morning, sped along thanks by Jonah's Focus Sites.

* * * *

I TOLD YOU HE'D MAKE IT OUT, Death said.

Byron of Sidius had smiled as a Dread Knight, and the effect had always been eerie because of the skull and his very nature. When Death smiled, the lesser Gods and Goddesses felt it in their core being, and all of them shuddered as one. And this smile could be said to come close to splitting his skull in half.

"Indeed, you did." Fate peered at the orb in his chamber. "How did you know? There were no guarantees."

Death reached into his robes and drew out Portenda's life timer. An immeasurable amount of sand filled the top bulb.

"Ah, so that's it. I suppose we each have our own ways of predicting such things. I wonder whose is more accurate?"

THAT DOESN'T MUCH MATTER NOW, DOES IT? I'M JUST GLAD THAT HIS BEING BORN HASN'T CAUSED A RIP IN REALITY. AND SINCE HE'S IN THE HISTORIES NOW, HE CAN'T JUST BE RUBBED OUT.

"Indeed. But he'll have to be spoken for. Who will be his deity? I don't think anyone is going to want to take the task."

HMPH. I KNOW SOMEONE WHO'S PERFECT FOR IT, Death moved toward the door leading out of Fate's room and back to the labyrinth that served as the home of the Gods. I'LL GO SPEAK WITH HIM NOW. AND DON'T WORRY, Death said as he opened the door. IF HE ASKS ANY QUESTIONS, I'LL TAKE THE FULL BLAME FOR THE BOY.

"So, who are you going to talk to?"

WHO ELSE? Death asked in his funeral bell tone. THE GOD OF WAR IS ALWAYS LOOKING FOR WORTHY CANDIDATES. WELL, I'M OFF, FRIEND. WE'LL TALK AGAIN.

"Yes, I believe we shall," Fate said. He looked over at his bed longingly. He so seldom ceased his tireless, endless study of the Histories. Maybe, just for a little while, he would rest. Of course, he had to do one more thing before he took that rest. "Um, Grim?"

YES?

"Is there any way I could convince you to clean up your dog's mess? He went on my pillow."

* * * *

Portenda's blood sped along the long and narrow racetrack of his arteries and veins, pressed on by the dual nature of his Simpa and Khan blood. As the sun's first warming rays of light touched his furry flesh, his mother's lineage awoke in his body, alive and alert.

His eyes snapped open, and to his surprise, he found the others of the small company already moving about the campsite to prepare their morning meals.

The Bounty Hunter tried to rise to a sitting position, but his entire muscular system shouted rather loudly at him in protest.

Gods, I hurt all over, he thought.

Still, he managed to get himself into a seated position, with his left arm stretched out to the side for additional support.

A slender shadow was soon cast down over him, and Portenda looked up into Jonah Staples's gentle smile.

"So, you're finally up big guy," Jonah said amiably.

A Hunter and his Prey

"How long was I asleep," Portenda asked.

"Probably about ten hours." Jonah took a seat and stretched out his legs in front of him a few feet away from Portenda. "That's a good three times longer than I've known you to sleep any given night. You've endured a lot over the last month. You've earned it."

Jonah passed Portenda a water skin.

The Simpa Bounty Hunter accepted it with little hesitation, breathing the crisp morning air before taking in much-needed liquid.

His physical condition had seemed solid before he passed out the previous night, but then, he didn't usually fall asleep so early.

"Did I miss anything when I fell asleep?"

"Not much," Jonah said. "I agreed to move back in with my sister and parents for a while, and Nareena's going to set up an Alchemy shop in Desanadron. I'll probably move in with her after a couple of months, if all goes well."

"You talked to her about that after Eileen was asleep, didn't you?" Portenda asked, already aware of the answer.

Jonah smiled wanly at him, comforted that the Bounty Hunter's powers of observation and deduction hadn't faded with his strength.

"Still not sure your family would approve of your seeing the woman who, apparently, tried to kill you a few years back. Smart move on your part." Portenda took another swig of the water before passing it back to Jonah.

A wisp of smoke plumed up into the air, a sure sign that the ladies and Kobuchi had started the early meal.

A deep, awkward silence settled between the thin, frail-bodied Human boy, whose favorite activities included scientific research, and the huge, thickly built half Simpa, whose favorite activity happened to be, in actuality, enjoying a spot of cuppa with a friend. But he did rather enjoy the thrill of the hunt nearly as much.

Portenda sniffed the air, and made a note of how close to being finished the meal was. He sensed that Jonah had something on his mind, but the boy seemed tense, expectant. He wanted to say something, or ask something of the Bounty Hunter.

"Out with it, boy," Portenda said flatly.

"Oh." Jonah jumped a little at the sound of that familiar, droning bark. "Well, I was sort of wondering, Portenda. What's next for you? I mean," he looked over his shoulder at his sister, the woman he had fallen in love with again, and the odd but clearly talented Kobuchi. "What do *you* do now? The mission's over."

Portenda looked Jonah in the eyes, boring as deep as he dared do so without gaining the boy's attention.

Observation, he always called it when somebody got an inkling of what was going on.

"The mission isn't over, Jonah."

Jonah simply raised an eyebrow.

"Not until Eileen is home, which should be in a little while. You've got your Focus Sites prepared?"

"Yes, actually, I have."

"Good," the Bounty Hunter said as he rose to his feet, ambling over to the rest of the company. "I'm going to need to get back to Ja-Wen quickly, in order to take care of some business matters. But I have to make a stop over in your hometown first, after we drop you all off."

"Business matters?"

"Yes," Portenda said evenly. "I have to purchase that apartment building our Kobold friends are in. I did say I was thinking about it."

Portenda sat down to the prepared meal before him.

"I'll be keeping the building in Ja-Wen, of course," he said to Jonah as he started eating the mildly prepared sweet meats and eggs that Nareena kept in her rations. "And I'll need your help to get back and forth a few times, Jonah. Your Focus Sites are a good deal less costly than Teleportation scrolls, eh?"

He gave the boy a gentle smile across the breakfast fire and Jonah saw for the first time just how natural and relaxed the hulking Bounty Hunter could be. Without a contract or mission, Portenda could possibly even be an easygoing sort of fellow, he thought.

"So, what are you going to do, Kobuchi?" Eileen asked the Kobold mage.

Kobuchi had seemed quite content since the fall of the tower, and hadn't bothered much with idle conversation. Conversation didn't come naturally to him after so much Alchemy had been used to suppress his free will. But he managed to respond in any event. After all, he reasoned, this Human girl was the only friend he'd had in years.

"I couldn't say for certain, but I think I may head for Palen. It's a city after my own heart, just drowning in magic. I can start looking for a new pack to join with when I arrive."

"Lots of Kobolds in Palen, are there?" Eileen asked.

"Not as such, but the ones that live there are all students of magic or science in some field. It'll be good for me, I think."

Portenda finished his meal, giving the few remains to Blink, who had been waiting patiently in his lap.

Eileen, quietly enjoying her meal and the company of her brother and friends, felt a little bad about the innocent creatures that had most likely died during the destruction of the tower.

"Well, I'll help clean up," Jonah said.

Jonah, Nareena and Eileen went about cleaning up the campsite while Portenda and Kobuchi rested around the dying fire.

"I see you've made a friend. What's his name," Kobuchi said to Portenda as the Bounty Hunter pet the Alchemy beast lightly on its small, canine head.

"Eileen named him Blink. He's taken to it quite well," Portenda said, carrying on an inner conversation with the rather intelligent animal. "As you know, he came from one of Genma's labs. She managed to send him to us for help when she tried to escape from the tower. Are you sure you're going to be able to make it all the way back east to Palen on your own?" Portenda asked.

Kobuchi waved a hand to dismiss the Bounty Hunter's concerns. "Trust me, I'm quite capable of doing so. We're closer to Palen than where you're headed, in any event. Of course, you do have Jonah's Focus arts to help get you to Desanadron. But don't worry." Kobuchi summoned a dagger of ice into his hand. "I've got a very handy arsenal of spells at my disposal. You shouldn't worry about me."

"Maybe not, but now I'm worried about the folks in Palen." Portenda gave the Kobold a sly grin. "They don't take kindly to newcomers who are better at magic than the local city guards right away."

Kobuchi chuckled lightly, and got up from his seat, hitching up the spare rucksack that the Simpa had given him.

"Well, I've got to say goodbye to Eileen," Kobuchi said. "She's a very special young woman, you know. With practice, she'll become a very powerful Q Mage. And Jonah, well, he seems very talented at what he does. Well," he said, offering his tiny, four-fingered hand to Portenda, who accepted and shook amiably. "Best of fortune to you, Mister Portenda the Quiet. May the Gods smile upon you."

He was quite unaware that one particular God was presently listening to a very important being make a case for the Bounty Hunter.

"And may they smile upon you as well," Portenda said with an easy smile.

Kobuchi walked away, pulling Eileen aside to talk briefly with her and thank her for her help.

They embraced one another briefly, and then Kobuchi was off, heading to Palen. The city would welcome him with open arms, and much would be accomplished thanks to his help. But that tale can be told later.

After the company from Ja-Wen and Eileen Staples could no longer see Kobuchi in the distance, Jonah set about making a large Focus Site in the barren dirt near the remains of the tower. When it was finished, everyone stood in the middle of it, and he clapped his hands together, bringing out the power of Alchemy.

A minute later, when he pressed his hands to the Site, the entire group disappeared from the region. Only one set of eyes watched them vanish from sight. Those eyes slightly misted over, and then turned their attention to the Allenian Hills to the southwest.

For a long moment, they stared at the label of a bottle of alcohol, before the hand holding it reared back and hurled the bottle into the distance.

"Never again," the Bounty Hunter's father whispered to himself. "Never again."

* * * *

"I'm impressed," the God of War said as he viewed the Keeper's record orb.

Death regretted that he had slipped the astral being out of Portenda's soul during such a peaceful period in the Bounty Hunter's days. But, it really was the best way to present his case. Portenda's Keeper, as with all Keepers, took on the shape and form best suited to the current host. This one named itself Talim, and took the form of a lion-tiger hybrid creature, adorned in blue fur, and golden riding armor. Its entire body appeared to be wound tighter than a clock spring, ready to pounce on anything.

I THOUGHT YOU WOULD BE, Death said.

"And you say he's partly related to you?" The God of War's raised eyebrows were barely visible behind the visor of his war helmet. "He shows more promise than most of my own loyal worshippers."

The orb wafted through the air back to the Keeper Talim, who swallowed the orb whole back into its body before disappearing back to its host's soul. "Very useful creatures, those Keepers. Fate's creations, right?"

INDEED. AND VERY HELPFUL WHEN I GUIDE SOULS TO THEIR FINAL DESTINATION. SO, WILL YOU ACCEPT HIM AS ONE OF YOUR OWN?

"Yes, Honorable Guest," said the God of War. "You seem in a bit of a rush, Grim. Something on your mind?"

OH, NOTHING MUCH. I'VE GOT TO GET HOME AND FEED THE DOG. Death opened a rift leading to his personal abode.

"Since when did you get a pet? Not that it's a bad thing," the God of War said with a grin. A pair of gray wolf hounds lay resting on either side of a hearth set in the wall of the God of War's main chamber, dressed in animal battle armor. "A lot of us have been saying for years that you need something to make you a little less, well, serious. And besides, dogs are great animals to have around, you know. Very loyal. What made you get him?"

I HAPPENED TO BE IN THE RIGHT PLACE AT THE RIGHT TIME, Death lied. It was a handy skill he had picked up from mortals over the ages.

Some mortals, the ones known to the world as Rogues, made an entire career out of lying. Death didn't care much for it, though, and reserved it for special occasions.

BESIDES, he said. EVERYBODY NEEDS SOMEBODY TO, UH. WHAT'S THE WORD I'M LOOKING FOR, he asked, perhaps directing the question to the God least suited to answering it.

"Love, Honorable Guest. I believe they call it, love."

YES, THAT'S THE TERM. WELL, I MUST BE GOING. KEEP AN EYE ON MY BOY, MARIKESH. I'LL BE RATHER SORE IF YOU DON'T.

Death left the God of War vaguely quivering as he disappeared through the rift.

As soon as he arrived on the other side, Maxi pounced on him, knocking him to the ground with a heavy HOOMPH!

He managed to get out from under the dog by rolling himself out, and brushed his robe off. COME ON, BOY. LET'S GO INSIDE AND GET YOU SOME FOOD.

A Hunter and his Prey

* * * *

Jacob Staples pulled the last of the encroaching weeds from his carrot patch, and wiped the sweat from his brow. "Well, that's the last of them," he said to himself as a flash of light and crackling, lightning-like noises burst from the air behind him.

His entire body stiffened, and when he turned around, he was looking at the Bounty Hunter, his son, his son's girlfriend, and, no, his eyes did not deceive him, his daughter!

He threw the gardening tools aside and dashed to embrace her, hoisting her into the air, giggling like a schoolgirl.

"Oh daddy! It's good to see you again," she cried out, the tears spilling freely now.

"Good, but you're crushing me," she gasped after a minute, and soon found her mother doing the same as her father.

The three of them turned quickly into a trio of smiling, crying heaps, kneeling together in the back yard and holding one another.

Jonah rubbed the back of his head, thoroughly embarrassed, but happy to see his family back together. Nareena gave him a peck on the cheek and put her arm around his waist.

"I'll be by later," she whispered in his ear. "I'm going to go see about renting out that shop."

Giving her a long kiss, Jonah felt warmth glowing out from his very core. He was home, his family was together, and he had a loving girlfriend. And his knowledge of Alchemy was growing daily. But one thing remained to be done, he thought.

"Mom, dad," Jonah said, and his family stood beaming at him, their eyes still glistening. "I'll be sticking around for a while, if that's okay."

"Don't be ridiculous, boy," Jacob said, smiling at his son. "Of course it is. And you, Mister Portenda," he said, taking on a more serious tone of voice as he stepped forward, putting a hand out. "We can't thank you enough for bringing her home to us."

"I had a good deal of help from your son," Portenda said, taking the offered hand.

Before he could react, he was pulled forward and embraced by the old Human Soldier, and before he had time to feel strange about that, Mrs. Staples was also on him.

"Um, you're welcome," he said as they pulled away. "I need to be going soon, to take care of some business. I'll need to borrow your son for a short while longer."

"Of course, Mister Portenda," Jacob Staples said with a smile. "You'll be back in time for dinner, right?"

Oh boy, Portenda thought. *How can I say no to that smile?*

Simple. You don't, Blink thought to him from his perch on his shoulder.

Humph, thought Portenda. *I wasn't talking to you, but thanks.*

"Of course we will." Portenda took Jonah aside. "Get the Sites ready, and we'll be as quick as possible."

"Don't forget that we should probably go get Talonz. Besides, what's the rush," Jonah said as he drew a new Site in the yard with his foot, setting the destination for Ja-Wen.

"I don't know about you," Portenda said with a smile. "But I'm rather looking forward to a home-cooked meal."

With that, the Bounty Hunter and young Alchemist disappeared.

A Hunter and his Prey

Epilogue

Sergeant Thompson of the Desanadron Police Department, 16th precinct, got up from his studies of a recent robbery when the knock came at his door.

He wasn't expecting company, but remembered when he looked at the calendar that the rent was due today.

Thankfully, the landlord didn't charge a great deal. In truth, this building had the lowest rent prices almost anywhere in the entire city. Moving in had given the sergeant the opportunity to afford better equipment for his job.

The landlord seemed a bit on the quiet side, but had a certain air of authority about him. And if the stories the Kobold tenants in the lower apartments told were true, he was a Bounty Hunter.

The sergeant opened the door, and found himself looking into the neutral glare of the landlord, a large, heavily armed Simpa with strange gray stripes on his arms, reminiscent of a Khan, the were-lions' natural enemy. He gave the hulking Mister Portenda a winning smile as he handed him a small leather pouch. "How's business going, sir?"

"Just fine, officer," Portenda said in that familiar, arctic tone. This alone unnerved Sergeant Thompson more than anything else about the landlord: it was as if the man constantly held his emotions in check.

"I won't be by on the normal day next month, officer Thompson," he said. "So I'll be by the next day for the rent. Any problems with the apartment?"

"No, not that I can think of," Thompson said.

"Good."

"Hey, is it true that you're the Bounty Hunter," Thompson asked before he could stop himself.

Portenda had been turning to move on to the next apartment, where he would be stopping in for a brief visit. He turned back to Officer Thompson, his gray eyes half closed. Thompson had come to notice that when the landlord looked like that, he was thinking carefully about his response. A good policeman notices these things, he thought.

"Yes, I am Portenda the Quiet," the Simpa said evenly. "Does the department require outside consultation?"

It wasn't uncommon for him now to get requests from the Desanadron police department for aid in apprehending a criminal. He'd been in the city for two months, and had already taken five jobs for the department.

"No, no, I just figured that's why you won't be by next month on the usual day," Thompson said.

At this, the landlord smiled, an expression that the Human officer hadn't yet witnessed on his leonine face.

Well, that's good to see, he thought. *He's not totally devoid of feeling.*

That would explain the strange pet he carried with him from time to time, too.

"No. Actually, my next stop to your neighbors across the hall is the reason. It's their wedding date, and I'm the guest of honor," Portenda said, audibly pleased.

"Oh, the Staples boy and the Elven girl," Thompson asked. "Well, good for them," Thompson said. "How's it feel to be the honored guest?"

"Pretty good," Portenda said, moving down the hall to Jonah's door.

As Thompson closed his apartment, silence wrapped around Portenda like a familiar blanket. "IT SORT OF RUNS IN THE FAMILY."

The End

We hope you've enjoyed A HUNTER AND HIS PREY by Joshua Calkins-Treworgy. Be sure to check with BooksForABuck.com or our distributors for other novels in Calkins-Treworgy's fascinating world of Tamalaria.